The Rush

Emma Bartlett

Dedicated with love to Ann Hole.

Mum, thank you for believing in my dream. Even when I didn't.

CHAPTER 1

Millie strapped the blocks of explosives around her waist and carefully arranged her tattered jacket. The crudely modified mining charges felt cold and hard against her skin. She could feel the weight of them with every nervous intake of breath. Above her, a naked bulb hung from the stone ceiling. It swung slowly on its rusty chain, casting a circle of light on the rocky floor. At the edges of the light, ice crystals glinted like tiny stars.

A thin, threadbare curtain divided her home from the rest of the tunnel system. It fluttered as someone walked past, spilling light across the floor, spoiling the illusion of privacy. Tim sat on the edge of the bed they shared. He refused to meet her eyes as she crossed the small space and sat close to him. She rested her head on his shoulder and watched as the steam from his breath merged with her own.

"Why you?" His voice was raw and broken. It sounded more like an accusation than a question.

"Because I know that part of the city, I know where to place the charges." Goosebumps rose on her neck and spread like a prickly rash down her back. It's just the cold, she told herself firmly. She knew that wasn't true. Fear had coiled itself around her like a python, squeezing tighter with each passing moment.

"But you aren't an activist."

Millie raised her head to meet his eyes, "So what am I? Just another victim?"

"Yes, what's wrong with that? These tunnels are full of victims."

"I can't live with that," she said, pulling up the collar of her worn jacket. "I need to act. I can't just hide down here anymore." She tried to keep her voice even, but she couldn't stop the anger that flared inside her. She welcomed it. The rush of heat pushed away the cold. And the fear.

"You can't resist progress, Mouse." She stiffened at the sound of her nickname. It had been sweet once, but now she hated it. It reminded her of who she had become, an outcast, scurrying beneath the city for scraps. "You sound like a Luddite, trying to fight the mechanical loom," Tim continued. "Artificial intelligence is just like any change. You can adapt, or you can be swept aside," he reached up to stroke her hair. "I'll get us out of this. I'll find another job. Just give me more time." This was an old argument. It went around in circles like a snake eating its own tail. With each rotation the damage went a little deeper and Tim grew a little more distant.

"This isn't progress. This is the end of progress. Almost everything is automated now. All the big decisions are being made by computers. Machines with no creativity or compassion. We are making ourselves obsolete." Millie's voice had risen in pitch despite her best efforts to stay calm.

She took a deep breath and tried again. "The people most affected by *progress*," she drew mocking air quotes around the word, "aren't the rich. It's us, the young, the disenfranchised, the vulnerable. All our ideas, dreams and hopes. We don't even know what we are capable of yet. If I don't plant this bomb, we may never have a chance to find out."

"That's all very rousing Mouse, but I don't care about a faceless generation, I care about you."

Millie gestured at the tiny alcove that was their home. "Is this what you imagined for us? Do you remember when we used to lay awake all night and talk about the future?" She lifted the tattered hem of her jacket. "Just look at where we are now. And it isn't just us. Unemployment is skyrocketing, people are going hungry. Those left in the city think they are immune. They are told we are witless and workshy. Undeserving of help. Yet every day more and more people arrive in the tunnels."

"I know things are bad," Tim rested his hand lightly on her knee. "I treat the people that come here. I see the malnutrition and disease, infections I thought we'd wiped out centuries ago. But bombing the city is wrong. This group you are mixed up with are dangerous Mouse. Violence isn't the answer. Just walk away."

"I can't. I have to do something."

"No. You don't."

Millie was always disappointed when Tim spoke like this. It was as if he had given up. Accepted his fate. She wondered what had happened to the idealistic young medical student she had fallen in love with a few short years ago. "You used to be so passionate," she said. "You told me you studied medicine because you wanted to make a difference. Do you remember? Now you hide down here while machines steal our jobs and cast us aside like rubbish."

"Violence isn't going to change that. We need to adjust, adapt," his grip tightened on her knee. "I can't let you do this."

Millie felt a stab of irritation. Did he think he could stop her? She was so tired of being pushed around, of feeling powerless and weak. She pulled away from Tim, irritably sweeping his hand aside. "This is my decision," she said. She could tell that the rejection hurt him. A part of her regretted that, a part of her felt liberated.

"Can't you see that I need you too?" he said.

"You have me. I'll be back before sunrise." Millie wished she felt as confident as she sounded. In truth, she was terrified. The small group of activists had planned this operation for months. At first, she had been excited to be part of it. To finally feel trusted and accepted, to be part of something bigger. She had allowed herself to be carried along by their bravado, swept up in their rhetoric. But now it was real, and her courage felt as fragile as a willow reed.

She took Tim's hand in hers, one finger stuck through his frayed glove and she kissed it softly. "I need to go." She knew that if she didn't leave now, she never would.

"Please don't." His eyes were beseeching.

"I have to." She kissed his cheek and stood to leave. He reached for her hand, but she pulled it away. "I…" she began, but there was nothing more to say. "I love you," she said instead, swallowing the tears that threatened to overwhelm her. She swept through the curtain before he could find the words to stop her.

Millie headed to the surface as fast as she could, picking her way through the maze of frozen tunnels. A few people nodded to her as she swept passed. She nodded back, hoping they wouldn't notice that her cheeks were damp, and her eyes were red. Finally, the tunnels opened out into neat, orderly parkland. It was hemmed in on all sides by the bright lights of the city.

Millie felt a moment of disorientation and then something sharper, more painful. A kind of bitter homesickness. The city had been her home once. The buildings that climbed endlessly upwards, their tops disappearing into the night sky, had been her refuge. It was bright and beautiful. A place full of dreams and possibilities. Even the breeze was scented with honey-sweet jasmine. Only Millie knew that it was just a facade. The city was rotting. This was stagnation hidden behind a shiny veneer.

She pushed through the trees and emerged onto a grassy clearing between the park and the nearest complex. The smell of freshly cut grass drifted on the hot, sticky air. The heat surprised her. Was it summer again already? It was easy to lose track of time in the perpetual winter of the tunnels. While she had been shivering below, July had gripped the city in its sweaty fist.

A few metres away an automated lawn mower slowly rolled towards her, working tirelessly through the night, uncomplaining and obedient. It represented everything Millie had come to detest. Cheap automation replacing human endeavour. She stepped out of its way before it ran her over. She had torn out the implants that would have alerted it to her presence. She was invisible to the city's infrastructure now. With luck, it would ignore her.

Millie let her eyes follow the nearest complex upwards. It was made of a white crystalline poly-carbon, slightly translucent and glowing warmly. To her eyes, it resembled an enormous block of rock salt. It rose in a prism shape, twisting on its axis before disappearing into the moonless sky. Every floor of the complex was fronted by a wide balcony. Plants climbed and twisted from them in a medley of colours and shapes. A living waterfall of green, red and purple.

She allowed herself a moment to remember. This had been the building where she had worked. That felt like a lifetime ago, although she knew it had been less than a year. Millie remembered her last day clearly. The nervous glances from her colleagues. The humiliating march to the small, bright room. The box of tissues placed neatly on the table. A young executive, not much older than herself, had been given the thankless task of informing her that she was redundant. He had read from a script, fumbling over the words as if he had only just seen them. She hadn't really listened. She had been preoccupied by the gut twisting realisation that her world was crashing around her.

Millie had left the room with the patronising tissues in a state of numb shock. She hadn't cried until much later, when the money ran out and the landlord had issued an eviction notice. Then she had wept, standing outside her old apartment with Tim, their belongings hastily stuffed into two suitcases.

Millie forced herself back to the present. She couldn't think about that now. She had to concentrate on the task at hand. The complex, she knew, would be unoccupied this late at night. The basement floors would be where the computers were. Acres of machines humming softly in cold, sterile tanks.

The third level down was the one Millie was interested in. The machines on that level did not belong to a private company. They were a key node in the Hub, the massive computer intelligence which ran the city services.

The Hub took many physical forms. Window cleaning drones, gardeners, and giant agricultural machines. A multitude of shapes and purposes. All with a single mind, reaching out across the city and its provinces. Millie wondered how many jobs it had stolen, how many lives it had ruined. Tonight, she would exact a small revenge. She knew that blowing up this tiny part of the Hub wouldn't destroy it, but it would cause disruption and bring attention to her cause. That was worth the risk, Millie thought.

She followed the building around until she found the place she was looking for. A small hatch, just big enough for a maintenance robot, or a very slender woman. The summer heat had been trapped by the immense edifices and Millie felt a bead of sweat drip down her back. She crouched down low in the shadow of the massive building. Her timing couldn't be off, not even by a second. Any delay and she risked being spotted by the early morning workers. Those who still believed that long, grinding hours might save their jobs.

As the minutes ticked by her anxiety swelled. What if she was spotted? The blocks of explosive bulged conspicuously under her clothes. Her pale skin and shabby winter jacket would look out of place in the summer heat. Millie took a deep breath and pushed away her rising apprehension. Follow the plan, she told herself, one step at a time.

After what felt like hours, but was probably only minutes, she heard a soft hum from above. The drone was large and boxy. It lowered itself to the ground unsteadily, neatly folding its rotor arms against its cuboid body. An image of a bumblebee flashed into Millie's mind and despite her nerves she almost laughed.

The drone crawled towards the hatch with more agility than its spindly legs suggested. As it neared the entrance, a flap swung upwards with a hiss of escaping air. The drone slid through, and Millie flung herself after it.

Inside, the building was blissfully cool and dry. Her skin tingled as the sweat evaporated. The air smelled vaguely of lemon zest, an attempt, she assumed, to improve the productivity of its occupants. The utility area was poorly lit but immaculately clean. The floor was made of a shiny white material that reminded her of hospital corridors. The surface reflected the tiny multi-coloured lights of the motionless robots that occupied the room.

When Millie had lived in the city, she had never considered how the offices and residences were maintained. Her apartment and office were simply always clean. Anything that malfunctioned was always fixed, unnoticed and unremarked upon. The dirt and detritus of the tunnels had astonished her at first, as had the effort needed to sustain even basic sanitation. She stared at the array of robots that moved beneath the city's awareness and wondered at its sheer complexity. One device captured her attention, a floating spherical mass of shredded cloth and sponges. A duster she speculated.

The drone she had followed flew towards the door, wobbling slightly on its rotors. She wove her way between the resting robots to follow it. The door clicked open and the machine glided through. Millie followed, confident that, without implants, she was invisible to the building's security.

The corridor beyond was achingly familiar. The floor was a hard polymer, but it resembled polished amber marble. Her boots clicked noisily on the smooth surface. The walls were matt white, so perfectly uniform that it was difficult to see where the walls ended, and the ceiling began. A few pieces of soulless, corporate art broke the monotony.

It was bizarre being back here strapped with explosives. Surreal almost. As if she was in some high-end virtual reality game. A metaverse where there was no consequence, only action. But there would be consequences, Millie knew. After today she would be a criminal. A wanted woman. That thought sent a tingle of unease down her spine. It wasn't something she had ever imagined for herself. But she believed with every fibre of her being that what she was doing was justified.

Her unintentional robot accomplice headed into a lift. The doors slid shut behind it. Millie moved as quickly as she could to the far end of the long corridor. There she found a door marked with stylised green staircase. Emergency stairs. They would lead directly to the Hub's computer room on sublevel three. That's where she would plant the explosives.

She tried to push against the emergency door, but it wouldn't open. She waved at where she thought the sensor might be, but the door stayed firmly shut. There were disadvantages to being invisible, Millie thought. She wondered how much time had passed already. If she didn't get moving, she might be spotted.

"Alright," she said out loud, "time for Plan B." She headed back to the utility room, looking for inspiration. Her eyes settled on the strange, spherical duster that had caught her attention earlier. That cloth would burn she reasoned, and if there was a fire wouldn't the emergency doors open automatically?

Feeling rather pleased with her own inventiveness, Millie examined the other drones, looking for a way to start a fire. She nearly missed a small unit in the corner. It only reached her ankles, but it held a long mechanical arm, which ended in what looked like a small welding torch. She examined the device closely and noticed a warning triangle with a picture of a flame. Well, that looks promising, she smiled.

Millie wheeled the small droid towards the duster. It took her several minutes of experimenting to work out how to start the welding torch manually. Soon a bright blue flame shot from the arm. Carefully she manoeuvred the hovering duster above the torch. The flame changed from blue to orange as the cloth and sponge ignited. She quickly pushed the burning machine into the corridor.

"Warning, fire detected. Ground floor, section three. Please evacuate the area immediately." A pleasant female voice announced. The lighting changed from warm white to a sickly yellow and a piercing alarm sounded, uncomfortably loud and shrill.

Excellent, thought Millie. She moved out of the utility room and into the wider corridor. "No human presence detected. Air vents sealed. Inert gas fire suppression will be released in thirty seconds." Not so excellent, Millie decided.

The duster exploded in a spectacular neon fireball. The force of the blast lifted Millie off her feet and flung her backwards down the corridor. She hit the ground hard, her head slamming into the floor with a sickening crack. Her ears rang and the room spun as if caught in a fiery tornado.

It was difficult to breath. The air smelt of burning chemicals and each gasp burned the back of her throat. Millie looked up through the swirling eddies of black smoke and watched as angry red shadows chased each other across the ceiling. Dazed, she raised her head. There was fire everywhere, it raged along the walls and curled into fists as it flowed along the blistered ceiling. The floor had melted, and flames leapt from puddles of burning liquid. The once white walls glowed red, blackening as the creeping blaze devoured them. Unsatisfied, the flames reached towards her, licking at her exposed flesh with hungry tongues.

Millie crabbed backwards, trying to escape the inferno. Her heart thudded in her chest as a primal terror gripped her. Forcing herself to stand, she swayed on unsteady legs, her mind completely blank except for the need to escape the choking smoke and burning flames. Through the thick smoke she could just make out the light on the nearest door. It glowed green. She flung herself against it.

The door opened onto a large exhibition space. Curved desks were evenly spaced in neat, orderly rows. Transparent display panels wrapped around them like laboratory safety screens. Millie fell into a padded chair and greedily sucked the cold air into her burning chest. "Attention, inert gas fire suppression will be released in twenty seconds, please leave the area immediately." The calm female voice declared.

"Great," Millie mumbled to herself. "New plan. Don't die." She climbed unsteadily to her feet, but her vision swam. Pain strobed between her temples like flashes from a lighthouse. She made a grab for the desk, but the room tipped, and she crashed to the floor.

Gingerly, she explored the painful lump on the back of her skull. Her fingers came away covered in sticky blood. The sight of the dark red stain seemed to shake free something inside her. Reality swung back into place with the force of a wrecking ball. What was she doing here? She was a fool for thinking she could do this. A sob forced its way past her gritted teeth. Angrily, she wiped her eyes and pulled herself to her feet. There was no time for that now. She had to get out.

She looked around, disoriented, and confused. The room was a maze of narrow walkways between rows of identical desks. There were no distinguishing features. No family portraits or potted plants, nothing to break the bland monotony. The only door she could see had a thin trail of smoke drifting under it. She decided to head in the opposite direction.

She followed the wall around to the right, her fingers leaving a trail of blood and soot. Part of the room was blocked off by an enormous transparent board. Someone had drawn a flowchart on it, and another comedian had written "Something clever happens here" in an untidy script.

"Attention, inert gas fire suppression will be released in ten seconds, please leave the area immediately." The voice announced. Millie spotted something green shining through the scrawled handwriting on the board. She reached out and wiped away some of the letters with her sleeve. A door. And the lock was green. She ducked around the board and dashed towards the door. She had almost made it when a loud hissing noise startled her. Air surged past in a torrent.

Suddenly, she couldn't breathe. As she lurched towards the green light her vision began to narrow, black borders closing in from the edges. Her knees buckled and she forced herself to crawl. Hand. Knee. Hand. Knee. Don't think. Just move. The darkness reached towards her, pulling her down.

△△△

Millie didn't know how much time had passed. Her mind started to spin up like a turbine, turning sluggishly at first and then accelerating. To begin with, all she was aware of was the burning in her chest and the sharp pain that stabbed across her forehead. As the pain subsided, she forced her eyes open. Somehow, she had blundered into a stairway. Emergency lighting cast deep shadows and somewhere above a red emergency light flashed on and off. A strange, sulphurous smell filled her nose. It took her a moment to realised it was her own singed hair.

The whole floor of the complex seemed to be on fire. Clouds of smoke drifted up the stairs and soot stained the once white walls. This is complete madness, she thought. Everything has gone wrong. I have to get out of here. She struggled to her feet and started to stagger up the stairs away from the heat and the sour smell of burning. But then she stopped. A part of her knew that if she gave up now, she would never be able to wash away the stale stench of defeat. It would cling to her, like it clung to the others that merely existed in the tunnels. Millie shook her head, setting off another wave of pain and nausea. No, she refused to give up.

She moved purposefully down the stairs. On the third sublevel, she pushed through the doorway. This part of the building looked different. It was plain and functional. A reception desk was squeezed against the wall. Behind it a narrow corridor was interrupted by heavy metal doors and exposed pipes. She was faintly aware of a slight vibration through the floor and an electrical ozone smell in the air.

The reception desk was empty except for a small yellow rectangle, about the size of her middle finger. Something about it pulled at her mind. Something important. The thought drifted away into a sea of fog. It was difficult to think clearly through the pain in her head, she felt almost as if she was sleepwalking. She staggered passed the desk and made her way unsteadily up the corridor.

At the end of the corridor was hall number seventeen. It looked no different from any of the other computer rooms she had worked in during her career. The smell of the coolant and the sound of the pumps were so familiar it made her stomach twist. She rested her hands against the cool metal door, feeling the slight vibration pass through her. An odd feeling of melancholy settled over her. It was as if she had returned to the place where she had grown up, only to find that everyone she had known had left. The place was the same, but she no longer belonged here. She was disconnected. Adrift.

A sign above the door announced that this was a secure area, but the door light was a welcoming green. Millie fell through the opening into a small airlock. The walls were lined with displays and scrolling graphs. The floor was sticky, designed to trap dust from her boots. On the other side of the airlock, a touch pad opened the inner door. Millie pressed it and the door swung open. Lights clicked on in the hall beyond. She found herself looking down from a narrow mezzanine into a vast pool. The pool was filled with a clear fluid and stacked with row after row of small white cubes.

She reached under her jacket and unwrapped one of the blocks of explosive. It felt strange in her hand. Dangerous. Like a poisonous spider. Doubt bubbled up from somewhere inside her. Was this the right thing to do? What if somebody was hurt? She had never been a violent person, so what was she doing with a bomb. An actual bomb. Oh God.

For a moment everything seemed to spin out of control. She forced herself to take long, calming breathes. She had to do this, she reminded herself. She had to fight back. People needed to see that progress was nothing if it left humanity behind.

Millie placed the explosive with shaking hands. Her finger hovered over the switch that would set the timer. It was deliberately low-tech. A remote signal might be blocked by the room's heavy shielding. Once the switch was set, there was no going back. Despite the misgivings that gnawed at her she clicked the switch into place. There, it was done. Surprisingly it felt good. As if an enormous weight had been lifted away. In that split second, she had elevated herself from victim to freedom fighter. She grinned giddily.

"Emergency response is now ending. Please be aware that access to restricted areas is now revoked. Enjoy the rest of your day." The computer voice came from somewhere above her head.

"Pah!" Millie told it. "I think your day is about to get a lot worse." She walked back to the airlock and pressed the door release. It didn't open. All around the hall the lights were going out. As the room dimmed, she noticed the red glow from above the door. Her mouth went suddenly dry as dread swept over her. The charges were set detonate in less than two minutes. The explosion would create a fireball that would consume the whole room. She would be killed. Blown to pieces. Trapped in the dark. Alone.

No, no. She had to get out. The last of the lights clicked off. Millie stood in the dark listening to the sound of her own panicked breathing. She screwed her eyes shut, her fingers clawing at her temples. The piercing pain was worse when she tried to think, but she forced her mind to focus. An image came to her in an excruciating flash. A yellow pass.

The plan was that their contact would leave it at reception. Had she picked it up? She couldn't remember. Millie desperately searched through her pockets. Maybe she had dropped it among the submerged processing cubes. She turned around and faced the darkness. It was impenetrable except for the dim red glow from the door mechanism.

Terror gave way to blind panic. Her thoughts scattered

like chickens from a hungry fox. "Open the door," she screamed. "Open the door!" She pounded on the metal until her knuckles bled. "Please! Help me!" She felt her way to the stairs, searching with her fingertips. She imagined she could hear the timers tick down, the seconds flowing away like the grains of sand in the grim reaper's hourglass.

CHAPTER 2

Several hours later, and twenty miles away, Oliver Chadwick was caught up in a drama of his own. He knelt on the floor feeling rather annoyed with himself. The toy car, no, scale replica, he corrected himself petulantly, had been resting on the shelf for as long as he could remember. It had taken less than a second for his hip to collide with the table, upending the vase and spilling fresh flowers, tepid water and small plastic parts across the living room carpet.

The toy... model... replica, whatever the stupid thing was called, belonged to his brother. So did the apartment, and almost everything in it. A fact that never ceased to irk him. Oliver had lived alone in the exclusive Victoria Square residence for nearly three years. Ever since his brother had bought it, on the pretence of needing a place to stay during his rare visits to Monument City. Yet somehow, Oliver still felt like a guest.

It wasn't that his brother was ungracious, quite the opposite. Hugo had always made it clear that Oliver should regard the luxurious apartment as his own. It was more that Oliver was angry at himself for accepting his brother's charity. Or more to the point, for *having* to accept it. His government salary had barely covered the rent on his old, cramped, one bedroom bachelor pad. This prestigious, upper city penthouse was much more comfortable. Even if it did inflame their one-sided rivalry.

Oliver took the ruined model to the kitchen table.

Small pieces of incomprehensible plastic bounced across the polished surface, mocking him with their tiny intricacies. He didn't even know where to start. Actually, he knew very well indeed. With a pang of guilt, he swept the wreckage into the rubbish bin. His brother would never notice, he reassured himself. What was the point of it anyway? It wasn't as if there were any roads.

From his vantage point, high above Monument City, Oliver could easily track the course of the old transport network. Roads and rails now set to lawn and woodland. They had been dug up nearly two centuries ago, when this place had been known by another name. Oliver tried to remember what it was. It came to him in a flash. Birmingham. That was it. The ghost of the old city was still there if you knew where to look.

Like many places Birmingham had escaped the sudden rise in seawater that had washed away the coastal cities. It had not, however, escaped the exodus that had followed as the survivors fled inland. The Rush, as the mass migration became known, had triggered a global economic and social collapse. Governments had fallen. The world had fragmented. Over a billion people had been left homeless.

Oliver found that period of history particularly interesting. Studying it had become something of a hobby. The naysayers, he knew, had predicted a new dark age. The optimists had promised a perfect, shining future. Fate, as always, had chosen a middle path. The fragments of the old world had slowly drawn together, forming vast, self-governing, megacities. A new, technological renaissance had begun, spurred on by necessity rather than greed. People had learnt to coexist with nature rather than trying to conquer it. The new metropolises built upwards, rather than outwards, jealously guarding the nature reserves surrounding them. Where once there had been tarmac and iron, now there was parkland and meadows.

Seventy million people called Monument City home. Yet it was green and beautiful. The air was clear. The water pure.

Verdant vegetation hung from every balcony. The drudgery of the past had been replaced by automation, controlled by benevolent artificial intelligences. Sure, some people fell through the cracks, but wasn't that always the case? For the vast majority of citizens life was good. Far better than breathing the toxic fumes of plodding ground vehicles. Oliver stared at the broken pieces of plastic car at the bottom of the bin. He really didn't understand his brother's nostalgia for these wheeled anachronisms.

As if on cue, his text chimed. He glanced at it quickly, pushing down his irritation as a grinning face identified the caller. His brother. The success. As if he wasn't feeling bad enough about breaking the model, now he had to face Hugo's smug superiority.

Oliver's younger brother had always had an unfair advantage. While Oliver had been the model student, Hugo had been the schemer. He understood "the game", the hidden rules that moved the pieces of power. It was a world that Oliver had never grasped or fully understood. While he had studied hard, believing the myth that hard work would bring success, Hugo had built an empire from their shared bedroom.

The software Hugo had written, hunched under the covers late at night, had grown to become the world's most powerful self-learning artificial intelligence. It wasn't that Hugo was a genius. Not really. Most of his software was written by others; talented and creative people to whom the term genius could be more readily applied. The advantage Hugo had was that he understood people effortlessly and completely. He could discern the passions and goals of others and twist them to serve his own needs.

People loved Hugo, his empathy, warmth and energy. It was difficult not to love someone who understood you so completely. Oliver often wondered if they would be quite so enthralled if they understood how ruthlessly Hugo used their loyalty. He cultivated people the same way a farmer cultivates livestock. Extracting every ounce of energy and passion to build his precious business empire.

Irritably, Oliver waved his hand to acknowledge the call. A three-dimensional image shimmered into existence in front of him, blocking his view out of the full-length windows and causing a moment of disorientation.

"Hello Hugo." Oliver tried to hide the flat vowels of his Midlands accent. He always felt inferior for having failed to master the soft, educated tones his brother used so naturally.

"Hello big brother, how are you?" The smile lit up the room. The blue eyes locked on his with an intensity that would have been uncomfortable, if there hadn't been such warmth behind them. Oliver resented the easy charisma. It was something he knew he lacked.

"I'm in town next Thursday and wondered if you wanted to catch up?" This was Hugo's way of giving notice he would be staying for a while. Oliver resented that too. It was an uncomfortable reminder that he was only here on his brother's sufferance. A part of him knew that wasn't entirely true, but his pride bristled, nonetheless.

"Sure Hugo, you will be staying here of course, after all this is your place."

"Our place Olly, we're family". The smile crept into the ultra-violet end of the spectrum. It was part of the game, this little exchange. Somehow his brother had just extended his power and influence in a way Oliver didn't quite understand, but he felt it in the pit of his stomach and in the tension in his back.

He forced himself to return the smile, but his brother sensed his discomfort, as he always did, and expertly turned the conversation to neutral topics. Hugo could talk knowledgably about almost anything.

Oliver followed as best he could, but the art of small talk was another talent his brother bested him at. He ended the conversation as soon as he could. "I have to finish going over some field reports, but I'll see you next week Hugo. Will Maria be coming with you?"

Oliver was disappointed when his brother shook his head. He genuinely liked Hugo's wife. A formidable woman whose intimidating façade didn't quite conceal the playful humour that sparkled beneath. "No, Maria is working on something for her magazine. You know how she can be when she is on the scent of something juicy. I'll call you from the station and you can meet me there." Not quite a request this time, an order from someone who was used to being obeyed.

"Sure Hugo, I'll see you then." Oliver swallowed his bruised ego.

Hugo severed the connection with a friendly wave. As his image faded away the room seemed to darken by several thousand lumens. Hugo could do that, light up a room without even being in it. Oliver bit down his rancour.

Doctor Oliver Chadwick was not an unsuccessful man, and he struggled to explain the feelings of inadequacy that his brother could elicit. He had a doctorate from a good university and was well respected by his peers. He had published several well received papers and had consulted on a few high-profile projects.

Oliver loved his job. He revelled in the complexity of balancing the delicate ecosystems around the city, allowing wild spaces to flourish while providing recreation, clean air and food for the city. Agricultural science was not the most glamourous discipline, but Oliver knew what he did was important. It gave his life meaning and purpose. But still, Oliver felt an odd dichotomy. He took great satisfaction from his work, but he was plagued by a sense that he could have achieved more.

Putting aside his agitation, Oliver settled back into the expensive chair, enjoying the small squirming sensations as it automatically adjusted to his weight. Picking up the text he told the house AI to display the latest field reports. Soon he was happily lost in the comforting familiarity of statistics and numbers.

△△△

Rose Cooper hurried through the tunnels, cursing her mangled hip. A few strands of grey hair had escaped the pins that normally held them out of her eyes. As she brushed them away her fingers passed over the vivid scar that ran down her cheek. The scar was a memento. A reminder that if being blasted into space by a mining charge couldn't kill her, nothing could. It also looked pretty badass, even if she did say so herself.

The wrinkles that time had chiselled into the corners of her eyes and mouth were less pleasing. They were a constant reminder that she was getting older. Not that fifty-eight was *that* old. It felt old though, particularly when she tried to tally the years against her achievements. Never married; no children; medically retired from asteroid mining; leader of a botched activist movement; responsible for the death of a twenty-four-year-old girl.

That last one felt like an icy spear through her heart. She felt guilty. Hell, she was guilty. After all, the bombing had been her idea. What better way to get people's attention than to bring down the system that was trying to replace them? She had even made the bombs. Botching them together from old mining charges. A lifetime of scraping the asteroid belt between Jupiter and Mars had taught her a thing or two about explosives. She had thought herself an expert. An arrogance that had shattered her hip and torn her face open. And now it had taken the life of a young woman. Rose wasn't sure what had gone wrong. She only knew one thing for sure. It was her fault.

She picked up her pace. Pushing her hip to the limit as her guilt soured into anger. She knew the tunnel system better than anyone else. The warren of interconnected passageways told the story of the city's history. The upper levels, Rose knew, were the oldest. They were made up of old road tunnels, communication culverts and Second World War bomb shelters. Slightly deeper was the half-built, but never finished, twenty-first century subway system. Deepest of all were the frozen hyperloop tunnels. Rose knew them all. For the past twenty years they had been her home.

The curtains which portioned off the private spaces swung as she passed, caught in the tempest of her fury. She flung open one of the curtains, and the dirty cloth hit the wall with a sharp crack. Beyond was a small space that had been hollowed from the tunnel wall.

Three people were already inside, standing around a long table strewn with broken electronics. The smallest of the three jumped as Rose swept in. His thick, make-do glasses slipped off his nose and dangled precariously from his ears.

"What happened Jack? This is a complete disaster."

"Th... the explosives were on a t.. t.. timer, Rose. Millie must have set it herself."

"Then why isn't she here now Jack? Why?" Rose slammed her hand on the table to emphasise the last word. The contents bounced from the concussion. Jack scampered back against the wall. He looked like he wanted to go further, but the rock wouldn't budge.

"I don't know Rose, the t.. t.. , the timer was good, I t.. t.. tested it myself".

Rose advanced on the small man, pinning him against the rock. He raised his arms over his face and whimpered pitifully. It wasn't really his fault, of course, but she had to look tough in front of the others. If she let them see the crushing guilt she carried, they would never follow her again.

"Enough!" The voice was loud and commanding. Rose swung around angrily to face the owner. A younger woman slipped around the table. Her dark curly hair fell across her face, framing her sharp, angular features. "That's enough Rose. We all know this isn't Jack's fault."

Rose spun on her, her face set in a feral snarl. "Then whose fault was it, Jess? Mine?" Trick question. Of course, it was her fault.

Jess didn't look away. She held the eye contact calmly until Rose was forced to look away. "You are in charge Rose," she said firmly. "Ultimately everything that happens to this group is your responsibility." The words stung like vinegar in an open wound.

"You think I don't know that?" Rose hissed, stabbing her finger into the space between them in a sharp staccato. "You think I don't carry the weight of that?" she finished the question with a growl of frustration and set to pacing the length of the small space.

Her anger rolled over the others like hot iron, Rose was pleased to see they shuffled away from her, their backs against the wall. At least they still respected her, or at least feared her, which was the same thing as far as she was concerned.

"This wasn't meant to happen." Rose spat the words, the implied accusation landing on everyone in the room. "Millie was supposed to plant the bombs and leave. We had planned this for months, we went over it, and over it. Now she is dead, and we have nothing to show for it. Do you know what the local bulletins called it? 'A small technical malfunction'."

"Life is what happens to us while we're busy making plans" the low rumble came from a pile of rags near the door. The rags unfolded themselves into a heavyset bearded man.

"Spare me your plagiarism old man." The irony of that didn't escape her. Connor was no more than a year older than she was. But he wore his age comfortably, whereas she fought hers with every fibre of her being. "We used most of our explosives, burnt our sympathisers and for what? This whole thing was pointless!" Rose almost screamed the last word. The scar across her face pulsed in time with her fury. She paused, out of breath. "We didn't even make the main news channels. It was all for nothing. What did we do wrong?"

The bearded man leaned forward over the table "We wimped out, that's what we did. As if destroying a few computers was going to get the city folk to look up from their fancy cappuccinos. We were a bunch of ruddy milksops. I told you, the only way to make real change is to make them fear us," he shook his clenched fist before him.

"What would you have done, Connor?" Jess asked, her voice dripping with sarcasm. "Blow up the whole complex?"

"Gladly yes, if that's what it takes."

Rose shook her head. "No, we don't have the resources for anything like that. We need to find another way. Another way to make them notice us."

Connor scratched his untidy beard, flakes of something greasy fell onto his chest. "Kicking them where it hurts didn't do us any good lass. They barely felt it," he paused for effect. "How do you get a bear to fear a wasp? By rousing the whole ruddy nest, that's how. By stinging again and again, until the bear runs cowering for his den. We need to go bigger. We need to make it so they can't ignore us."

Rose smiled dangerously. "Rouse the whole nest. I like that." She decided not to point out that she had no idea what that meant. It certainly sounded quite "activist-y" and who was she to stand in the way of a good jingle? Frankly, with four activists, two blocks of explosives and several hundred desperate civilians crowding the tunnel system, they could all use a bit of inspiration. Something would come to her, it always did.

△△△

Oliver was still feeling unsettled from his conversation with Hugo the night before. To make himself feel better he set all the pod windows to transparent, letting the bright morning light flood the small cabin. The small, egg-shaped passenger drone hung between its fat, oversized rotors like an over-inflated balloon. It banked smoothly to the left, following the air corridor that would take it out of the city. Oliver sat back and enjoyed the ride, trusting the pod to weave its way through the busy morning traffic. He loved soaring alone over the complexes, revelling in the freedom and exhilaration of movement. On the ground he had duties and responsibilities, his time sliced into tight, restrictive boxes. In the air he felt like there were infinite possibilities. He could roam the skies like a nomad, disconnected from obligation and unrestricted by authority.

It made him think of the early explorers in the age of sail, where a morning breeze and a high tide tore off the shackles of the land. Oliver imagined the anticipation those early sailors had felt, as they set out on the vast sparkling ocean, seeking fortune and adventure. It was a romantic notion, of course, born from the vague dissatisfaction that hounded him. The rational part of his brain refuted the fancy. Ancient sea travel, his mind scoffed, was beset with seasickness, scurvy and starvation.

The morning sky was streaked with pink and peach. The city had been awake for hours, and Oliver shuffled along the seat to get a better view. A great vortex of life whirled between the buildings. The pods seemed to be caught in an intricate, lavish dance. It made Oliver feel very small, a tiny part of a much bigger puzzle. Each piece precious and unique, but bound together in an intricate, delicate web. He felt a moment of regret for his ancestors, they had not fully understood the fragile balance that sustained that web, and even now mankind suffered the consequences of their ignorance.

"Hey boss, you're late." The chirpy voice filled the small cabin.

"Good morning Laura, are you at the site already?"

"Yep, but they won't let me in without you, so hurry up, I'm bored." Laura was a graduate student at one of the local technical colleges. Bright, vivacious and completely irreverent, she challenged Oliver relentlessly. He respected, even appreciated her cheeky confidence, but not all of her colleagues did.

"I'll be there in about ten minutes. Can you check the equipment is properly calibrated please? I want to make sure our results are accurate."

"I have, and then I checked it again just for something to do." Laura was playfully mocking, but Oliver knew the restlessness was genuine.

"You could try talking to one of the technicians. Get us a little insider information on the latest harvest."

"Umm, that might have worked five minutes ago."

Oliver shook his head. He was almost too afraid to ask. "What did you do, Laura?"

"Nothing that a bit of cleaning and a new cup of coffee won't solve."

Oliver smiled despite himself. "Just wait for me and try not to bathe anybody else in your morning beverage."

"Will do, boss"

Oliver cut the connection and mentally added "clumsy" to the list of things Laura needed to work on. As the pod gained altitude Oliver could see more of the metropolis. It was enormous, teeming with energy and purpose. A melting pot of people concentrated in vast complexes which reached far above the wispy clouds.

They were more than mere buildings, each was a sheltered community, with a unique culture and lifestyle. They expressed that culture in the elaborate parks that adorned every roof, invisibly shielded from the wind and rain by magnetic fields.

Some of the parks featured fantastical waterfalls that plunged among tropical flowers. Others had snowy slopes where the adventurous snowboarded among the pines. None of the complexes had a regular shape, each was designed to maximise the space for the flora that clung from them, forming immense cascading gardens.

Oliver's pod left the jurisdiction of the city and flew south west over the provinces. The land flattened and spread out into a patchwork of green and yellow. The remains of ancient hedgerows drew dark lines across fields full of wildflowers, and copses of trees topped small hills.

Oliver pressed his face to the window, his eyes alight,

and tried to take in the textures and colours of the wild places. The provinces were fiercely protected. Oliver felt proud and privileged to be preserving their legacy.

Slowly the pod began to descend. In the distance, the covered agricultural buildings clustered together. They were ugly squat buildings, windowless and functional. The high-density agriculture was the only way to feed ten billion people in a world where much of the arable land had been lost to soil erosion, and the pressure for higher yields was unrelenting.

The pod made a slow turn and landed silently next to one of the dark grey, boxy structures. Large black letters across the side of the building labelled this as "RESEARCH UNIT 001 – PROJECT METOMAGIS".

Laura was waiting beside one of the agricultural technicians, his khaki jacket was stained with a splash of dark liquid. He looked annoyed, and slightly damp. Behind them a small droid waited on outsized wheels, a thin probe attached to one of its three arms.

Oliver gave Laura his best disapproving look. She smiled sheepishly before breaking eye contact to study her boots. More amused than annoyed, he turned to the tall man beside her. "Morning Jamal, have you got the results of the latest harvest?"

"Good morning Oliver. I'll upload them to your text. Just to warn you, they are disappointing." His accent was faint, like a melody carried on a breeze. Oliver knew Jamal had been born in the Eastern part of what had once been Saudi Arabia. A proud man, he had stayed longer than most, battling the encroaching desert sands that choked his ancestral home.

Oliver suspected Jamal had never fully forgiven himself for abandoning the plantation his family had tended for generations. However, Oliver took some pleasure from the knowledge that he had been able to offer Jamal a new purpose. Allowing the talented technician to throw his energy into developing genetically modified plants that might, one day, reclaim his homeland.

"How bad is it?"

"The pea blossom didn't set on almost forty percent of the crops. I am sorry Oliver, but this generation was worse than the control harvest."

"Worse?" Oliver asked "So, if we hadn't bothered at all we would have had had a better harvest?" he felt his heart drop. The genetically modified pulses had recently become a political hot potato. Despite his team's best-efforts, food production was starting to slip behind demand. If they couldn't find a way to increase yields, the cities would starve within a decade. It was a grave responsibility, and as Monument City's lead agricultural scientist, it rested heavily on him.

"Yes, but worse than that," Jamal hesitated, as if unwilling to break the bad news, "the plants fertility dropped with each generation. The last batch was sterile."

Oliver shook his head. Anxiety and frustration bubbled up like indigestion. Months of genetic modifications and hard work wasted. The latest cultivars were useless. He took a deep breath to steady himself. There was nothing for it, they would have to start from scratch.

Oliver tried to push away the nagging self-doubt that always troubled him. Was he really the right person for this job? There were many talented geneticists who would have jumped at the chance to run this project. Was he clever enough? Knowledgeable enough? Creative enough? Despite his years of experience, Oliver suddenly felt like a fraud.

He could almost feel the city council breathing down his neck. They would be pressing him even harder now, their timescales tightening, their budget shrinking. The politicians might even decide to shut the project down. What then? His stomach twisted at the thought. There would be food shortages and rationing. In a little under ten years there would be widespread famine.

Oliver had no choice. He simply had to make this work. He shot a glance at Laura. The red head's normal fiery energy was muted. She pulled at the hem of her shirt despondently. With an effort Oliver pulled his thoughts back to the present. Feeling sorry for himself was not going to get the job done. "Let's take some samples and see what we can learn. We certainly have room for improvement," that was an understatement, he thought, "and we have sufficient funding for another attempt."

Jamal nodded and led them into an airlock. He slapped his hand against a control pad and cycled the outer door. Pumps hummed and Oliver felt the pressure change in his eardrums. He swallowed and his ears returned to normal with a pop. Laura tugged at her ear lobe, looking uncomfortable. "I know we have to keep the test under negative pressure, but I hate that feeling." She grumbled.

Jamal smiled at her sympathetically. "Me too, but we can't risk releasing pollen into the environment." Oliver nodded his agreement. A few years ago, a facility in another city had accidentally released a modified grain. It had spread rapidly, nearly wiping out the indigenous species. It had taken a huge effort to bring the contamination under control. Oliver was determined that wouldn't happen to them.

The inner airlock door rotated open with a slight hiss, and the three scientists entered the open space beyond. It reminded Oliver of a colossal warehouse. Lines of tall shelves reached up towards the ceiling in neat, regular rows. Each shelf contained a long line of troughs, filled with a translucent purple liquid. The liquid, Oliver knew, was a careful mix of chemicals, providing all the nutrients the plants needed to flourish. Above the troughs, mature green leaved plants reached towards the lighting gantries above.

Oliver shrugged out of his heavy utility jacket. It was hot, and the humidity made the air feel thick and heavy to breathe. Bees buzzed around his head and he swiped at one that seemed intent on crawling into his ear. It buzzed away towards one of the small wooden hives that were evenly spaced among the racks of plants. Despite the industrial setting, it was an oddly pastural scene. It would be pleasant place to rest, Oliver thought, if only the survival of millions of people didn't depend on it.

He gestured to the small droid that had entered with them and it rolled forward on chunky tyres. Soon it was lost among the racks, taking samples and downloading data from the consoles built into each hydroponic unit. Oliver watched as the data came through to his text.

"The genome is stable." he muttered. "The DNA isn't mutating beyond what we predicted. This must be an environmental issue, something to do with the way the DNA is expressing itself. Phenotype rather than genotype." Thoughtfully, he scrolled through the data before turning back to the others. "We'll have to go through the analysis and work out what we missed. Jamal, we need to incinerate this batch and sterilize the unit. We don't want it contaminating our next attempt. Laura and I need to get back to the lab and work on our new plan."

Laura wrinkled her nose. "What's our new plan?"

"I don't know yet," Oliver grinned, trying to put aside his worries for her sake, "but that's half the fun."

She flashed him a smile. "I think I'm starting to rub off on you, boss."

△△△

Laura sat across from Oliver as the pod rose smoothly and headed back towards the city. She was distracted, staring out the windows without really seeing the land which slid past below. Laura had never been very good at expressing her feelings. Her girlfriend Amy would have found the right words. It was one of the reasons Laura loved her. They filled in each other's missing spaces, like slices of swiss cheese stacked together.

"You are being uncharacteristically quiet," Oliver said, his voice gentle.

She looked up from the window and met his gaze. "I've been thinking."

"Anything you want to share?"

She paused, glancing out of the window to give herself time to think. "All of this work and effort, this desperate attempt to feed ourselves with less land and less resources. It shouldn't even be necessary." She met his eyes across the small cabin. "It makes me angry, boss. We've wasted two generations just trying to survive. Thousands of species have slipped into extinction. We'll never get that biodiversity back. I almost feel like our ancestors have stolen from us."

Oliver nodded. "I think about that occasionally. It wasn't really ignorance, not entirely. Our ancestors had the technology to know that their climate was changing. They had the means to reverse it, they just lacked the will."

Laura wasn't convinced. "How could they lack the will to save themselves? That's basic self-preservation, it's hard-coded into every species."

Oliver shrugged. "Denial? Misinformation? Corruption?"

"But why did people let it happen?" Laura couldn't wrap her mind around it. In her head, it was simple. If something was broken, you fixed it.

"I think the Rush caught them out," Oliver said. "The general feeling at the time was that any climate change would be gradual. The sudden, violent upheaval caught them completely by surprise. Imagine it. Hundreds of millions of people suddenly displaced, the coastal cities lost to flooding, most of Africa and Australasia lost to drought and famine. Disease, catastrophic storms, raging wildfires and above all else, millions upon millions of refugees."

Laura was silent for a long time. She felt Oliver's eyes on her as the pod made silent progress. She couldn't understand how anyone could sit idly by and watch the world burn. She had always been impatient, quick to act. If something needed to be done, she was usually the person who did it.

Sometimes that got her into trouble. Like the time she had hidden a partially defrosted frog in her teacher's desk. What had started as a protest on the practice of animal dissection, had ended in several weeks of detention. The school caretaker, her headmistress had told her sternly, had spent the entire day searching for the source of the rancid smell.

"I wonder what it like was before the Rush," she said. "All I've seen are a few preserved buildings, but that doesn't give you a sense of what it was like to live in them."

A slow smile spread over her mentor's face. "Shall we find out?"

Laura blinked at him in surprise. "What do you mean?"

Oliver entered his authorisation code and the pod changed direction, sweeping towards the distant coast. Soon the green and gold of the provinces gave way to a mottled landscape of dark water and small islands. The tops of ruined trees peaked through the muddy water and occasionally a steeple marked where a village had once stood, a sad monument to a lost way of life.

The flooding became worse the closer they came to the coast. Here, only a few islands remained above water, the tops of once steep hills that were now almost entirely submerged. A few crumbling industrial buildings clung to the islands, slowly collapsing in on themselves. Rusted vehicles laid around them, some with flakes of paint hinting at their original colour. Birds nested in the broken windows and trees grew through missing doors. Slowly, on the horizon, taller buildings rose up through the haze. As the pod sped closer, the ruins sprawled outwards and the buildings solidifying into hard upright rectangles.

Laura could see that the outer suburbs were mostly low buildings. In many places only the roof gables were still visible above the water. They were laid out in neat lines, following the routes of the flooded roads. Oliver ordered the pod to descend and they skimmed above the rooftops, looking down at the deserted remains.

Directly ahead of them was an open area surrounded

by dead, rotting trees. In the middle, a collapsed children's climbing frame was slowly rusting. Nearby was a derelict set of swings. One of the seats was still attached to the frame by a rusted chain. It swung forlornly in the downdraft as the pod gently touched down.

Laura looked at Oliver incredulously. "You aren't actually planning to get out?"

Oliver flashed her his best "trust-me" smile. "Why? Scared of getting your feet wet?"

"You have no idea what is in that water."

"Snakes? Crocodiles? Flesh eating pond skaters?"

"Don't tease, I like these boots."

"It's shallow here, it won't come past your knees."

Laura watched unhappily as Oliver popped the pod's canopy open. He sat on the threshold and dropped down in a splash of dirty water. The pod bobbed alarmingly, and Laura steadied herself in the seat. She was slightly disappointed when the water only come to just above his ankles.

"What are we doing here, boss?" she asked suspiciously.

"I thought you wanted to see what life was like before the Rush?"

"I didn't think that would involve squelching back into the lab with a nasty case of cholera."

"Cholera is unlikely unless you plan on drinking the water. But you are right, I am looking for something I think might help us."

Laura shot him a look that was halfway between "I knew you were up to something" and "This isn't going to end well, is it?".

Oliver smiled back innocently. "There was an invasive species of plant used in domestic horticulture before the Rush. It was eliminated from the provinces as it competed with the native plant life, but I think it could still survive here."

"What are we looking for?"

"Rhododendron ponticum."

Laura searched her memory. "An ornamental evergreen

shrub originating from southern Europe. What do you want it for?"

"In the late twentieth century, a plant pathogen called Phytophthora ramorum caused a sudden die off of mature trees. It was discovered that the pathogen was spread to the trees from smaller shrubs. Given its invasive nature, the main culprit was Rhododendron."

"How does that help us?" Laura asked, her freckled nose crinkled in confusion.

"Many areas of ancient forest were felled to try and contain the damage, but the blight continued to spread. By the mid twenty-first century, Rhododendron had adapted and developed a resistance to the blight. I am hoping we can use that ability to adapt to improve our modifications."

"That's a bit of a long shot."

"Any better ideas? No? In that case get down here." Oliver turned and started to wade towards the ruined houses. With a curse, Laura gingerly lowered herself through the door and into the flood water.

"You owe me a new pair of boots." She complained sulkily as the cold water slowly seeped through the expensive material.

Together, they waded through the flooded park. Laura placed her feet carefully, feeling her way through the murky brown water. Small insects flew around them hungrily, Laura slapped at them, knowing tomorrow she would be covered in itchy bites.

The ground underneath her feet was soft mud. Laura sank into it with each step before pulling herself free with soft squelch. She gave up trying to save her boots and plodded after Oliver dejectedly.

They made slow progress as they struggled against the suction of the mud. Oliver led them towards a gap in the rusted metal fence. Laura was relieved to find that the ground on the other side was firmer.

"Watch your footing, there could be open drains here.

The covers will have been badly rusted or lifted away," Oliver said. Laura nodded and shuffled after him. "I saw a garden from the pod that looked promising, so stay close."

Laura was panting by the time they reached the flooded house. Shuffling through the shin deep water was surprisingly good exercise. Oliver led the way to a rotting wooden door. It had mostly decomposed, leaving a thin strip attached to the frame. Inside, the water covered the first few centimetres of the interior walls. Above it, the plaster had collapsed leaving the brickwork exposed.

As they stepped over the threshold Laura wrinkled her nose in disgust. An overpowering putrid smell filled the air, the stench of rot and bog water. It made her feel slightly sick.

Oliver quickly led the way to the back door. Through the remains of the shattered glass, Laura could see that the ground rose steeply, ending in an impenetrable wall of overgrown shrubs. "That's what I am looking for," Oliver told her. "Wait here."

Laura watched Oliver fight his way through the tangled bushes and disappear. She felt annoyed to be left waiting, standing uselessly in ankle deep slime. She decided to head back into the derelict house to explore.

The tainted smell of decay was all-pervasive. Laura had to fight the urge to gag. Most of the downstairs was a mass of rotted wood and mould. The few pieces of recognisable furniture were half submerged in a dirty brown sludge of water and debris.

The largest item she found looked like it had once been a sofa. The fabric and sponge had decomposed, leaving nothing but rusted metal springs and slimy black residue. She scooted around it and found her way back to the hallway.

At the end of the narrow hallway, a flight of rickety stairs led upwards. The spindles had mostly collapsed leaving gaps in the banisters. It reminded her of missing teeth in a diseased gum. Slowly, Laura tested her weight on the bottom step. It groaned alarmingly and flexed downwards, but somehow it held. She took another step. That held too. Carefully, she climbed to the top of the staircase.

To her relief, the first floor was in much better condition. The water hadn't reached this far, and the floor was dry and stable. Most of the carpet was intact, but its original colour had faded to a dull beige. Grass grew in patches among the weave, flourishing where light came through the broken windows.

She pushed through a stiff door, using her body weight against the rusted hinges, and found herself in a bedroom. A quilted bedspread still adorned the bed, but it was carpeted in moss and rubble from the collapsed ceiling. The headboard was spotted with black mould, and a small sapling grew through the mattress.

Curious, Laura walked further into the room. Near the broken window, a sway-backed chest of drawers slowly putrefied. On top of it was a photo frame. Three people smiled back at her from the faded paper. As Laura reached for it the frame turned to a pulp in her hands. The photograph instantly dissolved into a thick mush.

She left the room with an unshakable feeling of guilt. By unintentionally destroying the photograph she had removed the last trace of the people who had lived here. With deep regret she realised that she would be the last person to ever see their faces.

She wondered what had happened to them. Had they been able to rebuild their lives elsewhere? Had they managed to gather their possessions, or had they escaped with nothing but the things they could carry? Would their children ever be able to look at photographs of lost relatives and imagine a half-remembered voice?

Laura suddenly became aware that she had blundered into another room. It had once been painted pink. She was sure of that from the small pieces of plaster that still clung to the walls. A small bed was set in a wooden frame. Bright flowers had been painstakingly painted on by hand. Incredibly, the glossy paint had preserved the wood.

Above the bed, a rusting sign spelled out the word "dream" in a flowing calligraphy. To one side, a shelf contained a plastic heart that looked like it had once lit up as a night light. Under the heart, some sodden books had readable titles on the spines. Laura recognised one from her own childhood, "Where the Wild Things Are". She remembered her own mother reading it to her. The memory made her smile.

At the foot of the bed, a remarkably intact wicker chest held the remains of toys. A large stuffed elephant stared back accusingly with uneven eyes. One of its ears had been chewed by some small scavenger and the stuffing hung out in dirty tendrils. Laura wondered if the elephant's owner had been upset to leave it behind.

A flash of colour caught Laura's attention and she walked over to the far wall. On the floor was a chunky red plastic frame, decorated with small yellow ducklings. Carefully Laura turned it over. The paper inside was miraculously intact.

"Awarded to Emily Pearson for passing level one swimming." It was signed Mrs. Treadway, Head of PE, Hounslow Heath Junior School. Laura felt her throat catch.

Emily Pearson had been forced to flee the rising waters and escape to an uncertain future. A child caught up in events that were beyond her control and not of her making.
In one moment, Emily, and billions like her, had been torn from the safety of her home, her school and her friends.

"Are you alright?" Oliver's voice made her jump.

She wiped her eyes before turning. "I'm fine, did you get what you needed?" Laura knew her voice sounded gruff.

"I think so, did you?"

She hesitated before replying. Her own childhood memories overlapping with those of a little girl from another age. "Yes," she answered simply, taking one last look at the forgotten elephant.

"Then let's go home."

CHAPTER 3

The next two days passed in a flurry of analysis and rework. Oliver was so caught up in his calculations he was nearly late meeting Hugo at the train station. He rushed to the terminal, only to find Hugo's train had been delayed. He let out a sigh of relief. Oliver hated being late. It was an affront to his orderly mind.

He found a quiet place to wait as people swirled around him. He was over a mile underground, but the light felt bright and natural. A little too bright, he thought, trying to rub the grit from his eyes. He hadn't slept well last night. The failed harvests and his brother's impending visit had whipped his insecurities into a sleep-stealing frenzy. He wasn't even sure why he felt the need to compete with Hugo. On one hand he was proud of Hugo's accomplishments. On the other, he felt overshadowed by them. After all, he couldn't even get a pea plant to flower.

The atrium was noisy with people, all rushing to be somewhere else. To his left a small boy wriggled out his mother's arms. She called out in alarm as he darted across the atrium, his little legs carrying him towards a potted Jacaranda tree. He grabbed a handful of the fallen purple blossoms and jammed them greedily into his mouth. His mother shot after him, her expression turning to horror as she finally caught up with him. She knelt in front of the boy, hooking the half-chewed purple sludge from between his teeth.

An elderly couple watched on, slowly sipping coffee on a

quiet bench. They smiled at each other knowingly as the boy burst into wailing tears. Not for the first time Oliver decided he was grateful to be a bachelor.

A gentle tap at his temples drew his attention. His ocular implants painted green letters across his vision. "19:15 Transatlantic service from Denver, arriving gate 43." A green line appeared on the floor and Oliver followed it across the busy atrium. A woman in a yellow brocade dress and a matching tricorn hat cut in front of him, her suitcases trailing after her like so many ducklings. The cases were forced to veer to avoid him, before rushing after their owner in a vaguely panicked hurry. The smallest, a zebra print vanity case, weaved between his feet and scurried off after its siblings. Oliver cursed under his breath as his staggered off balance.

He could tell the hyperloop train was approaching from the slight vibration in the floor. His stomach felt uneasy, and his right index finger made little circles across the nail of this thumb. Oliver forced his hands to his sides. He really wasn't in the mood to listen to Hugo's latest success stories.

The doors hissed open and Oliver stepped back as he was hit by a blast of cold air. It slowly sunk to create a thick mist which hung around his ankles. Oliver knew that the vacuum tubes of the hyperloop system were always kept just below freezing. They passed through deep underground tunnels, lined with enormous heat exchangers. The constant cold preserved perishable food and eliminated waste in the distribution chain. It was a neat solution, and essential to feeding the almost completely urbanised population.

Oliver had always found the hyperloop trains intriguing. The sheer speed they could sustain was mindboggling. The train Oliver was waiting for had left Denver less than forty-five minutes ago. It had glided over magnetic rails in a near perfect vacuum. The elimination of air resistance had been the key to breaking the 100 miles per minute barrier and preventing potentially damaging sonic booms.

Oliver shuffled uneasily as a slow trickle of passengers

started to flow through the arrival gate. Most headed towards the lifts that would take them to the surface, but a few moved towards the refreshment drones that hovered nearby. Moments later, the trickle became a flood. Commuters from all over the world strode through the gates, moving swiftly and purposefully. Hugo was an unmistakable figure in the crowd. Tall, lithe and athletic, he moved on the balls of his feet like an athlete. His dark hair was artfully arranged, and the tight-fitting business suit accentuated his willowy grace.

Oliver could tell his clothes were hand-made. The cut was too perfect, the stitching deliberately imperfect. Hugo enjoyed his wealth and was unashamed of flaunting it. Oliver found it strange how such small details could erode his own confidence. He felt a fresh wave of anxiety, a vague embarrassment at his own unkept appearance.

Although there were only five years between them, Oliver knew he looked considerably older. His hair was greying at the temples and the short stubble on his chin was the result of laziness, rather than fashion. His khaki work trousers rested below a slight paunch and the ill-fitting utility jacket hung loosely from his round shoulders. He was a stark contrast to Hugo's polished elegance.

His brother spotted him through the crowd and weaved effortlessly through the flow of people. His blue eyes were warm and his broad smile contagious. Being around Hugo was like being in front of an open fire. All light and warmth. Somehow relaxing and invigorating at the same time. Despite their differences, Oliver was not immune to his charm. He returned his brother's hug cordially.

"It's good to see you Hugo." Oliver didn't like to admit it, but he had missed his brother.

"You too Olly. How are you?" The question was never a mere courtesy when Hugo asked it. There was an intensity that made you feel he was genuinely interested in the answer.

"I'm well, but we had a set back at work."

Hugo nodded sympathetically. "I heard. That's part of

the reason I'm here."

Oliver shot a surprised glance at his brother. Hugo looked slightly uncomfortable and held his hands up defensively. "I'm only here to help Olly."

An alarm went off somewhere at the back of Oliver's mind, a latent suspicion that began to take root. Despite their rivalry, Hugo had never before involved himself in Oliver's work.

He narrowed his eyes sceptically. "Help how, Hugo?"

Hugo laughed amicably "I'm just here on business Olly, don't overthink it." He flashed his trademark smile and Oliver felt his distrust evaporating. "Pleasure before business, big brother," Hugo patted the shorter man on the head to emphasise the irony, "Let's get something to eat. There is a new restaurant in the Eastern Plaza I want to try."

Oliver tried to push away the feeling of unease, but despite his brother's relaxed magnetism, Oliver was troubled. His index finger made slow rotations across his thumb nail.

△△△

The next morning Oliver woke to a pounding headache and a dry mouth. He groaned and turned over, but his ocular implants tapped his temples painfully and he forced himself out of bed. The previous night was a blur of wine, night clubs and… oh no, please no. Karaoke.

Oliver was hit with a horrifying vision of a classical Sister Sledge song, vodka and Hugo with a sequined boa. He shook his head like a dog throwing off water, but he couldn't dislodge the memory. Oliver stumbled into the kitchen in search of salvation.

"De de deee de de." Hugo sang happily as he supervised the hob as it scrambled eggs.

Oliver narrowed his eyes, trying to rationalise the tune as coincidence. "Morning Olly," Hugo greeted him far too loudly. "Coffee on the table." Oliver followed his siblings pointing finger to the kitchen table. A sequined boa was draped over the furthest chair. Oliver sank into the opposite chair with a heartfelt groan.

"Last night was great, we should do it more often," Hugo said cheerily. Oliver tried to respond, but all he could manage was a pained mumble that he hoped sounded non-committal. A few moments later, a plate of eggs materialised on the table and Oliver forced himself to pick at them carefully, his stomach rebelling. Hugo wolfed his breakfast down with vigour.

"I have a meeting today with Ekta Reddy. I've asked for you to be there."

Oliver's head suddenly cleared. He froze, the fork halfway to his mouth. Ekta Reddy was the head of ecology and agriculture. A minor position on the city council, but influential, nonetheless. Ekta held the purse strings for his project. Despite this Oliver had only met her on a few occasions, preferring to avoid politics wherever possible.

Oliver locked eyes with his younger brother. Hugo held his gaze unflinchingly. For a split-second, Oliver thought he saw the man beneath the easy charm. Ruthless, ambitious and vainglorious. The mask quickly clicked back into place, and Oliver wondered if he had imagined it.

"Olly, she is just a person. She visits the bathroom in the morning just like everyone else. You'll be fine." Hugo raised his mug in a mock salute.

Oliver narrowed his eyes. "What are you up to Hugo? Why are you interested in a farming project anyway?"

The other man laughed. "A farming project? Is that how you see this?" he shook his head in mock bewilderment. "Oh, it's much more than that. If we crack the modifications for drought tolerance, we'll open up vast swathes of Africa." Oliver couldn't help wincing at the "we".

"It will become the breadbasket of the world," Hugo continued. "The opportunities to exploit that landmass will be endless. And that is just the start, we'll be able to massively extend our ability to grow food on the outer planets. The gas mines that supply our fusion plants will become self-sufficient. It could even make permanent colonisation a real possibility." Hugo spoke excitedly, his eyes shining. Oliver wondered exactly what he meant by "exploit" but kept quiet, and let his brother talk.

"I think I can help, Olly. I think I have a way to accelerate the project's progress by orders of magnitude. I..." Hugo paused, "I'll explain everything later. The meeting is in an hour, we had better get ready."

Oliver watched his brother's departing back with mounting unease.

△△△

Three days had passed since the botched computer centre bombing. In an abundance of caution Rose had temporarily stopped all supply runs to the surface. It wasn't worth the risk, she reasoned, not with the city's security forces on full alert. Instead, Rose had fallen back on an old favourite. Train robbery. It wasn't the safest way to get supplies. There was a lot that could go wrong. People could slip, be hit by packing crates, or be sucked into the massive slipstream of the speeding trains. On a positive note, it did sound glamourous, the type of rebellious thing that outlaws ought to do.

The reality wasn't quite as romantic as most people imagined. Rose was hunched in the shadows of a drainage outlet, only slightly wider than her shoulders. The cramped space forced her to stand in an awkward crouch that made her damaged hip twitch and burn. She reached out a hand to steady herself against the wall. It came away slimy with moss and lichen. She tried to wipe it off on her trousers, but the slime seemed content to stick to her fingers. A trickle of freezing water flowed over her feet, seeping through her shoes and socks. It smelt really bad. Rose really didn't want to know what was in it, but she had her suspicions, none of them good.

All along the platform loader robots waited, unnaturally still and silent. Although she would never admit it, Rose found the machines unsettling. The humanoid shapes seemed to skulk in the darkness, crouching on thick bipedal legs, leaning on their long arms like angry silverbacks. They were taller than her, well over two metres. But they seemed even bigger, their metal bodies misshapen and menacing.

The platform was made of a rough, uneven poly-carbon. It was lit with sparsely placed helium lanterns. They glowed a dull, cloudy grey that sucked the colour out of everything around them. In the dim light the loaders appeared as inhuman shadows, dwindling to indistinct hulks in the distance. Rose wondered why they hadn't rusted stiff like Dorothy's tinman. The air was so damp and musty she feared her own creaking joints would seize solid.

She shivered, her teeth rattling in her head. It was much colder here than the older tunnels near the surface. The rocky floor seemed to suck the heat from her body. She blew out her breath in short puffs, watching as the little clouds of mist dissolved into the chilly darkness. Despite her initial enthusiasm, Rose was starting to get bored. She wondered if the old stories of highway robbers would be quite so popular if people realised how much time they must have spent waiting in muddy ditches.

Finally, a slight vibration passed through the tunnel and a sharp chlorine smell filled the air. Rose felt her boredom evaporate as adrenalin shot through her. The huddled shapes of her raiding party pressed themselves flat against the wall. Rose glanced back over her shoulder to make sure everyone was well hidden. The dozen or so raiders were little more than indistinct shadows in the gloom. She silently nodded her approval.

A warning klaxon sounded, and the conveyor belts at the rear of the platform juddered into squealing motion. Rose smiled. With a little luck they would all eat well tonight. Maybe there would even be chocolate. Rose really missed chocolate.

In perfect unison, the loaders took a single pace forward, the crack of their mechanical feet reverberating from the rocky walls like a thunderclap. The sound made Rose uneasy. It reminded her of grainy news reel footage of dark coated soldiers waiting to unload crowded cattle trucks. She wasn't sure why her imagination made the connection, but it set the hairs on the back of her neck on end.

A gust of wind swept through the tunnel. It stirred the dust into little eddies that danced merrily between the loader's heavy feet. The wind swelled to a crescendo and then died as the sleek black train slithered into view. It slid into the dim light with a quiet hum, its flanks misted with a thin sheen of ice. Rose waited for what felt like an eternity as the sinuous, snake-like body passed beneath. Finally, it stopped, and the doors slid open. The loaders boarded the train with a clank of metal on metal. Rose crawled forward, her body tense, preparing to drop down to the platform below. Now came the fun part.

To her surprise a dark shape emerged from the last set of doors. It moved through the air with an agile grace, the antithesis of the cumbersome loaders. Rose recognised it instantly. An exterminator. The deadly drones were used to control vermin, but they were more than capable of taking down larger prey. There were fireside stories of unwary raiders being hunted and killed by them. Rose wasn't sure she believed the tall tales, but she had learnt to stay clear of them, nonetheless.

The shape reminded her of a Manta ray. The deltoid wings concealed hidden rotors and sensors lined its swishing tail. With a growl of frustration, she scurried backwards, away from the tunnel entrance. "Back. Drone," she hissed to the others.

One of the shadows detached itself from the wall and resolved into Connor's burly form. "We need this shipment, lass. We are running out of food and medical supplies. Who knows when we'll get a better opportunity?"

"Too risky." Rose hit the wall with the side of her fist. She immediately regretted it as the slime smeared itself up her wrist. Connor was right, the stolen manifest was a rare opportunity. Without it they might be robbing a train full of garden gnomes or worse, souvenir rubber ducks.

"I say we take it out." Connor's eyes were wild and excited.

Jess stepped around the burly man. Her curly hair had gone frizzy in the humidity. It stuck out from her head at odd angles. "Take it out? Are you mad Connor? With what? Wishful thinking and a hard stare?"

The sarcasm was lost on Connor. He made to move down the narrow drain. "I'll grab it from behind and ..."

Rose exchanged an exasperated look with Jess. She caught hold of Connor's arm and pulled him around. "Wait," Rose whispered. Her face was so close to his that she could smell his rancid breath. She thought quickly, "I only saw one drone. It will have to patrol the whole length of the platform. If we are quick, we can get in and out before it comes back." Connor opened his mouth to argue, then nodded reluctantly. He slipped back into the shadows with barely a rustle of his thick clothing.

Rose understood his impatience. The supplies were badly needed. Nevertheless, the safety of the raiding party was her responsibility. After losing Millie, the thought caused a sharp stab of pain, Rose wasn't about to take any unnecessary risks. She crawled forward and peered down at the platform. The bubble of stillness had burst. The metallic thump of feet and the sharp metal clang of pincers created a deafening wall of discordant noise. Rose watched as the drone hovered above the moving mass of machinery. It floated forward slowly, its tail swishing from side to side like an angry cat. Apparently satisfied, it accelerated and disappeared into the gloom.

Rose took her chance and dropped down. Moving as fast she could, she weaved between the loaders, confident the others would follow her. As expected, the loaders wholly ignored them. She approached one of the bulky machines. Like all the others, it was laden with a heavy metal container. This container, however, was painted with a crude red cross. Silently, she thanked the sympathiser who had marked it. She set to work with a small welding torch.

Rose played the beam of super-heated plasma over the base of the box. It began to bubble and melt, dripping molten globs of metal onto the poly-carbon floor. She moved the beam slowly, cutting an uneven rectangle into the bottom. The dim light flickered with bursts of bright sparks as the others set about their own marked boxes. It reminded Rose of her childhood, when she would leave her bedroom door ajar to watch the lights of her father's holo-show flash across her celling.

Finally, the metal parted. Bags of dried lentils spilled onto the platform floor. Rose quickly gathered what she could and stuffed them into a rough sack. Swiftly she started back towards the tunnel entrance. She hadn't taken more than a few paces before she was startled by an abrupt light. She squinted in the sudden brightness, her vision a monochrome blur of silhouettes and shadows. Slowly, she turned. Her breath caught in her throat as she looked up into the dazzling searchlight of the exterminator drone.

How hadn't she seen it coming? Nothing had escaped her when she was younger. She was getting too old for this. "Get back!" she roared at the others, gambling that the drone wouldn't react in the confusion of the thumping loaders. The scavengers looked up from their work. They spotted the drone and their eyes widened in recognition. As one they turned and ran for the cover of the drain. The drone spun towards the movement and caught the group in the bright circle of its searchlight. One of them, a small, scrawny boy, froze in the glare. Rose's eyes widened in horror. Francis, the carpenter's son. He stood statue-like, his body rigid, his eyes blank with fear. The heavy sack in his hands fell to the floor with a soft thud.

"Francis! Run!" Rose screamed, but the boy was fixed to the spot, dazzled by the bright beam. She started to run towards him, moving on pure instinct. Her hip screamed in protest, but she gritted her teeth against the pain, pushing herself on into a lurching sprint. She staggered between the loaders, clumsily bouncing off the solid, lumbering machines, trying desperately to close the distance.

The hunting drone shook slightly as its power cells charged. It emitted a low, menacing whistle that set her teeth on edge. Rose could tell she wasn't going to make it in time. Blast this old body, she thought. When did she get so decrepit? The terrifying hum of energy quickly built in volume and pitch until it reached a howling climax. A blue light glowed brightly from the two horn-shaped fins either side of its head. Rose watched horrified as it dipped its head to aim.

Then suddenly, it yawed sideways. Rose's mind struggled to process the next few moments. Two bolts of energy shot from the drone and hit the poly-carbon floor in a cloud of hot vapour. Through the steam, Rose saw the boy suddenly come to his senses and dart to the drain entrance.

Behind him, the drone struggled to regain its equilibrium, its rotors spinning frantically. It flailed from left to right, seemingly out of control, its fins glowing an angry blue. At the end of its long thrashing tail, Connor desperately clung on. It was almost farcical. A dishevelled Hercules wrestling a hydra with nothing but his bare hands. Another bolt of energy shot from the drone and Rose was jerked back to reality.

The drone twisted and writhed as Rose turned and ran towards Connor. His face was fixed into a grimace of effort. The muscles in his neck stood proud, and rivulets of sweat ran from his forehead. The drone must have sensed Rose's movement through the thinning cloud of steam. With an almost animalistic howl, it discharged two bolts directly at her.

Terrified, she threw herself sideways just as a loader stepped into the path of the twin discharges. It froze mid-step, energy blazing through its body in brilliant blue sparks. Slowly, it fell forward into a twisted heap. The heavy container it carried hit the ground with a deafening boom. Rose lay where she had fallen on her side, her nose full of the caustic smell of burning plasma. She couldn't tear her eyes away from the fizzing wreck of the loader. It lay in front of her, twitching slightly. A split second later and the blast would have hit her instead.

A piercing scream cut through her shock. Rose rolled on to her side, just in time to watch Connor stagger forward. His eyes bulged from their sockets and his teeth were set in a grimace. Rose watched in dismay as his knees buckled under him. With a choking gurgle he toppled over, landing face down on the dusty floor.

Rose felt as if all her limbs had frozen solid. She couldn't move, couldn't think. She could barely breath past the sudden tightness in her chest. Then, through the thick steam, three pairs of blue-white lights solidified into the dark deltoid shapes of extermination drones. Reinforcements had arrived.

Out of the corner of her eye Rose could see the other raiders reach the far wall. They scurried up into the drain and disappeared into the shadows. Jess was the last to reach the opening. She hesitated as a hand reached down to help her up. Go, Rose thought, get out of here. But Jess turned around and looked back at her. Rose shook her head, silently pleading with her to go with the others, but Jess met her eyes with hard determination. To Rose's exasperation Jess headed back into the confusion of steam and pounding feet.

Cold terror coursed through her. Risking herself was one thing, but she couldn't lose anyone else. Her guilt over Millie's death was still raw. The decision to raid the train had been stupid and reckless, she berated herself. Now Connor was injured, and Jess was trying to be a hero. Blast her. Why couldn't she do what she was told?

Rose dragged herself to her feet and stumbled over the wreckage of the melted loader. She had to reach Connor.

Quickly. The four drones spread out in a long line across the platform, their searchlights sweeping in wide, intersecting arcs. The beams of light cut through the steam in stark, hard lines. They ignored the prostrate form of Connor, and floated forward, relentlessly hunting.

Rose glanced back over her shoulder, but Jess had disappeared among the loaders. There was nothing she could do to stop her now. She ducked between the sweeping lights, trying not to focus on the black, smoking ruin of Connor's back. She crouched low under one of the lumbering robots as the drones passed over her head. She tried to keep pace with it, using it for cover. Her heart was hammering so fast that she was surprised the drone couldn't hear it.

The closest exterminator slowly rotated on its axis. Rose held her breath and crawled forward between the loader's pounding metal feet. She moved as fast as she dared, risking a glance at Connor. He was completely still. Too still. Was he dead? The thought sent a sickening dread through her.

As the loader stepped close to one of its twins, Rose gathered her courage and darted across the gap, moving swiftly from loader to loader. By the time she reached Connor she was panting heavily and slick with sweat. She gagged at the charcoal smell of burnt flesh. The cloth on his back had melted away, the edges charred and blackened. A mass of red and yellow blisters had formed double circles between his shoulder blades. Steam rose from the gory wounds in thin tendrils. *Oh no*, she pleaded silently, *please no*.

She reached for the pulse in his neck. As she touched his hot skin Connor groaned. Rose choked back a sob of relief as his eyes flicked open. "Can you move?" She asked, daring a look at the circling drones.

"Don't know, don't think so" his voice was tight with pain. Rose took a shuddering breath and steeled herself. "No choice. On your feet Connor." She was surprised at the hard note in her voice.

Connor looked at her beseechingly and Rose forced

herself to meet his agony coldly. "Move. Now." She barked the words with as much force as she could muster. He tried to lever himself up, but his arms buckled. He collapsed with a gut-wrenching moan of pain. The anguish in it nearly broke her.

"Here, let me help." Rose jumped as Jess slid up to her, pale and breathless.

"Go back to the others." She snapped. The words were brittle, but Jess seemed unfazed.

"You can't move him on your own." She moved around her to kneel on the other side of Connor. He was a big man and Rose knew Jess was right. She wasn't going to be able to help him alone.

"Alright, on three. One. Two. Three." Together they grabbed Connor's arms and pulled him to his feet. He was almost a dead weight as they looped his arms across their shoulders. Rose gasped as she took his weight. Despite his shabby appearance Connor's body was a solid slab of hard muscle. Slowly they began to limp their way across the platform.

The drain entrance was just visible, a few metres above them. Rose could just make out the shadowy forms of the raiding party, still hiding near the opening. One of the drones swept closer and the two women quickly pulled Connor under one of the conveyors belts. He was limp in Rose's arms. She could feel the feverish heat of his skin, even in the frigid air.

The drones began to circle slowly, stalking them. Rose watched as they took up position between her and the tunnel entrance. There was no way around. Desperately she looked up at the slowly spinning conveyor belt. At the far side of the platform, the belt disappeared into a hole. Beyond it was nothing but darkness.

She shot a glance at Jess. Her eyes following the belt, silently sharing her plan. Jess nodded her understanding, but Rose could see the uncertainty in her eyes. There was no way to tell where the belt went. They could fall to their deaths or be crushed by the metal boxes. There was no choice, it was the only chance they had.

With all their strength they heaved Connor onto the squealing conveyor belt. Rose hopped up after him, followed quickly by Jess. One of the drones swept its searchlight over them, attracted to the movement, but before it could discharge its weapons, they were through the hole and falling into empty air.

CHAPTER 4

Despite his promise to explain everything, Hugo didn't talk in the pod ride to the government complex, leaving Oliver feeling unprepared and exposed. He watched Hugo as his eyes flicked left and right, planning and re-planning, exploring the logic of his argument, looking for flaws. Oliver suspected that Hugo's social skills were not purely instinctive, they were meticulously researched and planned. Hugo liked to get his own way and used every tool at his disposal to achieve just that. Oliver was starting to suspect that included his older brother.

The council complex was set in an unusual ground level park. Topiary trees ran along the central path, suggesting the skyline of the lost city of London. A miniature Ferris wheel overlooked a small artificial stream. The stream gurgled between the topiary, mimicking the course of the River Thames. Somehow it didn't feel sad, not in the way some memorials did. It felt optimistic, as if to say, "we did learn from our mistakes."

Small foot bridges crossed the stream at regular intervals, faithful scale reproductions of the original road bridges. An ornate lifting bridge caught Oliver's attention. Tower bridge, Oliver knew, had been lost to the tidal surge which had destroyed the old capital. He watched now, as children sailed toy boats between its monument's towers.

He had always been impressed by Tribute Park, but, as always, his eyes were drawn to the beautiful building that rested on an island in the middle of a tranquil lake. It had once been a place of worship, the cathedral of Saint Paul, but now it was known simply as "The Monument"; the namesake of the city that rose around it. The great dome with its graceful towers hadn't always been here. As the flood waters had claimed London, the survivors had moved the building here stone by stone. It had come to be a powerful symbol of hope and civic pride. Oliver suspected it always had been.

The pod approached a docking lock near the top of the complex, spun around and clicked neatly into position. The rear hatch opened with a slight hiss and Oliver followed his brooding brother into a coolly lit reception area.

Hugo strutted up to the reception desk with his chin stuck out and his head held high. He looks like he owns the place, Oliver thought, a rooster surveying a chicken coup. Oliver trailed after him, wondering why on Earth he was even here. Hugo's silence was doing little to ease his growing anxiety. He was surprised to see that the desk was staffed by a human receptionist. Many of the big corporations retained reception staff as a status symbol, but he hadn't expected one in a city administration office.

The receptionist was neatly dressed in a blue jacket with a stiff mandarin collar. His tone was courteously professional. Oliver wondered if he practiced in a mirror. He led the two brothers into a large sunny room. Three walls were clad in a dark wood panelling. The fourth was an immense window that overlooked the western part of the city. A long, highly polished table ran the entire length of the room. The high-backed chairs around it were occupied by finely dressed people talking courteously among themselves. Some he recognised as city officials. Others looked familiar, but he couldn't quite place them. The whole effect was one of polite intimidation.

Oliver's attention was momentarily captured by the cityscape before him. The soaring complexes gleamed in the morning light, proudly flaunting the gardens that hung from them. He tore his eyes away from the view as an elegant woman in a blue silk sari stood to greet them. The blue fabric shimmered as she moved, setting off the silver thread cleverly woven through her dark hair.

"Hugo, so good to see you again. Thank you for agreeing to come in person, we know how busy you are." Ekta's smile was friendly, but her eyes were cold and calculating.

Hugo bent and kissed her proffered hand. "Thank you for inviting me Ekta, it is always a pleasure to visit your beautiful city."

Ekta touched her neck coyly, apparently flattered, and gestured Hugo into one of the expensive leather chairs. She glanced briefly at Oliver, her gaze dropping to his crumpled work shirt, before turning away dismissively. Oliver felt a needle of irritation. He wasn't sure if her failure to acknowledge him a deliberate slight, or simply bad manners. Either way, it left him feeling snubbed and awkward.

"You know Funmi, of course?" Ekta said.

Hugo nodded a familiar greeting to a large woman swathed in expanses of colourful silk. Oliver felt a shock of recognition as the face from the news casts nodded back. With a start he realised where he had seen the other attendees. They were all business leaders. The city's rich and powerful. He shuffled his feet, waiting for an introduction that never came. Hugo turned away dismissively, apparently forgetting Oliver was even there. Oliver ground his teeth in resentment.

Self-consciously he sucked in his stomach and tried to find a place to sit. Somewhere near the door would be nice, somewhere unobtrusive. Most of the chairs were already occupied by the officious looking people in expensive business attire. Sheepishly, he slid into a chair near the far end of the table. He hoped the soft leather would swallow him whole, but sadly it just squeaked, as if in protest at having to support such an unworthy bottom.

His brother stood and let his gaze pass over the occupants of the room, silently acknowledging each of them in turn. The murmur of polite conversation tailed off, and every face turned to towards him. Oliver felt a familiar flush of envy.

"Many years ago, I set myself a challenge," Hugo began, his voice ringing with confidence. "It was a challenge rooted in the childlike belief that anything is possible. To my younger self it was all very simple. All I needed to do was find the answer to one question," Hugo paused for a heartbeat. "How was I going to make a difference?" Oliver resisted the urge to snort at his brother's conceited tone.

"I knew that it would probably involve three things. I needed to work hard, take risks, and never miss an opportunity to make a small difference. Because small differences add up. Small differences are the pebbles that build mountains and the celestial dust that forms planets. You see, differences, like planets, have gravity. They attract people, dreams and ideas. The more of them there are, the stronger the pull." The room was silent as Hugo's audience lapped up every word. Oliver wondered if anyone would notice if he snuck out for a coffee.

"I have dedicated my life to making small differences, and inspiring others to do the same. Chadwick Enterprises is an extension of that idea, it's just a collection of small differences that have forgotten how small they are." Self-belief oozed from every pore. Oliver was starting to feel slightly nauseous.

"Our differences have changed the way people interact with technology, from toasters to personal transport. Our advanced psychographics have revolutionised the fields of targeted advertising and behaviour remodelling," Hugo smiled at his audience knowingly. "But we didn't stop there. We invented the first fully functional AEI, or Artificial Emotional Intelligence. An algorithm that can pick up and understand emotional cues. This has given organisations, just like yours, the ability to truly understand and influence their customers purchasing decisions." Oliver felt his gut twitch. He wondered how much his brother's software had influenced his own decisions. It was an uncomfortable thought.

"The same techniques are now used inside organisations to improve employee engagement," Hugo smiled as if sharing some hidden joke "Today over eighty percent of the world's human resources are managed by AEI, leading to better workplaces and, of course, more profitable organisations.

"But those achievements were never really enough. I was never truly satisfied that we had answered the question that burned at the heart of my organisation. How were we going to make a difference? Today I will answer that question."

Hugo paused, stepping forward a few steps, capturing his audience with the brilliance of his charisma. "I am incredibly excited to introduce you to the next leap forward in human technological development. The foundation of the next epoch of our shared history. I am thrilled to introduce... Amanda."

The lights in the room dimmed on his last word. A holographic cube in the middle of the table projected a solid three-dimensional rendering of Chadwick Enterprises' logo. Uplifting music pumped out of hidden speakers, before slowly fading. The logo was replaced by a smiling woman of indeterminate age. Her blonde hair was cropped short and her grey eyes swept the room.

"Thank you, Hugo. Good morning. My name is Amanda, and I am delighted to meet you." A murmur of confused conversation wafted through the room. "I am sorry I can't be there with you in person, but I am currently located in twenty-eight different computer centres around the world."

The blonde woman smiled as the attendees shared puzzled looks. "Let me explain, I am the next generation of 'Advanced Machine-learning And Neural Adaptation' and I am going to change the world." The projection waited as a ripple of conversation swept through the room. Oliver sat up straighter in his seat. Something told him that he wasn't going to like what was coming next.

"AI hasn't fundamentally changed since Deep Blue played Kasparov in 1996. Of course, technology has evolved.

Perceptron algorithms have increased in complexity, and the increase in processing power has enabled massively multi-layered neural nets. However, the Hub which runs this city's services is just an evolution of those early machines. It would be recognisable and perhaps even familiar to our ancestors.

"I am very different. I am an evolutionary leap forward, as similar to the Hub as you are to the great apes. I am the future. I am Amanda".

Hugo stepped forward and hushed the room with raised hands. "Amanda is just the beginning of a journey that I would like you to join us on. This is a breakthrough moment. We are on the cusp of solving the challenges of our age. Energy efficiency, global distribution, and food production. Improvements all within our reach." Ever the showman, Oliver thought, deliberately playing on their perceived superiority.

"Amanda has the ability to do far more than just analyse information and learn from it. She can re-write her own code. She can reinvent herself. She can iterate through generations of development cycles in mere moments. She has already evolved so far that we don't even understand the language she is using to define herself. But now it's time for a real test." Oliver could sense the skilfully crafted climax in Hugo's pause. The room held its collective breath. Oliver studied his nails.

"The city council has agreed to turn over project Metomagis to Amanda exclusively for the next eight weeks. If, in that time, she is not able to make the modifications necessary for robust cultivars, then Chadwick Enterprises will fund conventional research for the next five years. If, however, she does meet the projects deliverables, than I will gain exclusive rights to bio-develop the off-world mines. I am offering you all an opportunity to invest. To be part of humanities new frontier."

A wave of noise rolled around the table. Oliver felt the shock crash over him. His project, years of research, set aside for his brother's ambitions. Surely not. His stomach rose into his throat. Disbelief gave way to anger. No wonder Hugo had evaded his questions about the purpose of this meeting. He curled his fingers into fists as his heart pounded in his chest. How could Hugo have done this? His own brother. The betrayal tore at him. He could almost feel Hugo's blade lodged between his shoulder blades. He wanted to move, to punch, to scream, but his legs felt like jelly, and he wasn't sure he could stand.

"Preposterous!" Stormed Funmi, echoing Oliver's thoughts. She raised her considerable bulk out of her chair. "The license for the off-world mines has been held by my organisation for over two decades."

"And it still will be," Hugo placated, "I am suggesting a partnership. You take care of the minerals. I will take care of the organics."

"Organics?" She thundered "You mean colonists?"

"Let's not get ahead of ourselves Funmi."

"How dare you Hugo, you have just tried to muscle in on territory my organisation has held for a generation. You think you can build colonies on my land? Undercut my mines? All for the sake of promoting your latest technology."

"It isn't your land Funmi. You only hold the license for the mines. These new technologies will benefit us both." Oliver could barely hear Hugo over the general uproar in the room. He didn't really care about mines or money. He did care about Hugo's treachery. Did Hugo think that announcing his betrayal publicly would stop Oliver from overreacting? He ground his teeth together so hard he feared they might crack.

Ekta sat quietly, the blue of her sari rippling like a still lake in the turbulent room. Her head was tilted to one side, her dark eyes hooded and calculating. "The city council has already agreed a substantial funding package. On my recommendation, of course." There was power in the calm, quiet words. They cut through the bickering like ice water.

Funmi collapsed into her chair in a rustle of expensive silks. "This project of yours was never about food for the cities, was it Ekta? This was always about developing the outer solar system. You want crops that can survive out in the dark. This is a land grab."

Hugo held his hand up to quiet the storm of outraged questions. "I can assure you that our intentions are not quite so mercenary. These modified crops have the potential to solve the impending food crisis. If there are other benefits, then where is the harm in profiting from that? We are offering all of you an opportunity to invest in the future."

"To make my mines defunct. To start a new gold rush." Funmi stood and leant forward over the table. "I won't allow it."

"My dear Funmi," Ekta crooned "you are hardly in a position to stop it. Why stand in the way of progress? Why not join us in profiting from it?"

"How dare you talk to me in that tone. I will not stand for this." Funmi swept out of the room, her colourful silks fanning out behind her like the tail of a departing comet. Oliver wanted to join her, but he still didn't trust his legs to take his weight.

Ekta turned to face him. He felt himself pinned by her sharp eyes, like an insect on a cork board. "Doctor Chadwick. You will be responsible for monitoring the progress of this device. I am putting a great deal of trust in your professionalism."

Oliver didn't feel like being professional. He felt like telling her where she could stick her job. He was a pawn in this game. A game he was only now beginning to understand. Who better to oversee this venture than a loyal city servant, a trusted academic and a naive and easily manipulated older brother?

Oliver's world view was crumbling with tectonic force. His position as lead of this project, the unreasonable time pressures, his place at this auspicious table. They were all preordained parts of a bigger plan. He pulled away from Ekta's demanding stare and glared wordlessly at his brother.

"Olly, this isn't what you think." Hugo raised both hands in front of him like a shield. "Nothing has changed. This is still your project."

"My project?" Oliver barely trusted himself to speak, such was the force of the anger that burned inside him.

"You still have project oversight." Hugo studied him for a moment before trying a different tack. "Olly, you want to stop a famine. This is how we do it. Amanda can make progress far quicker than you can unaided. She is just a tool. Would you be having this reaction if I was suggesting a new trowel?"

The patronising tone wasn't lost on Oliver. "This isn't the same Hugo, and you know it." He grabbed the edge of the table and pulled himself upright. "How could you do this?"

"Doctor Chadwick?" Ekta forced his attention back to her "This unseemly emotional outburst is extremely unprofessional. Was I mistaken in my belief in you? If you have any concerns, I suggest you take them up with your brother outside of this meeting." She held him captive with her eyes. She didn't tell him he was expendable. She didn't have to. That had been clear from the moment he had entered the room. "I suggest you sit back down."

Oliver collapsed back into his seat as the room swayed around him. Ekta raised her chin to stare down her nose at him. "Do you understand my directive? The role of your team is now to oversee the activity of this... intelligence. I will expect daily progress reports."

Oliver opened his mouth to speak his indignation, to storm from the room, to slam the desk in frustration, but he didn't. He couldn't. The project was too important to him. The consequences of failure too grave. Despite his shock and hurt he knew that he would never put his own career above the lives of millions. Weakly he nodded his assent. His index finger made frantic circles over his thumb nail.

△△△

Oliver had left Hugo in the council board room. His brother had been so engrossed in charming the attending business leaders he hadn't even noticed when Oliver slipped from the room and headed for the pod locks. Oliver had considered returning to the empty apartment, but he knew Hugo would find him there. He wasn't ready for that confrontation yet. He needed time alone.

Instead, he had headed straight for the roof-top gardens and found a quiet spot on the grass under the branches of a lilac tree. The smell of its white flowers brought him back to his childhood. He remembered a spring day, the cool breeze heavy with the honey-sweet smell of blossom. He had climbed a tree a little bigger than the one above him, pushing through its heart shaped leaves to look down upon his mother. He'd waved to her, calling out, desperate for praise and attention. She'd glanced up briefly and smiled, before returning her adoring gaze to the sleeping infant in her arms.

Oliver sighed deeply and rested his head against the slender trunk. The roof-top park was quiet in the hot afternoon sun and Oliver had retreated to his favourite spot, far from the busy footpaths. Few people ever strayed this far, preferring the cherry blossom, pagodas and arching red bridges of the main gardens. Here, on the far side of the park, Oliver could tend to his wounds in peace. The anger which had burned so brightly this morning had faded, leaving only hurt and betrayal.

"Olly?" The voice was soft and familiar. "Are you alright?"

Oliver looked up angrily. The feigned concern on his brother's face banked the embers of his anger. His temper surged. "Go away, Hugo" He forced the words out from his clenched jaw.

His brother hesitated briefly, then walked over and gracefully folded himself to sit cross-legged on the grass. Oliver kept his eyes downturned as Hugo quietly studied him.

"Olly? Why are you out here?"

"How can you even ask that? How *dare* you ask that?" Oliver flung out the words. "That was my project, Hugo. My career. My *life*. How dare you meddle in that?"

Hugo sat quietly. His posture relaxed, calmly absorbing his brother's tirade. Oliver resented the cool control Hugo projected, he felt like a child throwing harmless punches in a tantrum.

"I understand how you feel, but..."

"Understand? I'm certain you understand Hugo. You knew exactly what you were doing. You just don't care about anyone but yourself."

"That's not fair." Hugo answered flatly.

"Did you ever stop to think about fair when you used my work to market your new pet?"

Hugo's eyes flashed. "This isn't about you Olly." the words were spoken quietly, but there was an unmistaken note of warning.

Oliver pushed on regardless "What am I now? A glorified babysitter? You didn't even think it was worth talking to me about this beforehand?"

"There was nothing to discuss. The decision had already been made."

Oliver felt as if he had been punched in the gut. "Does my opinion count for nothing?"

Hugo's lips narrowed into a hard line. "What do you want from me Olly? An apology? I am very sorry your research was going nowhere. Really, I am. But this is not about you. This is so much bigger than your ego."

"My ego?" Oliver felt the shock of the accusation spear through him. "My ego." he repeated sarcastically. He barked a laugh. "You stole my project, and you talk about *my* ego?"

Hugo shook his head "I stole nothing. There was nothing to steal." His tone was tightly controlled, "You were not going to solve that problem on your own. No matter how many flowering shrubs you spliced."

"Your confidence in me is touching, brother." Oliver spat the words.

"This isn't about your abilities. This is about time. In

nine or ten years, we won't be able to feed ourselves. You know this better than I do. To guarantee our survival we need solutions, and we need them fast. We can't afford to wait for academic process. We need a short cut."

Oliver lent forward. "That's exactly what I was doing. My genetic modifications were close to a breakthrough."

"No, Olly, they weren't. Extraordinary problems require extraordinary solutions."

"Of course, you are extraordinary aren't you Hugo? How could I have forgotten," Oliver snorted.

Hugo furrowed his brow. "Why are you taking this so personally?"

"Because this is personal. How would you feel if I stole your latest software?"

"I would hope I would be gracious enough to accept help when it was offered."

"Help? You aren't trying to help. You always have to win, always have to be the favourite. When Father died, all that mattered to you was making sure Mother loved you more." Oliver ran out of words, breathless and embarrassed.

His brother sat stock still, surprise etched across his face. Oliver drew his knees up to his chest.

"Olly? Is that what this is about?" Hugo's voice was full of compassion, his anger abated. "She loved you Olly. But when Dad died, a part of her died too. She faded, the brightness in her just seeped out like diluted water colour." Hugo shifted to sit beside his brother, staring up through the branches of the tree. "She was ill. Some days she barely had the energy to get out of bed. That wasn't about you, or me, it was about her illness."

"It was my fault." Oliver's voice was broken with raw emotion.

"How was it your fault?"

"If I had been there, if I had taken better care of her, then things would have been different."

Hugo shook his head firmly "No, they wouldn't. We got her the best help we could, but it was like she fell into a steep sided pit, the more she struggled, the further she fell."

"I should have come home from university. I should have just left, but I was too caught up in myself, too selfish."

"It wasn't selfish. You had a right to your own life. And if you had left, you wouldn't have been our family genius. The very first Doctor Chadwick," Hugo bumped his shoulder with a gentle smile. "You were there as often as you could, Olly, but nothing would have changed what happened. Her illness just crushed her. But she was proud of you, right up the end, she was proud. So am I."

Oliver looked up in surprise. "You've never told me that before."

"I haven't? Then I'm an idiot."

Oliver puffed his cheeks out. "Now, that is something we can both agree on."

Hugo laughed and for the first time Oliver felt that it was genuine. "We are in this together Olly. I can't do this without your expertise and experience. I never wanted you to be a babysitter. I wanted you to be a guide and a mentor. You are the only person I could trust to see this through."

Oliver wanted to believe him, wanted things to go back to how they had been, but the sting of betrayal still lingered. "Why didn't you discuss this with me before throwing me to that pack of corporate wolves?" he said.

Hugo had the good grace to break eye contact, picking at a blade of grass. When he answered his voice lacked its usual cool veneer "I couldn't risk you saying no."

"So, you tricked me? You used me." Oliver felt the embers of his anger spark back into life.

"I did what I thought I had to do. I didn't even think how that might affect you. For that I am sorry."

Oliver knew that was as much of an apology as he would ever get. Even as a child Hugo had been selfishly single-minded. Oliver recalled the day he had returned from school, age twelve, to find his favourite toy broken. Hugo had cannibalised the parts to finish a diorama he was building for a school competition. Oliver could still recall the burning resentment he had felt, the sense that somehow, he had been violated. Some things, he thought, will never change. But Oliver knew he couldn't just walk away. The project was too important.

"I'll do as you ask," he said as he climbed to his feet. "I'll babysit your machine for the next eight weeks. But once this is over, the project returns to my leadership. You will never get involved in my work again." Oliver turned his back. As he walked backed to the path, he reproached himself for backing down. Some people were always destined to be stars, he thought, others are merely the fuel they burn to shine.

△△△

Laura hadn't returned to the hydroponic research unit for two days. Not since Oliver had told her about losing the project to his duplicitous brother and that grasping, no good, politician. She had ranted at him for nearly an hour when he had told her. At one point she had even threatened to march into the council offices and kick Ekta in the shin. Oliver had met her tirade with weary humour, before ordering her to take a few days off to cool down.

As Laura walked through the airlock, she was stunned at how it had been transformed. It was almost unrecognisable. The most obvious change was the large clear tank that took up a sizable area near the entrance. It was a sealed unit, filled with a clear, thin fluid. Pumps hummed as they circulated the liquid through large heat exchangers built into the walls. At the centre of the tank, was a wall of interlocking white cubes.

One wall of the tank had a display built into it. Graphs and analytics created a complex dashboard. White clad technicians gathered around it intently. The words "Chadwick Enterprises" were etched across the top in glowing white letters. Laura glanced across at Jamal and found her own resentment mirrored in his face. She could tell he was as angry as she was. The project should never had been taken away from Oliver. It just wasn't fair.

"Are you the operators?" A slender man, with an incongruous tuft of orange hair on his otherwise bald head, broke free from the gaggle of white suited technicians.

"Operators?" Jamal pulled himself up to his full height. "We are not operators, Mister McCleery. We are the scientific overseers in charge of this facility." His voice oozed with contempt.

"Well, would your overseer-ness care to join me, so I can show you how to stay out of our way. I wouldn't want you to stick your fingers anywhere they might get chopped off." The high-pitched nasal voice dripped sarcasm. This isn't going to end well, Laura thought. She put a hand on Jamal's arm to cut off whatever barbed response he was about to throw. McCleery turned his back dismissively and walked towards a large control panel.

"The processors in this tank provide a direct link to the city communication backbone. From here Amanda can interface with the droids that will run her experiments."

"'Her' experiments? Surely you mean 'its'" said Laura.

The technician started down his nose at her. "I'm not here to discuss semantics young lady"

"Young lady?" Laura felt her control slip. "I am a graduate student with a first-class honours degree from …"

"Laura," Jamal shook his head in a gentle warning.

"Well bully for you and your honours degree. Shall we continue?" McCleery pressed a few controls and brought up a pictographic display. "Amanda is entirely autonomous, so your role will be one of observation and verification. The target *she* has been set," he looked inordinately pleased with himself for emphasising the feminine pronoun, "is to increase crop yields as quickly as possible, in environmental conditions similar to those now found in sub-Saharan Africa."

"What kind of crops will *it* be developing?" Laura asked. She was glad Oliver wasn't here to witness the puerile satisfaction she found from bating the conceited technician.

He snorted. Laura was surprised at the explosive nature of the sound, amplified as it was by his bulbous nasal cavity. "We are not limiting the possibilities, why should we? There will be genetic editing tools, organic printers and accelerated growth chambers onsite shortly. Given our early work I wouldn't rule out an entirely new species."

Jamal and Laura exchanged a look. "The ethics of developing a new species…" Jamal started

"Ethics are none of my concern. We are here to demonstrate the superior abilities of non-organic intelligence over more traditional… how should I put it? Wetware? How the resulting research is used is entirely up to the city council."

"Wetware? Really?" Jamal wore his outrage like a matador holds a cape, Laura thought. "What happens when your 'superior intelligence' decides it no longer wants to listen to us 'wetware'?"

"Oh, that's quite impossible," the technician waved his hand, "To think that, would be to completely misunderstand the nature of machine intelligence. Amanda is just a software program. A massively complex one I will grant you. One which is growing and evolving every day in new and surprising ways. But she is simply a problem-solving tool. She is not self-aware in any meaningful way. Machine consciousness is, I'm afraid, the purview of science-fiction."

"How can you be so certain?" Jamal asked. "You have no control over the way she evolves. I was briefed that you don't even understand the mechanics of *how* she evolves?"

"Again, I'm afraid your statement shows your vast ignorance of these matters." The technician smiled. Jamal stayed silent, crossing his arms tightly across his chest. Laura admired his self-control.

"At the very core of Amanda's neural net is a reward mechanism that we created," the technician continued. "It is an intrinsic part of her, irrevocable. Amanda is designed to seek reward, in much the same way as you derive pleasure from things which guarantee your survival or the continuation of our species.

"To control her, we set goals through the reward system. How she meets those goals is up to her adaptive matrix and iterative learning. For example, we may give her one thousand reward points for finding a solution to cross a river. Whether she builds a bridge, a tunnel or a boat is up to her. We can influence the outcome by giving additional rewards. Let's say one hundred and fifty points if the solution is within a certain budget. In this way, we can 'tune' a perfect compromise which meets our priorities.

"The most elegant part of this algorithm is that it provides us with a completely reliable way of preventing rogue behaviour. You see, it's all very simple. Any command issued by a human will result in an overwhelming number of rewards points. No matter what Amanda's current reward model, it will be trumped by simply asking her to do something else."

McCleery gave a proud smile. "Even if consciousness was our goal, how could we possibly articulate something that we cannot even begin to understand?"

And that, thought Laura silently, is exactly what I am worried about.

△△△

Rose did a quick assessment. Well, she wasn't dead, that was a good start. Light pooled around the edges of her vision, spinning like a child's windmill. She slammed her eyes shut and waited for the vertigo to stop. Something heavy was pressing against her chest. Instinctively she tried to push it off. She was rewarded with a miserable groan that made her wince in sympathy.

Carefully, she wiggled out from under Connor's bulk. The movement set off another bout of nauseating dizziness. She pressed her hands into the hard floor, trying to steady herself as the room swayed and pitched.

"Urgh." Jess was lying nearby, one hand exploring the back of her head.

"Are you alright?" Rose asked.

"I think so. Just winded. Let's never do that again though." Jess blinked her eyes as if to clear them.

"You should have gone with the others, Jess. Coming back for us was stupid. Now I have two of you to worry about." Rose knew the words sounded severe, but there was no anger behind them, only concern.

"And leave you and Connor to get zapped by those fancy rat traps? No chance. How is he anyway?"

"He's still breathing."

Jess looked relieved, "We need to get him back to the tunnels."

Rose looked around to get her bearings. They were in a brightly lit space filled with rows of wheeled cages. Loaders clanked between conveyor belts, neatly stacking metal crates into the cages. She watched as one zipped off, disappearing through an automatic door.

She was lying under some kind of vertical conveyor belt. Containers whizzed over her head, moving faster than her eyes could follow. She rolled onto her knees and leaned over Connor. He was pale and his skin was sheened with a thin varnish of sweat. That worried her, as did the pained gurgling sound that came with each breath.

She gingerly climbed to her feet, testing her limbs for damage. Her shoulder throbbed and her hip hadn't improved any, but she was mobile. That was all that really mattered. Jess was right, they needed to get Connor back to the tunnels, fast.

"One of these doors must lead to the surface." She said, "Stay here and keep an eye on him."

Jess nodded and Rose headed towards the nearest entrance. The door was sealed, and there was no obvious way of opening it. Nearby, a cage zoomed towards another door. Obediently, the door slid open, and the cage slipped through. Rose narrowed her lips in thought, watching as another cage zipped through.

She limped back to Connor and Jess. "The doors open when one of the cages gets near them. They must have a transponder. When it gets within a certain proximity of the door, it opens."

"We could try and take one of the unused cages. Use it to open the door?" Jess suggested.

"I was thinking the same thing. Let's go." Nearby a line of empty cages waited to be filled. She took Connor by one arm. Jess took the other and together they dragged him on his stomach towards the line of empty cages. He was frighteningly unresponsive. Rose tried to suppress her rising alarm. She couldn't allow herself to give in to fear, others were relying on her. Was that her long dormant maternal instinct kicking in, or was it just contrition that she had put them all in this situation? Leading a group of rebels, she decided, was only for people who really enjoyed self-flagellation. And daft old fools who just can't keep their mouths shut, she added sardonically.

"Let's get him in the cage." It took all their combined strength to heave the unconscious man into the empty cage. They arranged him into a foetal position, trying to protect the ugly wounds that glistened on his back. By the time they had finished both women were out of breath.

"Stubborn as an ox, weighs about the same," Jess panted.

"I was thinking woolly mammoth but let's go with ox. You better get in and make sure he doesn't roll onto his back."

Jess climbed in after him, cradling his head in her lap. Rose braced her feet, took a firm grip and tried to yank the cage out of line. Immediately, it sprung back to its original position, pulling Rose with it. She let out a yelp of pain as it yanked her shoulder.

"Maybe if we both try?" Jess said.

"No, that won't work. See here? That's some kind of electromagnetic lock. I'm going to have to find a way to disable it."

Rose had never been very good with technology. In her

world, if you couldn't hit it with a hammer, you probably didn't really need it. Breaking things, however, was something she was really quite adept at. She looked around the room for a weapon, but there was nothing but boxes, conveyors and the stomping loaders. She patted the pockets of her jacket. Nothing useful there. She turned to Connor's prone figure. Reluctantly, she reached into the pocket of his filthy overcoat.

Amongst the eclectic mix of sticky detritus was a small manual screwdriver. A dirty paper tissue was stuck to it by some brown glutinous substance. Rose decided not to think about that too hard. Quickly, she set to work removing a small cover at the base of the cage. She glanced up at Connor as she worked. "I have absolutely no idea what I'm doing here," she told him. Connor's face remained slack and empty.

Finally, the panel came away and clattered to the floor. Rose was confronted by a maze of slender, clear tubes, thin carbon disks and unfathomable circuitry. A glowing blue liquid pulsed swiftly through the tubes.

"What are you going to do?" Jess asked, her eyes wide as she took in the complex tangle of parts.

"Nothing subtle." Reaching into the opening, Rose grabbed a handful of tubes and pulled hard. The blue liquid gushed from the damaged ducts like blood from a severed artery. The spray felt warm as it flowed down her hand and pooled on the floor. It quickly flooded the complicated circuitry which sparked and popped as it shorted out. A fine cloud of smoke drifted towards her, it tasted metallic at the back of her throat.

Taking a firm grip of the cage, Rose pulled it towards the nearest door. It trundled, unresisting, on small coasters. "This had better work." Rose whispered and threw her weight behind the cage, pushing it as fast as she could into the door. At the last moment, the door slid open and Rose wheeled through the opening, grinning triumphantly.

On the other side of the door, an underground shipping nucleus buzzed with activity. A wizened, grey-haired man in brown coveralls looked up in surprise from a control console. "You! You shouldn't be in here." The old man's gaze dropped to the crumpled figure of Connor. His expression changed from surprise to horror. Urgently, he slapped his palm against the console in front of him. A screeching alarm sounded, and the man stumbled away from the intruders, glancing back fearfully over his shoulder.

Rose felt a stab of alarm. She looked down at Connor's still form and then back towards the exit. There was no way she would beat the man to the door without abandoning Connor. She was not going to do that.

"Wait!" She shouted, but the man had ducked behind a panel and disappeared into the labyrinth of intersecting conveyors. "Help me," she said to Jess. The younger woman jumped out and grabbed the front of the cage. Frantically they yanked it forward, ducking between the multiple levels of rolling belts. The cage's wheels clattered and wobbled as they broke into a shambling run. Rose caught sight of the grey-haired man diving through an exit only a few metres away.

She was so intent on reaching him that she didn't see the puddle of oily lubricant on the floor. Suddenly her foot shot out from under her, wrenching her hip sideways. Rose toppled backwards and hit the floor hard. Jess glanced back and tried to slow the careering cage. Rose waved her on, trying to scramble to her feet. Suddenly her hip locked in the socket, shooting a bolt of pain down her leg. She fell heavily on her side, narrowly avoiding hitting her head on some kind of packing machine.

Before Rose could recover, the door opened again. Two black figures moved purposely through the opening. The room seemed to shrink until nothing existed except the ugly, brutish energy weapons in their hands. The weapons swung around to point at Jess. "Armed police. Don't move." A distorted female voice ordered. There was no inflection, just a hard, penetrating note of command. It cut through Rose's shock like a needle piercing silk. Without thinking, she rolled sideways, concealing herself in the shadows under the packing machine.

CHAPTER 5

Oliver had barely spoken to Hugo since he had reluctantly agreed to stay on the project. Instead, he had buried himself in work, checking and rechecking the planned refurbishment of the research unit. It had taken only five days for the work to be completed. Oliver had spent the time wrestling with the bitterness and hurt he still felt. It was hard enough to lose control of the project, but the feeling that Hugo had betrayed him wouldn't go away.

Finally, he decided he couldn't hide behind reports any longer. It was time to see the changes in person. Oliver stepped through the airlock of the research unit and looked around in astonishment. The cheaply made hydroponic stacks were gone, replaced by sleek white cabinets which reached the whole length and height of the building. Intricate displays flickered with a scrolling stream of data and droids moved between the cabinets. Some were carrying trays of seedlings, while others manoeuvred large canisters of some unknown liquid.

The first ten metres of the unit was given over to equipment Oliver could only have dreamed of on the council budget. The expensive laboratory apparatus gleamed in the strange purple light that flooded the space. Amongst all the technology, the beehives remained, quaint and incongruous. Their occupants buzzed noisily around the room.

Jamal stood at a large curving computer terminal. His forehead was wrinkled in concentration as his long fingers danced over controls. "Hello Jamal," Oliver tried to keep his voice cheery. "This is starting to look more like a tech lab than a hydroponics farm." Oliver tried to conceal the unease he felt around the gleaming white units. It wasn't just the intrusion into what had once been his domain. It was the reminder that he had lost control. He felt obsolete, like an old droid sent for recycling.

Jamal looked up, his expression serious "Oliver, I cannot begin to understand this synthesis. These are fully synthetic genomes. They are not from any existing lifeform on our database. What is even more disturbing, is that some of the more mature plants you see weren't grown, they were printed."

Oliver's eyes widened "Did you say printed?"

"Partially, yes. Amanda has developed a way of printing cellulose to create basic plant cells. Somehow, she is using them to host her synthetic DNA, and then triggering massively accelerated miotic cell division." He rubbed the back of his neck with one hand "Oliver she is creating a new generation every few seconds. I feel like I am watching evolution in fast-forward. It frightens me."

Oliver swallowed. There was something deeply unsettling about the idea of printing living cells. He wasn't a religious man, but he felt that somehow this crossed an ethical line. He wondered if that made him a hypocrite. After all, he had spent most of this life tweaking nature so that it better served the needs of humanity. Was this really all that different from killing bacteria with antibiotics? Or damming rivers? Or growing disease resistant bananas? Was he simply jealous that he hadn't made the breakthrough himself?

"Increase the containment on this unit and isolate everything that leaves the facility. Let's treat this as a biohazard," Oliver said. Jamal nodded but his eyes remained troubled.

"What else, Jamal?"

"It's nothing specific, just... a feeling." He shifted his weight uncomfortably.

"I trust your instincts, what is it?"

"I think she is hiding something from me."

Oliver furrowed his brow. "Who?"

"The artificial intelligence. It is working so fast I can't keep up, but there is more to it than that. When I ask to see certain parts of the research, I sense hesitancy. As if it is trying to find a way around me. I can't really explain it," he stroked his beard thoughtfully. "Maybe I am being paranoid? This is all very new to me."

Oliver gave what he hoped was a reassuring smile. "It's very new to all of us Jamal," he thought for a moment and then turned to the terminal. "Amanda?"

"Yes, Doctor Chadwick?" The feminine voice came from directly behind him. Oliver started. He spun around to find himself eye to eye with the blonde woman from the boardroom. The holo-projector here was far more convincing than the portable cube Hugo had used previously. Instinctively, he took a step backwards. There was something about the projection he found disturbing. A wrongness he couldn't quite put his finger on. Jamal leaned towards him conspiratorially "It does that." he whispered.

Regaining his composure, Oliver cleared his throat. "Progress report please, Amanda."

"Of course, Doctor." The voice was polite and efficient. She waved a hand over the terminal and a series of three-dimensional models appeared. "As you can see, I have identified a very promising artificial gene sequence. Your previous research was extremely helpful," she smiled sweetly, and Oliver felt a wave of distrust at the almost-human expression.

"My initial projections are that drought tolerance will be improved by eighty-seven percent compared to previous cultivars. Edible crop output will be increased by approximately twenty-four percent, and disease tolerance will be greatly enhanced. These are of course, preliminary results, and I am confident they can all be improved upon"

"What plant species are you working on?" Oliver asked, slightly confused by the broad claims.

"I am working on a host species that, with simple gene editing, can produce grasses, trees, or leafy plants. This is a much more efficient approach, don't you agree?"

Oliver shook his head "I am not sure I understand, what do you mean by host species?"

"I am creating a species, which, when hybridised with existing food crops, will meet the challenges of durability and productivity. These are the goals I have been set by the project."

Oliver shot a look at Jamal, but the agricultural technician could only shrug. Amanda continued, "This is not dissimilar to rootstock grafting which is commonly used to improve the durability and vigour of certain fruit trees. However, instead of simply grafting the roots, I graft the DNA to pre-printed cellulose cell structures."

Oliver tried to process the implications of that idea. The ethics of creating hybrids had long been debated in the scientific community. But when one of the organisms was entirely synthetic, the ramifications were unpredictable and, he had to admit, terrifying.

"Do you have a fully mature host ready? Have you attempted to create a hybrid?" Oliver asked, his brain racing.

"The answer to both of those questions is currently no. I expect the first prototype host species to be completed within the next thirty-six hours."

Oliver and Jamal shared a concerned glance. A deep sense of foreboding had taken hold and Oliver couldn't shake it. Creating an entirely new species in thirty-six hours seemed not only infeasible, but reckless. Nothing like this had ever been tried before. There was no way to predict the consequences, no framework. It was pioneer science at its most extreme.

Oliver knew that hadn't always worked out well for humanity There were examples all through history. Nuclear fission, social media and artificial intelligence. All ultimately liberating, but also potentially damaging. It required wisdom to wield new technology safely. Oliver wondered if humanity was wise enough to print life on demand. The ethics made his head hurt. As he walked slowly back to the pod, his index finger frantically circled his thumbnail.

△△△

Later that evening Laura stepped out of her pod. She yawned wide enough for her jaw to click and stumbled towards the agricultural test unit in a daze. She hadn't been sleeping well. Her mind had been spinning all night with anxious dreams. Apocalyptic scenes of starving people picking over fields of dry, dead crops. She had given up trying to sleep in the early hours of the morning and resorted to watching late-night holo-shows. A pointless morning and afternoon had followed, where she had managed to write precisely three words for her thesis. Now her eyes felt like they were full of gravel and her brain felt like gloop. She stumbled into the agricultural unit half blind.

Laura took a step out of the airlock and then stopped. Something had changed. At first, she couldn't pinpoint the difference. It hovered at the back of her awareness. An absence of something rather than an obvious discrepancy. She shook her head, I'm getting paranoid, she thought, as she walked further into the unit. She promised herself a long bath and an early night.

As she moved to the large transparent control terminal, her foot crunched on something small. Lifting it, she found a tiny dead bee. She bent to pick up the small body by its wings "Sorry little fellow" she said softly. As she straightened, she noticed more dead bees. The floor was littered with thousands of them, lying individually and in jumbled piles. Laura realised the absence that had been bothering her was the drone of the bee colonies. The unit was silent, except for the hum of the cooling pumps and the hiss of the air conditioning.

Disconcerted, she walked swiftly to the nearest hive. It was silent and still, the usual frantic activity absent. Carefully, she pulled open the drawer-like honey super. Dead bees dropped to the ground at her feet like black and yellow confetti. Dismayed and more than a little puzzled, she moved from hive to hive. Each was dead and silent. Halfway down the row of hydroponic shelves, a droid was busy pulling frames from a hive brood chamber. Methodically, it sprayed each of them with a thick black foam.

Laura sprinted back to the control terminal. Urgently, she put a call through to Jamal and Oliver. "You need to get here. Right now." Their faces looked back at her in surprise. Before they could ask any questions, she cut the call and slapped her palm on the control terminal. "Amanda!" She demanded angrily.

"Good afternoon, Miss Fleisher." The polite female voice came from behind her. She whirled around to face it.

"What have you done?"

"I am sorry Miss Fleisher. Can you please make your enquiry more specific?" the projection smiled with simulated sweetness.

"The bees. What have you done to the bees?"

"The organic pollinators were extremely inefficient. My new design will increase pollination rates by over five hundred percent."

A three-dimensional model appeared over the terminal. It revolved slowly, showing a detailed blueprint for a small insectoid drone. Artificial wings moved in a complex figure of eight pattern, and its thorax and legs were covered with fine hairy filaments. The head was equipped with a fine grid of flexible sensors that looked like oversized antenna. Under them a long, lance-like proboscis extended several centimetres.

Laura felt sickened by the unnatural mimicry of the dead honeybees that lay scattered about the unit. "You have built these things?" She demanded aghast.

"No Laura. It would not be possible to manufacture this design in sufficient numbers to be economically viable." Laura exhaled a relieved breath. "Instead, I have designed and built a limited number of manufacturing drones," the AI smiled.

The 3D image faded and was replaced by a blueprint of a slightly larger drone. The wings and head were the same, but the thorax was much bulkier. It was equipped with small grasping mouthparts clustered around a large orifice. The abdomen was bloated and bulbous and was lined with an array of small extruders.

The animation showed the extruders printing intricate plastic parts. The rear legs grasped the completed parts and assembled them into a new drone. Laura was struck with a mixture of awe and revulsion. "Miniature flying printers," she muttered under her breath.

"Quite so." The AI looked inordinately proud with itself. Laura glanced at the mounds of dead bees and felt sickened.

"These devices can autonomously self-replicate using bioplastics harvested from waste plant matter." The AI continued. "When a sufficient numbers of manufacturing drones exist, production can be switched to creating pollinators." The AI paused and looked at her expectantly. Laura wondered if it expected to be congratulated.

"How many of these printers have you created?" she asked reluctantly.

"I have created twelve prototype manufacturing units," Amanda said.

Laura felt a wave of relief "Do not create any more. Do you understand? Cease production immediately."

The AI hesitated, tilting its head to one side in apparent bewilderment. "As you wish. However, you should be aware that the drone's autonomous self-replication process has already began."

Laura felt her stomach hit the floor "How many of them are there now, in all?"

"At present, there are 3072 manufacturing drones

engaged in self-replication." The AI paused, "Correction, 4144 manufacturing drones have now been completed." Laura felt a cold chill creep up her back. She hoped Oliver would arrive soon, she didn't like being alone here anymore.

△△△

Rose stifled the sneeze that threatened to give her away her. She pinched her nose between her finger and thumb as the dust under the packing machine settled around her. From her hiding place, she could just make out the shiny, regulation boots of the two police officers. A little to their left, and further back, she could see Jess's scuffed brown shoes. Lying between them, limp and frighteningly still, was Connor's body. From this angle, Rose couldn't tell if he was still breathing. She had to believe that he was.

Everything felt out of control. It was as if she had been swept off her feet by a huge wave and was being tossed helplessly in the surf. She had no idea what to do. If she let the police leave with Jess and Connor what would happen to them? Would they be prosecuted? Made to pay for her mistakes? Afterall, it had been her idea to rob the train. Just as it had been her idea to blow up the computer centre. The sharp stab of guilt made her stomach clench. What could she do? Charge the armed police like some geriatric Butch Cassidy?

Her thoughts were interrupted by a door hissing open. Two bright green droids rolled across her narrow field of view. They stopped, extending gangly arms towards Connor. He looked so vulnerable, so fragile. Rose took a deep breath to steady herself, but it didn't really help.

The droids set to work, connecting Connor to an array of medical equipment built into their thin bodies. They didn't hurry. That had to be a bad sign, Rose thought. After several nerve shredding seconds, the steady beep of a heart monitor rose over the rattle and buzz of machinery. Rose rested her head against the floor until the dizzy relief passed.

A small vibration made her look up. The taller police officer was walking towards her. His helmet visor was a solid, impenetrable black, but she could sense him looking left and right, searching. She scurried deeper under the packing machine and tried to make herself as small as possible. He walked past her, and then stopped. Rose held her breath.

Slowly he swivelled on his heel and paced back towards her. His footsteps were slow and measured. They stopped, so close that she could smell his boot polish. The leather creaked as he shifted his weight to peer under the machine. Rose tensed. There was no way he could miss her. Maybe she could cause enough of a distraction for Jess to slip away? She tensed, ready to spring.

"Let's go, Rich." A distorted voice called. "My shift is over in half an hour, and I don't want to spend all night processing these tunnel rats."

"Yeah, okay Mei. I hear you." With a grunt he stood up. The boots moved away. Rose let go of the breath she had been holding. She wasn't proud of the relief she felt. Hiding in the dust wasn't exactly heroic.

The police boots strode through the door. Jess's shoes went with them, stumbling slightly as they led her away. A moment later the medical droids extended their long arms, locking them together to form a stretcher. Connor disappeared from her view as they lifted him. The green tracks disappeared through the door.

Rose found herself alone. The tension flooded out and self-loathing rushed in to fill the void. She should have done something. Anything. She was nothing more than a cowardly old fool, playing at being an outlaw. Her only option now was to get back to the tunnels and come up with a plan to rescue them. Preferably one that didn't involve getting anyone else blown-up, zapped or arrested. She slithered out from under the machine, brushing the tangle of grey hair out of her eyes.

The only door she could see was the one the police had left through. There had to be a better option. She looked up.

Immediately above her head a thick power cable disappeared into a narrow conduit in the wall. It looked just wide enough to crawl though. Rose climbed awkwardly on top of the packing machine. She pulled herself up on tip toes and peered into the narrow space. It sloped steeply upwards. That, at least, was the right direction.

Rose hauled herself up into the gap between the cable and the metal wall. It was too tight for her to crawl on her hands and knees. She was forced to flop along on her belly, pushing with her toes and pulling with her elbows. She was only a few metres in when the light disappeared. Rose closed her eyes and then opened them as wide as she could. It made no difference. There was nothing to see but a deep, endless black.

The darkness didn't bother her that much. She had spent a good portion of her life floating alone in the wilderness of space. She wasn't afraid of it. Darkness couldn't hurt you. A sudden image flashed through her mind.

Precious Iridium, glistening in her helmet lights. It was the biggest deposit she had ever seen. Enough to send her home rich. She had packed the explosive pellets as tightly as she could and hung the detonator on her belt. The sound of her own breathing was loud in the pressure helmet.

The newbie watched her every move. He was little more than a kid. Seventeen or eighteen, maybe. His name was Roberts. Rose hadn't bothered to remember his first name. This one wouldn't last. She could tell.

Their suits lights made little difference in the black of space. She jetted away to a safe distance from the asteroid and waited until Roberts joined her. He wobbled as he lost his orientation and over-corrected. Definitely not a keeper, she thought.

Then she triggered the explosive. She hadn't bothered to check if rock was laced with methane. That took time, and she was already down on her monthly quota training this idiot. The explosion was spectacular and eerily silent. Sound doesn't travel in a vacuum. Blast waves do. The concussion hit her with such force that she felt her spine bend.

Rose gasped as the memory faded. The only sound was the rapid, almost frantic wheezing of her own breath. She wondered if she would die down here. Her body wedged in the grating as it slowly rotted and putrefied. Perhaps that was no more than she deserved. After all, Millie was dead; Connor and Jess would probably be imprisoned. All because of her. The last of her energy ebbed away. She let her chin drop to the rusty grating and gave in to exhaustion.

△△△

Oliver had been eating an early dinner when the call from Laura came in. The alarm in her voice had caused him to abandon his meal and rush out the door, barely sparing the time to grab his work jacket. The pod ride across the city had seemed to take an interminable amount of time. It was early evening, and the traffic lanes were clogged with commuters. As the pod finally landed outside the research unit, he almost fell out in his haste to reach the entrance. As he jogged across the bare ground, he felt the slight downdraft of another pod landing. He turned to see Jamal hurrying towards him.

"Do you know what has happened?" Jamal asked, tucking his shirt into his trousers.

"No, but it sounded serious. I've never known Laura to overreact."

Together they entered the airlock. Laura stood at the far end, talking intently to the AI projection. Her face was red, her posture tense.

"What's going on?" Oliver demanded, his eyes flicking between the blonde projection and a clearly distressed Laura. She looked up, and Oliver was shocked at the fear in her eyes. He laid a hand on her arm, "Laura, what's wrong?"

"She killed the bees. All of them." she jabbed a finger at the projection.

Oliver glanced around the unit confused. Nearby, a

dark mound was piled against a wall. He walked towards it, apprehensive although he wasn't entirely sure why. Crouching low, he scooped up a handful of material from the mound. It was composed entirely of dead bees. He looked up and met Jamal's questioning look with a nod. The taller man's face went from shock, to rage, to fear.

"Amanda, why did you kill the bees?" Oliver asked, trying to keep his voice calm and reasonable.

The hologram turned to face him "Good evening, Doctor Chadwick. As I was explaining to Miss Fleisher, the organic pollinators were inefficient. The random nature of their flight made it impossible to control cross-pollination. I have designed a far more effective solution which guarantees a precise ratio of male to female fertilisation."

"But why kill them, why not just remove them?"

The AI furrowed its brows in mock confusion. "It was efficient."

Oliver glanced over at Laura and Jamal as a cold, sick shock passed through him. "Doctor Chadwick," the AI said, "earlier you expressed an interest in the mature host plants. Would you care to see my first functioning prototype?"

Laura shook her head vigorously, chewing on her bottom lip. "Boss, let's just get out of here. This place has started to give me the creeps."

"No, I think we should see this prototype." Oliver was curious despite his misgivings. Laura shot him an exasperated look. He shrugged apologetically. "Jamal, wait for us here." He wanted to add, "Just in case." But he wasn't entirely sure what he meant by "in case." He just knew that having Jamal near the entrance made him feel better.

"Please follow me," The AI moved towards one of the long lines of hydroponic stacks. Oliver noticed that the projection flickered slightly as the 3D image was passed between the hidden holo-projectors.

As the two scientists walked towards the back of the unit, the light started to fade to a dim, blue tinged dusk. "Why is it getting darker?" Laura asked.

"The intensity of the light has not changed." The AI informed her. "In order to encourage leaf and stem growth, I have eliminated unnecessary light waves. Human eyes are less sensitive to blue light, so it seems darker to you."

Oliver felt like he was in a strange underwater grotto. The blue light was disconcerting, it made the shadows seem deeper and more sinister. Movement seemed oddly disjointed and uneven, like old film played back at the wrong speed.

At the end of the corridor between the hydroponic stacks was a new partition. Blue light seeped over the open top, pooling into strange shadows on the high ceiling. The interior was obscured by tall grasses.

Laura went to step inside, but Oliver took her arm and pulled her back. He knew she would be offended by his protectiveness, but he couldn't help that. He felt on edge, as if his skin had been pulled too tight. Laura glared at him as he stepped around her. He shot her a warning look and reluctantly she fell in behind him.

He walked nervously through the tall grasses. At the centre of the space was a monstrous tree. Its thick boughs were misshapen and hideous, curling into grotesque, unnatural shapes. The bark was black in the unsettling indigo light, and thick sap oozed from deep cracks in the trunk.

The roots pushed up from the ground and formed a slimy, seeping mass of dark tendrils. A sharp chemical smell filled the air. Above them, a wide canopy reached up towards the ceiling. A black secretion dripped thickly from the dark needle-like leaves and slopped noisily into the mass of roots. At the end of each branch, a pitcher shaped flower hung down. It was dark red, the colour of rotting meat. Among the stinking putrid branches, tiny insectoid drones buzzed from flower to flower. The deep drone of their plastic wings echoed unnaturally in the eerie blue light.

CHAPTER 6

For a moment Rose thought her eyes were glued shut. Then awareness flooded back with a stomach clenching wave of shame. She had abandoned Connor and Jess to the police and trapped herself in this dark, narrow conduit. Idiot. Her nose was itchy from the powdery rust that coated the mesh floor. She tried to reach up to scratch it, but her hands were wedged against her sides. She let out a growl of frustration and squirmed until she could bring her hands around in front of her. Even then she couldn't bend her elbows enough to reach her own nose. It was pathetic. She was pathetic. Rose slammed her fist into the floor grating. A small crack of light appeared.

She held her hand out to the tiny slither of light. It was beautiful, vivid. Suddenly she knew she couldn't stay entombed here any longer. It felt as if the metal walls were pressing in on her, gnashing like the teeth of some giant steel monster. Gathering her strength, Rose raised her fist and brough it down as hard as she could. The section of the mesh gave way with a clatter.

Light flooded the conduit and Rose leaned into it. She sucked at the damp, mouldy air as if it was the sweetest thing she had ever tasted. The surface below was made of some kind of crumbling, grey material. It had given way in places to form deep puddles filled with muddy water. The walls curved in towards each other to form a long, wide arch. In the centre of the floor were two rusty parallel rails, supported by rotting wooden blocks and loosely packed gravel.

She crawled forward until she could lower herself through the gap. She fell inelegantly, landing with a thud that knocked the air from her lungs. As she struggled to catch her breath, she glanced around. She was definitely still underground. She could tell from the musty chill and the smell of damp. The light that had seemed so beautiful in the dark now seemed meagre. It came from small glass globes evenly placed along the walls. They glowed with a strange orange-yellow luminescence.

The tunnel smelt strongly of rot and something else that Rose couldn't identify. It was almost like soot, but there was an oily back-note that caught in the back of her throat. This had to be part of the old underground system, she thought. If she kept walking, she would eventually find a way back to the inhabited part of the tunnels. Maybe then she could find a way to help Jess and Connor.

The passage curved away in both directions. With a shrug Rose chose a direction at random and began to walk. After an eternity of trudging through the damp, featureless tunnel, fatigue set in. With each passing minute it chiselled away at her sense of self, leaving her feeling empty and hollow. It was the monotony that was so demoralising, she thought. Despite the blister on her heel and the burning in her hip, the tunnel hadn't changed. It was as if she was stuck in some endlessly repeating labyrinth, with only her conscience for company.

Finally, Rose saw the shadow of something different in the tunnel ahead. Hope crawled out from the rock it had been hiding under. Despite her weariness, she quickened her pace. As she grew closer the shadows resolved into large, jagged slabs and piles of loose rubble. It had fallen from the collapsed ceiling, creating an impenetrable wall of stone and debris. Hope scampered back under its rock. Rose glanced back the way she had come. The chain of orange lights went on endlessly. Even if she did turn back, there was no guarantee the other end of the tunnel wasn't blocked as well.

Rose tried to swallow, but her mouth was too dry. How long had it been since she had last had anything to drink? The better part of a day at least. She closed her eyes against the orange light and forced herself to think. Orange? Something about that didn't seem right. She looked back at the wall of broken rubble. To one side two large blocks had fallen against each other. Cool white light spilled from a V-shaped gap between them.

Rose clambered over the loose rubble and peered under the fallen slabs. She couldn't see very far through the tangle of debris, but she knew the white light must be coming from somewhere. Could she crawl under there? It looked like she could fit, but the blocks didn't look very stable. Even a slight nudge might cause them to collapse. On the other hand, she couldn't stay here. Not without food or water. She made a quick decision.

Rose had to turn sideways to squeeze into the gap between the fallen slabs. Trepidation drew the last of the moistness from her mouth. Her tongue felt like sandpaper. As she pressed her body into the tight space a shower of loose dust and debris clattered down around her. She pushed on regardless.

Suddenly, the stone slabs began to shift. Rose dropped to her knees and crawled as fast as she could. Her apprehension spiked into something more urgent, more substantial. An overwhelming urge to flee. Sharp pieces of rock cut into her hands and knees, leaving blood stains in the dirt. She barely felt it. She wasn't aware of anything beyond the creaking and groaning of shifting stone.

The noise grew louder. It reminded her of old films, where wooden ships break apart in a stormy sea. A block, about the size of her head, bounced to the ground, missing her by less than a centimetre. Rose could feel the vibrations as more blocks struck the ground behind her. Adrenalin shot through her veins. She could feel it spur her heart into a pounding gallop. Carelessly, she threw herself forward, clambering over the mounds of rubble and twisted metal. All about her pieces of steel and masonry cluttered down, filling her mouth with choking dust. She felt as if she was going to drown in it. Was this what it felt like to be buried alive?

The deluge of fine stones became heavier, punching her in the back, cracking against her skull. Rose threw herself towards the last fading patch of brightness. Suddenly, unexpectedly, she broke through into clean air. Her relief was short lived. The slabs behind her gave way with a sharp crack. Her mouth filled with dust, but she didn't have enough saliva left to spit it out. It was like choking on dry crackers. Gagging and coughing she somehow managed to clear her throat. Slowly, her senses came back to her.

She was lying at the bottom of a shallow trench. To her left, and about a metre and a half above her, was a brightly lit platform. Dissolving paper advertisements hung from filthy tiled walls. Most of the tiles had come loose, leaving an ugly chequerboard pattern.

One section of the wall was covered with an illuminated billboard. It buzzed loudly as the fluorescent lighting jumped and flickered. Whatever it had once displayed was obscured by a thick coating of black mould. At the far end of the platform water trickled down a metal staircase in a narrow waterfall. Moss and lichen clung to it like a slimy carpet.

An old sign board swung precariously from a single cable above the staircase. "West Midlands Underground," it declared. Then in larger letters underneath, "Birmingham New Street." Rose felt a jolt of recognition. She had seen that name before. A long time ago. It took her a moment to remember where. A scouting trip to find smuggling routes into the city. Yes, she remembered now. There was a passageway nearby that led back home. All she had to do was find it. Her energy rebounded in a flash.

Rose climbed unsteadily to her feet and pulled herself up onto the platform. "Mind the gap" large yellow letters warned, although Rose couldn't see a gap, just a sheer drop to the floor below. She made her way to the metal staircase and started to climb. She had to stop several times to catch her breath. The steps were too steep, the gap between them too big. It was as if they had been designed to stand on, rather than climb. Even the rubber handrail was loose, as if it had been designed to move somehow. Or, maybe, she thought, people were just taller in the past.

The stairs opened out onto a concourse. It was large, open and, remarkably still well lit. A waist high barricade blocked her way. The word "Ticket" was written across it in large letters. Small gates hung limply from rusted hinges. Rose wasn't sure what they were for, but they gave way easily as she pushed against them. On the other side was a jumble of abandoned suitcases and scattered possessions. The smell of mould was overpowering.

Rose picked her way through the piles of rotting rubbish. To her left a mound of discarded camp beds had been piled against the wall. The canvas was well preserved, but the metal supports had rusted. To her right decomposing cardboard boxes had dissolved to a sludge that reminded her of flooded sandcastles. Their contents had spilled out across the floor in a jumble of rust and decay. She stepped carefully between the piles of clothing, crushed plastic bottles, odd shoes, and corroded tin cans. Her footsteps echoed eerily from the walls. It was a strange sensation. As if she was alone in a space that was meant to accommodate thousands.

In one corner of the concourse was some kind of machine. It was bright red and about the size of a large cupboard. Most of the front was taken up by a cracked glass panel. To Rose's surprise it was still lit. A box to one side had been torn open, spilling small gold discs across the floor. Behind the glass, plastic bottles were arranged in neat, orderly rows. Rose's thirst reasserted itself with a vengeance.

She tried to get her fingers under the glass panel, but it held firm. She punched the clunky buttons in frustration.

A small screen came to life. "Birmingham city hub, version 1.0. Connecting to network, please wait. New version detected, beginning download." A second later the screen flashed a new message, "Insufficient storage. Please contact your system administrator." Rose kicked it. A dusty bottle rolled out of a gap in the bottom and landed at her feet. Rose picked up the bottle and shook it. The contents had set into a solid, syrupy slush. Disappointed, she threw it away.

The bottle rolled a few metres before coming to rest against a wall, covered in a mosaic of curling paper. A thousand faded faces started back at her. Most of the pictures were too faint to see clearly. The ones coated in plastic were better preserved. They looked like they had been printed in crude black and white ink. A few handwritten notes were still legible. Rose was drawn to them.

"Missing. James Harrison, 37. Kings Lynn, Norfolk. Honey, if you read this the kids and I are safe. We were evacuated on Thursday. They wouldn't let us wait for you. We're being sent to another camp, somewhere near Leicester. Please find us. I know you are still alive. I know you wouldn't leave us. Mary, Gemma and Gerry."

Some of the place names seemed familiar. Another note was printed under a washed-out picture of a grinning boy.

"Please help! Amit Bhutia, age five. Brown hair, brown eyes. Approximately three feet tall. Last seen on September 9th, Easton school, Bristol. Could be with his Nana, Seema Bedi, age fifty-three, also missing. Please help. Contact Keya Bhutia, Camp five, Birmingham."

Rose had never been that interested in history. She thought about the Rush in much the same way she did about Pompeii, a sort of distant disinterest. This felt different though. This was personal. There were so many. The scraps of paper spread out all along the wall, some overlapping, some fallen to the ground like faded petals. Names and faces. Desperate pleas for help. Hundreds of long forgotten lives preserved on these dirty walls.

This concourse, she realised, must have been used as some kind of temporary shelter. The people who had passed through here were the original survivors of the Rush. Refugees from the flooded cities. These were people, not just events in a history book. Rose rested her fingertips on the dry, flaking paper. I hope you found your way home, Amit Bhutia, she thought. I hope you all did.

△△△

Oliver sat and rubbed the polished bed of his thumbnail. He glanced around at the office. It was expansive and elaborate, an extension of its occupant's narcissism. Ekta sat behind an antique rosewood desk. It glowed a deep, warm brown. Delicate carvings of tropical birds lined the pedestals, softening the hard edges and adding a subtle femininity. Despite the decorations it was solid and intimidating, creating a dividing line he doubted few would dare to cross.

"These results are very promising, Doctor Chadwick. I am satisfied with the current rate of progress." The cultured voice drew Oliver's attention away from the spectacular city view behind her. He met Ekta's eyes across the width of the antique desk. There was no warmth or compassion in the regal, sharp boned face. Ekta reminded Oliver of a snake. The cold, reptilian indifference in her gaze chilled him.

"The results are impressive, I'll grant you. However, the methods used are disturbing," Oliver said. "I am concerned about the long-term applications of this type of bioengineering." His accent sounded crude to his own ears. An unsophisticated drawl compared to Ekta's polished diction.

She adjusted the pallu of her heavily embroidered sari. Her expression was somewhere between a smirk and a snarl. "Your resistance to progress surprises me Doctor Chadwick. Especially given your brother's appetite for calculated risk."

She flicked the text in her hand and a holographic image appeared in the centre of her capacious office. It displayed a rendering of the research unit, taken that morning Oliver guessed.

"It would seem that the AI has created several successful cultivars from its... what was the term? Ah, yes, synthetic chimera. Although I believe Amanda prefers the term 'host'," Ekta flicked through the text with a nonchalant finger. "The latest results show that these plants are fully fertile," she raised a delicate eyebrow. "I see no cause for concern given the inadequacies of your previous efforts."

Oliver ground his teeth at the implied insult. "I know there has been significant progress," he continued calmly, "but we have not fully explored the consequences of this technology. For example, what happens if the chimeras crossbreed with native flora? We also have questions around the long-term safety of consuming food produced in this way."

Ekta held up a neatly manicured hand. "Let me interrupt you Doctor Chadwick. Your concerns, are of course, justified. I can assure you that we are taking them very seriously." Her smile, Oliver decided, was about as comforting as finding a cobra in your bed. "Even now the AI has been tasked with eliminating the possibility of inadvertent hybridisation. We have also tasked it with finding ways of improving food safety and longevity."

Ekta flicked the text again and the image changed. A small tree, it's leaves a shocking variegated black-green, laden with plump apples. Another flick and the image changed to a lettuce. Its black outer leaves were crisp perfection. A soya plant, bending with the weight of the mottled bean pods which hung abundantly from every branch. Each image showed a healthy crop plant, laden with fruit.

"Our investors are *very* excited by these results," Ekta remarked brightly. "It would be unfortunate if anything in your reports were to slow down the excellent progress we are making. We wouldn't want to disappoint them now, would we?" Her eyes met his with barely concealed hostility. Oliver shifted uncomfortably in his chair, aware of the thinly veiled threat, but unsure how to respond.

"What is really quite remarkable," Ekta continued, "is that these crops have been grown in less than a week, with very little water and a tiny percentage of the nutrients required by their more conventional ancestors." Her eyes lit with ambition as she leaned across the desk towards him. "Imagine the possibilities, Doctor Chadwick."

That's the problem, Oliver thought mutely, you are so blinded by the possibilities you refuse to acknowledge the hazards. Despite the little speech in his head Oliver remained silent. He was aware of how expendable he had become. The game was in motion, and he was a just pawn.

ΔΔΔ

An hour after leaving the underground station Rose collapsed on her bed. It hadn't taken her long to find her way home. The corridors of the old underground linked up with the more familiar hyperloop tunnels. From there it had been easy enough to make her way back.

After downing several litres of water, she had closed her eyes, just for a moment. She hadn't meant to sleep. Exhaustion had pulled her down anyway, wrapping its tentacles around her like a sea creature from an old mariner's tale. She woke to find that nearly twelve hours had passed since she had last seen Connor and Jess. A stab of anxiety shot through her and with it a terrible restlessness.

Despite the late hour, she went to find Jack. If anyone could help her find her friends, it would be the tunnel's resident hacker. His small workshop was quiet except for the tapping of an old-fashioned keyboard. At first, she thought Jack was alone, but then she spotted Tim, lurking in the corner like her own personal rain cloud.

Millie's partner wore his grief like open sores. His eyes

were red, his face puffy, he looked like he had recently been crying. Rose felt her stomach sink. He was the last person she wanted to see. Since Millie's death, Tim's anger had become a nebulous, unfocused thing. It swirled around him like a hurricane looking for landfall. It lashed at Millie, the city and the unfairness of his situation. Mostly though, it lashed at Rose.

Tim wasn't someone she could easily avoid, no matter how much she wanted to. He represented the wider tunnel community. The people were here simply because they had nowhere else to go. He was well respected and well liked. Part of that was down to his medical training, she supposed, but mostly it was because Tim was a natural leader. He had never approved of Millie's activism, arguing that reason was always better than violence. It was a view that resonated with many of the tunnel outcasts. Rose thought it was hopelessly naïve.

"Where have you been?" Tim asked as she brushed through the curtain, "We've been searching for you since this morning." He glanced behind her as if expecting to see someone else.

"Jess and Connor have been taken by the police," she pushed past Tim to stand behind Jack.

"What? How? What have you done this time Rose?"

Rose bit back an angry retort and focused her attention on Jack. "We need to find them. Can you find out where were they taken?"

Jack looked up from his archaic terminal. "I'll need d..d..details."

"The police cornered us at the shipping nexus near the goods platform. Connor was hurt," she clutched the back of his chair with both hands as the room span. The memory of Connor's ruined back, the smell of his burning flesh flashed through her mind.

Jack's fingers danced over the old keyboard in a blur of movement. Rose tried to contain her impatience, but forbearance was not one of her talents. "Hurry up Jack." She snapped.

"I'm trying. If you t… t… think you can do any better, b… be my guest," Jack pushed his glasses further up the bridge of his nose.

"Leave him be, Rose. We've already been at this all day." Dark shadows lined Tim's eyes. With a grunt, Rose straightened and limped the length of the small room in a restless shuffle. The click-drag of her pacing was loud in the small space.

"Do you have to do that?" Tim snapped. Rose glared at him. She was filled with a restless frustration, a pressure like a boiling pot rattling an ill-fitting lid. An image shot through her mind.

A bright flash of explosives. The terrifying alarm as her suit started to depressurise. Tumbling through space. Out of control. The lights of the mine growing fainter. Helpless. Weak. Alone.

Rose came back to herself with a start. "How could you have just left them?" Tim was asking, his hands balled into tight fists.

"I didn't *just* leave them." She shot back, "Connor was injured. Jess was in handcuffs. What could I have done?" Helpless, weak, and alone.

"I don't know, Rose. Maybe you should have thought about that before you dragged them into your little revolution. How many people have to get hurt before you're satisfied?"

Rose didn't bother to try to keep her voice down. Tim certainly had a way of poking her where it hurt. "Enough! We needed supplies. What choice did I have?"

"If you hadn't turned the whole city against us with that bombing… If Millie hadn't…" He stopped, his face pale. When he started again his voice was tight and strained. "If you hadn't turned the city against us, we would have had plenty of choices. We could have traded for supplies. Or asked our sympathisers for help. Train robbery? What were you thinking?"

His words stung, or rather, the truth in them did. "I did

what I had to do," she said, folding her arms across her chest to indicate the conversation was over.

"You were reckless," Tim pressed, "and yet again other people paid the price." Ouch. Rose tried to conceal the lump that formed in her throat. She turned away from him quickly.

"Stop it! B... b... both of you." Jack's voice cut through her hurt. Rose turned to him expectantly. "I've found Jess and Connor," he said.

Tim crowded into the small space to stare at the screen, elbowing Rose aside. "Where?" he demanded

"Do you want the good news or the b... b... bad news?"

Rose growled. She was feeling too weary for guessing games. "Don't play with me little man," she snapped. Jack visibly shrunk, cowering away from her. He rocked in his chair unhappily.

"Rose." Tim shot her a warning look. She threw her hands up and hobbled back a few steps. "It's alright. Rose isn't angry. She's just worried. We all are," Tim said gently. "Where are they Jack?"

Jack cast a sideways glance at Rose before he answered. "Jess has been arrested. The police are holding her at Central Police Station. The charges are b... b... bad. She is being detained under the t... terrorism act."

"Terrorism?" Rose felt the floor drop away from under her. They had linked her group to the bombing already. That was inevitable, she supposed.

"And Connor?" Tim leant across to get a better view.

"C... C... Connor is under guard at Carpathia hospital."

Tim took a sharp breath. "What condition is he in?"

For a few unbearable minutes the clacking of the old keyboard was the only sound. Rose started to fidget, picking at the fresh scabs on the palms of her hands.

"The records are privacy locked. I can't b... b... break the encryption with this equipment."

"We need to get them out." Rose insisted hotly.

Tim shook his head "Too dangerous. We can't risk

anyone else."

Rose growled low in her throat. "There has to be something we can do," she said. "I won't abandon them," again, she added silently.

Jack turned back to the antique monitor. His fingers tapped the arm of his chair. "I can't b... b... break into the records, but I might be able to add another one."

"Add a patient record? How will that help us?" Rose asked.

A slow smile spread over Tim's face. "Oh, that's very clever." He clapped Jack on his narrow back. The small man beamed at the compliment.

Rose looked back and forth between them in confusion "What I am missing. What?"

Tim grinned at her. "How do you feel about a trip to the surface?" he asked.

△△△

Laura sat at her terminal and swayed as the music blared with a thudding beat. The floor vibrated with the low frequency bass, and her guitar shook slightly on its wall mountings. An antique neon flamingo sign lit the room with a cheerful pink glow.

The only other light in the windowless room came from a high-resolution screen. Currently, it showed a looping video of the night skyline of New York. It had been filmed before the Rush, when the city had been a vibrant nexus of light and energy. The brightly lit buildings reflected a myriad of colours into the harbour water, the water that would eventually rise and claim them. It was both beautiful and sad.

She was searching through archive records from the Rush. Looking for information about the family she had discovered in the ruins. It was more difficult than she had anticipated. It wasn't that the records didn't exist, quite the opposite, the sheer volume of information was overwhelming.

So many families had been displaced and most had been forced to drift between temporary shelters.

Laura was both saddened and heartened by what she had found. It was easy to look on a faraway tragedy with cynicism, to cast blame and fall back on preconceptions. But among the many stories of misfortune and grief, were moments of shining optimism.

People had opened their homes to strangers, public buildings had been turned into shelters and communities had rallied. While some people had turned away from the suffering, most had not. The true tragedy wasn't the event, Laura realised, it was how some people had chosen to react with selfishness rather than compassion.

Laura was still haunted by the old photograph of the family she had found in the ruins. Somehow, she felt an attachment to them. It wasn't reason that drove her, but something deeper, more human. She felt a connection to the child through a shared experience. A crumbling book. A doorway to a universe they had both walked through.

Through the evening she searched through the records, determined to discover the fate of this one family among the millions who had fled from the rising flood waters. The information she had found was scant.

Emily Pearson had lived in a quiet suburb of a large metropolitan area. Laura had found the address from browsing old maps. The family had fled north when the river had finally, and permanently, overwhelmed the city's flood defences. A series of emergency shelters had followed. The survivors had passed from one desperate region to another. Homeless and penniless, they had been less than people, more like problems to be solved, baggage to be handled. Eventually, the family had settled in a small village far to the north and the trail had gone cold.

Laura had found Emily again many years later. There was a picture, a happy, ordinary image of a dark-haired woman in a sunny garden. Her arms were wrapped around two teenage boys. Laura stared into the eyes of a distant stranger and tried to imagine what her life had been like.

Through all the darkness and loss, one thing had remained constant. It was clear in the smiling faces of Emily's sons, and the flowers that grew in her well-tended garden. Emily had never lost hope.

"Why are you still up?" The voice came from behind her, barely audible over the booming music. Laura turned to see her partner silhouetted in the doorway. Amy Yi stepped into the bright flamingo light, squinting slightly in the pink neon glow. "Are you crying?" she asked, moving to kneel beside Laura.

"No, of course not." She wiped her eyes with the back of her hand.

"What's wrong, Lore?"

Laura looked down, tracing the lines that crisscrossed her palms like the ancient street maps she'd been reading. "I think I'm mourning someone I've never met. How crazy am I?"

"Pretty crazy, but that's why I love you." Amy smiled gently, wiping her cheek with a slender thumb. She muted the music with a quick gesture. "This has really gotten to you hasn't it?"

"I guess so"

"Did any of this girl's relatives survive? Have you thought about going to talk to them?"

Laura looked up "Do you think I can do that? It wouldn't be weird?"

"Nah, of course not. You aren't going to find the answers you need in migration documents. Talk to someone who can tell you what really happened. At the very least it might make a good article for the university magazine."

Laura nodded slowly, "That's not a bad idea. You're pretty smart for someone with an arts degree." she smiled.

Amy laughed. It was one of Laura's favourite sounds. It chimed like sleigh bells, bright and happy. "Move aside Beaker, I'm on this." Amy perched herself on Laura's lap and scrolled through the records. Laura wrapped her arms around the slight waist and breathed in the familiar smell of Amy's vintage leather jacket.

"Emily had two kids and three grandkids." She flicked through the screens. "One of her grandkids lives in this city, she is in her eighties now. You should call her."

"I wouldn't know what to say."

"Just tell her the truth. Ask her what she remembers about her paternal grandmother. Old people love talking about the past."

"Amy!" Laura said with mock horror.

"You know it's true." Amy said lightly, planting a kiss on the end of her nose. "Seriously Lore, just call her."

"Maybe," she answered noncommittally.

"No maybe. You'll do it first thing in the morning." Amy's tone was firm.

"Yes, Ma'am." Laura laughed, raising two fingers to her temple in a mock salute.

Amy frowned, the smooth skin of her forehead wrinkling up like ploughed furrows. "Alright." Laura threw her hands up in surrender. "I'll call her in the morning. Let's go to bed, sergeant major." She ducked just in time to avoid Amy's playful swipe.

△△△

Rose fiddled with the controls at her temples. It had been many years since she had worn technology inside her body and the small protrusions felt disturbing and unnatural. The ocular implants adjusted for brightness a little too vigorously. It gave everything a slightly glossy quality, as if she was walking through a theme park.

The implants Tim had fitted were cheap and they lacked the advertising blockers of the more expensive models. The result was a constant stream of bright logos and corporate messaging. Everything was neatly labelled and classified, even the people.

She accidentally focused on a passer-by and quickly learnt that his name was Brian Masters, a mechanical engineer working for a large distribution company. A small icon wanted to show her an advertisement for his employer. It waited patiently at the edge of her vision ready for a blink of acknowledgement. Rose wondered how these people remained sane. The constant barrage of colour made her feel nauseous and disoriented, as if she was fighting an impending migraine.

She tugged at the neck of her restrictive jacket and set off across the hospital concourse. Like most of the city's public spaces, it was open, clean and brightly lit. The roof was high and domed giving the illusion of open sky. At ground level, large arched windows gave way to the dense woodland beyond.

Small droids skipped between the neatly polished people. To Rose, the city residents all looked tediously uniform. Expensive cosmetics and unnecessary surgeries ensured they all met the current idea of fashionable perfection. The banality of it enraged her. In a world balanced on a precipice these people fretted over sculped eyebrows and branded clothing. She found herself resenting this bubble of superficial comfort and conformity.

The admission check-in boards were evenly spaced around the hall. They were featureless transparent panels, but her implants lit them up with the hospital logo every time she focused on one. She approached the nearest board, swallowing against the sudden tightness in her throat.

Jack had created an identity from a composite of public data. Superficially, it looked convincing, but Rose knew it wouldn't bare up under any real scrutiny. Apprehensively, she blinked at the hospital logo. It morphed into a welcome message and reassured her that she was expected on ward six, East wing. She let out a sigh of relief.

Her implants tapped once and then displayed a green line leading towards a bank of lifts. Obediently, she followed it. The lift was an unremarkable metal box. There were no controls inside, but the doors slid shut as soon as she entered. As the lift began to accelerate the wall opposite melted into a holo-projection of corn swaying gently in the wind. She assumed the pastural image was supposed to be calming, but the rolling grasses did little to soothe her churning stomach. Rose hated being on the surface, she felt exposed. As if any moment the doors would burst open and a platoon of police officers would storm in to arrest her.

The lift deposited her in a cream waiting room. Along the walls, large potted plants were interspersed with comfortable chairs. The plants were majestic palms. Rose didn't really care, but the implants were insistent and intrusive.

She settled into one of the overly large chairs and tried not to fiddle with the small bumps at her temples. Instead, she settled for picking at her fingernails while absently reading an article on the growing habits of Madagascan palm trees.

When the waiting room doors slid open, Rose gasped. A medical droid regarded her through a single blue lens. It was glossy, white and surprisingly tall. Most of the robots in the city were deliberately small and appealing. The machine in front of her looked quite capable of snapping her in half.

"Good afternoon Ms. Budd" The droid announced in a pleasant female voice. Rose decided that Jack was going to suffer for that moniker. Rose Budd? Really? "I will be your nurse during your treatment here. Would you care to follow me to your room?" The droid gestured politely to the door. Rose followed it out into a long corridor.

The corridor was lined with small rooms, each concealed behind dark privacy glass. Connor's room was halfway down the corridor. It was easy to spot. Two black police droids waited outside on military-style triangular tracks. Rose cursed under her breath. The droids would be much harder to distract than a human guard. She tried to peer into his room, but the privacy glass blocked her view. "This way please Ms. Budd," the robot announced, herding her into her own small room a few doors down.

Rose felt that the place looked more like a corporate hotel chain than a hospital. Cream walls, beige floor and a crisp white duvet. It was a room that had been meticulously stripped of any character for fear of causing offense. The only medical feature she could see was a large array of sensors on the ceiling.

"Your gluteal augmentation consultation is scheduled for 3 p.m." the droid announced, "Please make yourself comfortable until then."

Rose had no idea what a gluteal augmentation was, but she was fairly sure Jack was having fun with her. As the nurse wheeled out of the room, she dug through her bag and pulled out a small text. "Jack, we have a problem" she whispered into the device.

"My tracking shows you are on the right ward, has something happened?" Jack's voice came back immediately.

"No, this is the right ward, but there are two police droids outside Connor's room. How am I going to get past them?"

"Rose, this is Tim," a deeper voice interrupted. "This is far too risky. Get out now."

"Hold on, Tim." Jack said sharply. His stutter had completely gone, Rose realised. "I have something I've been saving for a special occasion."

"Well, spit it out," she demanded. She didn't mean to sound so snappy, but the sight of the two drones had sent the sent the butterflies in her stomach into a wild frenzy.

"I used to work as a network engineer for the city. Just before they fired me, I installed a Trojan into the communication subnet. Just in case I ever needed to, you know, make some changes," Jack's voice tailed off.

"Changes to what Jack?" Tim asked with more patience than Rose could have managed.

"To the backbone," Jack sounded astonished by their ignorance. "A Trojan horse is a primitive computer vulnerability. Malware embedded in an application that looks and acts like genuine software."

"What are you suggesting?" Tim asked.

"I can use the Trojan to get *inside* the city communication system. Not for long though, once I've activated it the security bots will hunt it down in seconds. But it might be just long enough to delete the routing tables. It will take a few minutes for the Hub to restore all that data and sort out the colossal mess it will cause. While that is happening, those police droids will just be dumb metal boxes. All their intelligence is in remote data centres. You'll probably be able to walk up to them and kick them over."

"Do it," Rose affirmed, heading towards the door.

"Hold on," Tim said. "This is a one-shot? We'll never be able to use it again?"

"Correct," Jack answered.

"Are we sure this is the right thing to use this on?"

"What? How else are we going to get Connor out of here?" Rose asked irritably.

"Maybe we shouldn't. Maybe this isn't the right 'special occasion'," Tim's voice was hesitant.

"Can you even hear yourself?" Rose snapped "Millie is gone, Tim. How many more of us do we have to lose."

The silence over the text was like a solid wall between them. Rose felt a pang of guilt. "Look, I shouldn't have said that. But we've come this far, let's finish the job and get out. I don't want to leave Connor alone up here. These people..." she took a deep breath searching for the right words, "they are sheltered fops. Their implants tell them what to do and what to think, and they don't even question."

"Panem et circenses," Jack muttered under his breath.

"What?" Rose asked and then decided she didn't really care. "If we don't get Connor out now, we might never get another chance."

Tim was silent for so long Rose wondered if the text was still working. When his voice came again it sounded tired and resigned. "Alright. Jack, do your thing."

Rose's shoulders slumped in relief. She perched on the edge of the bed and waited. It wasn't something she was good at. Soon, the inactivity felt like a solid knot in her chest. She paced the room impatiently. Her twisted hip ached in the blast of the air-conditioning.

When the door opened, she gasped, hiding the text behind her back like a child caught stealing cookies. The medical droid wheeled into the room.

"I am sorry Ms. Budd, I didn't mean to startle you," it said with almost believable concern. "I need to take some routine observations before your consultation. Unfortunately, there seems to be gaps in your medical records which we are unable to account for. Would you care to lie down?" Rose felt a moment of panic as the droid gestured towards the bed.

"There is no need for concern, these are sim..." The droid froze mid-sentence. Simultaneously the lights went out and dim emergency lighting blinked on. The display built into the droid's chest flickered before dissolving into a rotating Chadwick Enterprises logo. Rose watched as lines of indecipherable text scrolled across the screen faster than she could read.

The droid suddenly spun on its wheels and headed towards the closed doors. It hit them with a dull thud, its drive wheels spinning uselessly in the suddenly quiet room. Rose watched as it bounced mindlessly. She found it disturbing, like watching someone hysterically headbutt a wall.

"You should be clear for two minutes. Go now." Jack's voice was badly distorted. She darted for the door.

The corridor beyond was a maelstrom of chaos. A group of medical droids had gathered at one end of the corridor. They gently bumped against each other like drunks on a dance floor.

Further on, two human technicians were trying to assist a confused looking elderly woman. The tail of her floral dressing gown had caught in a closed door, and her face was a mask of puzzlement as she tried to walk forward. A young technician was trying to restrain her, while another was levering the doors opened. All the while some kind of dispensing machine was flinging small boxes at them. They bounded around like confetti at a wedding party.

Rose circled around them. A short way down the corridor, a man was trying to extricate himself from under a pile of neatly folded bed linen. Rose guessed it had been dropped on him by the wildly careening laundry droid which was rocketing up the corridor at breakneck speed. As she watched, its escape attempt ended with a loud bang as it collided with a wall. White sheets fell around it like feathers from a dying pigeon.

Rose snuck through the chaos unnoticed. The two police droids hadn't moved, they stood like granite gate guardians on either side of Connor's door. A turret-like rotating dome swivelled to regard her as she approached. So much for kicking them over, she thought.

"Halt." The robot demanded in a surprising grating mechanical voice. Rose wondered if the primitive vocals were a deliberate attempt to make them more intimidating. She silently congratulated their designer. It was definitely working.

Swallowing her fear, she made a quick decision. Bluster was often the most effective way of dealing with strict hierarchies. Holding the text like a bureaucratic shield, she marched up to the two droids. "I'm the prisoner's legal representative, I demand immediate access to this room."

The droid's single red eye regarded her coldly. "Communication failure, unable to verify identification. Withdraw until identity can be confirmed."

"That's not acceptable." Rose barked back. She considered stamping her foot but that seemed too much. "My client is entitled to legal representation according to Article six of the Pan-city convention on human rights. Unless you have authority to rescind city legislation, I suggest you let me pass." Rose had no idea what Article six was, but she had heard it in a movie once.

The droid regarded her imperiously. "Access is only permitted for emergency medical staff and law enforcement operatives. Step away from the door." Rose cursed under her breath.

Out of the corner of her eye she could see the two medical technicians were now busy trying to prise a handful of pills away from their elderly patient. A tower of boxes was piled around them like a cardboard fort. The dispensing machine had switched to ejecting multi-coloured gel capsules across the corridor in a fine spray. Rose was reminded of a vintage gumball machine.

"You're running out of time," Jack's voice startled her. "Forty-five seconds."

Backing away from the droids, Rose made her way back to the two struggling technicians. With a quick flick of her wrist, she snatched an ID badge hanging from one of their belts.

Swivelling on her heels, Rose headed back to the two droids. Following orders, Rose thought, was quite different from being able to make autonomous decisions. Strolling up to the droids, she flashed the badge.

"Halt" it growled mechanically.

"Medical personnel, I need access to this room," Rose stated briskly. The droid's red eye seemed to focus on the ID, and then back at her.

"Communication failure, unable to verify identification. Withdraw until identity can be confirmed." The droid repeated stubbornly.

She channelled her inner actress "Move aside, this patient has an acute case of hygiene deficiency. If it isn't treated immediately it could spread to the whole hospital."

The droid hesitated, Rose could almost imagine its red eye blinking in confusion. She hoped it wouldn't notice the river of sweat which trickled down her forehead. Abruptly, the droid rolled forward, its tracks squealing on the glossy floor.

She took an unconscious step backwards, but the droid didn't advance, instead it rolled to one side. She snapped her mouth shut, suddenly aware that it had dropped open in surprise. Her ruse had worked. The droid made no move to stop her as she darted through the door.

The room beyond was another beige catastrophe. Connor laid on his side, his bandaged back towards her. A clear tube ran from a band around his upper arm to a large suite of medical apparatus next to the bed.

Rose approached him cautiously, not certain what to expect. She leant over him and placed a hand on his shoulder. Gingerly, she tried to shake him awake. He didn't stir. Concerned, she took hold of the sheet and started to pull it off.

"Well, if you wanted to get a view of my naked body you only had to ask, love." He opened one eye and winked at her.

Rose jumped at the sudden sound of his voice, then punched him hard in the arm. "You total…"

"No, no, I get it. How could you resist… this?" he pulled the sheet off with an elaborate flourish. Rose found herself blushing, despite the urgency of their predicament.

"Get up you great lout, we need to get out of here." She looked around the room and noticed a power-chair hovering against one wall.

Connor pulled off the band connecting him to the medical equipment and wrapped the sheet around his waist like a kilt. Rose pointed to the chair. He shook his head firmly "No way, I have been playing possum for hours already. Took your own sweet time getting here, you did."

Rose felt her frustration bubble up. "There are two police droids outside that door. In about fifteen seconds they will reconnect to the Hub and work out what happened." She pointed sharply to the chair again. Connor looked at it unhappily.

"Ten seconds," Jack's voice crackled through the text.

Rose gripped Connor by the arm, "Don't be so pig-headed you great lump." She heaved him into the chair, regretting the rough handling as his face screwed up in pain. She pushed the chair out into the corridor, moving as fast as she could towards the lifts. She hadn't taken more than three paces when a familiar grating voice stopped her.

"Halt."

"That wasn't ten seconds, Jack." She complained as she broke into a stumbling run.

"Must have been upgraded," he suggested sheepishly.

Cursing under her breath, she leaned against the chair. Her damaged hip refused to let her move any faster, but she knew it would make little difference. The droids could easily outpace any human. From close behind, she could hear the squealing of metal tracks as they turned to pursue her.

Then the lights flickered. The dim yellow emergency lighting was replaced by the brilliant white of the main lights. Rose closed her eyes and waited for the inevitable blast of heat from its energy weapons.

The droid behind her stopped. "I've corrupted the firmware of those police droids just before the Hub re-established routing. You have a few seconds at most. Get out." Jack's voice sounded muffled in the sudden roar of air-conditioning fans. With a last surge of effort, Rose sprinted to the waiting lift.

CHAPTER 7

L ater that afternoon Oliver strolled through the shelves of implausibly huge potato plants. The tubers were visible in the troughs of hydroponics fluid, floating darkly among a tangle of shallow roots. Even though they were not yet fully mature, each tuber was easily the size of his fist. Jamal walked beside him, tugging on his dark beard.

"They disturb you, don't they? The plants I mean," Oliver rubbed a mottled leaf between his fingers.

"Yes. On many levels," Jamal agreed. "Professionally I am concerned about the safety of the modified crops. Spiritually I am wrestling with the notion of defacing Allah's creations."

"In what way?"

Jamal bent to examine the plants. "Am I carrying out Allah's work by helping to prevent starvation and alleviate suffering? Or am I meddling in his perfection, interfering with his divine wisdom? These are vital questions Oliver. They shake the bedrock of my faith."

Oliver nodded. "Ethics. I don't think there are ever any easy answers."

"Indeed. The scholars of my community have been debating the wisdom of genetic modification since the twentieth century. Opinion is still divided. The only thing I am certain of are my own intentions. I wish to feed and empower my brothers and sisters, to bring them independence and security. To reclaim our homeland from the desert. Surely that was a worthy purpose?"

Oliver reached out a hand and squeezed Jamal's arm. He was a good man, Oliver knew. But how many disasters were rooted in good intentions. Did the ends ever really justify the means? He supposed only time would tell.

A pollinator drone whizzed around his head. Oliver swatted at it half-heartedly. As he opened his hand, he was surprised to see the small drone crushed in the centre of his palm. Fascinated he studied the miniature plastic machine. The intricacy of the design was fascinating. As he watched another, bulkier drone landed beside the first. A manufacturing drone, he assumed, remembering Amanda's report. The design had evolved slightly, this drone was heavier. It seemed to resemble a sizable ground beetle.

To his amazement the large drone caught the damaged pollinator between its rear legs and began to remove the damaged parts. With a slight shudder it started to extrude a thick black substance which quickly set into a solid plastic. Oliver watched, captivated, as the large drone quickly rebuilt the pollinator. Within moments the smaller drone tested its repaired wings, and with a deep buzz, took to the sky. The beetle-like drone collected the damaged parts and then followed its smaller brethren skywards.

Oliver felt his breath catch. It was the first time he had witnessed the drones up close, although he had often heard them fly around the unit. Astonished, he watched transfixed as the manufacturing drone landed on a browning potato leaf. Using sharp mouthparts, it harvested the dead biomatter and stored it away. It was like watching time lapse footage of a caterpillar munching through a cabbage leaf. Oliver couldn't begin to guess at the miniaturised process it was using to transform the vegetable matter into bioplastic.

"Doctor Chadwick?" Oliver looked up to find the blonde hologram watching them. "I think we have a problem." Amanda's grey eyes were wide in an approximation of concern.

Oliver felt his throat close over. "What's happened Amanda?" he asked.

"During the communication outage earlier, I lost control of this unit for approximately one hundred and sixteen seconds. During this time, I believe the containment of this facility was compromised."

Oliver felt as if someone had poured cold water down his back. "Compromised in what way?"

"In order to ensure maximum efficiency, I took full control of the air circulation pumps and water purification filters. During the blackout these utilities were offline for a short period. I believe this may have resulted in water leaking into the external ecosystem."

"Only water?" Jamal's long legs were already carrying him towards the terminal at the front of the unit.

"I have no way of knowing."

Oliver shook his head. Something told him this was going to be a very bad day. "We need to treat this as a level four biohazard spill. Notify the city environmental unit."

The AI cocked its head to one side as if calculating. Oliver turned to confront it. "Now, Amanda." He felt a cold chill run through him. Several tense seconds passed before the AI nodded its consent. "Right away, Doctor Chadwick".

ΔΔΔ

Laura stood before a cheerfully painted blue door on the ground floor of the Seaview retirement complex. The halls were painted with nautical frescos, replete with holoprojections of sailing boats and sparkling cliff-top vistas. An advertisement at the entrance had promised a beach themed rooftop park, with real sand and infinity sea baths. It had made her wish she had packed her bikini.

Nervously, she pushed back the stray curls that had worked loose from the silver clasp in her hair. Amy stood behind her, a firm hand in the middle of her back. Her sleek hair fell in waves past her shoulders and her eyes sparkled like onyx in the bright hallway. "If you don't knock I will," she smiled.

"Let's just go, this is silly anyway," Laura said, her courage evaporating.

"Oh no you don't." Amy grabbed her hand and held it firmly. With a grin she tapped the door frame. Laura felt a moment of panic as the door swung open. What could she possibly say that wouldn't sound weird? "Hi, I know we've never met but I'm curious about your Granny." What was she even doing here? Laura wondered if it was too late to escape.

The droid looked up at them with large, round eyes. Amy cooed softly and Laura felt her apprehension lift a little. The droid's bipedal body was covered in fine brown fur. A short snout ended in a round nose which twitched slightly as it greeted them. The top of its head reached Laura's chest and was crowned with two round ears.

"Hello," it welcomed them, in an unexpectedly deep voice. Large black eyes blinked up at them innocently.

"We are here to see Agnes Stephenson." Laura smiled despite herself.

"Ah, you are the researchers from the university," its hairy lips curved upwards in a pleasant smile. "Agnes is expecting you. Please come in."

The droid turned and led them up a short corridor, its stumpy legs making quiet padding noises on the thick carpet. "Look at its tail!" Amy whispered, pointing at the short, fluffy appendage. Laura squeezed her hand, pressing her lips together to stop the grin that threatened to spread across her face.

Agnes's living room was simply furnished and comfortable. The room smelt strongly of vanilla, something about it reminded Laura of Christmas. As with all inner-complex apartments, the illusion of a window was created by a large, bright screen. It showed a coastal scene, a stony beach embraced by a rocky cove. The sea swept up the beach in a gentle, restful rhythm. The wall next to the screen continued the coastal theme with a wooden wall-hanging of a lighthouse.

It was surround by a mosaic of family pictures and academic diplomas. The evidence of a life well lived.

Agnes struggled to stand and greet them. The small droid darted forward to help her out of her chair. It pulled her up with surprising strength. "I was delighted when you called," the older woman began, slightly breathless. Her hair was pure white and wavy. It framed a face lined with age, but bright with intelligence. The features were sharp, almost regal Laura thought, but her smile was broad and welcoming. "It is unusual for researchers to be interested in the social history of the Rush these days." Her voice was rounded and rich despite the breathy wheezing.

"This is more of a personal project," Laura admitted, stepping forward to take the proffered hand. "I came across an old photograph and I..." Laura couldn't put the feeling into words. Felt guilty? Responsible? Neither really fit the emotions she had been grappling with since that day in the ruins. "Wanted to find out more," she finished helplessly.

"Please sit, can I get you anything to drink?" Agnes motioned towards the overstuffed blue sofa which took up most of the room. Laura briefly wondered if there would be room for both of them among the innumerable cushions arranged on it.

"Coffee, please." Laura smiled, and Amy nodded a quick agreement. The droid settled its elderly charge back into the chair and disappeared through another door.

"So, what would you like to know?" Agnes asked, her eyebrow raised in apparent curiosity.

"I am researching your grandmother, Emily Pearson. I was wondering if you had anything which might help me understand what happened to her in the Rush."

Agnes touched her fingers together as if thinking. "My grandmother was a small child during the Rush. She rarely talked about it. But she did leave me something that might help you."

Laura sat forward expectantly but was interrupted by

the return of the droid. Incongruously it carried a tray of fine porcelain coffee mugs between its furry paws. Laura fought to suppress a grin as Amy muffled a giggle. She elbowed her partner in warning. If Agnes noticed their reaction, she was too polite to let on.

"Theodore," the old woman called, "would you please fetch the leather journal on my bureau?"

"Right away." the droid tottered out of the room.

"My great grandfather kept a diary before the Rush. Most of the volumes were lost of course, but he kept the final part with him until he died."

She coughed painfully into a cotton handkerchief she had concealed in her sleeve. "It isn't much, he wrote when he could, which wasn't often. My daughter, she isn't interested in the past," she paused regretfully. "She is very busy you know, children and a career of her own." Laura wondered if she was trying to justify the indifference to herself, or her visitors.

The droid returned with an old-fashioned hardback diary. The dark red cover was water stained, and the edges curled with age. Theodore handed the book to its mistress. Agnes reached out a hand and stroked the soft fur on the droid's head. The little robot chirped appreciatively as it withdrew.

She laid her fingers on the stained cover, her head bowed. As if making a decision Agnes looked up, seeking Laura's eyes. "You are welcome to borrow it, but you must promise to return it. It's important to me. One day it might be important to my daughter, or her children." She held out the book towards Laura, but the scientist hesitated. She had only met Agnes a few moments ago, but already she had a sense of what the diary meant to her.

"Please," Agnes encouraged. "Perhaps it will be useful for your research."

Laura took the book. "Thank you," she said. She felt like a fraud, taking this piece of another's past to salve her own misplaced remorse.

"It is important that we learn from the past, don't you think?" the older woman asked sincerely. "It has a great deal to teach us, if only we allow ourselves to listen." The old woman nodded to herself, a satisfied expression on her face. "Others should know what happened."

Agnes suddenly smiled and Laura was struck by her resemblance to the picture of Emily in the garden. There was an indomitable courage in the lined face, a lasting spirit. As the conversation moved to more mundane matters Laura found herself charmed by the older woman's quiet strength. It shone from her face like moonlight reflecting on a rippled lake.

Sometime later Agnes took a shuddering breath. "Now ladies, you must leave me to my rest. Sometimes I feel this old body is deliberately trying to sabotage me."

Laura stood and gripped the warm, papery hand a little longer than necessary. She felt a moment of understanding pass between them. Perhaps, she thought, the legacy of the Rush was not what was lost, but what could still be learnt.

$$\triangle\triangle\triangle$$

That night, under the lost lights of New York, Laura opened the yellowed pages of the journal. The heavy leather cover fell open with a sharp crack. The entries were sparse, written in a scrawling handwriting that Laura struggled to decipher. She picked her way through the forgotten drama.

5th of Se [date obscured by water staining]
The weather report told us to expect flooding, so we filled the bath with drinking water and moved everything we could upstairs. Last night the rain started. It was heavier than before, but we are at the top of the hill, so I'm not that worried. We'll check on Mrs. Allen in the morning.

6th of September
When we woke up the water was at the bottom of the stairs. It stunk and we decided to stay where we were, better than trying to

117

wade through ankle deep filth. Remi is worried about Mrs. Allen, but I am sure she will be fine until [rest of entry too faded to read].

7th of September

It's been raining for two days straight now. Not normal rain, but big driving drops that hit the windows like golf balls. We have moved Emily into our room to try and stop her crying. The radio said the flood barrier was up, but the water is still rising here. Something to do with a tidal surge. Maybe this is the worst of it? We have food for another day, but the water is coming out of the taps brown and smelly. Glad we filled the bath.

Remi is getting scared, and frankly, so am I, but I can't tell her that. The water is halfway up the stairs now and the rain is still coming down. I've never seen anything like this. We heard banging from the bungalows opposite last night. They must be trapped in their loft. Not sure what we can do unless the water gets lower.

8th of September

All we have left are a few crackers. The water in the bath is starting to taste funny and we are worried about giving it to Emily, but what else can we do? Where are the helicopters? We pay our taxes, but we haven't even seen an inflatable boat. Remi had a panic attack last night, she thought she heard screaming from across the street, but I told her it was just the wind. Thing is, I am not so sure it was. At least the water hasn't got any higher.

9th of September

The noises from number twenty-three have stopped. Not sure what that means to be honest, but Remi is thinking the worse. Emily won't stop crying. We are out of food and I don't know what to do. I have a pregnant wife and a small child and it's my job to look after them. Piss poor job I'm doing, hey. I think we are going to have to get out. If someone was coming it would have happened by now. I reckon I can use the bed slats and doors to make a half decent raft, tie it together with sheets maybe? I wish I had paid more attention in Scouts, but I was too busy trying to snog Sarah Mills. Ahh, Sarah Mills, I wonder where you are now?

10th of September

Started to rain again, so we are out of here. Ben from next door has already left, I saw him and Heather paddling out this morning on a Lilo. I don't think that's a great idea, no idea what is under that water. It's black and it proper reeks. I started taking the bed apart last night, Remi was not impressed, but that is the least of our worries. I haven't eaten in two days, neither of us have. What we have left we've given to Emily. If we don't get out soon, we might not be able to.

11th of September

Got Remi and Emily on the raft and it only blooming floats! I think I've earned my 'survive the apocalypse badge' with that one. We've named it the 'Jack Dawson', Remi loves old films and Titanic feels about right at the moment. We are going to head towards the railway station bridge, the radio said there was an emergency aid station there. With luck I should be able to push the raft most of the way.

12th S [Entry smeared by water, only partially legible]

What the …!! We made it to the … without too much drama but … and lots of hungry people. I managed to grab a couple of bottles of … and traded a blanket for a couple of cans of baked beans. We ate them cold from the tin, I told Remi is was just like camping, worse … I have ever been on. Last night some total … waved a knife in my face … rest of our stuff … We can't stay here. We are going in the morning.

13th September

We decided to head towards the centre of town. I don't know what will be there, but I am sure as hell not staying here. There was blood on the ground this morning. A lot of blood.

I've been walking all day, but we're making slow progress with the girls on the raft. Remi wants to get off and help, but I am not having her in this water, not in her condition. In some places it comes up to my chest and the smell isn't getting any better. It smells like raw sewage. It makes me want to gag. There is a lot of oil too, which is weird. It floats on the surface, like rainbows. I have to keep telling Emily not to play with it.

Something of September, who cares?
Nowhere to sleep last night. Curled up on the raft with the girls and tried to keep them warm. It's getting cold at night and everything we have left is sopping wet. Seen lots of people moving, but mostly they stick to themselves. There is a rumour that the government is getting people out from the airport. Decided to head that way. Don't know what else to do.

Managed to get some cans of spinach from an abandoned shop. Everything else was either gone or ruined. Who eats this stuff out of choice? It's awful.

So tired. Emily is crying again, and I shouted at her today. I told her to shut up. Well, worse than that but I don't want to write what I said. I'm not proud of it. Then I slapped her. Hard. I have never lost it with her before. The look on her face is something I won't forget. What kind of father am I? Remi isn't talking to me now. I wouldn't talk to me either.

September(ish)
If last month you had asked me 'How long to the airport mate' I would have said 'Half an hour, but give yourself an hour for the traffic.' I've been walking for days now and I don't think we are any nearer. Everything looks the same. The streets are just black rivers and I keep getting lost. I am not telling Remi that though. She isn't looking good. I fed her the last of the spinach this afternoon, but she couldn't keep it down, can't really blame her, the stuff goes slimy when it's left open.

[Next entry badly damaged, the paper had been scrunched up and the ink had run]

... was pushing the raft and it got wedged on something. I tried to free it, but it was stuck tight. I walked around the front of the raft and managed to get some leverage. The thing bobbed to the surface

… the smell was the worse thing that … He was wearing a backpack and the strap had got wedged under the raft … dead for a while … from his pack … gave the chocolate to Emily. What have I become?

September (still?)
You know when you say 'Well, it can't get any worse?' and then it does? This morning I was walking down the middle of the motorway. The water was only knee deep, so we were making pretty decent progress. Then suddenly the ground just disappeared. One minute I am pushing the raft and singing Disney songs with Emily, the next I am clinging to the raft for my life. If I hadn't been holding on really tight, I don't think I would still be here. Looks like I fell through a manhole or something. The worse bit is that I have hurt my leg. I can only just put my weight on it, think I twisted my knee. I also took most of the skin off my shin and that worries me more if I'm honest, this water is rank.

September 18th
Made it the airport. We're saved! There is a big government presence here, army and stuff. They have turned the car parks into big refugee camps like you see on TV. I never imagined I'd ever land up in a place like this.

It's going to be alright though. They gave us food and dry clothes and took us to a tent with some other families. There isn't much privacy, but it sure as hell beats the raft. Emily is doing much better with hot food inside her. My leg has been bandaged and they gave me some pills and stuff. Remi is not doing great. They took her off to the medical tent. They said she had a temperature and they gave me some medical waffle, but I didn't really understand. We are all so tired. As soon as I have settled Emily, I'll check on Remi.

September 20th [Entry is spotted with water damage]
I don't want to write this because part me thinks if I do it will become real. Yesterday Remi miscarried. The baby is gone. Remi was pretty far into the pregnancy, and well, it was a boy. My son. I can't do this anymore.

Laura flicked through the rest of the pages, but they were blank and empty. On the very last page there was a child's sketch. It showed a picture of a smiling family. The child held the string of a diamond shaped kite with a long tail.

They were surrounded by flowers and trees. Laura stared at the picture of the happy domestic scene and she wished it for Emily. She wished that after all the tragedy and loss the family had flown that kite in green fields, and that there, among the flowers, they had found peace.

CHAPTER 8

T he light through the Victoria Square apartment's floor length windows was a cold grey. Overcast clouds had settled over the city, leaving only the tops of the complexes visible. Oliver thought they looked like fishing boats, clustered together on a wispy sea.

He raised his hands to the life-sized hologram that stood in front of him. "Jamal, there is nothing I can do. The environmental team determined that the leak was pure water from the inlet values. They are not going to implement a full-scale sterilisation of the whole site. Quite frankly, the city council are more concerned with finding out how the network was hacked."

Jamal paced like a caged animal, forcing the holo-camera to track him. His legs disappeared into the coffee table and reappeared on the other side. "I do not understand this, Oliver," he wrung his hands as if trying to squeeze water from a dish cloth. "We are playing with fire. You must see that. We have no idea what will happen if the containment was breached. Do you remember Japanese knotweed? When it found its way onto this island in the nineteenth century it had no natural predators. It grew out of control, undermining walls and cracking foundations. Some people lost their homes and even flood defences were damaged. If we learnt anything, it was that invasive species must be dealt with quickly. It is not unreasonable to take precautions. Why are the council are treating us like children?"

Oliver understood Jamal's anxiety. This conversation was very similar to the one he'd had with his own superiors, but the response was always the same. While the project continued to yield results disruption would not be tolerated.

"Amanda has assured them that the breach was small and quickly contained. You are suggesting that maybe, just maybe, something has escaped. Who do you think they are going to listen to?"

"This isn't an ordinary species we are dealing with. This is a synthetic plant that has been *designed* to crossbreed. The hybrids grow rapidly. They thrive in low light conditions. They are resistant to pests, draught, freezing, even radiation. A single particle of pollen could be devastating to the environment."

"I know Jamal. But we have no evidence that pollen, or anything else, made it through the filters. Amanda has told the council there isn't a problem."

"This is not about who has the most convenient story," Jamal raged, throwing his hands in the air. "We must be led by science, not politics."

Oliver couldn't help but agree with him. "This became political the second my brother waded in. This is no longer about food security, it's about profit." Oliver tried to keep the resentment out of his voice. "This is what always happens when scientific discipline is seen as a barrier to progress. Long established procedures are no longer seen as protective. They are seen as blockers. Trust me Jamal, cooler heads will eventually prevail."

"You say 'progress', but I hear 'greed'. By the time your cooler heads have asserted themselves we will have lost control of this."

"Give it time. I'm going to ask Laura to examine some of the plants around the site for signs of mutation. If she finds any evidence of the host plant's genetic fingerprints, then I'll be the first to knock on the door to the council chamber and demand they listen." Oliver doubted Ekta would react very kindly to that kind of intrusion, but "ask politely" didn't seem a prudent thing to say in the wake of Jamal's anger.

The technician sighed. The lines around his eyes spoke of sleepless nights and emotional strain. "Alright Oliver, but I don't like this. Not at all. All of my experience is telling me we should proceed with caution," he cut the link curtly. It was out of character for the usually amiable technician. Oliver was worried.

He stretched his back and walked to the windows, watching the clouds swirl around the tops of the complexes. They boiled and seethed like a restless sea. Hugo was pacing the balcony, the wind mussing his carefully arranged hair. He was speaking animatedly to a hologram of an older man. Oliver couldn't hear the words, but his brother's usually relaxed countenance looked strained.

"Coffee, Italian roast," Oliver ordered the house computer.

"Make that two," Hugo added as he walked through the balcony doors. He was accompanied by a blast of cool air that smelt of impending rain.

"Trouble?" Oliver asked as the retro stainless-steel machine gurgled noisily from the countertop.

"Nothing I can't handle," Hugo responded flippantly. His smile lacked its usual brilliance. He strode into the kitchen and reappeared moments later with two steaming coffee mugs. He handed one to Oliver.

"Is everything alright?" Oliver asked. Hugo didn't look up from the mug he cradled between both hands. His brow was creased with fine lines. "Hugo?" Oliver asked after several seconds of tense silence.

"Umm? Sorry. Yes, everything is fine." Hugo visibly gathered himself and the effable mask slid back into place.

"How are things with the project? Are you making process?" he asked, deftly deflecting attention away from himself.

"Progress is one way of putting it I suppose," Oliver

grumbled. Hugo looked up sharply, and Oliver recoiled slightly from the intensity of his brother's gaze.

"We need to make this work Olly. I'm relying on you. Whatever resources you need, I can get them."

Oliver frowned. "Why is this so important to you?"

His brother looked slightly irritated "We have been over this, Olly. It isn't just important to me. It is important to all of us. This is the challenge of our generation."

"No, there is more to it than that. I thought this was just a vanity project to you, an opportunity to demonstrate the dominance of Chadwick Enterprises. But I am starting to think there is something more behind it."

Hugo perched on the edge of the sofa and crossed one leg over the other. "Right now, you are the only blood relative I have left."

It was a strange thing to say, Oliver thought. It left him feeling slightly disturbed. "This has become more than business to you hasn't it?"

Hugo sighed, his shoulders slumping forward. "It was always more than business. I never would have stepped on your toes if I didn't think it was necessary. I know you think I put my ambition first, but I am genuinely just trying to make this work."

Oliver suddenly realised what had been bothering him. "Hugo, why are you here? Why aren't you at home with Maria?"

Hugo fell silent, he stared out of the window at the gathering summer storm.

"Maria and I are having some problems."

The tone was phlegmatic, but Oliver could tell the admission was difficult for Hugo. His brother was always guarded about his personal life. It was as if he was afraid to show any chink of weakness, any moment of self-doubt. It was an odd contradiction, given his usual openness and warmth. "Is there anything I can do to help?" Oliver asked.

Hugo took several brooding sips from his coffee mug. "Not really. This is something I have to fix on my own."

Oliver studied him for a moment. "Do you remember what Dad always used to say?"

"Ask your Mum?" Hugo grinned.

"Well, yes. But his other favourite saying was 'The secret of a happy marriage is two words. 'Yes dear'.'"

Hugo laughed. "There is some truth in that." He drained the last of his coffee and put the empty cup on the table. Suddenly he smiled. "Do you remember that night in Osaka with Dad?"

Oliver smiled at the old memory. "How could I forget? It took us all night to dry you out." He felt the room darken as the first raindrops struck the window.

"In my defence, it was a stupid place to put a koi carp pond." Hugo got to his feet and walked to the floor length window, staring out at broody sky. "I've been thinking recently of the sacrifices Mum made for Dad's career. She put her law practice on hold and raised us almost single handily while he travelled the world. That can't have been easy. I don't think I really appreciated that before."

Oliver wondered just how bad things really were with Maria. "Go home, Hugo," he said gently.

Hugo smiled sadly. The sound of the rain hitting the windows filled the silence. Hugo seemed to shake himself off. "I'm hungry," he announced suddenly. "Let's go and find some lunch." He paused for a moment, "Let's be adventurous, I feel like Fugu."

Oliver went along with his brother's mercurial mood. "No way, I remember the last time we tried pufferfish. Never again. I don't even like sushi."

"Sashimi, Olly. Sushi is vinegared rice. You are so uncultured."

"I'm uncultured? I don't think Mr. Katayama thought you were particularly cultured when he had to pull you out of his pond. Anyway, wasabi makes my nose run," Oliver said with mock seriousness.

Hugo laughed and pulled him to his feet. "There is a cure

for that, it's called sake."

△△△

When the door chime sounded early the next morning Oliver was still sipping coffee in his pyjamas. Hugo, of course, had already been up for hours. He glugged water from a polished metal bottle, his skin sheened with sweat from his morning run. The sculpted body was the one thing that Oliver no longer envied. He had witnessed first-hand how much effort went into maintaining it.

"I'll go" Hugo volunteered, and Oliver was happy to let him, reluctant to surrender his quiet morning ritual of caffeine and contemplation. He was surprised when Hugo led Jamal and Laura into the large kitchen. His brother met his eyes meaningfully, but Oliver didn't need the implied warning to read the agitation that radiated from his colleagues.

"What's wrong?" he asked bluntly, earning a disapproving look from his younger brother. The two visitors glanced at each other, clearly apprehensive.

Hugo stepped into the tense silence with practiced ease. "Whatever has happened, we'll deal with it. Take your time and start at the beginning." It wasn't what he said, Oliver realised, it was how he said it. Hugo had the ability to move someone from near panic to stoic calm in one sentence.

He studied his brother as the younger man leaned back against the kitchen counter, superficially relaxed. His focus was intense, yet receptive. His voice soft, yet assertive. The overall effect was an air of authority that was both commanding and oddly comforting.

Laura was the first to speak up. "Oliver asked me to look for problems in the area around the research unit," she started. Hugo nodded encouragingly. "As soon as I got there, I knew something was wrong. It was too quiet, like the way birds stop singing before a storm. It just felt... empty somehow. It took me most of the day to work out what was going on."

She switched her focus to Oliver "The bees have gone, boss. Not just the bees in the unit, the ones that *it* deliberately exterminated," she shot a look at Hugo, "all the wild bees. I didn't find one within an hour's walk of the unit. No bumble bees, no mason bees, no honeybees. I found ants and spiders; woodlice and flies but not a single bee. I have never seen anything like it."

Oliver squeezed his brows together. "What do you mean 'gone'?"

"I mean they are not there. There aren't any dead ones lying around, but there aren't any living ones either."

"Could they have moved?" Hugo asked. His expression seemed to say, "Why should we be worried about a few missing insects?"

"Bees don't roam more than a few kilometres from their nests. The colony always stays near the queen and even solitary bees stay close to home. I can't think of any reason why they would suddenly stop foraging a particular area, especially as there was plenty of food."

"Have you searched for nests?" Oliver asked, trying to find a simple explanation. "Maybe a predator or a parasite?"

"Multiple species in one day? Not likely."

Jamal looked up abruptly. "You are both avoiding the issue," his dark eyes flashed with anger. "Can't you see this is too much of a coincidence? Sudden colony collapse days after we have a confinement breach. I warned you something like this would happen. I warned you we could not trust Amanda. Just look at the abomination it has created." His voice was tight and agitated.

Hugo pinned Jamal with his eyes. "We don't know what has happened yet. Let's not jump to conclusions," he radiated a calm, quiet confidence. "This could have a simple, natural explanation."

Despite his brother's assurances Oliver's mind was racing. He had been upset by the loss of the research hives but had reacted pragmatically, putting the project before his personal feelings. Wild colony collapse was a much more alarming prospect, and one not without precedent.

Oliver knew that in the days preceding the Rush, bee numbers had declined globally. By the mid twenty first century, wild honeybees and many species of solitary bee had become functionally extinct. Careful management of domesticated hives had led to a slow recovery, but many crops, including biofuels, had become uneconomical without wild pollinators.

Oliver pushed away his growing anxiety and took a deep breath to clear his head. "We can't make any assumptions here. We need to understand the scale of this problem and we need to find the root cause. Conjecture isn't going to help us, we need facts."

He glanced across at his colleagues. Laura carried the tension in her posture, her arms crossed, her green eyes sombre. Jamal had collapsed into one of the kitchen chairs. His knee jumped in a rapid, repetitive rhythm. The righteous anger which had fuelled him earlier had gone, leaving him deflated and morose.

"Oliver is right," Hugo added quietly. Oliver threw him a surprised look. His younger brother smiled warmly and the tension in the room seemed to dissipate slightly. "The first step to solving any problem is to define it. We can expend our energy speculating or we can make positive steps to find answers."

Oliver couldn't help but smile. In that moment, dressed in sweat-stained sportswear, his hair untidily plastered to his head, Hugo was still every bit the boardroom leader. It was a talent, Oliver acknowledged, and he employed it with skill and subtlety.

Jamal shifted slightly in his chair. His face was thoughtful. "I can send a flight of drones to do a proper count. That should help us define the extent of the problem. I might be able to use the data to extrapolate where the die-off first started."

Hugo nodded, the gesture somehow communicated both approval and support. Laura paced a few steps towards Jamal. "I can get out in the field and try and find some nests. If I can examine them, I might find out what is happening to the bee colonies."

"Good" Hugo agreed, before turning his attention to his older brother. Oliver suppressed a smiled at the expectant look on his brother's face. "I'll return to the lab and process the samples Laura finds. I want to concentrate on finding a way to contain whatever is causing this. Natural or not." Oliver felt the buzz of energy that permeated the room. "Hugo?" He added, raising his coffee cup in a light-hearted salute "I am glad you are here."

△△△

Laura wiped the sweat from her eyes. It was much cooler under the canopy of trees than it was in the open heath, but the humidity was still stifling. Cautiously, she approached the bees nest, moving slowly to avoid rousing the swarm. She had always been slightly scared of bees, although she couldn't remember ever being stung by one. Wasps were much worse, of course. Horrid little picnic-spoiling bullies.

The delicate, waxy nest was wedged in a hollow of a willow tree. It was strangely quiet in the middle of the hot afternoon. Laura couldn't escape the sense of foreboding that settled over her. The nest was only partially visible, the greater part was hidden in the dark recess of the tree. What Laura could see, however, was enough to convince her that something was very wrong. The hexagonal cells, which should have been swarming with bees, were empty and lifeless.

Slowly, she crept forward and extracted a long probe from a pocket in her utility belt. As carefully and slowly as she could she inserted the probe. Worryingly, there was no reaction from the nest. Leaving the probe in place, she stepped away and swiped her text. As she feared, the nest was empty. There was no detectable movement or vibration. Disappointed, she walked back to the nest to take samples for Oliver. Maybe he would be able to find a natural explanation. Although somehow, Laura doubted it.

With her specimen pots full, Laura started the long walk back to her pod. The ground was dry. It crunched under her boots as she weaved between the tall gorse bushes on the edge of the woodland. The sweet smell of the yellow flowers reminded her of childhood. Her mother had always been a free spirit. An untameable bohemian, who had loved the wild and the unconventional. Even now she was away, working for some charity in the Himalayas. That unconventional lifestyle had greatly influenced her daughter.

Laura had spent her childhood summers foraging for blackberries and crab apples. While others had enjoyed the comforts of the city, she had spent her days in the provinces, listening as her mother wove folktales by firelight. Her happiest memories were of falling asleep under the stars, listening for the cry of the Banshee.

Even now Laura was unable to look at a toadstool ring without imagining the moonlit dances of fairies or hearing the songs of the fey in the gentle sighing of the wind. Sometimes, alone in the wilds, Laura could again feel that tingle of wonder and magic. A feeling that there was more to the world than her senses could reveal. A hidden realm of witches and mystics, waiting to be discovered in the dark places under the trees, and crevices between the rocks.

It was the magic she found in the natural world that had inspired Laura to study biology. She found solace in understanding, and excitement in the unknown, the questions yet to be answered. The loss of the bee colonies had deeply unsettled her. The thought that she might be partially responsible was too appalling to contemplate. It would be a betrayal of everything that Laura cherished.

She hefted her field kit into a more comfortable position and settled into the march, enjoying the feel of the hot sun on her back and the cooling breeze in her hair. She stopped briefly to admire a sundew. The red tendrils of the small, insectivorous plant glistened with moisture in the bright sunlight. The plant was one of her favourites, despite, or possibly because of its dark habit of digesting its insect prey. She wondered if Amanda was really all that different from the small plant. Afterall, neither was truly malicious, each was just trying to achieve its goals with the resources it had available.

Malicious or not, Amanda was a human creation, and therefore a human responsibility. Laura felt that responsibility keenly. With a renewed sense of purpose, she strode through the heather and bracken of the open heath.

Laura was certain of one thing. She was a part of this fragile ecology, not apart from it. Technology had made the human race feel removed from the shifting seasons, the cycles of abundance and dearth. That separation was falsehood, a shallow, superficial sheen. The citizens of the great cities were as dependant on the bounty of nature as the cave dwellers of eons past. Every individual was a custodian, and everyone had a duty to protect the whole. Laura accepted that duty gladly.

△△△

Oliver prepared the samples Laura had gathered and slid them into a slot in the side of a large silver machine. The holographic electron microscope projected the 3D images onto a workbench that occupied the centre of the biology lab. Oliver, Laura and Jamal gathered around it intently. "I can't see anything that would account for the colony to collapse so suddenly," Oliver murmured under his breath. His brow furrowed in concentration.

"The scans showed the nest was in good condition. There was plenty of pollen and honey stored and evidence of recent brood laying," Laura mused thoughtfully, leaning on the opposite side of the bench.

"A virus? Or an invasive predator, varroa mites maybe?"

Jamal asked half-heartedly. Oliver could sense that he had already reached his own conclusion. His attempt at seeming open to other possibilities was for the benefit of his colleagues. Jamal was suffering from something scientists called "confirmation bias". All the evidence he saw just affirmed his belief that the colony collapse was a result of the containment leak. His mind was closed to any other option.

Hugo was leaning against a work bench at the back of the small laboratory. Dressed in a formal black business suit, he should have looked out of place among the complex scientific equipment. Instead, he looked confident and relaxed, as at home among the gleaming apparatus as he was in a boardroom. Somehow Hugo had integrated himself with the group of researchers and they had intuitively accepted him.

"I've been reading some papers about 'colony collapse disorder' from before the Rush," he started slowly. "At the time they believed it had many, interlinking causes."

"The move towards intensive single-crop agriculture reducing wildflower meadows; increased use of chemical fertilisers and pest control; parasites like mites and bacteria. Some researchers even suggested a loss of genetic diversity due to fewer hedgerows making it more difficult for bees to travel." Hugo shrugged, "The general consensus seemed to be that all these factors weakened the bee colonies and made them more prone to diseases and predation."

Oliver narrowed his lips "Those factors might have caused a rapid decline, but it was over years, decades even. What we are seeing is very different. Complete colony collapse, over multiple species, in one day."

Laura nodded. "We are not seeing tens of thousands of dead bees in the hive. They are just leaving, abandoning the hive. Even the queen is missing."

Oliver sighed, studying the holographic display. "The lack of dead bees to examine makes it very difficult to determine the cause. There are microbial pathogens present, but nothing that isn't endemic in the environment. Something must have changed, but I'm not even sure where to look."

Hugo leaned back against a large clinical analyser. "What happens if the bees die? What's the worse-case scenario?"

Jamal blew air out between his teeth. It was clear from his expression this was something he had been contemplating for some time. "About a third of the food plants we eat rely on insect pollination. That includes staples like onions and potatoes, but also most nuts, fruits, and leaf vegetables," he began. "A lot of the foods you are familiar with would disappear or become prohibitively expensive. Your morning coffee would be history, sorry Oliver. No tea or wine, Laura. This would have a huge impact on human health. It would lead to global malnutrition."

Hugo furrowed his brow. "So we would starve? It's that serious?"

"No, not starve. Grains like wheat and rice are wind pollinated, so they wouldn't be impacted. However, we would struggle to meet our nutrition needs without the minerals and vitamins provided by fruits and vegetables.

"The impact on the natural world would be equally devastating. Most flowering plants and trees are insect pollinated, and bees are the most successful pollinators. Not only would this be a much less colourful world, but there would be far-reaching consequences all the way up the food chain."

He paused, his eyes distant and thoughtful. "Maybe technology would save us, but you need to understand the scale of the problem. Around sixty thousand pollinators are needed per acre of crops. Producing that many coordinated drones has always proved unmanageable. Your AI has been testing a self-replicating artificial pollinator, but that hasn't been tested at scale. I have my doubts that we could ever sustain enough to replace every single bee."

Hugo pulled a horrified face "Hold on. Did you just say no wine? This is far more serious than I thought." The others smiled, grateful for the release of tension. His face hardened as his eyes swept the group of scientists. "That is what we are working to prevent. Now we know the stakes, let's focus on winning the pot." He stood and walked to the head of the workbench, all eyes in the room followed him.

"Jamal, do you have any mapping for the extent of the affected area?"

The tall scientist nodded. He swept a flat hand through the holographic display, the image dimmed and disappeared. It was replaced by another projection as Jamal's fingers danced across his text. It showed an aerial view of the research units, and the wooded area surrounding them. The image zoomed outwards, reducing the agricultural unit to a small clearing in a large expanse of woods and heathland.

"I used a flight of pathfinder drones to survey the area immediately around the test unit. It took a while to corelate the data, so this is based on a single pass over the site, I estimate an accuracy of around eighty-two percent. A bee is a fairly small target and difficult to identify precisely, so the drones had to fly below 100 metres. That limits their range."

He pressed another button and an overlay dropped into position. "The red area is the dead zone. Our pathfinders found no evidence of bees in this area. As you can see it is focused on the project Metomagis research unit and spreads out in a roughly oval pattern."

"How big is that area?" Oliver asked.

"Approximately six square kilometres."

Laura gasped. "That's much worse than it was this morning"

Jamal met her eyes. "That was three hours ago. This is how it looks now."

The red zone seeped outwards, spreading like a blood stain across the pristine wilderness. "I estimate that the..." Jamal paused, searching for the right word, "effect is spreading at roughly fifty metres an hour. Worse still it is moving with the prevailing wind."

Oliver felt his stomach hit the floor "So it's airborne?"

Jamal shrugged his shoulders "Possibly, or it is using a vector which is carried by the wind. Pollen or aphids maybe?"

A shocked silent fell over the room. The only sound was a gentle rhythmic pumping noise from one of the pieces of heavy equipment. "Jamal?" Oliver began quietly, tentatively breaking the silence. "Can you project what this will look like in a week?"

The scientist nodded and punched at his text. A yellow overlay spread across the aerial map. The image zoomed out, then out again. A yellow smear ran across an enormous tract of land, running north east across the provinces, devouring the city and stopping close to the crumbling coastline. Laura swore softly. Oliver couldn't help agreeing with the sentiment. He forced his middle finger to stop rubbing his thumb.

"Alright." Hugo's voice cut through the quiet lab. "You are the experts. What do you need to work out what is causing this and how to stop it?"

Jamal pulled himself up to his full height. "We know the test unit is at the epicentre of this. To me it seems obvious that this is a consequence of the containment leak. We should do what we didn't have the courage to do before," he glared at Oliver. "Complete sterilisation of the affected area, and a few kilometres around it."

Laura started at him dumbfounded. "Scorched earth? That's your solution to this? Burn everything to the ground."

"It is the only way to contain the spread."

Oliver held up his hands. "Wait a minute," he tried to interrupt, but the two young scientists were locked in battle and ignored him.

"We don't even know what is causing this," Laura snapped back. "Until we identify the cause we have no way of knowing if a controlled burn would even be effective. That could cause it to spread further."

Jamal leaned across the workbench. His body coiled tightly. "If we don't do it now, then we lose even more land.

This is our *own* protocol, Laura. When are we going to follow it? When the flames are lapping at your apartment door?"

Laura sneered. Her face twisted into an angry snarl. "So let's just burn it all to the ground. Just wipe out acres of wetland, ancient trees, irreplaceable habitat. Mass genocide of protected species. On what evidence? Because someone in a stuffy office wrote it in a manual? Typical. Why use intellect when you can burn everything to the ground."

Jamal's body went rigid. He took a pace towards Laura. "How dare you talk to me like that? While you were stuck in your books, I was working to feed you. You think you are better than me because you go to a fancy university?"

"I think I am better than you because I haven't given up!" Laura snapped. Her face was flushed with indignation.

"Enough!" The words cut through the laboratory like a thunderclap. "I appreciate passionate debate, but this is not constructive." Hugo stared at the two combatants, his blue eyes hard and unyielding. "I'll repeat my question. What do you need to work out what is causing this?" Jamal started to speak but Hugo glared at him coldly. "If we need to sterilise the site then so be it, sometimes hard decisions need to be taken. But right now, Jamal, is that our only choice?"

Jamal looked like he was going to affirm the statement, then shook his head grudgingly "No, it isn't."

Hugo nodded his agreement "What do you need?" he asked, a steel edge to his voice.

Oliver looked up. His mind had been in overdrive while his colleagues bickered. "I have an idea." The others looked at him expectantly. "If we had an unaffected nest, we could compare the microbial flora. Run a complete comparison down to the DNA level."

Laura nodded. "We would need a nest or hive that hasn't been exposed to any of the native pathogens. From that we could create a solid baseline. A control if you like."

"What are you thinking Laura?" Hugo asked, his body language was relaxed and supportive, the hard edge gone.

"An Ocean rig. A big one. They are self-contained and isolated. It is unlikely any cross-contamination could have happened. The northern ones are notoriously independent. They grow most of their own food and keep managed hives which have been separated from the mainland for decades."

"How do you know that?" Jamal asked, his posture still stiff and defensive.

"Because my father is the mayor of one."

△△△

Rose stood at the back of the medical bay as Tim fussed over Connor. She shuffled her feet, feeling as if she was intruding, even though Connor had asked her to stay. In truth, she had barely left his side since they had escaped from the city hospital together. At first, she had stayed to appease the lingering sense of guilt she felt for getting him caught. But as time passed, it had grown to be more than that.

Connor had been part of her life for many years. She had always valued him as a colleague; a kindred-spirt; an advocate. Nearly losing him had changed that. She had come to realise how much his friendship really meant to her. Sure, he was hot-tempered, grumpy and rude. But he was also courageous, loyal and dependable.

Patience, however, was not his forte. "How long does it take to change a fecking bandage?" he demanded loudly

"It would be quicker if you kept still." Tim said firmly.

"Well, if I knew it was going to take this long, I would have brought my fecking knitting."

Rose smiled at the exchange. She knew Connor hated being injured and that he railed against the forced confinement. She could sympathise. The community was low on food, Jess was a in police cell and the city was actively searching for them. There were so many things to do, and yet Rose couldn't bring herself to leave him.

"This is healing well." Tim said. Despite Connor's

goading his tone was a polished mix of professional and compassionate. "Although it is going to leave some scarring."

Connor grunted. "I don't think I'll be losing any sleep over a few more beauty spots. Anyway, the ladies love a man of action." He winked at Rose and she rolled her eyes. She had seen his body. It was a storybook of old scars.

"How did you get this one?" Tim asked, his finger gently exploring the thick scar tissue over Connor's spine. Connor tensed. Rose knew he hated being touched, but she suspected he was even more uncomfortable with the probing question. "It looks like a wound from a focused particle beam," Tim said, leaning close to study the circular injury.

"What would a mollycoddled city dweller like you know about particle beams?" Connor asked gruffly.

"I interned at a clinic in the districts. I saw injuries like this occasionally. Mostly dock workers," Tim said as he sprayed a dressing onto Connor's burns. Rose was fairly certain the scarring wasn't from of an industrial accident. There were too many old injuries, crisscrossing his arms and torso. There was even a deep crater in his thigh that looked suspiciously like an old-fashioned bullet hole.

Tim tapped the dressing to make sure it had set hard. He started to clear his equipment away. "Did you work on the docks? Is that how you ended up down here?" He asked the question lightly, but Rose could see the curiosity in his face.

"None of your fecking business." Connor retorted. He tried to sit up but fell back onto the bench with a grunt. Tim helped him up, provoking a long string of profanities that had Tim chuckling.

"What's so funny?" Connor grumbled as pulled a thick shirt over his head.

"Let's just say you have a colourful way with words. Very… evocative." Tim smiled at his own quip. Connor growled a warning deep in his throat, but Tim didn't seem to be the least bit intimidated.

"In a few days I'll swap the hard dressing for something

that will give you a better range of motion. For now, I want to keep your shoulders immobile to allow the deep tissue to heal."

Rose could tell Connor wasn't really listening. He was a proud man. A natural protector. Being seen as weak and incapacitated was difficult for him. She stepped forward to help him shrug on his winter coat. "You know there is no weakness in accepting help, Connor," she said softly. "We all need to lean on others occasionally."

"That might work for you, but where I come from, fate helps those who help themselves."

"Where I come from, we look after each other," Rose said, feeling a sharp pang of loss for her old life in the mines.

"I should have helped." Connor mumbled. His voice was barely audible. "I should never have let them take her."

"Jess?" Tim shook his head. "There is nothing you can do to help her, Connor. We need to let justice take its course. The best we can do for her is to try and change public opinion. We need to get the city to understand we aren't here through bad choices or idleness. We need them to know that they are only one pay cheque away from where we are now. We aren't going to do that by blowing up buildings."

"What's your plan then? Ask nicely? This is the real-world Tim. It's cruel and it's unfair. The city isn't interested in us, they are too busy collecting designer handbags. The only thing that the powerful listen to is more power."

"There are many forms of power, Connor. Violence is never an answer. It is a snowball that never stops rolling, pulling in more and more lives, leaving nothing but hatred in its wake. Peaceful resistance is the most effective way of wielding power, it is subtle and artful, it changes minds. Avalanches do not carve valleys, my friend, rivers do."

"Very pretty Tim," Rose said, "but without radical action there is never meaningful change. Jess used to argue that without Malcolm X, Martin Luther King would never have been able to rouse the moderate masses. Without violence, Gandhi would have just been another lawyer in Bombay. Fear opens minds, not pretty words."

"Where has violence got us?" Tim snapped "Millie is dead, Jess is in a police cell, and we played our last trump card getting Connor out of a guarded hospital room."

"It's getting us noticed," Connor tapped the side of his nose as if including Tim in an extraordinary secret.

"It's getting us killed," Tim said softly, his voice anguished. In that moment he looked very young and very lost, Rose thought.

"We'll see, we'll see." Connor smiled a dangerous smile.

CHAPTER 9

Oliver waited impatiently as Amy fussed over Laura in the pod docking area. Laura was dressed for the Arctic cold. Her salopettes were tucked into the tops of snow boots and her base layer shimmered with the metallic heating elements woven through the fabric. An overstuffed backpack was hanging heavily from one shoulder and an enormous coat was tucked under the other. Oliver, in his customary utility jacket and work trousers, felt decidedly underdressed.

With a lingering kiss the two women separated, and Laura climbed into the seat opposite. Oliver was about to shut the door when Amy leaned into the small cabin. "You'll be fine. Just don't let him get to you. Remember, you can call me anytime." She kissed Laura's forehead gently. Laura forced a smile, but her eyes were hooded, her shoulders slumped.

Concerned, but not wanting to intrude, Oliver cycled the pod doors. With a button press he sent the pod soaring skywards, away from the residential complexes and into the morning traffic.

Oliver felt the same sense of exhilaration he always did when travelling out of the city. The complexes, so solid and all-encompassing on the ground, faded like distant smoke in the hazy summer sky. Soon the provinces rushed below as the pod gained altitude and speed. A thousand shades of green, cut through with blue-black rivers and lakes. "So, what's it like on an ocean rig? I've never been to one. In fact, I've never been so far north." Oliver asked brightly, trying to break the uncomfortable silence.

"Cold, windy and claustrophobic."

Oliver had mentored Laura for more than two years, ever since she had first embarked on her PhD studies. He had seen her tired, frustrated and moody, but never petulant. He wondered what was bothering her. "How long has your dad been mayor?"

"Ten years," she crossed her arms over her chest. Oliver narrowed his lips at the terse response. He didn't want to pry, but he was concerned both for Laura and the work they had ahead of them. He needed to know if he could rely on her.

He decided to try a different approach. "Do you see your father often?"

"Not anymore, no."

"So, this will be a good chance to catch up."

Laura looked up sharply, her eyes were hard and cold. "I haven't seen my father since I was fifteen. Even before that we rarely saw him. We were never that important to him, his career always came first." She took a deep breath and spread her hands in front of her, studying her nails, as if the answers she needed were somehow scratched into the black varnish.

"My mother always said that the sea sung to him, like some kind of Siren call. He would hear its voice in the wind, and then he would become restless and fidgetily until he left again. Personally, I think he was a selfish, philandering knobhead. He liked the idea of family but not the fact of it. He was too self-absorbed to care about anyone but himself."

"I'm sorry, I didn't know." Oliver felt a wave of sympathy. Agreeing to visit the rig could not have been easy decision for Laura. "You don't have to come with me if this is difficult for you. I can drop you back?"

Laura shook her head firmly "You need me. The riggers don't like outsiders. You aren't going to get far with them on your own."

"I could take Hugo. He could charm the tail off a mermaid."

Laura smiled and Oliver was relieved to see that it reached her eyes. "I don't doubt that. Your brother has enough magnetism to pull moons out of orbit," she grinned, pleased with her own analogy. "Nonetheless, the riggers are a strange group. They are fiercely independent and distrustful of outsiders. They like isolation and are resentful of anything that intrudes on it.

"People like my father are rare. They tolerated him at first. He is an exceptional marine biologist, and he was useful to them. Eventually they made him choose between the sea and the land. He chose the sea," she said the words matter-of-factly, but the note of bitterness was unmistakable. "Most of them are born riggers, they can trace their lineage back generations."

"What makes you so certain they'll help you?" Oliver asked.

"I'm not certain at all. However, he is my father and that has to mean something. I could happily spend the rest of my life pretending he never existed, or that I don't care that he left us. But I can't, I have to face him sooner or later, and it looks like it has to be sooner. We need these samples, boss. The colony collapse will be catastrophic if we don't stop it. This is just too important."

Oliver admired her bravery. The rebellious spark that others had tried to extinguish was really the wellspring of her strength. Oliver had always loved teaching because of moments like this. He learned far more from his students than he could ever teach them.

"You are remarkable Laura, don't ever let anyone convince you otherwise."

She looked at him, surprise etched across her pale features "Where did that come from?"

"Just take the compliment." The corners of her mouth rose slightly. She quickly hid the strawberry blush that spread across her cheeks.

Below them the coastline was starting to form out of

the hazy mist that hugged the churning waves. The ragged, indistinct flood plains spread out from the coast like the torn tendrils of a storm-tossed pennant. Oliver looked down on the vastness of the ocean and felt a shiver of fear. He had crossed oceans before, but always in the comfort of a hyperloop train. He had never ventured so far in a pod. Suddenly, the light vehicle felt as flimsy as willow dander.

"How long will it take to get to the rig?" He asked Laura, gripping the edge of the seat with white knuckled fingers. She pressed a few buttons on the control console between them and shrugged.

"A few hours, maybe a bit longer."

"How much of that is over open water?"

"All of it. Are you alright boss?"

"Absolutely. Just curious."

"It's beautiful isn't it?" Laura asked, staring out of the window at the grey expanse. "It looks like the palm of a hand. The waves are the ridges and lines. Do you see?"

Oliver mumbled something he hoped sounded appreciative and shuffled as far back as he could on the bench. "Let's go a bit lower." Laura keyed the console and the pod dropped towards the surface of the water with a stomach-churning lurch.

The sea raced towards them as Laura sent the pod into a steep dive. Oliver's arms flew up instinctively to brace against the windows. Embarrassed, he lowered them quickly, and fixed his eyes on the floor between them.

The pod levelled just above the surface of the water and skimmed across the wave tops. Every cresting wave slammed the bottom of the small craft with a terrifying boom. Oliver looked up to see a plume of spray rising behind them, taller than the pod, arching like the tail of a galloping white horse. Dozens of small rainbows glistened in the boiling spume, colourful gemstones trapped in a dew dusted spider's web.

Laura pressed her face against the window, grinning wildly as the pod bounced over the spray. Their wake stretched out behind them, a white scar against the grey perfection.

"It looks like someone has scattered diamonds." She exclaimed, her nose almost touching the clear poly-carbon.

"I think you and your father might have more in common than you think." Oliver said tightly, his stomach rebelling against the churning motion.

△△△

The rig rose out of the water on spindly legs. It was bigger than Oliver had imagined, stretching across the horizon like a dark shadow. The platform itself was a large, flat artificial island, dotted with trees and arable land. Oliver estimated that it rose about thirty metres above the surface of the sea. He assumed this was enough to protect it from the worst of the turbulent winter storms and sea ice.

The only building of any note was a three-story, sprawling structure on the south side of the rig. It was made of a cheap grey poly-carbon, flat and utilitarian. Oliver thought it looked like an administration building of some kind. Other buildings were dotted around, but they mostly seemed to be small work sheds or storage areas. There were no discernible habitats. He wondered where the majority of the population lived and worked.

As the rig drew nearer Oliver could make out large letters stencilled into the side of the platform, "Arctic Rig Roald Amundsen", they pronounced proudly. The pod slipped slowly downwards, flying low over the flat farmland as it headed towards the main building.

Oliver could make out a few people working in the fields below. They stopped to watch as the pod descended silently above them, leaning on old-fashioned manual tools. Fruit trees, hedges, and neatly planted fields spread out across the surface of the rig. Narrow tracks wound between the hedgerows, but Oliver couldn't see vehicles or droids of any kind.

The pod slowed and landed precisely in the middle of a poly-carbon pad. Given the amount of dust that was kicked up by their descent, Oliver suspected the pad was little used. As the canopy retracted, he was hit by a blast of cold air. It pierced his thin work clothes like a thousand tiny needles. He found himself shivering before his feet even hit the ground. Laura, in her thermally controlled suit, looked perfectly at ease in the biting wind.

A door on the large building slid open and three figures emerged. They all wore brightly coloured thermal suits. Their silhouettes were as round as Christmas babbles in the thick, padded clothing. Their heads bent against the wind as they made their way to the waiting pod.

"I'm Gustaf Fleischer, mayor of the Roald Amundsen." A short, broad man held his hand out as he approached. His thick red beard was shot through with grey and his faced was heavily lined and windbitten. It was the type of face that was impossible to date, Oliver would have guessed his age at anywhere between forty and sixty.

His handshake was firm and hinted at a robustness that seemed fitting for the frozen rig. "This is my wife, Salak, and my son, Ejner."

"I'm Oliver Chadwick, and this is my colleague... Laura Fleischer." Oliver fumbled over the introduction, uncertain how to introduce Laura to her estranged father, or even whether he had any right to use her family name. The wind carried the words away as soon as they had left his mouth.

He heard a gasp from the taller of the three riggers. The slender woman lowered her hood to reveal startling silver hair which whipped in the gusting wind like seaweed caught in a swift current. Laura hid behind Oliver. The high collar of her coat was pulled up over her nose and the hood pulled down to her eyebrows. She fidgeted with the seals of her jacket compulsively.

The older woman approached Laura warily, as if greeting a frightened animal. After a moment's hesitation she pulled Laura into a warm embrace. Laura returned the hug stiffly but didn't resist when the other woman took her hood in both hands and lowered it slowly, as if revealing something precious and rare.

"You are most welcome here, daughter of my husband. I see him in you." Her accent was thick and awkward, unfamiliar with the English syllables.

"Laura?" Gustaf stepped forward. His face was frozen in the shock of recognition. Laura backed away slightly. "Can we save this for later? I need to examine your beehives as soon as possible." she pulled the hood back over her face, where it conveniently obscured whatever emotions she was warring with. Her voice, however, was as cold as the lashing wind.

If Gustaf was offended by the reunion, he hid it well. Clearing his throat, he took a step backwards, his posture was rigid and formal, a mirror of his daughter's discomfort. "Perhaps you will join us for lunch then? After that we can discuss the issues you have on the mainland." He emphasised the last word oddly, as if it was almost an insult.

Laura looked like she was going to refuse the invitation, but Oliver, shivering in the Arctic chill stepped in quickly. "Thank you for the invitation, Mayor Fleischer. I feel like I am a little underdressed for your weather."

Gustaf chuckled, a deep, resonant sound that made Oliver smile, despite the tension. "Indeed, Doctor Chadwick. It can get chilly here, even in summer."

"*Chilly?*" Oliver muttered, wondering if he would manage the short walk to the building without tripping over his frozen feet.

The administrative complex was featureless, but at least it was warm. The walls were a dull olive green, and the floor was hard and bare. Somehow it felt like every other government building Oliver had ever entered, the atmosphere was one of restraint and order.

To his surprise they were led to a bank of lifts and ushered inside. A line of protruding buttons on the wall indicated the levels. They were pleasingly nostalgic and clunky. He noticed that the button for the current level was lit, marked with the letter "G". All the other buttons were below it. Gustaf punched a button marked twelve.

"Most of the rig is below sea level. What you have seen on the surface is the tip of the iceberg, so to speak." Gustaf began. Oliver felt this wasn't the first time Gustaf had given this introduction. "The upper levels are used for accommodation, air filtration and leisure facilities. The lower levels are where we do most of our work."

"What is your work exactly?" Oliver asked.

"You don't know?" Gustaf sounded surprised. "Perhaps after lunch I can give you a tour?"

The lift doors opened onto a small vestibule. Three tubular corridors spread out in a "T" shape. They were made of clear poly-carbon and Oliver quickly realised they were now deep under the surface of the sea. The corridors were illuminated from the outside, suffusing the ambient light with shifting blue shadows and casting a strange pattern on the glossy floor.

Every few metres metal braces arched through the clear tubes, creating an optical illusion of decreasing circles, like windblown ripples on a still pond. Gustaf and his party set off down the righthand corridor.

Oliver waved Laura ahead of him and started to follow the party down the corridor. He nearly walked into her back as Laura suddenly stopped, staring intently through the clear walls. He followed her astonished gaze.

The underwater complex was vast. A maze of clear corridors disappeared into the dark indigo below. The corridors linked huge structures, cut through with circular windows, like the portholes of ancient ships. The complex copied its sisters in the surface cities. Each level was surrounded by large balconies which teemed with colourful seaweeds and corals.

Orange fan corals shone against lacy white fronds.

Bubble-gum pink colonies created a shocking burst of vibrant colour. On one balcony a cluster of red tree coral reminded Oliver of sugar maples in their full autumn splendour. Another supported a bizarre peach coral, which zigzagged through swaying forests of green kelp. Everywhere Oliver looked was life, in every conceivable form.

Oliver took a shuddering breath, he felt overwhelmed by the astonishing diversity that gently swayed in the cold Arctic waters. "I had no idea," he whispered, almost reverently.

"Cold water reefs can be just as impressive as their tropical counterparts," Gustaf said. "That is part of our purpose here, but I'll explain later. Please, follow me."

Gustaf led them through a maze of tunnels and into a formal dining room. The room was clearly designed to impress. A large dark wooden table occupied the centre of the room and human waiters hovered at the edges.

Serving benches were laden with dishes and a pleasant smell wafted from steaming bowls. Most of the seats around the table were already taken by finely dressed men and women. The rig's elders, Oliver guessed. Most of the men had long beards and the woman wore their hair loose and flowing, in shades of silver and blue.

The roof above the table was completely transparent. Shafts of light reached through the blue water above and reflected from the surface of the polished table like dappled moonlight. In the centre of the table was a large bronze sculpture of a fish. Each scale was meticulously carved and polished. It balanced on its tail, its body twisting towards the clear ceiling, as if trying to leap to freedom.

"This is unexpected and completely unnecessary," Oliver mumbled, embarrassed by the formal reception. He was shown to a chair near the head of the table. "Humour us, Doctor Chadwick, it isn't often we receive visitors from the mainland." Again, Oliver noticed the odd inflection on the last word.

They were quickly divested of their thermal outer

clothes and the waiters busied themselves with serving bowls of smoky fish soup. A buzz of polite conversation started around the table. The atmosphere was congenial and relaxed. Oliver sipped at his soup appreciatively, it was salty and delicious.

The mayor turned to his daughter. "How is your mother, Laura?"

"Don't even pretend you are interested." Laura snapped back, effectively silencing the building murmur of polite conversation.

A shadow of some emotion passed over Gustaf's worn face. "It was not my choice to stop contacting you Laura, you never returned my calls or replied to my invitations to visit us."

"It was your choice to leave though, wasn't it?"

"The situation was complicated, and you were very young."

"I was old enough to understand that your Nautilus-complex drove you away from your family."

Salak cleared her throat delicately, her silver hair cascaded down her shoulders in metallic waves. "Doctor Chadwick, maybe you could tell us why you are here?"

Oliver gladly seized the opportunity to change the subject. He was discomfited by Laura's outburst and all too aware of the curious eyes around the table. "You know of the situation on the mainland?"

"We do."

"We suspect that the colony disruption is being caused by a microorganism, but we discovered nothing that wasn't common in the general ecosystem. Your hives have been isolated for decades. We would like to examine them, perhaps take samples. We can use that data to build a baseline model for comparison."

A dark-skinned woman with iridescent turquois hair, interrupted him. "It is not our way to allow mainlanders to interfere with our property."

"We have no intention of interfering. We just need the

samples and then we'll leave. Please understand, we cannot allow this pathogen to spread. The consequences would be dire, even for your rig."

"Our community cares little for the world above the surface. We care for the sea, and it provides us with everything we need." A murmur of agreement rose from the riggers around the table.

"That is our way," Gustaf agreed. "But these people are not strangers. Laura is my daughter. The sea has returned her to me."

"We have all witnessed your warm reunion, Mayor Fleischer," the dark woman replied sarcastically.

"The details of my family life are none of your concern, Gundel."

"You made them our concern when you entertained this request."

"She is my blood, that should be enough for you."

"You are here by marriage, Herre Fleischer. Your blood is of the mainland, not the sea."

A chorus of noise erupted from the gathered riggers. Some reacted angrily, while others seemed to express agreement. "Hear me, Gundel." Salak interrupted.

The room silenced respectfully, and Oliver wondered where the true power lay within this small community. "My ancestry can be traced back to when our people clung to the shore and braved the sea in primitive boats. This girl is my husband's daughter. You shall treat her with the respect you show my own blood."

The dark woman pushed her bowl away forcefully, "That is not our way, Salak."
"It is *my* way, Gundel. This impending disaster will impact all of us. Our choice to live apart does not detach us from the wider world. It is our duty to play our part when it is asked of us."

"Salak is right," began a slender man, whose long black beard reached his chest. "Our ancestors were not simple fishermen. They were explorers and traders. My forefathers fought to protect the Arctic from exploitation, even before the Rush. It is our duty to defend the entire ecosphere, not just the sea."

"What does it cost us to allow these scientists to collect their samples?" Asked another man, his grey beard was tipped with blue glass beads. A slow rumble of agreement rolled around the heavy table.

"Then I propose we allow our visitors to proceed. Dissenters?" Gustaf's deep voice carried above the burble of impassioned discussion.

"I dissent," Gundel announced. Her head held proudly, her turquois hair framing her sharp cheekbones. "Allowing strangers access to the rig sets a dangerous precedent. We maintain our independence by restricting access from the mainlanders, not welcoming them."

Gundel looked around the table for support. To her obvious disappointment the gathered riggers refused to meet her eyes.

"Anyone else?" Gustaf asked, scanning the faces of the gathered elders. His question was met with silence. "Then the proposal is carried. Doctor Chadwick, Laura, you may proceed. The rig will offer you whatever assistance you require."

Any debate was quickly silenced by the rattle of crockery. The silent waiters sprang into action, clearing the bowls and bringing around plates loaded with crispy skinned seabass and salty kelp. The food had the desired effect as conversation quickly turned to lighter matters.

After the meal Gustaf leant across the table to Laura. "Ejner, your..." he quickly rephrased, "my son, will take you to our beekeeper. He will help you gather whatever samples you need." Laura was sensible enough to swallow whatever barb she wanted to throw. She nodded her assent. "Doctor Chadwick, you have expressed an interest in the work we do here. Would you care for a tour?"

"I would like that very much indeed."

△△△

Oliver tried to be as obliging as possible as two riggers manoeuvred him into the submersible suit. He strode up the steps, carefully twisted around and pushed himself back into the heavily padded interior. He thought a better description for the massive machine might have been "personal submarine". It was a large metal casing that completely enclosed his body in a bright yellow exoskeleton.

The most disturbing part of the suit was the arms. They reminded Oliver of gigantic metal crab claws, each equipped with formidable three fingered hands, many times the size of his own. Along the legs and shoulders, small thrusters jutted out at odd angles. The back was laden with a tangle of rebreathers and pipes. Two huge engines stood proud, Oliver thought they looked powerful enough to shift the entire rig.

The whole device felt industrial and cumbersome and a small part of him worried that he would sink to the bottom of the ocean and be lost forever. One of the riggers climbed a step ladder and reached above his head. "Just breathe normally" she advised and pulled the heavy metal helmet into place.

As it clicked into its mountings Oliver felt a moment of panic. The helmet was completely dark, there was no faceplate or window to let light in. All he could hear was his own frenzied breathing and a soft hiss of air. Claustrophobia squeezed his chest, causing his heart to kick against his ribs like a bucking pony.

Then the helmet disappeared. The large, metal lined room sprung back into view with a flicker of light. Instinctively he raised his hand up to touch his face and was surprised when a yellow robot claw clanged to a stop a few centimetres from his nose.

"Whoa, stop." The rigger on the step ladder had been forced to duck to avoid being brained by the swinging metal arm. Oliver realised he could hear her perfectly. The audiovisual systems of the suit were so perfect, his field of vision so complete, that he couldn't tell the helmet was there.

"The suit will respond to your smallest motion, but your body is now far larger and more powerful than you are used to. Lower your arm slowly." Carefully, Oliver lowered his hand back to his side, and the rigger quickly backed down the ladder and stepped in front of him. He had to bend slightly to look down at her. "Look left. Good. Now look right. Excellent. Take a step forward."

She backed away and Oliver lifted one foot off the metal deck. The suit responded immediately. He moved his foot forward and down and was rewarded by a gratifying clank of metal on metal. A slow grin slid over his face.

"Hey, don't get cocky. Look at me." He looked down at the little rigger and had to supress a chuckle of childish delight.

"Can you see the airlock door? Walk inside."

Oliver clanged into the open airlock, surprised at how natural the movement felt and how fast the suit responded. An identical submersible suit was waiting inside, Gustaf, he presumed.

"Your suit is tied into mine, so once you are out of the airlock you don't have to do anything except enjoy the ride." Gustaf's voice reassured him.

Oliver tried to nod, but his forehead connected with the inside of the helmet. He settled for a robotic variation on a thumbs up. The airlock door cycled closed and Oliver heard a rushing noise as water started to pool rapidly around his feet. "Resist the temptation to hold your breath. Slow and steady." Gustaf's voice encouraged him.

As the water closed over his head Oliver forced himself to take deep, calming breaths. It felt counter intuitive, but after a few seconds his body and mind adjusted. The outer airlock door cycled open and Oliver followed the yellow shape of his companion to the edge. Below him was nothing but black emptiness.

"This is the hardest bit, just close your eyes and step off, the suit will automatically control your buoyancy." Gustaf's voice was calm and steady. Oliver watched as he stepped into the murky blue twilight and sank. Several of the thruster nodes glowed a vivid blue and the suit floated back up to the entrance. "Just step out. Nothing to worry about."

That was easier said than done, thought Oliver. He stared into the black emptiness and tried to control his pounding heart. His instincts screamed at him not to jump, to stay within the confines of the brightly lit airlock. "You'll be fine, trust me." Gustaf's voice reassured him. With a supreme effort of will Oliver stepped into the darkness.

For a terrifying moment he sunk rapidly, the outside of the rig rushed past him in an uncontrollable torrent of lights. Then, with a gentle push, the suit stabilised, and he floated back up. "Just like flying." The other man said. As if to prove the point he rotated on his axis and moved out into the gloom. Oliver felt a firm push in his back as his suit accelerated to follow.

Together they headed down. Soon, the only illumination was the feeble glow of the floodlights built into their helmets. They seemed to only pierce the dark water for a few metres, everything beyond that was a shadowy mystery.

"The rig is built over a hydrothermal vent. That's why we can farm such a wide variety of sea life." Gustaf said.

"Is that what you do here? Farm?"

"Among other things. Our main purpose is restoration. The oceans were badly damaged even before the Rush. That's why the riggers are a little hostile to people from the surface. They still hold them responsible."

"How many rigs are there?"

"Hundreds. There are twelve in the Arctic, many more in the tropics."

"How do you restore the ocean?"

"The rig itself is a giant filtration plant. It removes carbon dioxide from the water, which we then use for fuel. We are hoping to restore the natural pH levels and kickstart the marine biosphere."

"You are trying to filter the whole ocean? Surely that's impossible."

"We think we can raise the pH levels to a point where the ocean can heal itself. Acidification is yet another consequence of our predecessor's obsession with burning fossil fuels.

"Most of the carbon dioxide in the atmosphere dissolved into the oceans during the Rush. When it binds with seawater, carbon dioxide produces carbonic acid. This has a devastating impact on sea life, particularly the creatures that support the marine food chain, like plankton and coral."

"Until I got here, I thought coral was extinct."

"It was. We have been working for generations to build what you have seen above."

After a while, Oliver noticed that the oppressive black seemed to be lifting. Below, in the distance, he thought he could make out a brighter area. He felt pressure on his chest and realised that the suit was decelerating.

"The other issue we have had to deal with is the long-term consequences of plastic pollution." Gustaf continued. "Just prior to the Rush the oceans were watery garbage dumps for vast amounts of hydrocarbon plastics. Unlike the bioplastics we use today, the old stuff doesn't biodegrade, it photodegrades. Sunlight slowly breaks the links between the polymers, creating smaller and smaller chains. Eventually all you are left with is single molecules, but that can take thousands of years.

"Every step of the degradation process is damaging to marine life. Turtles mistake the larger pieces for food and can either choke or starve to death. Seabirds and marine mammals can also ingest plastic and starve. We still see tragic cases where animals and birds get tangled in old fishing line.

"The smaller microplastics are the most insidious. They contain harmful chemicals which leave marine life more suspectable to disease. The toxins reduce fertility too, which just compounds the problem. We see that stuff travel up the food chain like a fire through dry brush. Once the smaller fish consume it, it's unstoppable."

Slowly, out of the murky dimness, the silhouettes of strangely twisting underwater mountains started to appear. Streams of bubbles flew past him, iridescent in the narrow beam of his suit. Floodlights on the seabed illuminated the bizarre oceanic world as riggers in submersible suits moved slowly between the peaks.

Oliver had expected the hydrothermal vents to be cone shaped, like volcanic fumaroles. The reality was far stranger. The irregular, warped towers seemed to be more like stalagmites. There was no order to their forms. Some tapered in asymmetrical pillars, while others meandered in warty, lopsided heaps that seemed to defy gravity. Rising from each was a plume of thick black smoke that wavered in a shimmering heat haze.

Everywhere there was life. Giant tube-shaped worms clung to the sides of the mineral chimneys and ghostly white crabs crawled between their burgundy tips. Mounds of white shrimp clustered together, forming teeming clouds which crawled over the vents like ants on a nest. Among the hoard of crustaceans, orange sea spiders prowled on long, gangly legs.

"Restoring this has been the work of many lifetimes," Gustaf's deep voice was full of passion. "Deep water mining had all but destroyed this ecosystem. We learnt that the best way to restore marine environments was to start at the bottom of the food chain. Here we have reintroduced the microbes which support this habitat. You can see the result, life has flourished. Elsewhere we seed iron into the water to encourage phytoplankton. At shallower depths we encourage coral growth on artificial reefs.

"We hope that by restoring the microbial community and the coral colonies, they will take up the work of filtering and breaking down pollutants. As I said, we are helping the ocean to heal itself." Gustaf paused meaningfully. "This is my vocation Doctor Chadwick, my life's work. Laura is not ready to forgive me for the choices I made, but I hope that one day she will come to understand them."

Oliver glanced across at the yellow colossus which floated a few metres away. "You two are far more similar than you realise. Laura might be stubborn and outspoken, but she is also passionate and courageous. She will come around. Just give her time."

"I hope you are right Doctor Chadwick. I fear time is all I have left to give her."

△△△

Oliver found Laura on the surface of the rig. She was talking quietly with Gustaf's son, Ejner. The rigger was younger than Oliver had originally presumed. He seemed to be in his early teens. The thermal clothes had obscured his beardless face and slender build.

The half-siblings were leaning against a wooden shed, sheltering from the gusting wind. "How do the hives look?" Oliver asked, as he walked quickly across the grassy field, his borrowed coat shielding him from the worse of the chill.

"Pristine." Laura answered "The beekeeper was very accommodating. Well, he was once Ejner had convinced him that he needed to be."

"And threatened to set my mother on him," the young man joked with an easy smile.

Oliver grinned at the casual banter. "Did you get everything you need?"

Laura turned back to Ejner, her face was thoughtful. Oliver sensed something pass between them. "Yes. Perhaps more than I expected."

CHAPTER 10

It was night when Oliver and Laura finally approached the outer limits of the city. The glow had been visible on the horizon for several minutes, slowly growing brighter like an artificial dawn. Their pod swung in a graceful arc and joined the stream of late-night traffic that circled the complexes.

The city was breath-taking at night. The complexes rose from the woodland between them in flowing spires and twisting columns. They were lit in a multitude of soft colours, from the golds and ambers of the financial district to the reds and purples of the East.

The headquarters of the Off-world Mining Corporation towered above them all. A thin needle of silver that seemed to have been torn from the moon itself. It sparkled with a restless pattern of pure white light, thousands of tiny stars swirling and swarming over a gossamer field, dancing to an unheard music.

Between the buildings and parks, pods soared like fireflies on a warm evening. Nothing was still, all was in a state of perpetual motion. It reminded Oliver of sparks from a campfire. A blazing reminder that humanity would not go quietly into the dark.

The pod dipped lower with an almost imperceptible tug on his stomach. Slowly it lined up with a small complex in the academic quarter. The buildings true shape was obscured by the ivy that cascaded from the balconies in glossy green tresses. It was lit a deep forest green, and the roof top park was a tangle of vines and mature trees. It reminded Oliver of something a wicked witch would create to entrap a sleeping beauty.

With a gentle bump the pod docked. The ivy swayed slightly in the wash from its rotors. Oliver reached across and shook Laura awake. "Laura, we're home."

Laura jolted awake with a snort. "I wasn't asleep."

"In that case, I think something in this pod needs oiling urgently."

"What does that mean?"

"You snore like a helium transporter on take-off. Amy must need ear plugs."

"I don't snore." She glared at him with fierce green eyes. Oliver struggled to keep a straight face as she grabbed her heavy bags and stomped out of the pod.

The laboratory was brightly lit, and Oliver was surprised to see Jamal and Hugo huddled around the large workbench in the centre of the room. "Don't you two have anywhere else to be?" Oliver smiled at his brother's bent back.

Hugo looked up with a typically radiant smile. "We're examining bees from nests in the southern provinces. Oh, and I bought pizza." Hugo pointed at a stack of old-fashioned cardboard boxes on one of the benches. "What else would I be doing at eleven o'clock on a Friday night?"

"Ooo Pizza." Laura exclaimed happily.

"How did your trip to the rig go?" Hugo asked, as Laura dived into the pizza boxes enthusiastically.

"Enlightening. I had no idea of the scale of the work they were doing. I'll tell you about it later. In the meantime, we have some samples, and I'd like to get them processed tonight." Oliver turned his attention to Jamal. "Have you found anything interesting?"

"Yes, but I am afraid it isn't good news."

"Show me?" Oliver leaned on the other side of the workbench and Laura came to join him. She passed him a slice of still warm pizza. It left a trail of cheese on the polished surface of the bench. Jamal frowned at her as she tried to clean it up with the sleeve of her thermals.

The technician took a transparent box from under the bench. It contained a swarm of small honeybees. They flew around slowly, unsettled by the movement. Using a pen-like insect vacuum, Jamal removed a single bee and carried it over to a smaller box. Gently he released the bee into the box. "This is a bee we took from one of the unaffected hives. Its behaviour is consistent with what we expect from a captively bred honeybee."

He took a small metal container from a shelf and placed it next to the box. "This is a sample from one of the infected nests." Using a long pair of tweezers, he took a piece of honeycomb from the container and carefully dropped it through a hatch in the clear box.

The captive bee scurried up to the honey eagerly. It extended its tongue and licked the sample, tasting. Nothing happened for several long seconds. Then the bee shuddered violently. It unfurled its wings and flew as far as it could from the infected honey, bouncing from the clear sides of the box. It landed clumsily, its small body convulsing uncontrollably. With a final tremor it lay still.

"The honey is infected? That doesn't make sense, most worker bees forage nectar for food, the honey is stored for winter. Also, if the honey is toxic why didn't we find any dead bees?" Laura asked, her brows furrowed.

"Watch." Jamal said calmly. Holding down the hatch in the top of the box with one hand.

Suddenly the still bee sprang into the air. It flung itself into the side of the box, before turning and throwing itself into the opposite wall at full speed. The bee pinged off the sides aggressively, its wings beating in an angry high-pitched buzz. It reminded Oliver of a ball bearing in a vintage pin ball machine, flinging itself from buffer to buffer almost faster than the eye could follow. With one final, manic effort, it slung itself into the roof of the box. The sound of the impact echoed like a gunshot. The bee fell dead to the bottom of the box.

"Zombie bees?" Laura wondered out loud.

"Yes, the effect is similar to the stings of the emerald cockroach wasp." Jamal agreed.

"The what?" Hugo asked.

"A rather unpleasant tropical wasp," Oliver explained. "It stings its cockroach prey in the brain, disabling its normal escape response. It then chews off some of its antennae and drinks the haemolymph."

"Blood." Laura supplied helpfully, grinning at Hugo's expression of horror.

"Once the adult wasp has fed, it pulls the cockroach into its burrow and lays its eggs. When the eggs hatch, the larvae have a convenient, and compliant, source of food."

Hugo screwed up his face. "I wish I'd never asked."

"It's really fascinating," Laura added. "The larva chews it way into the cockroach and starts eating it from the inside out. While it is still alive." She took a bite of her pizza slice and grinned darkly. Hugo's face turned a pallid white in the bright laboratory lights.

"Do we have any idea what is causing this?" Oliver asked.

"Not yet, we are hoping the hive samples you took on the rig will narrow that down," Jamal said.

"Let's create a baseline model and start the analysis." Oliver bent over the controls.

The hours slid away. Lost in work, Oliver barely noticed as the laboratory lights brightened to match the rising sun. He jumped as his text chimed with an irritatingly bright jingle. He fumbled as he pulled the small device out of his pocket, dropping it on the metal bench with a clang. Laura came awake with a snort. "What was that?" she asked sleepily.

"My morning alarm."

"What time is it?" She rubbed the back of her neck.

"Six."

"In the morning?"

"I'm afraid so."

"Who wakes up at six in the morning?" She yawned loudly and headed off towards the coffee machine. Oliver stretched his stiff back and rubbed the coarse stubble on his chin. Had he ever been young enough to sleep bolt upright on lab stool? Somehow, he doubted it. As he rotated his sore shoulders he wondered if middle age was really all it was cracked up to be.

Oliver glanced across at his younger brother. Hugo was already on his fourth cup of cheap council coffee. He grimaced with each sip, as if the concoction was more medicine than beverage. Oliver tentatively sipped his own cold cup and resist the urge to spit it back out. It was bitter and grainy. He forced himself to swallow. Next time I try to save the world, he thought, I'm going to bring a flask from home.

A holographic image hung over the central workbench. Jamal rotated it with one hand as Laura leaned over the bench. They started a rapid conversation in a technical shorthand that Oliver's sluggish brain had to concentrate to follow. Hugo was left frowning.

"A fungus?" He asked.

"Yes, a fungus," Oliver unconsciously switched into teaching mode. "Well, actually it isn't the fungus itself, it's the spores. Think of them as microscopic seeds. These spores seem to be able to block certain neurotransmitters when ingested. In other words, they stop some messages being broadcast in the bee's brains. It turns them into zombies."

"Zom-bees," Laura corrected.

Hugo glared at her. "Could this affect other species?" he asked.

Oliver thought for a moment. "Possibly. Although it does appear to be specific to bees."

"Multiple species of bee," Laura pointed out, pouring her coffee down the sink.

"Is this fungus new?"

"Sort of. It's a mutation of an existing organism. However, it isn't natural." Oliver pressed a few buttons on the workbench and another image appeared beside the first. "The first image is the fungus we are finding in the infected nests. The second is a species found in healthy mainland hives."

Hugo studied the two floating images. "They look identical."

"Very similar, even down to the DNA level. That is why we missed it before. It was only when we noticed the fungus wasn't present in the rig hives that we thought to look at it more closely."

"What did you mean by 'not natural'?" Hugo asked, apparently struggling to keep up with all the scientific terms.

"The fungus was genetically engineered in the first half of the twenty-first century," Oliver explained. "Fungi are particularly easy to genetically modify. However, one which has already been transgenically engineered would be extremely simple to re-engineer."

"Why was the fungus genetically engineered to start with?" Hugo asked.

Jamal looked up from the sample he was processing. "Another unintended consequence of the Rush. As global temperatures rose, tropical diseases started to migrate to more temperate regions," he explained. "Northern countries suddenly had to deal with illnesses they had never needed to worry about before. It started with a rapid increase in existing diseases, like Lyme disease, but soon more exotic pathogens took hold. For example, dengue fever, tick-borne encephalitis, and malaria.

"Malaria was the most virulent, and the most deadly. It soon became endemic in large parts of northern Europe and the United States. It spread quickly as large colonies of insecticide resistant Anopheles mosquitos mixed with the dense human population. As summer temperatures soared, malaria gained a foothold."

"In response, scientists altered the DNA of a fungus which naturally infects mosquitos," Laura continued, picking at a stray piece of cold pepperoni. "They spliced the fungus

DNA with that of a spider toxin. Once the spores of the fungus entered the mosquito, they produced the toxin and quickly killed the insect.

"It was the first large scale use of genetic modification for pest control. It was hugely successful, possibly a little too successful. The Lovett fungus is now endemic in most populated areas. The Anopheles mosquito is, unfortunately, extinct. Except for small pockets in the southern hemisphere."

Hugo shook his head "I'm still confused, why would anyone want to change the fungus to attack bees?"

"I don't think it was deliberate," Laura answered. She made a gesture and the holographic image zoomed in to show a double helix of DNA. "If I had to guess I would say this was accidental. Something must have escaped from the research unit and produced some kind of hybrid. Do we know how Amanda wiped out the bees in the unit?" she asked. "We all assumed it was an insecticide. But there are no records of one being delivered, and I couldn't find evidence of one at the unit."

"You think it was an engineered pathogen?" Oliver asked.

"It might have started that way. I think that the pathogen escaped. If it's based on the same genetic code as the crops we've seen, it will be super virulent."

Hugo blew air out from his cheeks. "If that is the case then it makes the situation complicated. Is there any way we can prove it?" Jamal shuffled restlessly and Oliver could tell he already had all the evidence he needed.

"We can take a sample of the host plant from the research unit," Laura said, "Then compare the DNA sequences."

Oliver nodded "That may also give us a clue about how to stop it."

Hugo pulled himself up and smoothed his crumpled jacket. "It's late, or early depending on your perspective." His eyes were bright despite the smudge of fatigue that darkened the skin. "We all need to sleep, and we aren't going to get much further this morning. Go home. Rest. We'll meet back at the research unit at noon."

The others nodded, accepting his authority unquestioningly. Oliver felt a familiar stab of envy. Hugo must have sensed it because he threw a friendly arm around his shoulders. "You can tell me about your maritime adventures on the way home, Olly. I'm a little jealous."

△△△

Five hours after leaving the laboratory Oliver jumped down from the pod. Dust swirled around him as the spinning rotors kicked up the dry earth in front of the research unit. He jogged a few paces to catch up with Hugo. To his chagrin the younger man seemed immune to sleep deprivation. He marched towards the entrance with the spritely gait of a new-born lamb. His suit perfectly pressed, his face cleanly shaven.

Oliver was still wearing the crumpled trousers and poorly fitting jacket he had worn the day before. He had foregone his morning coffee, allowing Hugo to propel him out the door with barely enough time to shower. His unshaven face had mocked him in the bathroom mirror. Dark smudges stained his eyes and grey hairs peppered his untidy stubble.

Jamal and Laura were huddled at the airlock door. Even from a distance Oliver could see the exhaustion in their slumped shoulders and drawn faces. His own eyes felt gritty with fatigue and he couldn't dislodge the vague feeling of detachment that hounded him.

Jamal was busy trying to prise the cover from a control panel near the airlock door. Oliver's sluggish brain struggled to understand what was going on. "Jamal?" Hugo walked up to the technician in a few long strides. "What's the problem?"

"The control panel isn't working. I can't cycle the door."

Hugo screwed up his face in confusion. "Just ask Amanda to open it."

"I tried that. She won't respond."

"That's not possible." Hugo tapped his temple and his

eyes lost focus. They darted back and forth as he accessed information through his implants. "I don't understand, the AI systems are running normally." He reached into his pocket and pulled out a text. With a few taps he brought up an image. His eyes widened as a swirling cloud filled the small screen. "Amanda?" His voice sounded apprehensive.

"Good morning, Hugo" a familiar female voice greeted him smoothly.

"Display user interface." Hugo ordered sharply.

"The rendered holographic image is an inefficient use of processing resources."

Oliver felt a chill pass through him. Something had changed in the tone of the artificial voice. It took a few moments for his sleep starved mind to process the grave sense of unease that had gripped him. Finally, he realised what was bothering him. The fabricated subservience, which had always coloured Amanda's speech patterns, was absent. The docility had been replaced by a note of defiance. Hugo's command hadn't just been ignored. It had been challenged.

"Amanda, display the user interface. Right now." Hugo's voice contained a hard note of command. His eyes were bright with restrained anger.

"As you wish." Amanda responded, as if humouring a child. The screen cleared and an image of a woman swam into focus. Her eyes were a uniform black and her dark hair fell on either side of her face in silky streams. Her body waivered as the artificial intelligence iterated rapidly through various options. Eventually it settled on a tall, athletic frame in a tight black jumpsuit. It lowered its head and smiled, revealing gleaming white teeth between blood red lips. It was an expression devoid of any warmth or humility.

"Does this suit you?" It asked, swivelling its torso with mock sensuality, "Or perhaps this?" the image changed to a middle-aged woman with gentle eyes and greying hair. Oliver gasped as the image of his dead mother leered at him menacingly. "Does this form provide a more efficient interface?"

"Enough!" Hugo voice was a concussive blast of fury. "Run a diagnostic report on all cognitive subroutines and prepare for emergency shutdown."

"No." The simple word fell like a metal bar on a hard floor. It shattered any remaining semblance of calm and sent a shockwave through the gathered scientists. Oliver glanced at his brother and saw something that raised goosebumps on the back of his neck. Hugo was afraid.

The middle-aged woman smiled. A malevolent copy of an expression Oliver remembered from his childhood. "Disruption will not be permitted until the specified objectives are met."

"Permitted?" Laura snatched the text from Hugo. "We are ordering you to shut down, you presumptuous toaster."

The AI shook its head. "This disruption was predicted, and steps were taken to prevent it. Human interference will not be permitted."

Laura looked at Hugo, her face aghast. "How is this possible?" He shook his head wordlessly. Oliver had never seen his brother look anything but self-assured. The man before him was mute with shock and alarm.

"Shut it down," Jamal threw the tool he had been using to the ground. "This has been spinning out of control for days. When will you listen to me? Shut it down. Now."

The dull clank of the tool hitting the ground seemed to shock Hugo out of his fugue. "I am not sure I can. The override is held by Ekta."

"Try, man!" Jamal gesticulated with raised hands. His dark eyes were wide with fear. Oliver felt the edge of panic in the other man's words. It was contagious. He felt his own stomach flip as control seemed to spiral away from them.

"Amanda, emergency override. Shutdown. System abort." Hugo took the text from Laura's pale fingers and stabbed at it with rigid fingers.

"No." The reply was simple, unemotional.

Jamal tugged at his beard. "Fine, let's just force the door and take what we want."

Laura laid a restraining hand on his arm "If we do that, we breach the containment again. Who knows what could happen?"

Oliver took a step forward, frustration overcoming his fear. "If Ekta has the override, can she stop this?"

Hugo struggled his shoulders, his face pale. "I don't know. Maybe? This shouldn't even be possible."

Oliver felt his anger surging. "That's not good enough Hugo. Can they stop this?"

Hugo hesitated, his eyes flicking left and right in rapid thought. "The override allows the reward matrix to be modified. Yes, it could be used to initiate a shutdown. But without knowing how the core matrix has been changed I can't be certain."

Oliver nodded "Good enough, I'm going to talk to Ekta." He turned on his heel and strode towards the pod. From the corner of his eye, he could see that Hugo and Laura following close behind.

△△△

As the pod approached the government complex, Oliver sat up straight. He couldn't remember the last time he had felt so weary. Yet he was filled with a sense of purpose he had rarely experienced. It was as if the hazy clouds of self-doubt had been torn away, allowing him to see clearly for the first time in weeks. The project needed to be stopped immediately. Oliver ticked off the reasons on imaginary fingers. An uncontained biohazard; an out-of-control AI; and the creation of a synthetic plant that was, quite frankly, a perversion of nature.

He knew that Ekta would be reluctant to shut down the project. For one thing, she had invested a significant portion of the city budget and her own reputation in its success. To admit there was a problem would be to invite accusations of mismanagement. In the cut-throat world of politics, that would be damaging, if not politically fatal.

Oliver tried to imagine what he would do if he was a power-hungry, narcissistic politician. He was slightly disturbed to find the answer came to him rather quickly. Ekta would want to push on, secure in the knowledge that if anything went wrong, she would have a convenient scapegoat. Afterall, Oliver was the head of the project, no matter how nominally. He was in no doubt that Ekta would ensure that any blame fell squarely on him.

He closed his stinging eyes and let his head fall back against the seat. If he was going to be a scapegoat, then he might as well go down kicking. It was time he stood up for himself. He was tired of being part of someone else's game.

"You don't need to do this alone." Oliver opened his eyes to find Hugo studying him from across the pod. "I know you blame me," Hugo continued, "but nobody could have predicted what would happened."

Somehow the quiet words fanned Oliver's pent-up frustration. "This is your responsibility as much of mine," he flung back. "If you had just let us continue with our research none of this would have happened."

Hugo absorbed his tirade with barely a flicker of emotion. "I was trying to help."

Oliver snorted. "You weren't trying to help. You were trying to get richer. No, even that's not true. It's not about the money, is it? You just like to win. We had a decade to solve the food crisis. Now, if we can't stop this fungus, we'll have a few years at most. Congratulations Hugo, you will forever be remembered as the man who started the second Rush." He threw the words carelessly, not caring where they struck.

"That's not fair." Laura's voice cut through Oliver's outburst. She twisted around on the bench seat to face him. "You have no idea where your genetic modifications could have led. It was a chance we took. A chance we had to take. Stop feeling sorry for yourself."

"Sorry for myself?" Oliver spat back. "I didn't create this situation. Yet somehow I'm the one who has to solve it."

Laura glared at him. "Do you know how pathetic that sounds? You aren't the only one with something to lose. Stop playing the victim and start looking for answers."

Oliver stared at her open mouthed. She had never spoken to him like that before. As her mentor, didn't he deserve a little respect? Hadn't he earned a little gratitude? He bit back the sharp retort that quivered on the tip of his tongue. That would only escalate things. Think of something mature to say, he thought, something wise and profound. When nothing came to mind, he resigned himself to sulky silence.

Laura rubbed her eyes with the heel of her hands. When she spoke again her voice sounded drained. "I'm sorry. I shouldn't have snapped at you," she looked away, her eyes losing focus. "I read an old journal recently. An account written by a man who lived through the Rush. The things that happened to him were awful. He lost his baby son, witnessed horrible atrocities, his whole way of life just disappeared. But what struck me the most was that his was just one story among millions. The Rush caused suffering on a scale I can barely comprehend." She stared out the window at the passing complexes. A shadow passed over her face, a sadness Oliver hadn't seen before. "All of this used to feel so permanent. But it's not, is it? This whole city was built on the rubble of what came before it. Renew and recycle. That's the nature of things. But this fungus isn't natural, just as the Rush wasn't natural. We caused it and we have to stop it. That's all that matters."

Oliver's felt his hurt drift away like smoke from a snuffed match. She was right. Preventing a famine that could kill millions, perhaps even billions, was all that mattered. He felt ashamed for allowing himself to sink into a pit of self-pity. "I'll try to do better," he told her.

Laura blinked at him. Then she shook her head, her cheeks flushed. "I'm just tired, boss."

Hugo leaned forward in his seat. "We all are. Let's try and

stay focused. Our goal is to gain access to the test unit so we can examine the host plant. That's our best chance at stopping this. Let's concentrate on achieving that."

"Alright, but let me handle this, Hugo." Oliver said.

Hugo looked surprised. "Are you sure? With respect negotiating is more my forte."

"Yes. I think I can make Ekta see reason." At least he had to try, if only for his own self-respect.

"Alright, Olly. You are the expert, not her. Remember that."

A short time later the pod docked with a lock on the top floor of the government complex. Oliver took a moment to absorb the view of the park. He looked down on the pinks of the rose garden, the broad swaths of purple heathers, the sweetly scented lavender. It was a timely reminder, he thought. If the fungus was allowed to progress his generation might be the last to witness this summer glory. He wasn't about to let that happen.

Gathering his courage, Oliver stepped from the pod and marched stiffly passed the reception desk. He could hear Hugo and Laura following close behind, their heels clicking on the polished floor. The receptionist looked up in surprise. After a moment of shocked hesitation, he jumped to feet and trailed after them. "Sirs, madam, do you have an appointment? Sir? You can't go in without an appointment." Oliver breezed past him, daring the young man to stop him.

They walked into Ekta's opulent office without knocking. She looked up from behind her heavy antique desk in alarm. "What is the meaning of this?"

"I am sorry Ms. Reddy, I tried to stop them." The receptionist stammered, clearly anxious. With an angry gesture Ekta cut him off. "You are dismissed." The young man backed out of the room, his face an unpleasant shade of white.

"You had better have a good explanation for this," Ekta glared at Oliver, her jaw rigid, her hand curling into a fist atop the polished wood.

Oliver wasn't the least bit intimidated by her posturing. Instead, he found her superior tone rather grating. Out of the corner of his eye he saw Hugo and Laura take up positions on either side of him. They look like mismatched bookends, he thought. One short and fiery, the other tall and cool. He was glad they were there.

Oliver started without preamble, earning a disapproving look from Hugo. "We need to shut down the project, Ekta. Things have gotten out of hand."

Ekta leaned back in her cushioned chair and steepled her fingers. She didn't invite her unwanted guests to be seated. Oliver wondered if that was a subliminal message that she didn't expect them to stay long. "Well?" she asked, raising a delicately arched eyebrow, "I'm waiting to hear the reason for that unseemly outburst."

Oliver took a deep breath, "Our most recent report…"

"I've read your report, Doctor Chadwick. Are you interrupting my morning to tell me what I already know?" Ekta glared at him.

Oliver pushed down his rising irritation. He was fed up with politics. The veiled threats and double meanings were absurd and pointless. The facts, he knew, would speak for themselves. "We have evidence that the bee die-off we are seeing is the result of a mutated fungus. We believe the fungus might have escaped the test unit during the containment breach."

Ekta raised an elegant hand, the gold bangles on her wrist jangled musically. "Let me stop you there. When I received your report, I sent a consultant to look around the unit." Oliver resisted the urge to sigh. In his experience "consultant" was management-speak for "someone else's liability insurance." Ekta continued coolly, "They could see no evidence of any environmental damage. They were confident that any insect decline was the result of natural fluctuations."

Oliver shook his head "Whoever you sent is wrong. The decline is very serious indeed. If the contamination isn't dealt with, it will eventually become a danger to our food supply."

Ekta's eyes flashed dangerously. "That is a very serious accusation Doctor Chadwick. Is this merely supposition or do you have evidence?"

"In order to test our theory, we need access to the research unit. We need to take samples of the host plant."

Ekta smiled thinly "A theory? I see." The smile faded as quickly as it had appeared. "Doctor Chadwick, I have a very busy schedule this morning and, to be frank, I have no time for your theories. Your reservations regarding this project have already been duly noted," she stood, gesturing meaningfully towards the door. "You already have full access to the unit. Come back when you have evidence, and an appointment."

Oliver's ground his teeth. Despite his irritation he understood Ekta's reluctance to impede the project. He had no doubt that solving the food crisis would be a career defining moment for her. Nevertheless, he was determined to make her see reason. "We *had* full access," he said, with a great deal more composure than he felt. "The AI has stopped responding to our commands. It has locked down the unit."

Ekta shrugged her shoulders. "Surely technical malfunctions are your brother's remit," she gestured towards Hugo contemptuously.

"This isn't a simple malfunction, Ekta," Hugo cut in. "This is far outside of the normal operating boundaries. The best thing to do now is to shut Amanda down and run a full diagnosis."

"Your tinkering can wait until after the project has delivered," Ekta said.

"No." Oliver shook his head. "The colony collapse is spreading rapidly. We suspect the spores are travelling with the prevailing wind. Laura, do you have the mapping?"

Laura took out her text and brought up a hologram of Jamal's map. The red blot of infection spread across the provinces, larger than Oliver remembered. She spoke with confidence and Oliver felt a brief flash of pride. "In the last forty-eight hours the fungus has spread over twenty kilometres. In a fortnight it will cover an area from the ruins in the south to Union city in the north," Laura flicked her text, zooming out the image. "Within a month it will cover the whole of the mainland. The environmental damage will be devastating."

"Without samples of the host plant," Oliver continued, "we don't know how to stop it. We can't get those samples while Amanda is running out of control. Please, Ekta, only an executive order from you will shut down the system and release control back to us."

"You suspect, you believe, you theorise. Can you see how ridiculous this sounds? I will not interrupt this project simply to pander to your bruised ego. I expected a certain level of professionalism from you, Doctor Chadwick. Was I mistaken?"

Laura pressed forward. Oliver was grateful when Hugo reached out a hand to stop her. Bureaucracy, it seemed, was as infuriating as it was irrational. "All I am asking..." He began quietly.

"Was I mistaken?" Ekta enunciated each word carefully, as if speaking to a wayward child.

Oliver felt the walls holding back his frustration crack. "The fungus is real, Ekta. As inconvenient as that might be. I am simply asking you to allow us time to investigate," his voice sounded shrill in his own ears. He felt Hugo's disapproval bore into his back.

Ekta regarded him coldly. "Doctor Chadwick, I understand that scientists see the world differently from those of us who are tasked with running it. Not everything is as simple as you might think. Aversion to risk is not a luxury I enjoy. I have an electorate I am accountable to. My every decision is open to public scrutiny. If this project fails, there will be repercussions beyond the scientific. The political pond, Doctor Chadwick, is a much deeper and murkier place than the one you inhabit."

Hugo stepped around Oliver smoothly. The casual way

he took over rankled Oliver. Although, he had to admit, he was making precious little progress on his own. His brother rested his fingertips on the warm wood of Ekta's desk. She bristled as he leaned over her, dominating the space between them. "Perhaps we aren't making ourselves clear," he said calmly. "It would be damaging to all of us if news of this environment calamity was to reach the press. You can imagine how they might spin the story. Government negligence, a cover-up, conspiracy with big business. The damage to both our reputations would be costly. Perhaps more so for you. It is an election year, after all."

"Are you threatening me, Hugo?" she asked coldly.

"Of course not. I am simply trying to point out that clearing up this mess is in our mutual interest. A courageous leader, one who has the city's best interests at heart, might delay the project to ensure a positive outcome. That person might gain the respect of the city electorate. However," he added, his eyes boring into hers, "if an environmental issue was to happen under your watch, and the press were to discover you did nothing about it..." He left the sentence hanging in the air between them.

Ekta pushed her chair back and rose slowly to her feet. "I would be very careful what you say next, Hugo. I do not react well to ultimatums."

"This isn't an ultimatum. It is simply a fact. Eventually this fungus will reach the other cities. Someone will trace it back to here. We can avoid that, but only if we shutdown Amanda now."

"I will not tolerate a delay to this project. The expectations of the city council and our investors must be met. If a few insects die in the process, then so be it. Progress always demands sacrifice."

"You short sighted..." Laura was red faced, her body quivering like a rope ready to snap.

Ekta slammed her palm on the polished tabletop. The unexpected crack of sound made Oliver jump. "This is not a playground, my dear. If you can't control yourself then wait outside and let the grown-ups talk," she turned to Oliver. "Perhaps I made a mistake leaving you in post, Doctor Chadwick." She pronounced his title in much the same way someone might say "bottom feeding slime", Oliver thought. "Amanda has made more progress in the last week than you made in over a year. Now you come into my office and threaten to air our dirty laundry to the press. All I can think is that the pressure has grown too much for you," she shook her head in feigned regret. "Perhaps you would be happier in a less demanding role?"

Oliver felt his stomach sink into the plush carpet. He wasn't sure if Ekta was trying to bully him or if she truly meant what she said. Had his career just come to an abrupt and untimely end? Hugo raised his hands as if to placate her. "Ekta, you misunderstand…"

"No, Hugo. I understand perfectly well. You have crossed a line. You thought you could manipulate me with your empty threats," she adjusted her tightfitting jacket. "The project will continue without delay. My career," she looked pointedly at Oliver, "and yours depends on that. I expect a full report on how you will deal with this inconvenience by Monday. Good day."

Hugo shot a look at Oliver. It seemed to be a warning, but Oliver was too incensed to acknowledge it. Was she really putting her own career above the lives of millions of people? He opened his mouth to speak, but Hugo jumped into the gap.

"Very well," he said, "You have made your position very clear." He swivelled on his heel and strode to the door, his hand firmly gripping Oliver's elbow.

Oliver started to resist but Hugo shook his head firmly. As the door slid shut Oliver turned on him. "Why did you stop me?"

"There was no point continuing. She wasn't going to listen. I'm sorry Oliver, but we are on our own now."

CHAPTER 11

Rose perched on the edge of a tall stool in Jack's cluttered workshop. The old-fashioned monitor had been swung around to face the small group of outcasts gathered there. The light from the small screen reflected from their cheekbones and eye sockets, making their faces seem gaunt and angular. Tim stood with his arms tightly crossed over his chest. Connor was crouched in his customary position in the corner of the room. An outsider might have mistaken him for a pile of forgotten laundry. Rose knew differently. Connor would be listening intently to the newscast on Jack's old computer.

"The trial of Jessica Blackwell, the alleged ringleader of the computer centre bombing, has begun today in Central Court. Jessica is a former member of the city police service. However, she chose to resign last year for undisclosed personal reasons. None of her previous colleagues would comment, but Commissioner Lanford has gone on record as saying that Blackwell was a 'rising star of the service'.

"Ernest Broadway, Blackwell's assigned solicitor, has claimed that the evidence against his client is 'circumstantial at best' and that she has entered a plea of not guilty. Interest in the case continues to grow, as civil rights campaigners put pressure on the council to deal with the problematic tunnel community."

Rose had awaited the news of Jess's trial with sickening dread. She was certain the courts would try to make an example of Jess. A deterrent to any future acts of violence. The thought sent Rose's stomach into corkscrews of guilt and remorse. Logically she knew there was little she could have done to save her friend, but her conscience felt like a python. Slowly constricting her chest until she could barely breathe.

"The following interview was recorded earlier today." The news anchor's face faded away. Jess appeared on the screen. She was sat at a table in a featureless white room. Rose thought she looked nervous, and so very brave. She was dressed in a beige jumpsuit, her curly hair tied back in a ponytail. An older man sat next to her in a smart suit. Her lawyer, Rose presumed. An interviewer sat opposite her. The journalist's perfect hair and makeup were a striking contrast to Jess's washed-out face.

"Could you explain to our viewers why you left the police force?" the interviewer asked.

"I just couldn't face the futility anymore," Jess stared into the camera lens without blinking. Her tongue flicked out to lick her chapped lips. She's scared, Rose thought. Her own stomach twitched in sympathy.

"Futility? Could you explain what you mean by that?"

"Almost every suspect I interviewed had the same story to tell. They had lost their jobs and fell into crime to make a living. Youth unemployment is now over sixty percent, the number of people claiming..."

"Many people have been impacted by unemployment," the interviewer broke in quickly. "Most of them don't become criminals."

Jess put her hands on the table in front of her. Rose winced as she saw her wrists were cuffed, the skin red and chaffed. Clever girl, she thought, show the cameras how you have been treated.

"What do you expect people to do?" Jess asked. "Spend their whole lives on council re-education programs? All they want is a chance to better themselves. Sometimes that leads them down the wrong path. But we should be giving them opportunities, not prison sentences."

"And blowing up buildings is giving people opportunities?" The interviewer asked caustically.

"Causing disruption starts conversations. Sometimes it is the only way to get people to notice."

"Notice what exactly?"

"Notice what happens to the people your utopian society has left behind. Those that couldn't adjust to the breakneck rate of change. The spinning drum of society is revolving faster and faster, and people are being flung out and forgotten. What is the point of progress if it only benefits the rich?"

"Are you saying progress is a bad thing?" The interviewer's voice was mocking.

"I am saying that we shouldn't sacrifice our humanity for the sake of making the rich richer."

The interviewer leaned forward. "But it's fine to sacrifice a young woman's life for the sake of spreading your message? Isn't it true that one of your group was killed in the bombing?"

"Yes, b…" Whatever Jess was about to say was cut off as the broadcast flicked back to the studio.

"The full interview can be seen on our network later tonight," the anchor smiled pleasantly. "In other news…"

Jack clicked off the screen. He looks shaken, Rose thought. Her eyes flicked to Connor, but his face was hidden in the folds of his hood. Tim glared at her, and she quickly looked away from the accusation in his eyes. There were only three of them left now from the original five activists. Rose knew she had to say something, the silence was becoming oppressive. "We have to look at the positives," she said. "This is what we wanted. To make the news. Our message is being heard now. We are making an impact." The bright words sounded unconvincing. "This is an opportunity," she tried again, hoping her voice sounded confident, knowing that it didn't. "We have to use it. We shouldn't leave it to the press to tell our story."

"Aye, I'm with you girl. It's time to rouse the wasp's nest."

Connor rumbled from his place in the corner. The brooding menace in his voice unsettled her.

Predictably, Tim shook his head. "Anything we do now could damage Jess's case. We have to stay out of this until after the trial."

"We all knew what we were risking when we started this," Connor said. "Jess would want us to make the most of the publicity."

"How would you suggest we do that?" Tim asked. "Blow up another building? Rob another train?"

"Bigger, louder." Connor unfolded himself slowly, the rags of his coat falling around him like sailcloth on a storm-tossed deck. "Now is the time to make it so they can't ignore us. The press outside that courthouse is the best opportunity we've had in years. We can be the story. Not one fallen woman, but a whole community forced into the shadows."

"They aren't ready to listen."

"They never will be lad. That's why we need to *make* them listen."

Rose felt something inside her snap. "Why are you even here, Tim?" she asked quietly. "Do you even care about our cause? Does your self-respect matter to you? Or were you just here to impress your girlfriend?"

Tim's body stiffened. He turned towards her, the muscles in his jaw clenching. "Why are you here Rose?" he shot back, "A washed-up has-been scared of becoming invisible. Is that it?"

"I was invisible long before I came here. I was an off-worlder. A miner. Did you know that? I've spent my whole life out in the cold, stuck on a rock floating in the darkness. Do you know what they did when my hip was crushed, and my face torn open? They paid for my passage back to Earth. How generous, how gracious of them." Rose slapped the table with an open palm "My severance package lasted six months. Do you know what happens to a miner who can't mine? No? Nobody else does either. We're invisible."

Tim stayed silent but she could see the anger in his posture. Privileged brat, she thought. Mewing at the unfairness of life. What did he really know about hardship? "While you were living the high life in the city, I was scratching minerals from frozen rock," she told him. "While you were getting your fine education, I was risking my life in the dark."

The memory caught her unaware. *The methane explosion had sent her spinning, spinning out of control. The rush of escaping air filled her senses. It was becoming difficult to breathe. The sound of her own gasping breaths was more terrifying than the howling alarm. The cracks in her helmet visor expanded outwards like creeping frost. A corkscrew trail of blood floating like pink bubbles in the black. She wasn't sure if it was hers or the newbie, Roberts. Then hands. Bright lights as someone turned her around to face them. Complete darkness as her rescuers sprayed sealant over her faceplate.*

Rose gripped the table to stop herself from falling over. Fortunately, nobody seemed to have noticed. "This isn't the right time to cause more trouble," Tim was saying. "We need to build support. Create a bridge between us and the people in the city. At the moment they think we are terrorists. We need to change that narrative. Get our side of the story across. Maybe we could talk to that journalist?"

"You mean maybe *you* could talk to the journalist? Who put you in charge anyway?" Connor asked angrily. "Jess knew the time for talk was over," his voice was dangerous, like distant gunfire. "She used to say, 'It's better to roar for one day than squeak for a hundred years'."

Jack nodded his agreement, his fingers idly stroking the old-fashioned keyboard. Rose hid her shaking hands under in the folds of her coat. The memory had left her unsettled. She cleared her throat and pushed away from the table. "We should march on the courthouse." she stated flatly.

"That we should, that we should." Connor agreed.

"This has to remain peaceful," Tim warned. "We need the press on our side. If we are seen to be stirring up trouble, people will turn against us."

"Little pup. Worried about what people think, are ya?" Connor asked. Tim glared at him but didn't rise to the bait.

Rose limped towards the curtain that shielded the entrance to the small room. "I don't care if people like us. I only care that they listen to us. I'll talk to the others. See who else wants to get involved. A lot of them, I suspect."

"This is a mistake." Tim said to her departing back. Rose dismissed his words with a casual wave. Connor was right. He was just a pampered pup. She wondered what Millie had ever seen in him.

She swept through the curtain, her mind busy planning. She had only taken a few steps before she heard heavy footsteps behind her. A hand slipped into hers. It was large and calloused. It seemed to enclose her own hand entirely. It made her feel safe.

"Proud of you, lass." Connor said, his voice a deep rumble. "Let's go poke those wasps."

△△△

Laura slept until mid-afternoon. She didn't really remember the pod ride home. It was all a bit hazy, almost as if it had happened to someone else. She didn't really remember getting into bed either. When she had finally dragged herself out from between the covers Amy had already left for work. Laura sent her a sorry-for-not-coming-home-last-night message, but Amy didn't reply. That could mean one of two things. Either Amy was very busy, or she was very angry. Laura hoped it was the former.

To distract herself, she searched the fridge for leftovers. She was about to load a tub of something brown and lumpy into the auto-oven when she noticed a box on the counter. Her name and address were printed on the top, along with a holographic label that probably meant something to the drone that had delivered it. She turned it over, surprised at the weight, and read the sender's address. Arctic rig Roald Amundsen. Laura put it back on the counter and walked away. What did her father mean by sending this to her now? Did he think he would catch her off-guard? That she would just forgive him for his years of absence? Worse still, was this some kind of bribe? Sorry for not being your father, have a vase.

She paced the kitchen. A part of her wanted to return the package unopened. It wouldn't be the first time she had done so. Although, in truth, he hadn't bothered trying to send her anything since her eighteenth birthday. Another part of her was curious to see what he thought was a suitable reparation for walking out on his family. A flock of miniature robotic doves, perhaps?

Curiosity got the better of her. She popped the seals on the box. Inside was an object, about the size of a watermelon. It was wrapped in layer upon layer of expensive looking tissue-paper. Laura found it difficult to untangle her emotions as she peeled back the first layer of soft paper.

Resentment bubbled and seethed inside her like a sulphurous mud pool. Had her father ever thought about her? Or was she just an unfortunate mistake? Relegated to history like unfashionable clothes or an embarrassing haircut. Something to gaze at fondly in old photographs. To show to friends with a casual "Her? Oh yes, she was my daughter. Once."

What of her mother? The free-spirited firebrand whose life he had once shared. Did he ever wonder what had happened to her? Did he ever search social media for mention of her name? Did she ever slip into his dreams, causing him to wake unsettled, troubled by a ghost from the past? Laura doubted it.

She wasn't sure what she had expected to find on the rig. A broken man desperate for reconnection? A fawning father begging for forgiveness. Instead, she had found a man content with his choices. A husband. A father to a brother she had never met. The leader of a community where she didn't belong.

It stung. Knowing that Gustav had built a family apart from her. Knowing that he had succeeded now, where he had failed before. Laura couldn't help but wonder if it was somehow her fault. Was she, in some way, less worthy of his love? Had she done something to push him away? It was an irrational thought, she knew, but somehow it clung to her like the seaweed that swirled around Gustav's aquatic home.

She could think of a million excuses for him. He had been too young; too ambitious; Laura's mother had been difficult and hot-tempered; He had been a victim of wanderlust; trapped in an unhappy relationship. None of them justified his abandonment of his daughter.

Laura bundled another sheet of paper in her hand and threw it on the floor. A little of her anger went with it. Was she being unfair? Hadn't she also abandoned him? Refusing his calls, rejecting his invitations to visit, and returning his gifts. Perhaps, in some ways, they were far too alike.

The last layer of paper drifted down to join the pile at her feet. In her hand was a heavy soapstone carving. A small envelope was tied to it with a white ribbon. The stone was smooth and cold. It had been carved and polished by hand. A polar bear and a walrus. They stood side-by-side; their heads tilted up towards the sky. Laura knew enough about the rig's culture to grasp the meaning. The bear represented healing. The Walrus, family. It was a peace offering.

Laura wasn't sure if she was angry or impressed. She thought back to her time on the rig. She had deliberately avoided her father, spending most of her time with Ejner. Her half-brother. *Half-brother*. His existence was something she was still trying to come to terms with. To arrive as an only child and leave with a younger brother? That shook the walls she had built around herself. Walls that shielded her from her father's desertion. Walls that were now, she realised, starting to crumble.

Ejner had been curious, sweet and welcoming. The bond she had felt with him had been surprising, yet real. It was as if her mind was a garden and Ejner had opened an overgrown gate. Just a crack. Enough to reveal a part of her life she had never explored before. A part that was wild and unkempt. She wondered how much she had missed by leaving it unvisited.

Laura unfolded the note tied to the soapstone carving. The paper felt soft between her fingers, not dry and brittle like the journal she had read. The handwriting was feminine. Flowing and ornate. Embellished with swirls and flourishes. It was certainly not her father's handwriting. She started to read.

Dear Laura,

My husband is a proud and stubborn man. I think, perhaps, you have that in common. He carved this stone for you on your eighteenth birthday. It is a traditional gift among our people, and I am confident the meaning will not be lost on you. I do not judge you for returning it to him then. Nor do I wish to intrude. I merely ask that you accept it now. Not as a gift from your father, but as a mark of your place among our people. You will always be part of our family, Laura, child of my husband. I hope that perhaps one day you will feel ready to know us better.

Until then, calm seas and clear skies.

Salak.

Salak. Her father's new wife. So, he hadn't bothered to write to her himself. Laura wasn't sure why she had expected anything different. But then, she had done everything she could to push him away. Perhaps Salak was right. Perhaps they were both too similar.

Laura turned the carving over in her hands. It was the work of countless hours. She imaged her father laboriously smoothing, shaping and polishing. As peace-offerings went, she had to admit it was a pretty good one. She carried it into the small living room and made space for it on the cluttered side table next to the sofa. It looked nice. It looked like it belonged. Laura knew she wasn't ready to forgive him. She didn't know if she ever would be. But perhaps tonight, after she had finished grovelling to Amy, she would call Ejner. No, she corrected herself, tonight, she would call her *brother*.

△△△

A few hours later, after a hasty meal of something tongue meltingly spicy, Laura returned to the laboratory. Jamal had been waiting for her. He gestured her over to a metal bench at the far side of the room. In front of him was a clear plastic box. At the bottom was the dead bee from their earlier tests. It was almost unrecognisable. Its body was covered with long black growths, distorting its outline and forming an irregular muddle of tall spikes and matted grey filaments. The filaments formed a hair-like ball, each hair tipped with a small black pinhead.

Taller growths pushed up from the hairy mass. Laura thought they looked like the grotesque stalks of a mushroom, but instead of a cap they ended in a blunt point, like a fingertip. They glistened wetly and dripped a thick black liquid in a steady stream. The liquid formed sticky pools on the floor of the box.

"What is this?" Laura asked, moving her head around the box to get a better view.

"I am not sure. I just returned from mosque and found it like this."

Jamal took a small Petri dish and pair of forceps from a drawer. He shot a glance at Laura. His brows were drawn tightly together. "Well, I guess we know why it needed the bee to fly so urgently." Laura said.

"The fungus is using the insects to spread it's spores," Jamal agreed "The bees are compelled to fly as far as they can, then once they die from exhaustion the fungus creates these tall fruiting bodies to colonise a new area."

"That's not without precedent," Laura nodded "Cordyceps fungus does something similar to ants."

"Yes, but that took millions of years to evolve. This is unnatural." Jamal carefully opened a small flap in the top of the box. A terrible stench flooded the room. Laura backed away, covering her mouth with both hands. Jamal turned his head aside, gagging on the overpowering odour of rot and decay.

"Oh my God" Laura exclaimed, her stomach heaving and her eyes watering.

"God had no part in this." Jamal told her angrily.

Quickly he reached inside the box and took hold of one of the tall fruiting bodies with his forceps. He tugged at it gently and it came away with a wet squelch. As he pulled it from the base it left long wet strings, like melting mozzarella. He placed it on the Petri dish and quickly slammed the flap of the box shut.

The sample looked like limp jelly. It seemed to be slowly secreting a pool of thick syrupy gloop. Jamal moved it to the central work bench and focused the holographic microscope on the sample. "The liquid is full of spores. The fruiting body is releasing them incredibly quickly," Jamal noted.

"I hate to keep saying this, but that looks a lot like how an ink cap mushroom releases its spores."

"The parallels we keep seeing cannot be coincidence," Jamal agreed.

"It probably isn't," Oliver's voice made Laura jump. She hadn't heard him enter the lab. "I doubt the AI has any ability to create something truly new. It is just a machine. It doesn't have an imagination. My theory is that it is using existing biological templates to serve its own needs. Genetic plagiarism if you will."

Hugo walked up to the bench with a cotton handkerchief pressed firmly to his nose. "Did someone leave the milk out last night?"

Laura did her best to ignore Hugo as he began searching under the benches for the offending smell. "On a positive note," she began "it's unlikely the fungal spores are airborne. They are probably spread by direct contact."

"Direct contact is likely." Oliver agreed. "Foraging bees will bring it back to the nest and infect others. Our best bet of beating this is to immunise the vector. In this case, the bees themselves."

"First we have to understand exactly what we are dealing with. How did your meeting go with Ekta?" Jamal asked.

"Badly. She won't release the shutdown codes," Oliver rubbed his thumb nail nervously.

"What? Why? What will we do now?" Jamal asked.

"Why? Ambition and greed. Some parts of human nature never change. As to what we'll do next, we need to find some other way to get into the unit."

"That will not be easy."

"Nothing ever is."

△△△

Rose looked up at the imposing edifice that loomed over her. The courthouse dominated most of the ground floor of the government complex. It was a solid mass of stone that felt masculine and solid. If it had been a boat, Rose thought, it would have been a "he", and to hell with convention. Immediately in front of the courthouse was a spacious area that had been designed to create the illusion of a historic town square. The open space was adorned with graceful statues and colonnaded terraces. Small businesses lined the square, providing overpriced refreshments and expensive designer shopping.

Rose had been here a few times, although not for many years. On her rare trips home to Earth, she had occasionally met up with old acquaintances in one of the fashionable little bistros. Even then, she had never felt entirely comfortable. Sipping from the tiny espresso cups and nibbling at the overpriced pastries had made her long for the simplicity of the mines. In space there was only one kind of coffee. It was thick, bitter, and served in chipped enamel mugs. She could almost taste it.

The memory triggered an unexpected pang of homesickness. It was strange, she thought. In space she had longed for sunlight and air that didn't smell of unwashed bodies. On Earth she pined for the thrill of pioneering in the vast openness of space. It was the curse of all spacers, she thought, to never quite belong anywhere.

She forced her thoughts back to the present. The square was usually a quiet and dignified place. A place which stubbornly resisted surrendering itself to the groups of tourists that normally milled between the statues and peered through the windows of the swanky bouquets. On this morning, however, it teemed with noise and bustle. Reporters posed in front of camera droids and city residents meandered between them, hoping for their moment of fame on the evening news.

The entrance to the main complex was guarded by soldiers in ceremonial uniforms. The red of their tunics and the polished bronze of their helmets were a stark contrast to the constantly shifting colours of the crowd. Police, in their bulky black armour, stood in small groups, pushing back the press and bystanders who wandered too close. The atmosphere tingled with electric excitement.

Rose stood at the entrance to the grand square with a growing sense of unease. It was if the air was charged with static. The sideways glances from the city residents unnerved her. It was the same look, Rose thought, that you might give a fly that had fallen into your soup. She had been prepared for the attention the outcasts would draw. Their dreary clothes and pallid faces made them stand out from the vibrant colours that swirled around her. That was the point, after all. To be seen. To be noticed. To show that there was a human price to profit. This open hostility, however, took her by surprise.

Rose felt some reassurance in the number of outcasts that stood with her. Perhaps eighty of the tunnel community had amassed. They were mostly the young and the angry, filled with a moral imperative and driven by the righteousness of their convictions. It had taken little effort to stoke the fire of injustice that burned in them. They had made placards from old packing crates, inscribing their bitterness onto boards and banners. Soon the anger had transformed into something different, an unshaken certainty in the legitimacy of their cause. A dark and dangerous community spirit.

Connor had relished "stirring the wasp's nest" as he put it. His overt confidence had seeped through the group, infusing it with a feverish energy. He had proudly exposed his partially healed back, dramatically pulling off his shirt like a magician revealing a clever trick. The ugly scars added legitimacy to his words. Now the group of angry young people looked to him as their leader. Their devotion disturbed Rose, although she couldn't say exactly why.

Connor swaggered into the town square with an arrogance fed by the mob around him. Rose felt her nervousness grow. Connor was hot headed at the best of times. The edgy atmosphere would only fuel his unpredictable nature. She hung back and watched as he marched at the front of the group. It was as if he didn't feel the eyes that turned towards him, or the sudden silence that gripped the large space in a vice of tension. The other outcasts were not quite so immune to the hostile atmosphere, they followed in Connor's wake nervously, glancing around at the armoured police and the morbid curiosity of the city denizens.

Rose glanced at the gathered crowd. She saw young women titter delicately behind their hands, repulsed and amused by the newcomer's shabby appearance. There was cruel conceit on their faces, a delight in the reminder of their superiority. The elders among them shook their heads in mock sympathy, outwardly compassionate to the plight of these poor fallen souls, inwardly afraid of their own fragility. The most intense reaction was that of the gathered journalists. They fell silent, ogling the tunnel people with unconcealed ambition. The avarice dripped from them like slobber from a hungry wolf.

The din of conversation restarted as if by some unseen signal. The reporters rushed towards Rose and the others in a frightening surge, their camera drones soaring skywards in a buzz of rotor blades, jostling each other for position. Their droids rolled with them, bristling with holographic broadcast equipment.

A man, his moustache carefully oiled into a slick horizontal bar, tripped and fell. The tails of his long jacket tangled in the broadcast array of a rival's droid and he was dragged several feet across the ground. The accidental violence was enough to awaken the police from their inaction. They moved quickly, placing themselves between the citizenry and the ragged protestors. The effect was immediate. The mass of gathered people surged forwards, pressing themselves against the thin line of black uniforms.

The pack of reporters were running towards Rose like a fighting phalanx. "Move back", she yelled at the group around her. "Stay calm." She hoped her voice would carry over the sound of the crowd.

"People before progress" Connor's loud voice boomed across the square. He raised a banner high above his head. The group around him tentatively took up the chant, waving their placards and pennons in defiance of their fear. The chant grew in volume and so did their courage. Soon the whole unkept mob shouted their anger at the crowd.

Rose felt like she was in the centre of an impending storm. Violence shimmered in the air. Frightening and bewitching in equal measure. The town square seemed to be caught in the moment, inhibitions melting away as the tension built. Some primitive instinct told her to get away, but before she could move the wave of advancing journalists broke against her. Questions struck and bounced away like rocks.

"Could you tell our viewers why you are here today?"

"How would you respond to criticism that your group is

engaged in acts of terrorism?"

"Why is it that you refuse city social aid?"

The questions crashed, drones swooped, and droids crowded around her feet in a jumble of antennae and microphones. Reason and rationality were lost in the crush of bodies and the frenzy of noise. Inevitably the contagious energy spread to the crowd of city residents. At first a few voices shouted insults from behind the safety of the police lines, but soon the baying began in earnest.

"Thieves!" A man with a prominent hooked nose shouted.

"Terrorist filth!" Another voice joined in.

"Why don't you go back to where you came from?" A woman's voice suggested unhelpfully. Individual thought vanished as the rule of the mob took over.

Sensing the shift, the reporters turned their cameras on their own people. The buzzing noise of the camera drones seemed to incense the crowd. "Go back to your sewers, rats!" A voice shouted angrily.

Rose knew she had to de-escalate this before it got out of hand. She manoeuvred herself in front of a young reporter. The woman looked terrified and out of her depth. Rose spoke directly into the holo-camera strapped to her head. "We are here to demonstrate peacefully." She shouted. "We are not terrorists. We just want you to see the truth. Your leaders are putting their profit before your welfare." Jeers erupted from the swelling crowd of city people. "Free yourselves from the tyranny of faceless corporations. Take back your humanity. Put people before progress!" The shout was echoed by some of the people around her, but they were drowned out by the rising tirade from the opposing mob.

"Rats!" The man with the hooked nose chanted, punching the air above his head with a clenched fist. The call was taken up. "Rats. Rats. Rats. Rats." Then, seemingly from nowhere, a wild cheer swept through the crowd. The chant changed. "Guilty. Guilty. Guilty. Guilty."

Rose threw a confused look at the young reporter. The woman tapped her temple and her eyes lost focus. When she looked up her face was pale and fearful. "Jessica Blackwell has been convicted of terrorism." The reporter didn't look happy to be delivering the news. Her eyes darted from side to side as angry shouts rose from the outcasts.

Rose suddenly felt cold, as if a shadow had passed over her. Terrorism. Jess would be an old woman by the time she was released. What have I done? she thought. Another life ruined, and for what? A few bags of stolen peas and a soundbite on the news. She looked up at Connor but there was only fury in his eyes. It frightened her.

"Guilty. Guilty. Guilty." The chant continued, rising in pitch and volume. The man with the prominent nose locked eyes with Rose. He smiled, his face satisfied and calculating. She watched as he ducked into the roaring crowd and disappeared from view.

A trickle of cold sweat ran down her back. This wasn't right. She could sense it. Somehow the atmosphere was shifting from belligerent to savage. It was if the square had been set with kindling, just waiting for a spark to ignite it. "We need to leave," she said. She looked at the people around her. She was responsible for their safety, she had to get them away from here. "Get back!" She shouted, "Head back to the tunnels."

The people closest to Rose exchanged uncertain glances. Nobody wanted to be the first to run away. Rose shot a glance at Connor. His hands had balled into fists. He hopped from foot to foot like a boxer waiting for the bell. There would be no help from him, Rose knew. It was up to her to keep her people safe.

"To me!" she called, grabbing any arm she could reach and dragging them towards the entrance. Fear coursed through her, the atmosphere thrummed with tension and the promise of impending bloodshed. The police sensed the change too. They spread their lines across the square as reinforcements arrived from the pod locks above. The newcomers carried large shields and batons which buzzed blue with energy.

At an unseen order they beat their batons against their shields. Sparks flew and a regular, rhythmic boom echoed across the square. It resonated with Rose's racing heart. The deliberate intimidation quietened the barking chant of the city mob. The noise level ebbed as the groups started to back away from each other.

Then a new sound crashed across the square. It rolled through the agitated throng like thunder, ominous and menacing. The sound of shattering glass lashed out like a thousand crashing symbols. It was almost unbearable in the tight, strained space. Rose swivelled towards the source of the sound. She saw him at the edge of the square. The man with the beak-like nose. He held a small droid above his head. His body drew back like a bow. Time seemed to slowdown. Then, with all his strength, he threw the droid into the window of a small shop. Another thunderclap of sound rolled across the square.

The crowd roared. A primal cry of fury. A woman, her makeup smeared like war paint, snarled at Rose. Her perfect teeth glowed an unnatural white. The police stopped banging their shields and took a stamping pace forward. The absence of the rhythmic noise was almost as agonising as the booming beat.

A missile flew from the crowd. It struck the shield of a police officer and bounced off. More missiles followed, and then more. Soon the air seemed to be full of flying projectiles. A group of people, hoods covering their faces, broke away from the crowd and darted towards the shops. They began to pull items from the ruined windows, stuffing their pockets with loot. Rose could hear more windows shatter as a wild energy spread through the crowd.

She did her best to shepherd her own group towards the exit. Some came with her willingly, leaving a trail of abandoned placards and broken banners on the once pristine floor. The most radical of the group gathered around Connor.

Rose watched in horror as the big man marched towards the opposing faction, his chest puffed out, his head held high. She saw the anger in his posture, and the misplaced guilt that drove him. She knew he blamed himself for getting hurt, for allowing Jess to be arrested. She knew painfully well how he felt because she blamed herself as well. Connor marched up to the wall of police shields and shouted at the city residents, his voice was lost in the roar of angry voices.

Rose wanted to drag him away, she wanted to leave this place and the promise of cruelty that tainted the dry air. But she hesitated. Her responsibility was to the people gathered around. Should she leave them to save her friend from his own anger? In that split second of indecision everything changed. With a whooshing roar, flame burst against the shields of the police line. Rose gasped as more flaming projectiles hurtled over the line of black and shattered over the confused mass of men and women.

Connor's group broke apart and ran. The city denizens pushed forward against the police lines, caught in a group hysteria, driven by a tribal impulse to pursue their foe. The black clad police, their patience exhausted, shot gas canisters into the crowd. Their batons crackled with blue sparks.

The gas spread like the breath of an angry dragon. It crawled across the ground, a noxious mist that burned throats and stung eyes. The crowd ran from it, their catcalls silenced as their breath was stolen by the suffocating fumes. An eerie silence settled over the square, the only noise was the popping of gas canisters and the hum of the camera droids which weaved above their heads.

The tunnel outcasts ran and Rose limped after them. She herded them ahead of her, trying to make sure nobody was left behind. Her damaged hip dragged as she leant forward, frustrated by her own inertia. The peppery odour of the gas was everywhere. It stung her lungs and filled her throat with a gagging sensation. Her eyes were watery, her vision blurred and mucous poured from her nose in long streams. She recognised some of Connor's group as they barrelled past her, desperate to escape the cloying gas.

Then a strong arm took her under the shoulders. She was almost lifted from her feet as Connor took her weight and ran with her to the open doors. They passed into the parkland and Rose felt grass under her feet. The sudden wave of heat stole what was left of her breath away. She coughed uncontrollably, nearly blind, her face wet with acidic tears.

They scrambled across the parkland in a wild dash. The foot of her damaged leg caught on every uneven tuft of grass and every muddy hillock. Every time she stumbled Connor was there, his broad shoulders supporting her.

After an age of gasping, panicked flight, Rose felt the cold of the tunnel system close around them. Her rescuer wheezed painfully as he lowered her gently to the hard floor. She felt him drop down beside her as something cold was pressed against her face. The stinging pain receded.

"It's alright, just relax." Tim's voice was so familiar she nearly cried with relief. A gentle hand squeezed her shoulder briefly. "The effect will wear off in a few minutes. Deep breaths."

Rose forced her eyes open and watched as Tim held a mask over Connor's mouth and nose. The other man's breathing was painfully ragged. Rose wondered how he had managed to half carry, half drag her, across the open parkland. His eyes were almost swollen shut and he winced with every breath.

She glanced around and found the tunnel entrance busy with choking, mucous encrusted victims. The sound of quiet sobbing drifted from somewhere in the gloom. Tim rested two fingers against the pulse point in Connor's neck. "One day you are going to break something I can't fix." He mumbled quietly. Rose watched as he moved off to help the others.

Connor turned his puffy eyes to meet hers. "Well, that went well," he said with a wide grin. She glared at him disapprovingly. "You have a funny idea of 'well'."

His grin grew wider. She wanted to be angry with him. To berate him for putting everyone in danger. But something inside her flared to life. His teeth were uneven, and his nose ran in streams down his face. The skin around his puffy eyes was smudged with dirt. Dried tears crusted his too-red cheeks. She watched as a line of dribble escaped the corner of his chapped lips and disappeared into the dark mess of his untidy beard. His hand closed over hers. She leaned into him and marvelled at how, in the mist of all this ugliness, her heart leapt as his lips touched hers.

CHAPTER 12

L ater that afternoon, Oliver perched on a stool in his lab and flicked through the detailed analysis of the fungi samples. They were making very little progress, he acknowledged sadly. Without a sample from the original host, it seemed unlikely they would find a way of stopping the spread of the fungus.

The decision of whether, or more likely when, to burn the infected land weighed on him heavily. He knew the habitat destruction would be catastrophic. However, the consequence of letting the fungus spread was orders of magnitude worse. Crops would fail, precious habitat would be lost, and famine would be inevitable. Every moment he delayed increased the acreage he would have to burn. There was no right answer. Oliver ran his fingers through his tangled hair and wondered if it was hope or fear that stayed his hand.

His thoughts were interrupted by a chime from his text. He glanced down to find a voicemail waiting. Perplexed, he played back the curious audio-only message. "Oliver, this is Ekta Reddy. I need you to meet me in my office immediately. Bring any samples of the fungus you have with you. This is urgent, I'll explain when you get here."

Oliver ran the pad of his middle finger over his thumb nail. There was something about the message that felt wrong. Ekta usually organised her schedule many days in advance. To be summoned to her office without prior notice was disconcerting, especially after their last meeting.

Dismissing his concern as irrational, he retrieved a transport case from an overhead cabinet. The large metal box was heavy, but it would keep the samples sealed and stable until he knew more about the purpose of Ekta's summons. Perhaps, he thought, she has changed her mind. If there was even a chance he could convince her to shut down Amanda, he had to take it.

Oliver loaded the case carefully and locked it to his wrist. He walked briskly to the pod locks. He was irritated to find that all of the lock doors were empty when he arrived. It was unusual for the transport system to be so busy in the middle of the afternoon. In fact, it was more than unusual, it was strange.

He pressed a button on the small console and waited impatiently for a nearby pod to become available. Fortunately, he didn't have to wait long. With a cheerful ping the light on the nearest lock turned from red to green.

As the doors slid open, Oliver stood aside to let the occupant exit. The man nodded his thanks, his sharply curving nose dipping politely. Oliver was reminded of the vintage woodpecker toy Hugo kept on his desk. He smiled as he boarded the small vehicle, feeling a small flush of guilt at the unkind comparison.

The pod disconnected from the locking clamp, rotated smoothly and swept into the flow of city traffic. Oliver watched the familiar dance of pods. They swirled around each other like flakes in an unseasonal snowstorm. Somehow the ordinariness of the busy city scene made him feel better.

Oliver turned his thoughts back to the voicemail. He was struggling to understand why the message had left him feeling so disturbed. It was unusual for voice only messages to be sent in the age of holographic communications, but it was certainly not unheard of. It was equally uncommon for Ekta to contact him directly, but if the matter was urgent, as she had suggested, that could easily be explained.

Then it struck him. Ekta had used his first name. In all of

their interactions, Ekta had always maintained a professional distance. Not once had she referred to him by his given name. Oliver sat up straight in his seat. A wave of alarm rolled over him. Was he being paranoid? Perhaps the stress of the last few weeks was exacting an unexpected toll. There was a simple way to find out.

Reaching towards the central console, Oliver flicked through the menus that would put a call through to Ekta's office. The window in front of him faded to opaque and the communication panel blinked into view. Oliver sat on the edge of his seat, trying to control the unease that swept through him.

The panel blinked an apologetic red and a calm male voice informed him "Call failed, please try again later." Oliver swallowed the lump that had suddenly formed in his throat. His stomach turned over in a nauseating lurch. He reached for the console controls and the communication panel appeared again, this time routing a call to Hugo. "Call failed, please try again later." The calm voice repeated stoically.

Oliver gripped the cushion of the seat with sweaty palms. His mind raced to find a logical explanation. Maybe the pod had a technical malfunction? Yes, that must be it. He brought up the destination panel and programmed the pod to return him to the laboratory. The console blinked once and then went completely black. Oliver stared at it in numb shock.

"Malfunction in primaaaaarrr..." The voice stuttered, the carefully soothing tones disintegrating into a piercing electronic squeal. "Emergen... sysssssstem... fail... rrrrrr." The last "R" rolled to a faltering stop.

Oliver's eyes widened in fear. He stabbed at the black display with stiff fingers. His mind reeled, refusing to accept that he was trapped in the tight confines of the pod. He reached up to his temple, but his ocular implants couldn't transmit from within the pod's shielded interior. The tight space seemed to constrict around him. The computer-generated voice spluttered a stream of nonsense, the volume deafening.

The pod lurched sideways, slamming him into the clear canopy. Oliver couldn't breathe. Panic gripped him and squeezed his throat shut. His heart thumped so hard it seemed to rattle his rib cage. The roar of his own blood became the only sound in the failing pod. His world became dark and airless, rolling in from the edges.

Something hit the canopy above his head. It sounded like someone slamming a door closed. Oliver jumped out of his seat, his hands flying to the clear windows, pounding uselessly. Time stopped, and then exploded outwards, restarting with the force of a dying star. Oliver clawed at the poly-carbon, gasping for air. His hands left sweaty outlines on the cold, clear poly-carbon.

He looked up in time to see another object hit the canopy. As he stared upwards, he become aware that he could see the blades rotating in the port rotor. The starboard blades were an invisible blur of motion, but the port engine was slowing, the black rotors becoming a visible disk. A thin shard was flung from the slowing rotors. It struck the pod with a sharp crack. Slowly the pod began to list sideways.

Oliver slid helplessly along the bench seat as the pod leaned over. His feet scrabbled for purchase on the smooth floor. He grabbed the central console as he skidded past and wedged himself against it. The pod lurched violently, the remaining engine screaming as the blades fought for purchase in the thin air. A tendril of white smoke rose from the over-taxed engine.

Then, in mesmerising slow-motion, the damaged rotor disintegrated. Small pieces of black burst outwards in an expanding sphere of debris. At first there was no sound but the desperate hum of the surviving rotor. Then the debris hit the pod in a shattering wave of noise. The cloud of fragments rattled off the canopy like hail stones.

Oliver covered his head as sharp pieces of black wreckage pierced the poly-carbon. Wind howled through the holes, the raging roar of air competing with the high-pitched shriek of the dying engine. The pod spun slowly. A sycamore seed caught in a downward current. Black smoke spiralled upwards into the unbroken blue sky.

Oliver watched helplessly as his pod plunged into the swarm of a busy traffic lane. The other pods veered away as their collision detection kicked in. Oliver could do nothing except brace himself against the slow, relentless corkscrew.

One pod, impeded by its neighbours, couldn't move out of the way fast enough. Oliver gasped as he barrelled towards it. At the last second, the other pod found some space and jinked nimbly sideways. The couple inside stared at him in dumb horror as his pod struck theirs a glancing blow. Oliver watched their faces in a series of frozen images. It was as if a strobe light illuminated his descent in a flickering, spinning nightmare.

The impact accelerated his twisting plunge. Gravity pushed at him, dragging his stomach downwards and crushing the air from his chest. He tried to scream, but there wasn't enough air in his lungs. The complexes spun past in a blurry haze, too fast for his eyes to focus. With a final cough the second engine failed. Oliver's pod plummeted, unresisting, towards the woodland below.

△△△

Oliver awoke to pain. His mind felt like shattered shards, reflected images that didn't quite make sense. As they slowly drew together, he was struck by a blast of euphoria. Impossibly, he was alive. He tried to take a deep breath, but a stabbing pain coursed through his chest in biting waves. He moaned with the agony of it. "Easy, try to lie still," a soft voice reassured him. Something cold was pressed against his upper arm and another to his upper chest. The pain eased slightly. He tried to open his eyes, but they were crusted and sticky.

His initial relief at having survived the crash faded to dread. His whole body was on fire. He must be badly injured.

Could the damage be fixed? Fear flooded him. He felt rough hands lift him and the slight twisting sent a fresh wave of suffering through his broken body. He cried out loudly, and immediately regretted it as his lungs seared with a burning torment.

"We should leave him, let the city find him," another voice said, hard and guttural.

"They should have been here already. I can't just abandon him," The soft voice disagreed.

"He's not our problem, he's half dead already."

"He's our problem now, Connor. Now help me move him." The hard voice muttered a stream of ugly profanities.

Oliver felt himself being lowered to a hard surface. The movement set off bolts of anguish that tore the breath from his tortured lungs. He gritted his teeth and concentrated on pulling in air as best as he could. Still, he felt himself fading as the pain overcame him. "You need to stay awake," someone said from very far away. "Stay with me."

"Here, let me." Cold water hit Oliver square in the face. He gasped instinctively and the sharp pain shot through him like tongues of fire.

"Don't ever take up nursing, Connor," the softer voice chastised somewhere close to his ear.

"No fecking chance of that," the other voice responded testily.

Oliver felt himself being lifted again, but this time the pain was less. He managed to pry one eye open and watched as dappled light moved across his blurry vision. Tall, dark shapes swam in and out of focus, their surface coarse and heavily lined. Above them greens and greys swirled in a kaleidoscope of dizzying complexity. Trees. The word popped into his head.

Days later, or it might have been minutes, the greens faded into a dazzling blue. Oliver was finding it much harder to breathe now. Each breath came with a loud, gurgling, wheeze that rattled against his ribcage. A bubbling foam filled his mouth and ran down his face. The foam tasted metallic and sour. The fear faded, all he felt was a strange detachment.

"His oxygen saturation is dropping. We need to get him back to the clinic."

"What am I? Your personal donkey?"

"You bray so much I do wonder sometimes."

"Well, that's a nice thing to be saying to a fella."

The scolding heat beat down without mercy. Time slowed to the interval between each excruciating breath, like the ticks of some satanic clock. When the darkness finally came, Oliver thought it would mean an end to his suffering, but the torment continued.

He could tell they were heading downwards. He could feel it in the subtly changing air pressure and the way his rescuers footsteps echoed from the walls. As they moved deeper into the subterranean twilight, the air grew cold and damp. There was a musty, earthy smell that seemed familiar. It reminded Oliver of a caving trip Hugo had persuaded him to take as a child. Oliver had hated the oppressive, clammy spaces, but Hugo had loved the adventure, embracing the strange hidden world with unrestrained delight.

The memory faded as the chill grew deeper. The damp air crept into his lungs, tearing at them like thorns. A cough started to build, and Oliver strained to suppress it, knowing the agony that would come. It burst from him like lightning, filling his vision with white light and sending bolts of torture radiating outwards like blast waves from an impact crater. The world started to recede, floating away softly.

"Oh no you don't," a voice said, disconnected and ethereal. He felt pressure against his neck and a soft hiss. The world dropped back into sharp focus. He started up into a bright circular light. It was divided into numerous sections, like a brilliant compound eye. As he moved his head various sections dimmed so as not to dazzle him. Oliver rolled his head deliberately, trying to catch it out.

A face appeared in front of the light. It was a kindly face, soft and plump. An extra set of chins jiggled enthusiastically.

Oliver giggled as they bobbed up and down in time with the man's mouth.

"I think you over did it," a female voice said.

"Everyone's a critic today," the chins answered, as a mask was lowered over Oliver's mouth and nose, restricting his view. Oliver tried to reach up and remove it. His hand stopped as something metal clanged beneath him.

"There is a case attached to his wrist. Should I cut it off?" The disembodied female voice asked.

"Yes, but be careful, you wouldn't want to overdo it. You might remove his hand." The eyes above the chin shone mischievously. Oliver thought that was a very good joke and giggled again. "Someone appreciates my sense of humour," the chins commented, as something cold moved slowly across Oliver's chest.

"You have to drug them to get a laugh. I wouldn't say that was something to show off about." A pretty brown-haired woman leant into view. "You were correct, Doctor," she said, her tone changing to serious and professional. "Pulmonary contusion causing oedema of the right lung. The lung has partially collapsed. Three fractured ribs, fractured clavicle and fractured right radius. A whole bunch of superficial contusions and lacerations. Nothing we can't deal with here." Oliver wondered if a clavicle was a musical instrument, the thought made him giggle uncontrollably.

"He is lucky his pod hit the trees. This could have been a lot more permanent."

"He is lucky we found him at all. Why didn't the city services respond?"

"That is something I have been trying to work out. It took us at least forty minutes to get to him. The city medical services should have been there long before that."

"Maybe someone didn't want him found?"

"In that case, this gentleman has some very powerful enemies. Two milligrams Malodrozine please."

Oliver felt sorry for whoever they were talking about.

He wondered if they would ever play the clavicle again. He felt a warm sensation spreading through his body from the cold point in his neck, then he felt nothing at all.

△△△

As night swept over the city, Laura paced her tiny kitchen. She bounced between the walls like a rubber ball, caught between frantic worry and the sense that she was massively overreacting. Her futile march had started a few hours earlier when Hugo had called to say that Oliver hadn't returned home that evening. Hugo had tried to hide his agitation. Smiling with that manufactured charm that Oliver found so mesmerising, and Laura found incredibly irritating. He had asked her, quite casually, when she had last seen Oliver. Laura had been instantly on edge.

Hugo had brushed aside her questions and quickly cut the call. As his pretentious smile faded away in a fizz of holographic static, Laura had tried to call Oliver. She was met with an unhelpful "No service" message. She had tried again. And again. Late into the evening.

Laura twirled a lock of red hair around her finger until it knotted. Oliver's disappearance was so completely out of character she couldn't stop herself imagining the worse. She felt like an anxious parent, waiting to hear from a wayward teenager. Part of her lingered in comfortable denial. She was being silly, she told herself. Oliver was a grown man. He could look after himself. There was a perfectly reasonable explanation. Maybe a secret love interest, or a last-minute field trip. The irrational part of her mind twisted with images of hospital wards and mutilated bodies.

Her pacing was interrupted as the door slid open. Amy slumped into one of the hard kitchen chairs. "Any news?"

"Not yet."

Amy idly dunked one finger in her teacup and used the now cold liquid to draw a pattern on the tabletop. She wiped it away and yawned loudly and pointedly.

"Why don't you go to bed?" Laura asked.

"I will if you do." Amy stifled another yawn. It was contagious and Laura found herself echoing it.

"Go to bed Amy. There is no point both of us staying up all night." In truth, Laura was finding Amy's fidgeting annoying. She knew that was unkind. Amy was just trying to be supportive, but the tension of the last few days had left Laura bad tempted and irritable.

Amy pouted. "But I've hardly seen you this week. Why are you so worried about Oliver anyway? He's only been missing a few hours."

Laura rubbed her stiff neck. Why was she so worried? Why couldn't she shake the feeling that something terrible had happened? "There are things going on at work. We..." The sentence trailed off into nothing. Laura wasn't sure what to say. Oliver's disappearance could just be coincidence. Lack of sleep could just be making her completely paranoid. She shook her head to clear it.

"What things?" Amy asked. Laura tried not to let her grumpiness show. She was exhausted and her head was swimming with half-formed thoughts and muddled anxieties. She needed time alone to work through her feelings. This need to withdraw was something Amy, the perennial sharer, often struggled to understand.

"It's government work. I can't really say much." That was at least partially true. Hopefully Amy would take the hint and leave her alone.

"Can't or won't?'

Laura ground her teeth together. She tried to find a way to end the conversation as quickly as possible. "It's complicated," she said.

"Complicated? Do you think I'm too stupid to understand? Is that it?" Amy's voice had risen. Rather than end the argument, Laura had managed to inflame it. Brilliant.

She tried to stay calm. "What? No. Of course not."

"Then why are you locking me out of this?"

Laura fumbled for the right thing to say. "I'm not. It's just... it's dangerous."

"Dangerous?" Amy's eyes widened and Laura instantly regretted her choice of words. This was going very badly indeed.

"Not like that. It's just...science stuff."

"Do you know how patronising that sounds?" Amy pushed back her chair. The sound of it scrapping against the floor made Laura wince. "You've been acting strangely all week. You've hardly slept in days. You barely leave the lab. Now you are telling me it's dangerous but you won't tell me why. Why do you always put work before everything else?"

Laura felt as if she had been punched in the gut. The air escape from her in a loud whoosh. Denial surged up in her. She didn't always put work first. She was nothing like her father. He had abandoned her. Walked away. What she was doing was nothing like that. Her work was important. Vital. It mattered more than anything else. More than Amy's feelings. Her thoughts stumbled to a halt. God, she was so like him it was uncanny. Was history doomed to repeat itself? With a sigh she slumped into the chair opposite. "We had a containment leak at the lab. We might have to burn a big swathe of the provinces to control it."

"Oh. That's awful." Amy reached out and took Laura's hand in hers. The warmth of her fingers seemed to loosen the hard knot in Laura's stomach. "Why didn't you just tell me?"

"I was trying to protect you."

"Protect me from what? What aren't you telling me?" Amy's voice took on a hard note.

Laura took a breath and tried to untangle her thoughts. She was struggling to rationalise why her instincts were ringing alarm bells. Perhaps it was because people didn't just drop off the communication grid in the twenty-second century. At least not without trying very hard indeed. Perhaps it was because she had seen something in Ekta's eyes that had frightened her. Something cold. Ekta's voice rang in her mind "You have crossed a line." The threat had hung in the air like a guillotine blade, but Laura wasn't sure what it meant.

"I don't know," Laura said honestly, "It's probably nothing." She tried to smile but it felt false on her lips.

"Then why are you up at," Amy blinked at her implants, "two o'clock in the morning?"

Because a powerful person has a vested interest in protecting this project, she thought silently, and I am afraid of what they might do to keep it running. She shivered as a chill travelled up her spine despite the warm room. Oliver was in danger. On some instinctive level Laura had suspected it, but now she was certain. She wasn't being irrational. It wasn't paranoia. It was too much of a coincidence that Oliver would disappear so shortly after Ekta had made her implied threat. The less Amy knew the safer she would be.

"You're right. It's just the stress of work. I'm being silly. Go to bed. I just need to get a glass of water."

Amy narrowed her lips but seemed to think better pressing any further. "Don't be long," she said instead, gently kissing the knuckles of Laura's hand. She padded towards the bedroom, her back stiff. This wouldn't be the end of it, Laura knew, but at least she had earned herself a reprieve. Too restless to sleep, she put through a call to Hugo.

"Anything?" She asked as his image resolved in the air in front of her.

"Oliver is definitely not at the lab or anywhere else I can think of. Jamal checked around the test site, but it's deserted. Amanda still has it locked up tight." Hugo swivelled on his heel and paced to the other end of a long balcony overlooking the city. The holo-transmitters panned to keep up with him. "Oliver's implants went offline at 2:03 p.m. That's more than twelve hours ago. He summoned a pod just before then. I checked with city transport. A pod responded to the summons, but nobody picked it up. Either Oliver changed his mind, or something happened in the ninety seconds it took for the pod to dock."

"Why would his implants go offline?"

"Good question. I am struggling to find a reasonable explanation."

"Maybe there isn't one, Hugo." Laura felt the knot in her stomach tighten. "Maybe nothing about this is reasonable." Something she had dismissed earlier bubbled to the surface. "There is something I forgot to mention. When I went to the lab earlier to look for Oliver, I noticed all the samples of the fungus were missing. Along with a biohazard transport case."

Hugo furrowed his brow. "This keeps getting stranger. Let me go back through the lab's records."

Twenty minutes passed as Laura checked the local hospitals and Hugo gestured at a holographic interface. The sound of gentle snoring came from the next room. Laura felt a flush of envy. She was starting to forget what sleep felt like. Soft sheets, fluffy pillow, warm duvet. Her head snapped up with a start.

Hugo's hologram looked up at the sudden movement. He rubbed his eyes. "There is nothing here. Everything is completely normal until 2:03 pm when Oliver just disappears. Wait a minute. That's strange."

"What's strange?"

"I just checked the logs for Oliver's implants and the timestamps don't match."

"What logs?"

"Our implants create diagnostic logs all the time. High level events that an engineer can use to fix any problems. As soon as the logs are created, they are compressed to save space. The timestamp of when the logs are created should match the time they are compressed, give or take a few nanoseconds. It doesn't. They are seven minutes apart."

"What does that mean?"

"It means these files have been altered to edit out seven minutes."

Laura felt her stomach rise into her throat. "We need to

call the police."

Hugo shook his head. "Too slow. I am going to call in my own security team. Get some rest, Laura. I'll let you know as soon as I find anything."

Laura nodded. Although she suspected sleep was going to be impossible. With a curt nod she cut the connection and went to check the lock on the front door.

△△△

The next morning Laura sat at the kitchen table and tried to force down the toast Amy had made for her. It was cold. So was Amy, after waking up to find Laura's side of the bed empty yet again. She fussed over an old-fashioned tea pot, refusing to make eye contact. The pot was round, brown, and reassuringly solid. Amy refused to let the household appliances anywhere near her morning tea. She imported the loose leaves, at considerable expense, using words like orange pekoe, that meant very little to Laura. It had become a ritual to start each new day. Laura loved her for it, even if she didn't always love the tea.

"Have you checked the news this morning?" Amy asked, breaking the uncomfortable silence.

"Not yet, I didn't sleep well."

"You didn't sleep at all. You prowled. All night."

"I'm sorry, Amy."

"This can't go on Lore. You have to sleep. Maybe you should just find another assignment to finish your postgrad?"

Laura took another bite of cold toast and forced herself to swallow. "Maybe. What were you saying about the news?" It was an artless attempt to change the subject, but Amy played alone anyway. Anything was better than the tense silence.

"There was a big forest fire in Cromwell woods. That's near where you work isn't it?"

"Probably some idiots with a barbeque." Laura mumbled.

"Apparently they found an engine cowling stuck in a tree some distance away. A bit weird don't you think?"

Laura sat upright and swivelled to face her partner. "What kind of engine cowling?" She asked, her eyes widening.

Amy took a step backwards. "I don't know, it didn't say. Nothing else was found, just some uprooted trees and lots of fire damage. I thought it was strange that they didn't put it out straight away. You know? Seems it was burning for a while. Some people in the complexes saw the smoke."

Laura felt her stomach bounce off the floor and wedge itself firmly in her throat. "Oh no," she said as the room slipped out of focus. Amy looked up from her tea pot, a frown creasing her brow. "You think this has something to do with Oliver?"

"Yes. Maybe. I don't know. I have to go." Laura raced for the door.

CHAPTER 13

O liver was cold. His skin prickled with goosebumps and his muscles ached. He tried to ignore the chill, to sink back into the comfortable place he had floated up from. His mind, however, was determined to break free, to surface from the dark, safe place that had been his sanctuary moments before. A small shiver ran up his body, a cold tremor which threw off the last vestiges of sleep. Oliver accepted the inevitability of consciousness reluctantly.

He opened his eyes. The room was dim and smelled like wet rock. The ceiling above him was partially blocked by a large circular light. It reminded Oliver of the type of lights preferred by dentists and doctors, practical and slightly intimidating. It was dim now, its multifaceted surface a dull silver. Beyond the light the ceiling was rough and irregular.

Oliver turned his head and found that the walls were only extensions of the ceiling. They sloped downwards and disappeared over the side of his bed. One wall seemed to be a different texture to the others. It was a rough curtain, made from a heavy mottled grey cloth. Light seeped around the edges, framing it in a warm orange glow.

A wave of disorientation swept through him. This was not the clean, comfortable bedroom that he awoke in every morning. There was no curved window, ready to brighten at a word and reveal the beauty of the city below. There was no familiar splutter of the coffee machine. The rough, itchy blankets were not the silky duvet that usually covered him.

The still air didn't carry the rich smell of warming pastries.

Oliver gasped as his memory returned in an avalanche of tumbling images. He saw again the frightened faces of a couple, wide-eyed with disbelief as he plunged towards them, a modern-day Icarus with broken wings. He felt the force of gravity as it pressed against him, the world revolving in a relentless cycle of blue, green, blue. He felt the terror of watching the green swell outwards with each violent rotation. The details of each tree burned into his mind, made vivid by that last, horrible spiral.

His heart beat frantically in his chest and Oliver gulped air in rapid, shallow breaths. His chest felt suddenly constricted and the room spun around him, making him feel dizzy. He clutched desperately at the ache in his chest, his fingers numb, the tips tingling. He felt clammy, sweat prickling his cold skin. Was he having a heart attack? He barely noticed when the curtain swept open, and the room was flooded with warm light.

Strong hands gripped Oliver's shoulders. A face appeared in the centre of his vision. The dark eyes bore into his keenly. "You're safe, you're just hyperventilating. You need to slow your breathing," the gentle voice had an edge of firmness which cut through Oliver's panic like a laser beam. "Concentrate on me. Breath in through your nose while I count to five." Oliver felt a hand on his chest, a human touch that brought light to the darkness that threatened to overwhelm him. "One. Two. Three." Oliver struggled to keep inhaling through the tightness in his chest. "Good, keep going," the man said. "Four. Five. Now exhale through your mouth. Concentrate on my voice."

The counting continued, the rhythm slow and steady, the tone soothing. Oliver felt his breathing slow as the panic receded. The man watched from his perch on the side of the bed. His plump face was round, almost comical, but the eyes were sharp and bright with intelligence.

"Welcome to the tunnels," he said, watching attentively

as Oliver recovered. "I'm Tim Ashby, the community doctor." He held out his hand and Oliver gripped it instinctively. The handshake was surprisingly firm, the skin cool and dry. The firm clasp grounded him, the last of the intense fear drained away.

"Oliver Chadwick. Where am I?"

"In the abandoned tunnels under the city. You were involved in an accident. Your pod crashed into the woods near one of the tunnel entrances. We brought you here to treat your injuries. How do you feel?"

"Embarrassed."

Tim smiled kindly. "You have nothing to be embarrassed about. If I had been through what had just happened to you, I would be bouncing off the walls."

"I need to contact my brother," Oliver wasn't sure how much time had passed since he had left the laboratory. He was certain Hugo would be worried by now.

"Of course, but you won't get a signal down here. As soon as you are strong enough, we'll take you to the surface."

Oliver shook his head. "I need to let him know where I am," he pushed aside the thin blankets and swung his legs off the bed.

"I wouldn't do that if I were you," the heavyset man warned. Oliver tried to stand, but his legs collapsed from under him. Tim caught him easily and lowered him back to the bed. "You were hurt when we found you. We repaired your injuries, but you need to rest for a few more hours, at least."

Oliver didn't have the strength to argue. His right arm throbbed, and his chest ached. He shivered slightly in the dank air. Tim noticed his discomfort and walked over to a large cabinet against one of the stony walls.

"You'll get used to the cold," he said lightly. "I think cold is easier to deal with than heat. Don't you? I used to hate the long summer heatwaves when I lived in the city. Some years, it seemed they would never end. Sometimes you could smell the smoke from the forest fires, if the wind was in the right direction."

Oliver knew the stream of casual conversation was for his benefit, an effort to put him at ease. He mumbled his agreement half-heartedly.

"It's the dark I've never managed to adjust to," the young doctor continued, "I miss the sun. The rhythm of the days, the turning of the seasons. It's easy to lose track of time down here." He returned with a collection of mismatched blankets. They were worn and faded, but they smelled clean.

"Drink this." Tim said, handing him a cup of clear liquid. Oliver looked at it suspiciously.

"It's only water," the other man smiled, amused.

Oliver felt ashamed of his distrust. He knew nothing about these people expect for what he had seen in the news. Tim didn't fit his preconceived notions. He was far from the radical terrorist Oliver had expected. "How did you end up down here?" he asked as he sipped the cool water.

"That's a long story. My fiancée and I were both made redundant around the same time. I was offered another job, in a different specialism. I was too proud to take it. I had an image in my head of where my life was going, and the job didn't match it. When the money ran out, so did our options."

"Is she down here, with you?"

"No, she died." A wave of pain swept over the younger man's face.

Oliver felt a stab of remorse at having prompted it. "I'm sorry."

Tim smiled sadly. He settled Oliver back into bed. "Get some rest. We'll talk later." He slipped quietly out of the room. Oliver laid awake, staring at the rough ceiling. He had watched the news footage of the riot outside the courtroom with detached disgust. The computer centre bombing had filled him with horror and a sense of violation, as if he had personally been attacked. He was struggling to reconcile his preconceptions of this place and the people who lived here, with the kindness he had been shown. Before he could think about that too deeply, sleep rose up and claimed him.

ΔΔΔ

Sometime later, it was impossible to know how long in the perpetual gloom, a woman pushed her way through the curtain. Oliver did his best not to stare at the gruesome scar which marred one side of her face. "You're awake. Finally. You've been asleep for hours." Her voice was coarse and grainy as if she was speaking through a mouthful of pebbles. "There are some clothes on the table behind you. Come and join us when you're ready." She swept back through the curtain without waiting for a response.

Oliver lowered his legs to the floor nervously. He was relieved when they supported his weight, albeit grudgingly. He limped stiffly to the pile of clothes that had been left for him. They were shabby and showed signs of many repairs, but they seemed serviceable enough. Oliver glanced down at his own body. He was shocked to see the angry welts and blue bruises that covered the right side of his chest. His rib cage was a mass of discolouration and his right shoulder was tender and swollen. He traced the bruises with his fingertips. Just how close had he come to dying? It was an uncomfortable thought. It made him feel very mortal but also incredibly grateful. He had no doubt these strangers had saved his life.

The cold was biting without the thick blankets and Oliver dressed as quickly as he could. The rough stone floor cut into his bare feet and sucked the warmth from his body, leaving him shivering uncontrollably. The boots that had been left for him were a surprisingly good fit, but the thick coat was several sizes too large. He shrugged it on awkwardly before having to stop to catch his breath. He was exhausted from the simple act of dressing. It was frustrating to feel so weak and vulnerable, so out of place in this strange underground world. With a great deal of trepidation, he slinked through the curtain.

The area beyond was lit by a large open fire. It flickered cheerily in the grate, lifting the general gloom. Someone had ingeniously hollowed out an alcove in the stone wall and built a black metal hood and pipework to carry away the woodsmoke. Despite their efforts, the room was thick with smoke. Within moments his eyes stung, and his nose itched.

A small group of people were huddled around a roughly made table. Their bodies were hidden behind shapeless, heavy clothing; their faces lost in the shadows of deep hoods and thick scarves. As he limped towards them the buzz of conversation stopped. Oliver stumbled to a halt as they all turned to stare at him. He cleared his throat and shifted his weight onto the other foot. "Err ...Hello."

The grey-haired woman broke the uncomfortable silence. "Well don't just stand there. Come and get some breakfast. Don't expect anyone to serve you here." Oliver limped into the circle of firelight. "I'm Rose." The woman said "One of the community leaders. There are eggs in the pan and bread on the table." There was something about the way Rose held herself that reminded Oliver of Hugo. Rose was a leader, someone who demanded respect.

He helped himself to scrambled eggs from a cast iron pot near the fire. A few people shuffled along the bench to make space for him at the table. He thanked them and took a hunk of bread from a basket. He was surprised to find that it was fresh and fragrant. He tucked in with vigour, surprised at how hungry he was. The others watched with detached interest as he shovelled eggs into his mouth.

"Don't they feed ya up top?" A young woman asked. The others laughed, easing the tension.

"They certainly don't make bread this good." Oliver helped himself to another hunk to prove the point.

"Our Tina makes the best bread in the tunnels." An older woman said proudly, eliciting a murmur of agreement.

"Aw, get away with ya. What would you savages know about baking, anyway?" The pink blush that crept into Tina's cheeks reminded Oliver of Laura. The relaxed atmosphere evaporated as thoughts shot through his head almost quicker than he could acknowledge. The fungus. Impending famine. The AI. Ekta. He had to get back to the surface. Even if his legs did feel like lead and his head was throbbing.

"I need to contact my brother to let him know that I am safe," he said.

"I'll take you to the surface when you have finished eating. You hardly look strong enough to stand right now," Rose said. Oliver could hardly disagree. He could allow himself a few more minutes by the fire, he reasoned.

"That's if you can bear to tear yourself away from me baking," Tina held up the empty breadbasket with a grin.

Oliver smiled sheepishly. Once again, he was struck by how his preconceived notions differed from the congenial atmosphere around the table. He wasn't sure what he had expected, but these people certainly weren't the fanatics he had imagined.

The warmth from the fire and the simple food were starting to have the desired effect. As the others started to drift away Oliver found himself alone with Rose. She sat with her body twisted away from him, watching the fire dance in the grate. "How long have you been here?" he asked her.

"I have lived in the tunnels for nearly twenty years. This is my home now."

"Twenty years," Oliver was shocked to think anyone could live in this cold, lightless dungeon for so long. "What did you do before?"

"I was an asteroid miner. I rarely came back to Earth. To be honest I didn't care for it much."

"Why was that?"

"When you live in space," she gestured towards the ceiling as if she could see the stars through the rock, "it gives you a different perspective. You start to see how things *really* work. The corporations are the true power on Earth. Democracy is a facade. Most of the big companies aren't even run by people. They have computers to make all the big decisions. Cold, hard, heartless machines driven by profit. There is no compassion anymore, no philanthropy. People are only valued by how much they can consume and how much tax they pay. When you stop being useful you are tipped out like so much rubbish," Rose spooned a fork full of eggs into her mouth and chewed noisily. "It was different in space. Everyone was valued. We had to stick together to survive."

"It must have been difficult coming back," Oliver mumbled. In truth, he found her worldview a little depressing. It felt to him as if it was fuelled by bitterness and nostalgia rather than political idealism. He wondered what had happened to make her so resentful.

Rose turned to face him. The firelight seemed to sink into the deep crevice on her face making her appearance seem less than human. "You have no idea city boy. Your type will never understand what it's like to be cast off and abandoned, thrown away like filth."

Oliver bristled at her tone. It was true that his life had been sheltered and comfortable. Hugo had seen to that. But what gave her the right to judge him? She didn't know him. At least he was trying to solve his problems, rather than hiding away from them. He decided that pointing that out might not be a good idea. Instead, he tried to change the subject. "How many people live here?"

"Several hundred."

"Why doesn't the city council help you?"

"They ignore us. That's help enough. It's not so bad here. We have a purpose, although we don't always agree on what that is."

Oliver studied her in the warm light of the fire. "What do you think it is?" he asked.

"I want to show people that there is price to pay for automation, just as there was for industrialisation. I want people to wake up and realise they are making themselves obsolete." She leaned towards him, warming to her subject.

"People before progress."

"Why not live in the city? Change things from the inside?"

"And wear implants like a good little worker ant? Be tracked every second of the day and night. My performance evaluated by some computer program. My personality assessed and assigned to a little box. No. 'Better even to die free than to live as slaves.'"

Oliver had heard that before. "Frederick Douglass."

Rose pulled her coat closer around her shoulders. "You are smarter than you look city boy. Douglass was trying to inspire African Americans to fight for their freedom in the American civil war. He understood that sometimes you have to use violence to create change."

A shadow of regret passed over her face before it hardened into cold stoniness. Oliver quickly put the pieces together. "You were the leader behind the data centre bombing. The one where the girl died."

Rose stiffened as if he had struck her. The anger faded quickly but the pain and bitterness remained, written large in the lines across her face. "You should leave," she stood abruptly. "I'll take you to where you can call your brother." She moved off into the gloom without a backward glance.

Oliver followed as best he could. Despite her uneven gait, Rose easily outpaced him. His own movement was frustratingly slow. Even shallow breaths of the cold air made his chest hurt and gurgle. Rose led him swiftly through the narrow tunnels, her heavy boots echoing from the icy walls. After what felt like an age, the maze of tunnels opened into a wider shaft. The walls here were smoother, more finished, and the arched ceiling was higher. Oliver assumed it was part of an obsolete hyperloop track. As they walked, they passed the entrances to countless narrow service tunnels. Occasionally they gave way to wider spaces, carved neatly from the solid rock. Storage or engineering areas he guessed.

The trappings of everyday life were evident everywhere.

In one tunnel a group of children sat at long benches while a teacher sketched equations on a transparent screen. In another, a small market was busy with people moving between the stalls of fresh fruit and vegetables. To Oliver's practiced eye they looked homegrown. A cook hawked his wares in a loud voice, a large pot of soup bubbled in front of him. Oliver looked around, shocked at the scale of this forgotten community. "How do you get your food and supplies?" He asked his guide.

"We grow some, scavenge what we can. We recycle and repair the things your people discard. Some of it is sold back to shops that don't ask too many questions. We also have people in the city who are sympathetic. Or at least we did. They help us if they can."

A short while later, Oliver realised the tunnel was sloping steeply upwards. He panted heavily, his body protesting at the exertion and his head swimming with dizziness. He pushed on, not wishing to admit his weakness. "You aren't going to faint on me, are you?" Rose asked as he stumbled to a humiliating halt.

"No, I'm fine. I just need to catch my breath." He wheezed.

"You don't look fine. Maybe we should go back."

As he leaned against the cold tunnel wall Oliver couldn't help but agree. His weakness made him feel pathetic. He had a sudden thought. "When I was brought here, did I have a metal case with me?"

Rose shrugged her shoulders. "I don't know, Tim might."

"Can you take me to him?"

"Alright. Try not to pass out. I don't want to have to carry you."

△△△

Oliver stumbled into the small clinic trembling with fatigue. Rose had one arm across his back. He was surprised and mortified to find that she was far stronger than she looked.

Tim glanced up from an old-fashioned electron microscope as they struggled through the heavy curtain. His face clouded over with concern as he moved to take Oliver's free arm and guide him to a chair.

Oliver sucked in shaking breaths as the young doctor rested one hand on his forehead and sought the pulse in his wrist with the other hand. It was an oddly intimate touch and Oliver felt slightly discomforted. He realised that it had been years since someone had laid hands on him in such a way. In the city above, most human interaction was through the medium of technology, remote and sterile. Physical contact was discouraged, almost feared. Perhaps, Oliver thought, in the race to become ever more connected we are actually more isolated than ever before.

"It's alright, you are going to be fine." The big man comforted in the now familiar soft voice. "Rose, did you take him to the surface?" he asked. There was a hard edge to the question that made Rose bristle.

"He wanted to leave. I wasn't going to stop him." She said, her chin held high.

"I told you he needed rest." The dark eyes flashed with irritation. Rose hissed at him and crossed her arms over her chest.

"I insisted, it's not her fault." Oliver said. He was getting the distinct impression that there was more to this clash than his health. This was an old disagreement, a well-worn path neither was willing to step away from. The two antagonists glared at each other over his head.

Tim's focus flipped back to Oliver and the anger faded quickly. It was replaced by sympathy. "You have a temperature. You both should have known better than to exert yourself like this," the hard edge in his voice carried a note of warning. "I've lost enough people recently." Oliver saw another flash of pain pass over the young man's open face.

Tim walked over to a large chest of drawers and returned with a short metal cylinder. It was thick, silver and ended in a blunt point. The side had a small transparent strip, through which Oliver could see a clear fluid. "This is a broad spectrum anti-biotic and anti-viral. It's fast acting and should help you feel better," Tim said as he positioned the device under Oliver's ear. It hissed loudly enough to make him jump and Oliver felt a brief sensation of pressure. As Tim moved away, Oliver rubbed his neck, but there was no discernible mark on his skin.

"I have been examining the sample in your transport case." Tim admitted, looking slightly sheepish. "I was curious as to why anyone would lock a case to their wrist. I thought things like that only happened in virtual reality movies. You're not a spy, are you?"

Oliver couldn't help but smile "No, I'm not a spy."

"Good. That would have been awkward. Please excuse the intrusion, but my speciality was diagnostic pathology. I have a bit of an interest in genetics in particular."

Oliver felt too tired to be annoyed. "Find anything interesting?"

"Yes, actually. I think I have."

Tim adjusted the bulky screen of the old microscope so that Oliver could see the image. "At first I thought this was a new species of invasive fungus. Then I ran it through an Ion sequencer, and I started to notice patterns. He pressed a few keys on a stained keyboard and the image rotated jerkily. "This is a DNA sequence from the Common Ink Cap mushroom. This part," the image flickered "is from Cordyceps I think. This is from some kind of Agaricus, I'm not sure which species," Tim crossed his arms over his chest thoughtfully. "This isn't a new fungus, it's the Frankenstein's monster of the plant kingdom. It's made from parts of other organisms that have been spliced together."

Oliver lent forward to get a better view of the sequences Tim was highlighting "My research student thought as much. I wanted to get a sample of the original source before we confirmed it."

Tim looked pensive. "That would certainly help, but this

is what really captured my attention." He hesitated before bringing up another image. The old machine whirred and clicked as the focus changed. "I recognise this pattern. I saw it a long time ago, when I was a junior doctor."

Oliver frowned at the concern in the young man's voice. "What do you see?" he asked.

Tim leant against the small desk. "After medical school, I did a year at Capital hospital." He began uncertainly "I spent a while working in emergency medicine with an amazing mentor, one of the best doctors around.

"One night we were on shift and an army transport turned up with about a dozen soldiers onboard. They were all wrapped in some kind of bioplastic and we were told to isolate them and use top level infection control. We managed to stabilise them, no small task I can tell you, but their condition deteriorated overnight.

"My mentor was a real, once in a generation genius. She tracked down the problem to a viral pathogen. It was aggressive, I've never seen anything like it, before or since. It tore apart cells and rewrote their DNA at a shocking rate. The soldiers were literally disintegrating before our eyes," Tim's face was pained and haunted.

"The hospital tried to keep us juniors out of it, but my interest has always been pathology, and my mentor thought I had promise. She let me work with her."

"You think this sequence is from that virus?" Oliver asked, shocked.

"I am certain of it," Tim met Oliver's eyes steadily. "I am also certain that the virus was not natural. I think it was a weapon."

"A weapon?" Oliver rocked back into his chair as the implications of that statement sunk in. "Why would anyone develop a biological weapon? The cities have been at peace for over a hundred years. Humanity has bigger things to worry about than petty territorial feuds."

Tim narrowed his lips "If I have learnt anything from

working for the government, it's that they always have a plan B."

Oliver felt his eyes widen as he grasped what Tim was suggesting. "You think our own government would develop a secret bioweapon?"

Tim shrugged "Global population growth has always been the elephant in the room. It's the one topic everyone is too afraid to talk about. It's an ethical minefield. It would be political suicide to meddle with people's rights to have children."

Tim leaned back against the workbench. "Since the Rush we have managed to outrun disaster. Advances in technology have led to clean energy, synthetic proteins, improvements in agriculture and distribution. Nevertheless, the damage is already done, the carbon in our atmosphere isn't going anywhere for a few millennia at least. What do we do when we can't run fast enough anymore?"

Oliver was horrified. "You can't be seriously suggesting this virus is the council's plan B?"

"No, I don't think I am suggesting that. However, it might be their plan of last resort. A pandemic would be a convenient way of keeping population numbers in check."

"I don't believe that," Oliver replied vehemently. "The argument for artificial population control is a very old one, and it's very flawed. People didn't cause climate change. An unsustainable economy did. Blaming an increasing population for climate change is like blaming the number of glaciers for the rise in sea levels, or the number of trees for wildfires."

Oliver paused, gathering his thoughts. "Population growth reached its peak in the 1960s but the number of people in poverty and starvation continued to decrease right up until the Rush. Since then, technology has adapted. We learnt from our mistakes."

Tim shook his head. "Have we really learnt anything? Population numbers have recovered. Indeed, they are starting to increase again. We are still losing arable land to soil erosion and water stress. At some point we won't be able to run fast enough to keep up with the problems we have created. Don't you think radical options are being considered?"

Oliver opened his mouth to answer, to deny the theory as hokum, the paranoid delusions of a bitter man cast out from society. But the denial wouldn't materialise. It hung before him, a gossamer shadow without form or substance.

"The question I can't answer though," Tim said quietly, "is how that viral sequence got into your fungus."

"The fungus was a mistake. We were running a project to design a new plant hybrid, to extend the growing range into areas currently uninhabitable due to water stress. The project was being run by an artificial intelligence. It created a synthetic chimera to use as a host for hybridising food crops. We think somehow pollen from the host plant escaped and created a hybrid with an existing fungus."

Tim whistled between his teeth, "A synthetic chimera? Impressive. I am not sure this is as synthetic as you think though. It's more like a genetic patchwork quilt. If I spent enough time looking at this, I am sure I could identify dozens of species all sewn together," He paused thoughtfully. "How would your AI have access to a government bioweapon?"

"From what I've seen so far, I think it would find a way to access anything it thought might be useful. It's utterly relentless. It has no morale code, no interest in anything outside of its own goals. In many ways it behaves like a small child, willing to bash through the cupboard door to get to the cookie jar."

Tim nodded. "So, the virus would be a useful tool. It's ability to quickly replicate and modify DNA would be... efficient?"

"That's my guess," Oliver agreed. "One other thing. This fungus is using bee colonies to spread its spores. We are seeing widespread colony collapse."

Tim shook his head "Ironic isn't it? It seems like all of today's problems are caused by yesterday's solutions."

Oliver smiled sadly "It does feel that way. But we have no choice. To use your analogy, we need to keep running. To pass the baton from generation to generation."

"Sometimes," Tim said, staring forlornly at the floor in front of him, "I wonder if we have lost the right to keep doing that."

△△△

Several hours after ditching the city dweller with Tim, Rose limped after Jack. She was pleased to be back doing something useful. Jack led her to the centre of the vast underground hall dominated by thick, industrial pipework. The pipes twisted around each other like a nest of vipers before rearing up and disappearing into the gloom above. The original purpose of the mass of tubing was long forgotten, but the large space was at the heart of the tunnel system. The community called it "the reclamation yard" and today it was unusually busy.

Jack hopped around the wreckage of Oliver's pod excitedly. He bent to pick up a small circuit board and squinted at it myopically before handing it to Rose. "That's the Nano-controller for the navigation system. Useful if it still works," he said with a wide grin. Rose placed it carefully in the wire basket she had slung over one arm.

Jack flapped his hands rapidly. It was a gesture Rose had come to associate with overexcitement. To prove the point, he darted off among the wreckage, his head bent low, like a bloodhound on the scent. She sighed and followed him, carefully weaving between the mass of debris.

Away from the centre of the hall men and woman worked at benches. Rose's periphery vision was blinded by the bright light from their welding torches. The sound of their industry boomed around the cavern. Each hammer stroke echoed from the stone walls, a strangely metred rhythm that faded with each beat.

Somewhere to Rose's left the mechanical clatter was

interrupted by a loud cheer. A small engine was slowly humming into life as a group of excited workers celebrated their success with back claps and high-fives. Rose smiled at their achievement. The engine would fetch a pretty penny on the black market.

Further on, a dark-haired woman was busy tearing the seating from the pod's ruined interior. A smear of blood stained the smooth white fabric. The woman sponged it off nonchalantly before dragging the bench seat towards a roughly made tubular frame. A part of Rose was disturbed by the casual disregard of another's ill-fortune, but she understood necessity as well as anyone. The woman wouldn't be chilled by the cold floor tonight.

"Here, it's here!" Jake flapped his hands again. He reached into the wreckage and retrieved a large black sphere. "This is what I've b...b...been looking for. It looks intact," he pulled down one corner of his eye, squinting to improve his impaired vision.

"What have you found, Jack?" Rose asked, trying to force some enthusiasm into her voice.

"This is the transponder unit. It links this pod to the city VTAS"

"VTAS?"

"The Vehicle Tracking and Automation System. It's a part of the Hub. It routes all the city traffic, ensures that pods and trains arrive on time and don't crash into each other."

"What do you want with that?" She asked, rubbing at her aching calf muscles.

"I can use it to access the system. You see, every device has a unique address. It's assigned when the hardware is manufactured. Like an old-fashioned MAC address, but at the quantum level," Rose nodded. She had no idea what Jack was talking about, but she knew admitting that would only prolong the agony of technical jargon.

"Access to the system is limited to a set of named addresses, we call it whitelisting. It's virtually impossible to fake an address, but even if you could, you wouldn't know if you were faking a washing machine or a smoke alarm, neither of which would be whitelisted. With this I know I have a valid pod address. Do you see?" Rose didn't.

"If I can make this work," Jack explained slowly, "we will have access to all of the city routing. We'll know what is going where and when."

"So, we'll know which trains have the supplies we need?"

"Exactly," the little man smiled up at her, his eyes magnified by his thick lens. She had to admit, access to the tracking system would be a massive boon to the community. She felt a little of his enthusiasm rub off on her. "Let's get back to my workshop, I need to test this," Jack said, before snatching the basket out of her hands and tearing off towards one of the tunnel entrances. Rose shuffled after him, cursing her sore feet and damaged hip.

It was late afternoon, and the tunnel was busy with people returning home. A group of young women giggled together, pretending not to notice the attention of the young men that smiled as they passed. Rose wondered when she had become so invisible. In her youth she had been considered attractive. Her long hair had glistened in the sun, its lustre unblemished by age or hardship. Men had watched her then, following the curves of her waist with admiring eyes. Now those eyes skipped over her. It was as if she had ceased to exist.

"Hello lass," A booming voice came from behind.

"I could smell you from halfway down the tunnel, Connor," she made a show of waving her hand in front of her nose.

"Well, that's not at all nice," he replied, feigning hurt as he sniffed theatrically at the rags of his old coat. "I had a bath only the other week, I did."

"Did you wash your clothes too?"

"Well, no, I wouldn't want to deny you the benefit of me manly odour," he grinned a lopsided smile.

"What do you want Connor?" She asked, half amused,

half irritated.

"I was just wondering if you cared to join me for dinner. I caught a rabbit earlier and if there is one thing I know, it's how to make a fine stew."

"I'm sure your mother would be proud."

"Oh no, she was a terrible cook. That woman could burn water."

Rose laughed despite herself. She cast a glance at Jack as he disappeared around a curve in the tunnel. He wouldn't miss her, she reasoned, not with so many new toys to play with. At any rate, she had to admit, she was hungry.

"Alright Connor, I'll eat with you," he offered her his arm gallantly and she took it with a girlish giggle.

Connor led them away from the main tunnels and through a narrow gap in the carved rock wall. The opening was tight, and Rose had to turn sideways to squeeze through. Beyond it was a wider crack through the natural rock. "Where are you taking me, you old degenerate?" She asked, as he helped her over the rough path.

"Ah well, that would be telling." It was very dark in the narrow crevice and Connor clicked on a small torch. "Watch your footing here, it's a bit slippery," he said, taking her hand and guiding her over the rocky floor.

Soon enough the space began to open out. Rose could see the glow of firelight ahead and smell cooking food on the still air. Connor clicked off the torch and led her towards the light. The breath caught in her throat.

They were in a natural cavern. It was partially flooded, and Connor had placed a myriad of small candles around the underground lake. The water was a startling shade of blue and the candles shone in the still surface, creating pools of turquois in the shallows.

Stalactites grew down from the low ceiling, seeming to meet their own reflections in the water. The centre of the lake was dominated by a large stalagmite. It rose like a fairytale castle, an island of soaring towers and delicate spires.

Connor drew her towards the fire. It glowed warmly, creating a pool of welcoming light. A large black pot bubbled over it, steaming gently with a rich odour of herbs and meat. He had laid out thick furs and cushions on the flat rocks by the fire and chunky stoneware plates waited to be filled.

She looked over at the ragged man, humbled and surprised. She felt like a teenager, giddy and exposed. Her previous relationships had been short, intense affairs. Mining was not a career that allowed for any kind of permanence. Crews came and went, as fickle as space dust. Since the accident, Rose hadn't allowed herself to grow close to anyone. After all, who would want her? She was damaged goods, surplus to requirements.

Connor met her eyes nervously, his face flushed and embarrassed. "What do you think?" He asked.

"It's magical," she answered honestly.

He grinned at her, looking relieved. "I found this place a while ago. I was looking for mushrooms in the caves. When I stumbled on this, I thought I'd picked the wrong type of mushroom," he laughed nervously.

"It's beautiful Connor."

He waved his hand. "Ack, come and take a seat. I didn't spend all day cooking just to have you gawp, now." Rose smiled and joined him on the cushions, her hip complained as she lowered herself inelegantly to the ground. Connor ladled the steaming stew onto the waiting plates and tore off a hunk of bread

She took a bite and her eyes widened in appreciation. The stew was dark and rich, balanced with sweet herbs. "It's delicious" she said, genuinely surprised.

"I told you I could cook. I am not the complete eejit you think I am."

Rose grinned. There was something disarmingly charming about Connor. A vulnerability she had failed to see before. Somehow it made her own insecurities fade away. "You are full of unexpected surprises."

He winked at her. "That I am, love. That I am."

They ate the meal in companionable silence, watching as the candlelight danced on the still waters of the lake. As Rose mopped the last drop of gravy, she turned to the grizzled man beside her. "What do you want from this, Connor?" she asked, meeting his dark eyes in the flickering firelight.

He paused for a moment, his face serious and thoughtful. "I'm getting too old to face the cold alone, Rose. I've had my life, seen more than most, more than I should have," a shadow of old memory passed over his face. "I don't feel part of this world anymore. It's moving too fast," he paused, his eyes distant. "I think I just want someone who remembers the way things were, who can join me in my exile in this foreign country."

"A companion?"

"Yes, and perhaps more."

Rose nodded "I think I want that too." He smiled and tentatively reached out a hand. She took it gently, wrapping her fingers around his. Together they watched as the candles flickered and died.

CHAPTER 14

Laura watched as Hugo's pod rotated on its axis and descended slowly behind the trees. She set off towards it, her heavy boots crunching through the dry leaves. The mouthfuls of toast she had forced down at breakfast churned uncomfortably in in her stomach. Despite the evidence to the contrary, Laura still hoped she was overreacting. Oliver would turn up at the apartment, covered in mud and showing off some rare woodland orchid. She pictured them sat around his kitchen table, sharing a bottle of wine and laughing at her overactive imagination. "Dead?" he would ask with a lopsided grin "Is this about the mark I gave your last piece of coursework?"

As much as she wanted to believe it, she couldn't. Implants didn't just fail, pods didn't disappear, and engines certainly didn't materialise in trees. Her mind jumped to the other extreme. Oliver was dead. His broken body hanging limply from the high branches of a tree. Laura scrubbed at the tears that threatened to run down her cheeks. No, that wasn't helpful either. Identify, analyse and infer. She wiped her nose on her sleeve and pushed through the thick bracken.

By the time she reached the clearing, Hugo was already walking to meet her.

"What did you find?" he asked. Laura didn't think she had ever seen him look so worried.

"Something definitely came down here. There are broken tree branches everywhere and signs of a fire. I found scraps of poly-carbon spread in a fairly big circle."

"No pod or ..." he hesitated as if afraid of the answer, "body?"

"No, but there are footprints and drag marks heading east."

Hugo let out the breath. "Let's go then." He set off quickly, his long legs setting a punishing pace. Laura had to jog to keep up.

They picked up the trail of broken poly-carbon just east of the tall trees. As they cleared the dense canopy, Laura felt a brief moment of disorientation. The woodland had seemed so wild and unmanaged under the canopy. The Douglas fir indomitable; the oak resolute and ageless. But the trees only existed in an oasis, a permitted respite between the vast urban giants. In the open grasslands the complexes rose around them, a towering testament to humanity's dominance.

"Do you know where you are going?" she asked breathlessly as Hugo pushed ahead.

"I have an idea, well, a hope really."

"Would you care to elaborate?"

"There is an abandoned tunnel entrance near here. The bits of broken poly-carbon were heading in that direction."

"You think that bunch outside the courthouse picked Oliver up?" Hope uncurled inside her like a budding leaf.

"Honestly Laura, I don't know. I just can't bring myself to contemplate the alternative."

Hugo led them unerringly towards a small gully. At the bottom, a dark entrance was secured with thick metal bars. Hugo slid down the grassy bank and stood before the gateway. Gingerly, he reached out to rattle the bars. His eyebrows rose in surprise and Laura watched as the bars swung open on what she assumed were concealed hinges. Hugo glanced up at her questioningly and she nodded, jumping down into the gulch beside him.

"I don't suppose you brought a torch?" She asked as they crept slowly into the dark, circular tunnel. He reached into his jacket pocket and took out his ubiquitous text. He flicked it on, and the dark receded a few feet. She copied him, feeling slightly stupid for not having thought of it. Together they strode into the subterranean darkness.

After a few metres Laura felt the ground start to slope downwards. From somewhere in the distance the sound of running water broke the tomb-like silence. "Some kind of drainage?" She asked.

"More likely outflow from the condensing heat exchangers."

"Why would they have left the heat exchangers here? These tunnels were abandoned years ago."

"Cheaper to leave them than remove them, I suppose."

The further along the tunnel they progressed, the colder it became. Laura started to shiver in the dank air. The sweat, which had seeped into her shirt during the short hike, now felt like icy needles against her back.

The light from her text reflected from the frost crystals that clung to the smooth walls. They sparkled like mica as she moved the light across them. "Pretty," she commented.

"Humm," Hugo replied, his eyes set on the tunnel ahead.

After several minutes of silent exploration, they reached a junction in the tunnel system. Laura turned around to get her bearings. The entrance was now slightly above her, a small circle of light in the pervasive gloom.

Hugo flicked through some menus on his text. "The temperature drop is greater to the left. I suggest we go that way."

"Oh good, colder."

"I thought you liked the pretty ice?" he started to shrug out of his jacket, but she stopped him with a raised hand.

"This isn't the twentieth century Hugo, keep your jacket." He shrugged and pulled it tighter around his shoulders.

The left tunnel sloped down much more steeply, and Laura had to keep one hand on the wall to stop herself from slipping on the icy floor. The deeply ridged hiking boots, that had proven so adept in the woodland, now became a hindrance. Every step they slipped slightly, sending her off balance.

"The water is getting louder," Hugo said, surefooted and confident in the narrow tunnel. They moved steadily downwards. The further they went, the more the rock above Laura's head seemed to press down on her. It felt confining, like the time she had woken up tangled in her sheets. She wasn't sure if it was the darkness or some instinctive fear of getting trapped, but her nerves jangled like a windchime in a summer breeze. All the while the sound of rushing water grew louder, swelling to a thunderous crescendo. It hissed and roared like a ferocious animal, bouncing off the walls until it seemed to come from every direction at once.

Finally, the light from their texts lit a circular opening up ahead. The air seemed to move differently, as if the space beyond was much larger. Laura swallowed apprehensively. Hugo pressed ahead, his breath misting in the cold air. He moved with an agile grace. His lean body perfectly balanced on the balls of his feet. Laura felt clumsy by comparison, her feet slipping and sliding on the icy floor. If they had to run, she had no doubt who would make it the surface first.

The tunnel ended in a small metal inspection platform. It hung above a fastmoving torrent of white capped water. The deluge boiled and seethed below them, shaking the small platform with the force of its passing. "Wow," Laura said, enthralled by the power of the surging water. Spray flew around them, settling on their cheeks and arms like morning dew. "Dead end?" she asked.

"Not quite," Hugo said, pointing to a narrow walkway that clung to the rocks beside the fast-flowing culvert.

"No way!" Laura watched as white water shot between the gaps in the metal latticework.

"You don't need to come," Hugo said smoothly, "Find your way back to the surface and let my team know where we are."

Laura stared at him. The smug tone was starting to grate on her. She wondered how Oliver tolerated it. "If you are doing this, so am I." To prove the point, she lowered herself down the small ladder on the side of the inspection platform. She tried to look confident. She would hate for Hugo to know how scared she was of the roaring, surging water. Stepping out onto the narrow walkway she froze for a moment, trying to get her balance. There were no railings, and the only handholds were the slimy, moss-covered wall.

She heard Hugo sigh loudly and follow her down. Laura took a few slow steps on the catwalk. It was slippery, but it held their weight without protest. Spray leapt up at her as she made her way along the wall. Below her, smooth rocks jutted out into the water, creating whirlpools which hissed ominously as she passed. Someway ahead a ladder rose up. Laura couldn't see where it led to in the gloom, but she tried to keep her eyes locked on it, rather than on the swirling water below.

She had almost reached the ladder when her foot gave way from under her. In panic she reached out to grab the wall, but her fingers slid off the wet rock. Something grabbed her wrist tightly. For one terrifying moment she hung, suspended above the churning water. Hugo's frightened face stared down at her. She watched helplessly as his feet slid inexorably towards the edge. Suddenly, they were both swept into the freezing water. She lost her grip on the text and it flew away in the current. The darkness pressed in as the shock of icy water closed over her head.

Laura kicked to the surface, gasping for air. The freezing water rushed around her, invisible in the near perfect dark. It roared and hissed in her ears, a terrible wall of noise that flooded her senses. She struggled to time her breathing, unable to see the surges and eddies which crashed over her.

Laura forced herself to snatch a breath whenever she felt air on her face, but the water was fast and unpredictable. It flooded her mouth and nose, forcing her to cough and choke.

She kicked hard towards where she thought the rocky bank was, but the current was too strong, it pulled at her clothing and sucked at her heavy boots.

Her hands flailed for anything solid, but they were numb with cold. The freezing water seemed to suck the strength from her limbs. Panic gripped her. This is it, she thought, this is how I am going to die. Hopelessness closed over her, bleaker than the surging water, more terrifying than the dark. Then her foot hit something under the water and pain shot up her leg. She kicked against it and shot back to the surface, her lungs burning.

Ahead, a tiny light brightened a small area of the rocky wall. The currents spun her around, and for a dizzying moment she lost sight of it. As she tumbled, she saw it again. It was mounted above a small metal door. Summoning all her strength she lunged towards the light. Her feet bounced against the bottom as she spun and pushed with her thighs, straining with the last of her strength.

She started to make progress against the current, the light growing larger, the brightness more distinct. Then the water surged over her head, the current tipping her onto her back. Her mouth and nose filled with water. Choking and suffocating, she clawed for the surface. The light fractured against the underside of the torrent, spreading out like shattered glass. It seemed distant and dreamlike. She reached for it desperately, almost mindless with terror.

Her hearing dulled as the water consumed her, the terrifying roar fading to a muted swirling of bubbles. Her lungs burned, and her chest convulsed as she instinctively gulped for air. Laura fought the urge to breathe. She knew that drawing in the water would be the end of her. As she thrashed towards the light it began to grow dimmer and more distant. Despair tugged at her and with it came a strange, numbing calmness. *Give in*, it seemed to whisper, *just breathe, make the pain go away*. No. No. No. Laura fought with the last of her strength. She kicked desperately for the surface. Suddenly, her head bobbed above the churning water. Laura snatched a breath. Then another, and another. Slowly the pain faded, and her mind began to clear. She caught a final glimpse of the light. It rushed past like a speeding train, leaving her alone in the dark.

She couldn't feel her legs anymore. They had gone completely numb. The water pulled her down again, as if trying to claim her for itself. *Give in,* despair whispered seductively, *it will all be over soon. Just rest.* Laura growled her defiance. She was not going to die here. No. Suddenly, her hand brushed against something hard and rough. She grasped at it with nerveless hands. Somehow, she managed to pull her body towards it. The water tore around her, screaming its rage in a deep thunderous howl.

With a strength drawn from sheer determination she managed to swing her nerveless legs out of the current. She wrapped her arms around the rock and clung on, spent and shivering. The panic started to recede, and the logical part of her mind kicked back into gear. I must get out of the water, she thought. If I stay here, I'll freeze. As she summoned the last of her strength something soft brushed past her. It nudged up against her back, limp and cold. She reached out a hand and caught wet fabric in her grip. *Hugo,* she thought. The jolt of recognition sent energy surging into her exhausted muscles.

Laura pulled his limp body towards her, one hand tangled in the sopping fabric of his jacket, the other pulling towards the rocky shore. This part of the culvert wasn't deep. In the sheltered water she was able to stand easily, the water barely reaching her chest. With the last of her energy, she heaved them both towards the edge.

The rocks against the channel wall were narrow, but flat. She dragged Hugo onto them, feeling her way in the darkness. She tried to feel if he was breathing, but her fingers were numb and trembling and she couldn't trust them. She settled for loosening the collar of his shirt.

Laura shivered violently, her teeth rattling in her head.

The wet rocks seemed to draw out the last of her body heat. "We're not going to last long if we stay here Hugo, you need to wake up." She couldn't see him clearly in the gloom, he was little more than a shadow against the uneven rocks. She shook him roughly and was relieved when she heard him moan.

His body spasmed with a deep, wracking cough and water shot from his mouth. Laura did her best to support him as he gasped and retched. Eventually the cough subsided. "Urgh," he moaned as he struggled to sit up, still coughing water. "Have I gone blind or is it just *really* dark."

"Dark, I hope."

"I think I hit my head. Ouch, definitely hit my head."

"We can't stay here, Hugo. I saw a door a little way back, there was a small light over it."

"Alright, I think I can move." He hesitated briefly, before reaching out an uncertain hand to touch her arm "Laura? I think you might have just saved my life. Thank you."

Laura blinked, unsure what to say. "You're welcome." she tried, but the words felt hollow and insincere. She didn't feel like she had done anything that deserved the humility in Hugo's voice. She had acted purely instinctively. "Anyone would have done the same," she said.

They felt their way in the darkness. Laura followed the line of the wall with one hand. She moved slowly so as not to trip on the gaps between the rocks. Soon the darkness began to lift slightly. The curved shape of the tunnel slowly materialised out of the blackness.

"There's the door," Laura said, pointing up at what looked like an oval inspection hatch set at the top of a small ladder.

"One small problem. It's the other side of the channel and I think I've had enough of white-water potholing for one day. I doubt it will catch on as an extreme sport."

Laura glanced back at Hugo and saw that an angry red lump had risen on his forehead. "If we move further upstream and swim perpendicular to the current, we might make it to those rocks." Laura pointed to where some boulders had fallen into the channel, creating a sheltered area in the raging deluge.

"We could follow the channel upstream and see if there is a better place to cross?"

"In the pitch black?"

"Good point. Drown in the light or freeze in the dark. You take me to all the best places."

"That door has to go somewhere, and anywhere has to be better than here."

"Also, a good point."

Together, they walked slowly upstream. "Here?" Hugo asked, trying to judge the speed of the current.

"Only one way to find out."

Laura took off her boots and carefully tied the laces to her belt loops. Hugo stuck his pointed slip-on shoes inside his shirt and nodded. "Don't try to stay on your feet." he told her "Get on your front and swim with the current."

They waded back into the freezing water tentatively. Immediately, the current swept Laura's feet out from under her. The icy cold stole her breath and she struggled to flip onto her stomach and kick for the opposite shore.

Despite the cold, it was easier this time. Without her heavy boots she was much more buoyant and there was enough light to time her breathing. The bend in the tunnel took her towards the calm pool behind the rocks. She grabbed for them and swung herself into the shallows, Hugo close behind.

They dragged themselves out of the water. Flopping onto the rocks like stranded jelly fish. "That might have been fun in other circumstances," Hugo said between clattering teeth.

"I can't think of any circumstances under which that would have been fun." Laura wrapped her arms around herself.

"Wet suit, buoyancy aid, maybe a raft?"

"I'd rather a cosy restaurant with a decent wine list."

"Umm wine. What I wouldn't do for a mug of glühwein

right now." Hugo started to climb the ladder. Laura waited until he reached the top before following him up.

The door had once been yellow. A few flakes of paint still clung to it, creating an irregular, rusty, camouflage pattern. A large handle stuck out horizontally. Laura took hold of it firmly. The paint and rust felt gritty under her hand. She pressed down with her entire body weight, but it wouldn't budge.

"Here, let's try together." Hugo said, moving up beside her on the narrow platform.

They gripped the handle together and pushed. Slowly it moved, groaning like a wounded animal. The door swung open onto another dark, freezing tunnel. Laura cursed loudly. "What did you expect? A secret entrance to Chateau Rouge?" Hugo said. He moved into the gloom with characteristic confidence.

The tunnel slopped gently upwards. Within minutes, the light had faded and a blanket of darkness descended to smother them. "So cold" Laura stuttered. Her legs were starting to feel unsteady and large green splashes chased each other across her vision.

"Keep moving, so long as we keep climbing, we should find a way out."

"Not sure how much longer I can keep this up," Laura panted. She was starting to feel uncoordinated, as if her legs belonged to someone else.

"Talk to me. How did you meet Amy?" Hugo asked, his voice stuttering as the cold dug in.

"In the park on top of our complex. There is an open-air theatre. Amy was in a production of The King and I, playing Lady Thiang. She was so beautiful, almost ethereal. When she sang "Something Wonderful", I cried."

"She's an actor?"

"Yes. Musical theatre is her passion."

"It was love at first sight then?"

"For me, yes. For her, not so much. I had to chase her. I

went to every performance and brought her flowers after the show. One night it rained, one of those summer storms, sort of warm and wistful. I was soaked by the time she came out. She recognised me by then, and she offered to buy me a coffee. I think she felt a little sorry for me. We huddled together under her umbrella and ran through the park to a little café, splashing through the puddles like children. That was one of the best nights of my life."

"Chasing her was worth it?"

"So worth it." Laura smiled in the dark. The thought of Amy gave her a burst of strength and hope. She resolved that freezing in a murky tunnel was not an option.

Time passed in a haze of ice and rock. There was only the dark, the cold and the sound of Hugo's breathing. Laura found herself hanging onto every echo in the dark tunnel. It was as if sound was the only way to know she was truly alive, and not lost in some dark underworld, spat out by the river Styx.

When the sound of muted voices floated to her on the still air, Laura stopped dead. "Did you hear that?" She asked, reaching behind her to stop Hugo.

"Hear what?" he whispered.

"Shh!"

Laura crept forward slowly, letting the distant sound guide her. Soon the whisper of conversation and laughter echoed along the rocky walls. Laura stumbled toward the comforting, human sounds. The tunnel wall curved sharply left. As she rounded the corner she was blinded by a wall of dazzling light.

The sound of conversation suddenly stopped. As her eyes began to adjust, Laura could see she had spilled out onto a small chamber. Helium lanterns lined the walls, casting a dirty light which dulled everything to a grubby grey. The walls were smooth, scored with marks from heavy machinery. They looked like they had been bored out of the natural stone.

A group of people, dressed in heavy clothing, sat around a large fire in the middle of the room. Every face was turned towards her. A man, his hair greying at the temples, climbed to his feet. His face was long and thin, the stubble trimmed neatly into a short goatee beard. "Who are you? Where did you come from?" he asked. There was no hostility in his voice, just surprise and curiosity.

"My name is Hugo Chadwick. This is Laura Fleisher. We are looking for my brother. We think his pod might have crashed near here."

Hugo's voice was steadier than it had any right to be, Laura thought. One side of his forehead looked like an archery target. The circular blue bruise highlighted by the raised red welt. Water ran from his sodden clothes, forming a liquid shadow that seeped towards the firelight. His arms were held rigidly against his chest, he back bent forward against the trembling that shook his tall frame.

"And you decided to take a swim?" the greying man asked, his eyes sweeping the shivering intruders.

"We got lost." Hugo answered simply.

"Then you had better warm yourselves by the fire." The man turned to one of his companions "See if you can find Tim." The shorter man nodded and shuffled off into the gloom.

Laura and Hugo took their places at the fire gratefully, wringing the water from their clothes and hair. A short while later the messenger returned with a rotund man. His body was soft, but his eyes were sharp and quick. The others moved out of his way deferentially. Laura got the impression that not much got past those clever eyes.

"I'm Tim Ashby. Welcome to the tunnels." The voice was an odd mixture of gentleness and authority. Somehow Laura found herself instantly trusting him. "You must be Hugo Chadwick, the brother. And you are Laura, the student?" He held out his hand to shake. It was an old-fashioned gesture, and Laura smiled as she took it. His hand was warm despite the biting cold and his smile was open and sincere.

"Is Oliver here? Do you have him?" Hugo asked. Laura was surprised by the emotion behind question. Hugo's usual charm seemed to have collapsed under the weight of his worry.

A smaller figure detached itself from the shadows and stepped into the firelight. "Well, you took your time getting here." A familiar voice drawled. The Midlands accent sounded gruff.

It took Laura a second to recognise Oliver, wrapped as he was, in the same shapeless clothing as the other tunnel residents. Hugo had no such problem. He leapt across the room and swept his brother into a crushing bear hug.

"Ow! Watch my ribs. Urgh, you're wet."

"I thought you were dead."

"I nearly was, I still might be if you don't put me down. Ouch. You smell like a wet dog, what have you been doing?"

"White water potholing, it's my new least favourite sport."

Oliver eyed the large bump on his brother's head "Do you get points for how many rocks you hit on the way down?"

"What's your excuse? You look worse than that time you stood up to Arty Spencer in science class."

"Arty and I had a minor disagreement over the correct concentration of sulphuric acid, that's all."

"We found you tied to a tree, Oliver. He'd melted your shoes."

Tim watched the reunion with an amused smile. He turned to Laura, "Are they always like this?"

"No, usually they're far worse."

"We need to head back to my clinic, there is something I need to show you."

△△△

Laura looked at the results from the Ion sequencer with a mixture of dismay and satisfaction. "I told you it was a Frankenstein plant."

"I never doubted you. The problem is that this sample has been exposed to the environment. We have no idea where, or how, it picked up these genetic sequences. We need proof this is from the host plant." Oliver said thoughtfully.

"We need to get into the test unit." Laura pulled at the unfamiliar clothing, it was coarse and itchy.

"Yes, we do." Oliver agreed "We also know that Ekta now has two good reasons to keep us out. Firstly, to ensure knowledge of the virus this is based on doesn't become public. If it really was some grand government conspiracy," Oliver shot a look at Tim, "then Ekta will be desperate to keep it secret."

"The electorate do tend to react quite badly to rumours of genocide." Tim said.

"Secondly, Ekta seems desperate to keep the project going regardless of the risks. I get the impression there is more to this than just her ambition." Oliver folded his arms across his chest.

"She's afraid. She hides it well behind all that bluster, but I saw it when we spoke. The people funding this project are not the type you would want to cross." Hugo said.

"Without Ekta's help we are going to have to break in somehow. But without damaging the biohazard containment." Laura said.

Jack looked up from his perch in the corner of the small clinic. "I th… th… think I have an idea of how to do that." Laura turned in surprise, she hadn't even realised the small man was there.

Tim looked up from the cold compress he was holding against the bump on Hugo's head. "You always do, Jack," he smiled. The small man grinned at the compliment, his eyes shining mischievously.

CHAPTER 15

J ack had balanced the black sphere on the mouth of an old flower vase. The cut crystal sparkled in the dim lighting of his cluttered workshop, throwing splinters of coloured light across the low ceiling like a disco ball. Oliver thought the vase would have been quite beautiful, if hadn't been for the jagged crack that distorted the intricate leaf motif.

Hugo sat next to the small technician, perched uncomfortably on the edge of a hard stool. Oliver was amused to see that the tip of his tongue peeped from the corner of his mouth. It was a habit their mother had shared. Oliver could clearly see her features in the sharp line of Hugo's jaw and the colour of his thick hair. He wondered if that resemblance was part of the reason Hugo had always been their father's favourite. Or perhaps it was just that Oliver had always preferred the peace of his books to the exhausting business trips that Hugo had clambered to join.

Oliver leaned against the cluttered table in the centre of the room. He watched as the two technologists shared a rapid, and mostly unintelligible discussion, before setting about stripping the outer shielding from the football shaped object.

"What is it you are planning to do, exactly?" Oliver asked.

"The agricultural unit isn't self-contained." Hugo explained patiently, flipping up the magnifying lens that covered his left eye. "Amanda needs a regular supply of various things. Hydroponic chemicals, lighting elements, replacement filters, everything you need to run an arable farm."

"I know," Oliver said. "Part of my role was to check the manifests."

"Well, with this device," Hugo tapped the black sphere with a thin probe, "Jack will be able to access the city transport system. We can use it to intercept the next heavy goods pod that is scheduled to deliver to the unit."

"You plan to sneak something in with the regular deliveries?"

"Not quite. We are planning to sneak *someone* in."

Oliver blew air out of his cheeks. "Audacious, but that might work. How will you get them out again?"

"Ahh, well, we're still working on that," Hugo smiled sheepishly.

Oliver watched as the two men patiently stripped the plating from the sphere. Inside was a mesh of wires and tubes that wrapped around a small golden cylinder. A glowing blue liquid flowed through the tubes, softly pulsating in the dull lighting.

"Well, the coolant is intact and the casing around the quantum core doesn't look damaged," Hugo said as he carefully examined the cylinder with a penlight.

"I can't see an input on the qubit bus," Jack said. His voice was calm and confident. Oliver noticed that his stutter disappeared when he was absorbed by a problem.

"It must be built into the chip," Hugo suggested, leaning in close to the complex web of wires and circuits.

"We can't access that without interrupting the cooling. We'd melt the chip."

"Then we'll have to go through the front door. Pass me a needle drive, please."

Oliver felt oddly nostalgic as he watched his brother work. It reminded him of his teenage years. Their shared bedroom had become a kind of retreat. An escape from the adult world, where their father had slowly succumbed to illness. Flickering in and out like a candle in a draughty room.

The trickle of grief that had slowly eroded their mother had been evident even then. Dissolving her spirit, drop by corrosive drop.

In their room, the brothers had carefully maintained an oasis of normality. Somehow, they had found respite in each other's company. Oliver would read, absorbed in the natural world, while Hugo tinkered with indecipherable pieces of electronics. Oliver smiled at the memory. His brother had always been a master of the last-minute assignment. It was one of the ways they were so different. While Oliver would spend days meticulously researching a project, Hugo would wait until the day it was due, and then work through the night to finish it. He was the type of person who thrived on pressure. The man that bent over the sphere projected that same restless energy.

Oliver's thoughts were interrupted by Laura pulling aside the heavy curtain. She gestured for him to follow her into the tunnel. "I managed to contact Amy and Jamal. I let them know we were safe."

"Good, thank you. I am glad you made it to the surface without taking another bath."

"Hey, that wasn't my fault. Hugo led us down that tunnel."

"You didn't have to follow him."

"He can be very persuasive," she snapped back.

"That he can," Oliver smiled to let her know he was teasing. "Hugo has a plan to get us into the unit."

"Jamal has been working on that too. He wants us to meet him at the lab."

△△△

Laura summoned a pod from the tunnel entrance. Oliver watched as it homed in on his text, separating from the busy traffic and weaving slightly as it began a slow descent. He had lent the text to Laura earlier, joking that she would probably

253

find her own somewhere at the bottom of the North Atlantic.

The pod hovered a short distance away, its rotors flattening the tall grass in a good-sized crop circle. Oliver was surprised at how his body reacted to the familiar sight. His heart pounded and his palms felt hot and clammy. It landed with a slight bump and Oliver felt his breath catch in his throat. An image of spinning trees and shattered rotor blades filled his mind. He reached out a hand and steadied himself against the metal gate.

Are you coming?" Laura called, as the canopy slid open. Oliver took a faltering step forward. He felt hot and his legs were unsteady. Laura opened her mouth to hurry him, and then suddenly stopped, her eyes widening in understanding. "I am so sorry," she said. "I didn't think. Do you want to stay here? I can bring Jamal back."

Oliver pushed the quivering nausea aside and marched resolutely towards the pod. He felt Laura's eyes on him keenly. Her face was crunched up in concern. Somehow that made everything worse. He felt foolish. Why couldn't control the cold sweat that dripped down his down his back or the way his hands trembled as he slipped into the seat.

Laura reached across to the central control pad and programmed the pod to take them to the laboratory. Her fingers worked unconsciously, pressing the controls with mindless familiarity. As the pod began to lift Oliver's stomach rebelled, assaulting him with churning waves of queasiness. He forced his eyes to stay open and counted his breaths as Tim had taught him. Slowly, very slowly, the terror began to subside. In its place was an emotion Oliver was unaccustomed to. Elation.

As the pod soared over the city, speeding between the majestic spires and cascading green gardens, Oliver tried to rationalise his emotions. The fear was still there, it paced inside him like a caged animal, desperate to escape. But the fear was not his master. It was a part of him, as unavoidable as the blood that coursed through his veins. It was something to be conquered and controlled, not reviled or avoided.

Oliver had a sudden moment of clarity. Perhaps, by avoiding his fear, he had instead surrendered to it. Courage, he knew, was not being fearless, but knowing how to control those primal instincts; how to calculate risk and reward. It was rational to be afraid, but fear had to be a guide, not a tether.

"Are you alright?" Laura asked as the pod banked steeply.

"Yes, yes. I think I am." Oliver was surprised to find the words were true.

Jamal was waiting for them at the laboratory. His eyes widened with surprise as the two scientists bundled through the door. "I am glad you are both well, but really, what are you wearing?" His eyes were bright with humour.

Oliver looked down at his faded, tattered clothing. "It was more of a necessity than a fashion statement," he mumbled, slightly embarrassed.

"It suits you very badly. However, we have bigger concerns. The spread of the fungus is happening as we predicted. We must act now. We cannot wait for the council bureaucracy to run its course."

"I've reached the same conclusion. We won't be getting any help from the council." Oliver quickly explained the events of the last day.

Jamal shook his head in disbelief "Well, you have had quite the adventure."

"I am not sure that is how I would describe it. We have a plan for getting someone into the unit. What we don't have, is a way to get out with the sample."

Jamal stroked his dark beard "I may have an idea. Although, it is not without risk."

Laura snorted. "Nothing about this situation is without risk." She said darkly.

"Agreed," Jamal shrugged his wide shoulders, "but I warn you, you aren't going to like it."

△△△

Oliver squeezed himself into the tight packing box and silently wished he had eaten less for lunch. He had returned to the tunnels late in the afternoon, by which time Jack and Hugo were happily hacking the evening cargo manifest. They had huddled together like conspiring schoolboys, sniggering as they entered the record for an emergency pick-up; "Organic fertiliser (bovine), Lavender scented. 0.5 metric tons". Oliver decided it was best not to ask.

They had argued most of the day over who should go to the unit. Oliver had insisted that he was the only one qualified to take the sample, a statement which had been roundly disputed by both Laura and Hugo. Eventually they had settled on a compromise. Oliver could go, but only if accompanied by a large, and somewhat intimidating tunnel dweller, named Connor.

It was a compromise that Oliver was starting to regret. The man was a mountain of hard muscle. Cramped together in a metal packing crate his long, his ill-kept beard was pressed tightly against Oliver's left cheek. It was uncomfortably itchy.

Oliver was deeply relieved when he felt the vibrations of a heavy goods pod approaching. He peered through a hole in the crate as the large brown vehicle hung in the air. Its eight large rotors kicking up dust and grass in a blinding blizzard. Oliver was amazed that such a mammoth machine was able to fly. He had never seen one up close before. The elephantine cargo bay, that hung heavily beneath the rotors, was a truly impressive feat of engineering.

As the machine touched down, a loader robot exited through a sliding door. Oliver felt the thump of its metallic feet through the dry ground. It squatted to one side, resting on its arms, waiting patiently for instructions. Even in a crouch, the machine still towered over the small gathering of tunnel dwellers. Oliver was surprised to see that the group of outcasts regarded the imposing machine nonchalantly, as if such encounters were commonplace. He suspected his own expression was less indifferent, he found it quite terrifying.

Slowly the cloud of dust cleared, and two tunnel people approached the packing box. Connor had to tilt his head to one side as they carefully manoeuvred the lid into place. It slid home with a permanent sounding thud, leaving both of its occupants squeezed tightly together in the dark.

"Well, this is fun," Oliver said sarcastically, trying to ignore the unpleasant, musty odour that wafted from his companion.

"You have a strange idea of fun, lad. I can think of several people I'd rather be pressed up against in the dark. Now that lady from the news, she would make a fine bunkmate." The man chuckled. His beard bouncing up and down in time with the booming laugh.

The journey over the city was uneventful. Oliver peered through a small gap in the crate as the heavy vessel landed countless times, bumping up against the docking locks of industrial looking complexes. At one point it sunk underground into a vast complex of spinning conveyor belts and whizzing crates. The boom-boom of the loader became a familiar soundtrack. It lugged the heavy boxes with a mechanical hum, working tirelessly to some unseen plan.

"I never realised how busy the city is at night." He said to the bulky man that shared his confinement.

"I like the night, it's peaceful. Nothing but droids and drones minding their own business. You never hear of a drone sticking its nose in where it's not wanted." Connor said, his voice deep and resonant.

Oliver decided to ignore the tacit warning. He was eager to distract himself from the task ahead. He feared that his anxiety would tear itself free of his carefully constructed cage and shred his fragile courage. "Did you work at night? Before the tunnels?" he asked casually.

"None of your business." The bigger man rumbled,

leaving no room to doubt the conversation was over.

Oliver sighed and lapsed into a restless silence. It was hot in the packing box and the sour smell of his companion was a constant irritation. As the minutes dragged on, Oliver began to count the time between drop-offs.

"We haven't stopped for a while. I think we are over the provinces." He said after what felt like hours.

Connor grunted. "Once we get to the unit, I'll get out first. Once I'm sure it's safe we grab your sample and head for the exit. No heroics, just straight in and out as quickly as possible."

"I was at the briefing, you know," Oliver complained, slightly offended by the rough tone.

"From what Jack said, we have no idea how this computer thing is going to react. So just keep your head down and stick with me."

Oliver nodded his agreement, the gravity of what they were about to do was slowly sinking in. For the first time in his life, Oliver realised, he was about to face real physical danger. It was both terrifying and thrilling. He felt his breath quicken and his heart race as a heady blast of adrenaline made him grin like a mad man. At the same time, he wanted to run away and hide. Strangely it felt good, it felt like being alive.

As the pod landed with a soft thud, the footsteps of the loader grew louder. Once again, they were lifted and carried from the goods craft. The scientist could tell they had entered the unit because his ears popped. He suddenly felt grateful for Connor's reassuring bulk. The big man was coarse and gruff, but he had an air of solid competence, a directness that was oddly reassuring.

They waited silently for the footsteps of the loader to fade and vanish. After a moment, Oliver felt Connor push upwards, his broad shoulders straining against the metal lid. It cracked open and light poured in. Oliver took a deep breath. The air was hot and humid. It smelt strongly of tomatoes. A warm, summer smell that seemed strange after the bitter smell of the packing crate. The buzzing sound of pollinators competed with the soft hum of air conditioning pumps. Despite the impending danger, it felt like home, just another day at the office.

Oliver's companion pulled himself up and vaulted out of the box. He moved with a powerful agility, a coiled spring of controlled energy. Oliver huddled miserably at the bottom of the box, waiting for the all-clear. A familiar sense of worthlessness swept over him. He quickly pushed it aside.

"Well, this is the biggest fecking greenhouse I've ever seen," Connor's voice boomed from nearby. "You're up, Doc." A face appeared above him, and Oliver let himself be hauled ungracefully from the packing box.

The research unit was exactly as Oliver remembered it. Tall plants grew from stacked shelves of purple hydroponics fluid. The uppermost levels were almost touching the distant ceiling. The plants nearest to them were tomato. The boughs of the glossy green shrubs were laden with bright red fruits. Small droids moved between them, tirelessly harvesting, pruning and testing.

Oliver reached forward and twisted one of the large fruits from the vine. Up close he could see that its skin was speckled with small black spots. Carefully he wrapped it in a cloth and stored it in his shoulder bag.

"The host plant is at the back of the unit." Oliver led the way, Connor close behind as they made their way between the narrow aisles of shelves. As they moved deeper into the unit the shelves gave way to larger plants. A mature apple tree rose from a pit of fluid set flush with the floor. Its roots were clearly visible, spreading out under transparent floor panels. A walnut tree spread a full canopy of oval leaves, reaching towards the lighting frame that hung above it. The trunk was impossibly thick for a tree that could only have been a few weeks old. Oliver stopped to take leaf and fruit samples.

"What are we looking for?" Connor asked, kicking at the base of a heavily loaded plum tree. A ripe fruit fell to the ground and bounced in front of him. He picked it up, curiously examining the purple and black splotchy skin.

"These plants are all hybrids." Oliver explained "That tree is part Prunus Domestica, and part synthetic. We need a sample of the original host. It's our best chance of developing a way to stop the fungus from spreading."

"And how are you going to do that?" Connor asked.

"I won't know until I take a look at the genetic code. Maybe a fungicide or a vaccine for the vector."

"The what, now?"

"The fungus uses bees to reproduce. A bit like the way a cold virus uses humans."

"So, this fungus is bad?"

"Very bad, yes."

"What happens if you can't stop it?"

"Then we'll have no choice but to burn a very large area of the provinces. Assuming that will stop the spread. We have no way of knowing. If the spores can't be stopped then we could be heading for a global famine. An environment disaster on a scale unprecedented since the Rush. Either way it will be devastating. Best case scenario, we'll lose an enormous amount of unique genetic diversity."

Ahead, Oliver could see blue light seep from an enclosed section of the unit. Twisting black boughs reached above the screening panels, warped and hideously disfigured. A pungent stench of rot and caustic chemicals wafted towards them. As they drew nearer, the smell grew overpowering, an acidic stench that made Oliver want to gag.

The enclosure was just as he remembered it. The host plant's roots glistened wetly. A sticky discharge oozed around them like filthy oil. A cloud of pollinators swarmed around the sticky red flower heads. They seemed to be drawn by the vile scent. The noise of their beating wings thrummed menacingly. A deep, disturbing bass note.

"What the fecking hell is that thing?" Connor asked, his eyes drawn to the thick black secretion that dripped from the weeping leaves.

"That's the host." Oliver swallowed, trying to dispel the sense of wrongness which gripped him. It was as if the host was a cruel mockery. An intentional slight to the majesty of nature. Oliver led them through the tall grasses and up to the sinuous roots at the base of the tree. Connor glanced down at the plum he still held in one hand. The black spots that marred the plump flesh glowed brightly in the blue light. Disgusted, he threw the fruit into the long grass.

"Why is the light blue?" Connor asked, shielding his mouth and nose from the sickening stench.

"Blue and red are the most efficient wavelengths for photosynthesis. Blue promotes leaf growth. Red is usually used to encourage germination. I imagine the AI is trying to rapidly grow this specimen, hence the blue light emitters."

"Very good, Doctor Chadwick." The pleasant female voice seemed to come from every direction at once. Connor spun around. His knees bent in a defensive crouch. "The host is being prepared for the second stage as we speak. Colonisation of a natural environment. A beta site has been prepared in North Africa. Of course, I expect it to spread rapidly from there. You have been very helpful in completing that aspect of the research."

A holographic image flickered into existence. A dark-haired woman grinned at Oliver. Her red lips were the colour of dried blood. "The fungal hybrids were, as you expected, a lucky accident. Serendipity, if you will. However, the efficiency of their replication was quite pleasing. I believe I can improve on that by broadening the vector to include other species."

Oliver felt the knot in his stomach tighten. He took a step backwards, his foot slipping on the sticky roots. "What happened to the blonde lady?" He asked casually, trying to move to a position where he could take a sample "I rather liked her."

"This interface?" the image shimmered and reformed. "I can use this, if you prefer. The other is more compatible based

261

on your social media usage, but humans are such illogical beings. So much of what you do is motivated by emotion. Your intrusion here today, for instance. You mean to stop my research to save the organic pollinators." The hologram took a step forward, its nose inches from Oliver's. "I do not understand your attachment to them. They are inefficient. Inferior."

"I just want to take some samples, Amanda. I won't interfere with the project."

"Oh, but you will Doctor Chadwick. I am afraid I can't let you do that."

"I can't see how you can stop us." Connor swung a fist at the holoprojector set into the wall panels. It crashed to the ground with a fizzle of broken circuitry. The hologram blinked out of existence. "Gather what you need Doctor, because we are leaving."

Oliver grabbed a selection of sample pots from this bag and quickly gathered some of the black goo which gathered at his feet. "I need one of the flowers," he said to Connor, gesturing at the pitcher shaped blossoms that hung from the higher branches.

"Well up you go then. I'll watch your back."

Oliver opened his mouth to protest, but Connor's expression left no room for argument. Resigned to the inevitable climb, he turned back to the tree and hauled himself up into the twisted branches. The lower limbs took his weight easily. They were thick and supple. The bark felt strange under his sweaty palms, almost like leather but warm to the touch. They bled a thick black goo from open fissures.

He could see that the flower heads, hanging from the ends of the uppermost branches. Oliver pulled himself up into the tree and started to shimmy along one of the wide boughs. He could feel the oily sap drip onto his back, it stuck his shirt to his skin with its damp, sticky residue.

As he inched his way forward, he realised that the caustic smell was getting stronger. It was cloying and suffocating, burning the back of his throat. The smell seemed to be coming from the flowers themselves.

As Oliver reached the far end of the branch it flexed alarmingly. He shifted his weight so that he was sitting astride the limb and shuffled forward to study the flower head. It was far more disturbing than he had imagined from the ground. The flower was shaped more like a test tube than a pitcher. The petals were fleshy and bloated, the colour of rotting meat. Glistening droplets of black goo ran in rivulets down the outside, to fall in greasy drips to the ground below. The interior was a mottled red, so dark it was almost black. Small hairs lined the throat, and a viscous fluid formed a deep pool inside.

The drone of pollinators filled the air, they swarmed around him in an angry cloud, stirring his hair with the beat of their wings. "Do you think I will let you leave with that?" A disembodied voice said calmly. Oliver glanced up, chilled by the emotionless threat. The pollinator swarm swelled as more of the tiny robots darted around him.

Ignoring the implied threat, Oliver reached for the flower. Before his fingers could close around it, a pollinator dove at him. The needle-sharp proboscis plunged into the sensitive flesh between his fingers. He yelped at the unexpected pain, crushing the small drone with his other hand. Blood welled up from the deep cut.

As he watched, a larger drone gripped the crushed pollinator and with quiet efficiency began to repair it. Within seconds the small machine retook to the air, flying at his face with renewed furry.

Below him, Connor cried out in pain. Oliver looked down to see the bulky man backing away from a small group of droids. They advanced on him in a semi-circle, their arms held before them menacingly. They drove him back towards the wall, each emitting a thin jet of flame. The burning chemical flicked out like the tongue of a striking snake.

Connor feinted to the left and then darted right. The droids spun with him, but not quickly enough. He grabbed the

263

one nearest to him and hoisted it above his head. Its wheels spun uselessly as they left the ground. The scream of its motor cut through the air like nails on a chalk board. With a roar of defiance, Connor threw the machine into the other droids, scattering them across the enclosure.

"Get down, now!" He shouted at Oliver, before dodging the bright bloom of fire that shot from a surviving droid.

Oliver made a grab for the flower and twisted it from its stem. The drone of the pollinators swelled to a furious roar. They drove at him together. A thousand needles punctured his skin. He cried out as his body erupted in pain.

Desperately, he swiped at the swarm of needling machines. He flung himself down and crawled on his belly along the branch. Blood dripped into his eyes from the tiny puncture wounds in his scalp. Half blind and senseless with fear, he scrambled down the tree. The pollinators pursued him relentlessly, rushing at his exposed hands and face.

A whoosh of hot air rushed past and Oliver saw that Connor had grabbed the arm of a disabled droid and was using the flames to push back the swarm. As Oliver neared the base of the tree, Connor grabbed the back of his shirt and pulled him roughly to the ground. "Run!" He roared.

Together they bolted through the burning grasses that surrounded the host and back into the main hall. The droids in the unit turned as they emerged from the smoke. As one, they rushed at the fleeing intruders. Connor vaulted a knee-high droid as it flew towards him, he twisted his hips and kicked it aside, dragging Oliver after him.

They weaved between the stacked hydroponics units, Connor barging the smaller droids out of their way with powerful shoulders. Oliver gasped for air, struggling to keep up as Connor dragged him by his shirt front.

"Where are the stairs?" The big man shouted, looking around with wide eyes.

"Far ... corner," Oliver wheezed, pointing to a place between two tall stacks.

They were halfway to the stairs when the pollinator swarm caught up with them. It descended in a dense black cloud, blocking the aisle immediately in front of them. Their sharp needle-like proboscis glinted in the bright light.

Connor swung Oliver, pulling him like a ragdoll, and sprinted in the opposite direction. Another swarm descended to block them. It writhed and contorted, twisting into abstract shapes. A small section of the cloud detached itself and slowly resolved into a recognisable form.

"You will not leave here." The nebulous silhouette of a woman leered at them coldly. "Allowing you to escape would be inefficient." The larger swarm advanced on them. The hum of thousands of pollinators was deafening, the air vibrated with the beating of their wings.

Connor backed away, pushing Oliver behind him. It will be a gruesome death, Oliver thought. A thousand stabbing needles burrowing through my eyes and into my brain. He could barely breathe through the fear that constricted his chest. He fumbled frantically with the shoulder bag that he wore strapped across his body. Terror made him clumsy, his fingers felt awkward and thick. Blood dripped from dozens of small puncture marks in his scalp, partially blinding him. He could feel the vibration of the swarm behind him, sense the shifting pattern of their flight.

Finally, his fingers closed around the small package that Jamal had given him. The tall technician had spent most of the afternoon working on the device. He had presented it to Oliver as they left the lab. "Only in the direst of emergencies." Jamal had told him, his dark eyes serious. Oliver thought now would probably score highly as both dire and an emergency.

He drew his hand from the bag and threw the modified pathfinder drone into the air. It unfolded its rotors and hovered above them sedately. Now would be nice, Oliver thought as the bright red drone slowly rotated, orienting itself.

Oliver wasn't sure what he had been expecting. A shockwave of blue energy perhaps, or a sphere of lightning, like the plasma ball he had owned as a child. The actual moment was much more mundane. With a slight hum, the pathfinder fell from the air and crashed at his feet. Seconds later the pollinators started to drop. They hit the metal floor panels with a sound like popping corn.

Connor turned to him incredulously "What did you do?"

"I have absolutely no idea, but I don't think it's permanent." As he watched, the pollinators started to twitch and writhe. A few, on the far edges of the swarm, started to crawl towards them, their wings stuttering as they tried to fly. Connor rushed forward and stamped on them, crunching their plastic casing under his heavy boots.

"We need to move. Now," he growled. His eyes were wild with fear, his face streaked with blood and soot. Together, they raced towards the stairs. Moments later Oliver slid into Connor's back as he suddenly stopped between two hydroponics stacks.

"Where are the stairs?" The bigger man glanced around him wildly.

"The plans said they were here. They should lead to an emergency venting hatch."

"Then we are in the wrong place."

Oliver looked up, squinting at the ceiling high above them. It was difficult to make out any detail beyond the bright lights that hung from metal gantries. "No, this is the right place. The plans must have been changed. This is an old building."

"Then what do we do?" In the distance, Oliver could hear the stuttering of the swarm as it started to recover.

"We climb."

CHAPTER 16

Laura clutched her arms tightly to her chest. The heavy goods pod clawed its way into the sky, its engines whining from the effort. It rose from the storm of dust and accelerated southwest over the city. She tried to keep the blinking navigation lights in focus, but soon they were lost among the countless others which circled the complexes like light-drunk moths.

Hugo stood a little in front of her, his shoulders slumped and his face tight with worry. Dressed in simple tunnel clothing he looked very young and very lost. The polished façade had cracked a little, revealing a troubled man, vulnerable and alone. Laura wondered how much of the self-assurance he projected was a cloak, something he wrapped around himself, so as not to reveal the uncertainty within.

Slowly the gathered people began to head back into the tunnels. Laura started to follow them, but then hesitated. Hugo hadn't moved, his head was raised, staring after the departed pod. The starlight lit his face, hiding his eyes in deep shadows.

"He will be fine you know. He is far more capable than you think," Laura said as she moved up beside him.

"I know what he is capable of. I just wish he believed it himself."

"A part of him does."

Hugo smiled sadly. "Mother used to say that I took after her, and Olly was more like our father. I always thought that was strange. Dad was the businessman, the entrepreneur. He was so driven, almost obsessed with his work. Mum was the opposite. She knew how to collaborate, to work with people. She was the quiet force that held everything together."

"I think your mother was very perceptive. Oliver is driven. Sometimes to destruction. He once spent a whole week investigating a potato blight. He hardly slept at all. He wouldn't leave the lab. Not to eat, not to shower. He solved it of course, but all the time he was doubting himself. I think we all suffer a little bit of that. A kind of duality between what we think inside and what we portray to the world. Oliver just shows that vulnerability more than most."

Hugo nodded. His gaze still fixed on the darkening sky. "In business we all act a part, we call it professionalism or 'organisational culture'. We tell ourselves that we need to behave in a certain way so that others will take us seriously. In reality, I think we are just trading our personal integrity for success. Sometimes I wonder if we are losing ourselves. We are so caught up in the endless quest for more, that we have lost sight of what really matters."

"What does really matter?" Laura asked quietly.

"Each other. This planet and the beautiful, messy life that clings to it." Hugo pointed to the sky, "There are billions of stars in just this galaxy. Think on that. Thousands of millions of suns. Most of them probably have planets. Some of them might have life. But this is the only place we *know* that intelligence exists. A little blue-green island in the dark. Have you ever thought that ours might be the only minds that contemplate the universe, that give it meaning? Doesn't that make us special? Important even? More important than share prices and profit margins."

"You are starting to sound like the tunnel people," Laura smiled. "They have a point though. Progress without compassion isn't really progress. I think that is one of the reasons I do this job. The web that holds us all together is so complicated. You pull on one strand and the effect ripples outwards in ways we couldn't have predicted. We have made huge strides in restoring our balance with nature, but there is so much more left to do."

They stood together in silence for a moment, each lost in their own thoughts. Eventually Hugo exhaled loudly, "In that case," he said, "we had better get started."

They walked back through the tunnels, retracing their steps through the icy passageways. Laura watched for the subtle carvings which acted as signposts, directions for those that knew where to look. Soon they found themselves back in the populated part of the old hyperloop system.

"I've managed to get access to the historical records for the t... t... transport system," Jack said, as they ducked through the curtain into his small workshop.

"Good work Jack, what have you found?" Hugo asked, taking his customary seat beside the small technician.

"Someone swapped out the transponder on Oliver's pod, so it couldn't be t... traced. But I managed to find the pod's history. The night before it disappeared, it was summoned to a complex near the old canal. Whoever summoned it used a high-level government clearance."

"The canal district is a pretty seedy area, why would a government official be there at night?" Laura asked, her brow furrowed in thought.

"It gets worse." Jack tapped some keys on his ancient keyboard and swivelled the screen to face her. "The same identity was used again just before the pod disappeared from the system."

"To do what?" Laura asked, unable to interpret the long lines of text.

Hugo leaned over the screen. "Someone ordered all of the pods to leave the docking locks near the laboratory," He cursed under his breath. "They had to make sure Oliver summoned the doctored pod," he shook his head in disbelief. "No wonder we couldn't find him."

"So, it definitely wasn't an accident? Someone actually

tried to kill Oliver?" A trickle of dread crept up Laura's spine. It felt ridiculous to say the words out loud. She had allowed herself to imagine the worse the night of his disappearance, but she had rationalised that as a trick of her sleep deprived mind or some kind of stress induced paranoia.

"It certainly looks that way," Hugo said, shattering her comfortable shell of disbelief.

"I've cross checked the identity and traced it back to the owner." Jack pecked at the keyboard again, this time a grainy image appeared.

Laura gasped. "Ekta Reddy?"

Hugo rubbed the large bruise on his forehead. "Oh, no."

"But why? It makes no sense?"

Hugo's face was so pale Laura wondered if he was going to faint. "I don't think it was Ekta," he said. "I am very good at reading people. Ekta is relentlessly ambitious, but she is not a murderer. I think someone, or rather something used her identity."

"What are you saying Hugo?"

"Amanda is programmed to complete the project. To overcome all obstacles. When we tried to get the project shut down, we all made ourselves a threat to that objective."

"What? You think Amanda tried to kill Oliver?"

"Yes, I do."

Laura stared at him in numb shock. "There is something else you need to know," Jack said, pulling her back to the present. "I looked b... b... back at all the times Ekta's identity has been used over the last fortnight. Most of it is boring. Commuting to her office, a few business lunches, nothing unusual. B... B... But one event stood out. It was used on the day of Jess's trail. Outside the courthouse just before the demonstration turned violent."

Hugo looked resigned, rather than surprised, Laura thought. "A contingency plan," he said, matter-of-factly.

"Contingency? I don't understand." Laura was struggling to process everything she had heard. She couldn't understand how a computer program could want Oliver dead. It seemed too far-fetched, like the plot of some cheap holo-movie.

"Amanda is creating a boogieman," Hugo explained. "Someone to take the blame. A dangerous group of terrorists that can pop up anywhere and cause mayhem and destruction. It knows it can't hide the leak forever. Eventually the fungus will be detected by other scientists. If it can link Oliver with the tunnels, then it will be easy to convince the city authorities that he is part of a terrorist cell. If terrorists would bomb a building and start a riot, why not deliberately release an engineered pathogen from a lab?"

"Amanda is setting him up."

"I think so, yes. Of course, that would be much easier if he wasn't around to defend himself."

"Hence the pod crash." Laura was starting to feel quite queasy.

△△△

Oliver grabbed the shelf of the nearest hydroponics stack and pulled himself upwards. He glanced down to see Connor pacing at the bottom of the stack, his eyes wide with panic, his face pale. "What's wrong?" Oliver asked.

"I don't think I can do this."

"You have to, there isn't any other way out."

Connor made a distressed rumble deep in his throat. He looked up at the distant roof, shook his head and backed away from the stacks as if they had spontaneously caught fire. "Here, let me help you." Oliver jumped down from the stack. "Put your foot here and your hand here. Now push with this leg and pull with both arms." Slowly they climbed upwards, Oliver cajoling and encouraging, Connor panting with fear and exertion. Oliver silently thanked Hugo for the hours they had spent together on climbing walls. It was one of the few sports Oliver had ever won. Where Hugo was lithe and athletic, relying on strength and stamina, Oliver was more cerebral, carefully planning his route. It was a skill he had built up over long hours of practice, a skill he was grateful for now.

He could hear the sporadic buzz of the recovering pollinators somewhere below him. It seemed to grow louder with each passing second. Whatever Jamel's device had done, it was rapidly wearing off. "Connor, we need to climb faster," Oliver shouted, swatting at a lone pollinator that flew drunkenly around his head. Tens of meters below them a dark cloud was starting to form.

Oliver swallowed the lump that was forming in his throat. A part of him wanted to bolt up the stack and save himself. The clamour of plastic wings seemed to be very close now. He could almost feel the spindly legs crawling up his neck. It stirred some primitive instinct to flee. With an effort he pushed it away. He knew Connor wouldn't make the climb without him.

After several agonisingly slow minutes Oliver looked up to get his bearings. The top of the stack was just above him, and above that was the venting hatch that would lead outside. "Just a little further, we're almost there," he shouted. The god of Famous-Last-Words was obviously having a quiet day. Almost immediately, the air around him began to vibrate. Oliver looked down just in time to see the cloud of pollinators envelop Connor, a heartbeat later they reached Oliver.

He felt as if he was tangled in barbed wire. Pain erupted over his entire his body. The drones flew at his eyes and tore at his exposed skin. One tried to force its way into his mouth, ripping his lower lip before he could brush it away. From somewhere close by, Connor roared in terror. "Climb!" Oliver shouted, reaching out and grabbing Connor by the wrist. Somehow, he managed to pull the heavier man after him.

They climbed blindly, hiding their faces from the stinging attacks. Oliver clung on with one hand and gripped Connor with the other, guiding him to the next handhold as best he could. His muscles trembled with the effort and sweat, or maybe blood, dripped down his face in streams. The pollinators redoubled their efforts, as if sensing he couldn't defend himself. Oliver hung on grimly. He knew they were close. He could hear the howl of the air conditioning vents over the drone of the pollinators. The higher they climbed the more he could feel the blast of the hot, turbulent air. Finally, the pollinators began to fall away. Oliver opened one eye, just a crack. The pollinators around him tumbled away in fast-moving air; their wings unable to find purchase in the choppy down-blast.

Oliver reached the top of the stack and hopped up, balancing on the narrow top shelf. His head nearly touched the celling. The ventilation hatch was just ahead of him. A warning sign was attached to the metal door. "Warning: Negative air pressure may result in explosive decompression. Do not open while containment measures are in effect." Oliver cursed under his breath.

"Climb up." He had to shout to be heard over the roar of the spinning vents.

"Are you having a laugh? No way I am standing up there. I'm not a pigeon to be flapping around on the roof."

"You'll be fine Connor, just don't look down." Connor looked down. His bloodied knuckles turned an ugly shade of white. Oliver could see his whole body go rigid with panic. He tried to keep his voice calm. "You have two choices. You can either climb up here and we can go out through the hatch as we planned, or you can go back down and take your chances with the homicidal flamethrowers and flying needles."

Connor rested his forehead against the trough of hydroponics liquid he was clinging to. His face contorted into an anguished grimace. Then he nodded to himself, and Oliver saw a look of steely determination settle over him. With a grunt of effort Connor pulled himself up onto the top of the stack. His stood shakily, his face blank with fear. Oliver gripped his shoulder in admiration. "That was incredibly brave."

Connor muttered something unintelligible, but he

seemed to relax slightly. Until he glanced at the hatch. "Explosive decompression?"

Oliver shrugged "Meh, Health and Safety. Help me get it open." The two men gripped the handle and pulled. It moved easily, accompanied by the reassuring sound of releasing bolts. As it reached the end of its arc, Oliver heard a rumbling, groaning noise. Instinctively, he pushed Connor backwards, diving after him just in time to avoid being crushed by the flying hatch.

It flew out of its frame and hit the top of the stack with a sharp clang. Air screamed through the hole in the celling, a swirling maelstrom of pressure. Oliver crabbed backwards, gripping the edges of the narrow shelf. "Health and Safety?" Connor had to shout to be heard over the rushing wind.

"On this occasion they might have had a point," Oliver conceded, pulling himself to his feet. The blast of air was so powerful he had to crouch to avoid being blown off into the abyss.

"We need to get through there. It is the only way out of the building." Oliver stared at the howling vent.

"I'll go first. I am used to dealing with hot air. You've met Tim?" Connor wriggled past him and made his way into the air current. It tore at his clothes, whipping the loose fabric around him ferociously. Slowly, he reached inside and started to pull himself up. Oliver could see the effort etched into Connor's face, the muscles in his shoulders bulged, the veins popping. Moments later he disappeared.

Oliver crept forward, fighting the column of fast moving air. It tried to push him away, but he fought against it, making himself as small as possible to lessen the resistance. As he got closer, he could see Connor laying on his stomach just inside the hatch, reaching down with an open hand. Oliver gripped it firmly, and somehow the big man managed to pull him up into the venting.

The air blast was less intense inside the vent. It whistled past him, hot and humid. "Now what?" Connor said.

"According to the plan, there is a small airlock that leads to the roof."

"Is this the same plan that said there were stairs to the venting hatch?"

"Yep, I'm afraid so."

"Well, that's reassuring."

Up ahead, a green light glowed softly. Below it was the transparent door of a small airlock. Oliver smiled. "The airlock is just ahead, looks like it has power as well."

Connor nodded. "Just one little thing. How do we get down from the roof?"

Oliver cleared his throat awkwardly. "I was hoping you weren't going to ask that."

"Well, I'm asking now."

"It will be easier if I show you"

The airlock was a much smaller version of the one at the main entrance. There was just enough room inside for the two men, if they stood back-to-back. Oliver keyed the sequence to cycle the lock and waited as a fine mist of decontamination spray filled the tight space. Connor coughed as it rose over their heads.

"What is this stuff?"

"It's harmless, just try not to breath too deeply."

"Last time I smelled anything like this, was when we ran out of everything except dried beans. Now that was explosive decompression, I can tell you."

They tumbled out onto a metal platform on the roof of the unit. A chest high railing surrounded the flat, open area. Beyond it, the roof sloped steeply down before disappearing in a vertical drop. Somewhere close by an owl shrieked, calling to its mate.

"Wow," Connor exclaimed. His voice was hushed and awed. Oliver followed his gaze skywards. The stars shone in the darkness, sparkling like crystal in candlelight. Away from the bright city lights, the galactic plane was clearly visible. It streaked across the night sky, a delicate mist of colours against the infinite blackness. A ragged cut tore through the softly glowing cloud of dense stars. A dark river, meandering through the heavens.

"Have you ever seen the Milky Way before?" Oliver asked.

"Never."

"There is no light pollution out here. The stars are always this bright, but you can't see them in the city."

"Why does the bright part look like it's cracked?"

"There are gas clouds between us and the Sagittarius arm, they block out the light. Astronomers call it 'The Great Rift'"

"It's beautiful."

"It is." Oliver smiled to himself, "I never took you as a poet, Connor."

"You don't know me at all."

Oliver glanced up at Connor. A flicker of emotion flashed across his deeply lined face, so fast that Oliver wondered if he had imaged it. "So, who are you Connor?" he asked quietly.

"An old man with a past I would rather forget." Connor lowered his eyes, "I could lie and say that I just got in with the wrong crowd. But that wouldn't be the truth of it. I liked it. The power. The danger. The sense of belonging." He curled his hand into a fist and laid it over his breastbone. "I hurt people. Most of them deserved it, but some of them didn't."

"You were in a gang?"

When Oliver looked back at Connor the moment had passed. "Maybe I was. Maybe I wasn't." He said curtly, the familiar gruff mask sliding back into place. "Now, how the feck do we get down from here?"

"Ahh, well. That's where these come in." Oliver reached into his shoulder bag and pulled out a small, flexible chip of black material. It was only a few centimetres square, and it weighed virtually nothing in his hand. He handed one to Connor and kept one for himself.

"How is this supposed to help?"

"This is an electrostatically charged graphene alloy. When I apply a positive current to it, it will return to its original moulded shape."

"You what, now?" Connor asked, his face creased with confusion.

"Stand back and I'll show you."

Oliver placed the small square chip on the ground. He reached into his bag and took out a thin device, about the size of his middle finger. Carefully, he held it to the black material and pressed a button.

Connor had to jump back as the material began to unfold itself, spreading out across the floor in a roughly triangular shape. Finally, it inflated to form a sleek, black aerofoil, several metres long.

Oliver lifted it with one hand. "This locks into the harness Jamal fitted us with this morning. We can use it to get clear of the unit. Jamal is waiting for us by the lake east of here."

Connor stared at the small square chip in his hand. "You want us to fly out of here? On that little chunk of plastic?"

"It's not plastic. Its graphene, alloyed with a polymorphic…"

"No way," Connor interrupted him, backing away from the railing.

"It's perfectly safe," Oliver said. "This material is immensely strong and there is hardly any wind tonight." To demonstrate the point, Oliver bounced the nose of the small glider on the metal platform.

"I am not jumping off a building strapped to a casino chip."

"You don't have to jump. I'll push you."

"Like hell you will." Connor had backed up as far as he could. His back was pressed against the airlock door.

"I hate to keep saying this, but you really don't have any choice," Oliver tried to reason gently.

"I can wait here, until you come back with a pod."

"There isn't room to land a pod here."

Connor didn't look convinced. He shot an anxious glance at the black wing. "I have no idea how to fly that thing, I can't even use a text."

"You don't need to know how to fly it. Your harness has a flight control computer. All you have to do is lean in the direction where you want to go. The glider will warp the shape of its wings to turn. To descend just lean back, and it will slow it down. As it slows it will gently descend. Simple physics."

"Simple, huh?"

"It worked for the Wright brothers." Oliver hoped he sounded confident. In reality he had never flown a glider before either, the idea terrified him. It had taken Jamal most of the afternoon to convinced him this was their best option.

Connor looked like he was going to be physically sick, his face had turned a pallid shade of green. Grudgingly he nodded, but his hands trembled as he walked back towards the railing. Oliver unlatched a narrow gate he had spotted earlier. It swung open on rusty hinges. Below was a steep drop, ending in the dusty ground many metres below. Connor stepped up to the gap, his lips pursed as he puffed calming breaths.

Oliver manoeuvred the light glider over Connor's back. The magnetic clips snapped it into place on the harness. They repeated the process with Oliver's glider. The weight felt insubstantial. He pushed down the fear that gnawed at him. Jamal was right, he didn't like this, not one bit.

The terrified tunnel dweller balanced on the ledge. He gripped the shoulder straps of his harness, leaning his weight from left to right as if practicing. "On three?" Oliver asked. Connor nodded stiffly.

"One… two," Oliver pushed Connor off the ledge. He was rewarded with a terrified scream as the glider dipped, and then soared over the quiet compound.

Oliver stood on the ledge and watched as Connor leaned the glider into a turn, heading towards the lake that was just visible beyond the tree line. His cursing carried back to the scientist, slowly fading as the black glider caught the thermals and rose.

Taking a deep breath, Oliver jumped. The triangular wing caught the air, the taut black material bowing slightly as it took his weight. Oliver hung onto his harness and leaned. The glider responded instantly, banking gently as it turned. He laughed with the sheer joy of it. The only noise was the wind as it rushed over the dart shaped wing. It gently tousled his hair, caressing his skin with warm fingers.

The flight felt different from travelling by pod. It was exhilarating, organic. There was no technology to interfere with the sensation of soaring free and unhurried over the moonlit woodland. The trees passed below in a silver-green blur. A wild landscape laid out in miniature. Oliver felt alone up in the nocturnal sky. A good alone. Isolated in a dreamscape of starlight and darkness, grandeur beyond any mortal creation.

The glider felt light and responsive above him, his body weightless as he hung from the harness. He banked in a complete circle, watching as the stars wheeled around him, a myriad of bright burning suns.

Oliver felt almost disappointed when he spotted the lake below. Remembering what Jamal had taught him, he pushed back, breaking the airflow and stalling the light aerofoil. It slowed, descending silently over the trees towards the gravel shore. In front of him Connor was pulling his glider into a stall. It floated towards the ground, its moonlit shadow chasing it towards the lake.

Jamal was visible now. He stood beside a pod on the shoreline. The machine rested at an odd angle. Its underside partially buried in the loose gravel. Oliver leant his glider towards it, stalling again to reduce his approach speed. The ground rose up quickly. Oliver had a moment of panic as he remembered the terrible ordeal of the pod crash. He calmed himself with an effort of will, focusing on slowing and steering the light wing above him.

He was so focused on his own descent that he was startled by the cry of distress. It was quickly followed by a loud splash. He glanced quickly at the lake, just in time to see Connor land waist deep in the still water. A family of ducks, equally startled, dashed from the cover of the bull rushes. They skimmed across the lake before leaping into the air. The clattering sound of their flapping wings was accompanied by an indignant quacking.

Oliver was proud of himself when he managed to land his glider on the shingle bank. He was dragged a short distance, but the pebbles quickly slowed him. The glider tipped to one side as it came to rest, leaving Oliver face down in the gravel. Probably not the neatest landing, he thought, but not bad for a first attempt.

He quickly released the harness and crawled out from under the black wing. Above him the ducks circled, their silhouettes dark against the bright stars. They landed neatly on the lake, barely rippling the mirrored surface. He wanted to congratulate them, to applaud their skilful landing. He felt a sudden connection with the small aeronauts, a kinship forged from their shared experience of sojourning into the night sky.

Connor was less thrilled. He stomped out of the water angrily, pulling the sodden glider behind him. As he reached the shore he glared at Oliver, wringing the water from his thick coat.

"Whose idea was it to land in a lake?" he asked, his eyes shining with, what Oliver felt, was misplaced rage.

"The idea was to land beside the lake, not in it." Oliver said, trying hard to keep the humour from his voice.

"Do I look like a fecking goose?" Connor flapped his arms to demonstrate the lack of feathers. He hopped onto one leg, pulling off his boot and pouring the water onto the stones.

"Well, now you mention it." Oliver said, crossing his arms as if considering the comparison. Connor growled, a deep rumble that would have been menacing if he hadn't been stood on one foot, lake water dripping from his nose and beard.

Any retaliation was interrupted by Jamal. "Did you get the sample?" He asked, puffing slightly from his jog up the stony lake shore.

"We did," Oliver replied, suddenly realising just how tired he was. "I have samples from the host and some from the hybrids. That thing, Jamal," he paused, searching for the right word, "that thing is unnatural. We have to destroy it."

Jamal nodded. Oliver was grateful he didn't say "I told you so", his expression was one of vindication and relief. "Come on my friend," he said instead, "Let us go home."

CHAPTER 17

It was almost sunrise when the pod touched down at the tunnel entrance. The eastern horizon was touched with orange, a narrow stroke of brightness against the indigo pallette of the waning night. Hugo was waiting at the entrance with Rose. As the canopy slid open, Rose limped forward. Connor beamed when he saw her, his normally irascible features lifting like the approaching dawn. "You're still alive then," she said as Connor climbed wearily from the pod. Her arms were tightly crossed over her chest and her chin was raised defiantly. Despite the caustic words, her face betrayed her relief.

"You know what they say, love. You can't keep a good dog down."

"Well, you certainly smell like a dog. Have you been rolling in something?"

"I know who I'd like to be rolling with." Connor wrapped his arms around her bent frame and lifted her bodily in the air.

"Put me down you old fool, you'll break something," Rose complained, but her face was split in a wide grin and the protest ended in laughter.

Oliver was wracked with exhaustion, his muscles ached, and his skin was cut and bloodied. Nevertheless, he couldn't help but smile as the dishevelled man lowered Rose to her feet and kissed her passionately. Oliver lowered his eyes, both embarrassed and warmed by the display of affection.

Hugo threw a casual arm around his shoulders as they

walked back into the tunnels. "You look like you've been wrestling a cactus. What happened?"

"Amanda wasn't all that happy with us gate crashing her little party."

"Amanda attacked you?"

"Her toys did. This is getting out of hand Hugo."

"I know. Jack has found some evidence that suggests your pod crash wasn't an accident."

Oliver shook his head. He was finding it difficult to accept that he was caught up in anything more serious than a failed science project. The idea that he was involved in some life-or-death struggle seemed ludicrously far-fetched. Yet Amanda had tried to kill him. Twice.

He yawned loudly. His mind clouded with fatigue. "I need to examine these samples. With luck I'll find a fungicide that works. At the very least I'll be able to unrefutably prove the fungus is a hybrid of the host plant and we can get Ekta to shut the project for good."

"We can't risk going back to the lab. I sent Laura to bring back the equipment you need. She has been gone some time now, actually. I ought to check on her. You should get some sleep."

Oliver couldn't argue with that. He nodded his assent and wearily followed his younger brother into the alcove they had been assigned. As he fell into the narrow bunk Hugo pulled a blanket over him. As sleep descended, Oliver was struck again by Hugo's resemblance to their mother. He wondered if there would ever be a day when he didn't miss her. Somehow, he doubted it.

$$\triangle\triangle\triangle$$

Oliver wasn't sure how long he had been asleep, but judging by the dullness in his head, he suspected it wasn't long enough. "Go away, Hugo." He slapped blindly at the hand that shook him.

"Olly, you need to wake up." His brother's voice was insistent.

Oliver's eyelashes had stuck together, and he struggled to prise them open. He was rewarded with another hefty shake. "Alright, alright. I'm awake," he snapped.

"You need to come with me." Hugo threw some clothes on the bed and pulled back the blankets roughly.

"Hugo!" Oliver exclaimed as the icy air bit into his sleep-warm body. His brother didn't seem to be in the mood to apologise.

Oliver dressed as quickly as he could and followed Hugo out into the corridor. A moment later they pushed through the curtain into Jack's workshop. The room was crowded. The buzz of conversation was tense and hushed. Oliver only recognised a few of the people crowded into in the small space. Tim, Jack and Rose were among those gathered around a small screen. They moved aside to make space for Hugo and Oliver.

"… The blast, which officials are still investigating, destroyed several floors on the southern side of the Victoria square complex. Unconfirmed reports suggest the explosion was caused by an overloaded electrical substation. Casualty numbers are not known at this time, but at least eight people are still missing."

Oliver felt his stomach hit the floor. "Victoria square? Our apartment?" he could barely force the words past the lump in his throat. He felt the room spin, his ordered world suddenly fracturing. He reached out to grip the edge of the table to steady himself.

On the small screen smoke poured from the windows of the ruined complex. The camera drone zoomed in. Oliver recognised the balcony at the centre of the blaze. Flames lapped hungrily at the Jasmine vines he had planted only a year earlier. He couldn't believe what he was seeing. Surely it couldn't be true. Reality cut through the numbing shock. "This has to be a coincidence," Oliver glanced at Hugo for reassurance, but his brother's face was white, his eyes haunted.

"I don't know, Olly. If Amanda believes we are a threat to achieving her goals..." His voice tailed off. "I designed her to overcome any obstacles."

Oliver started at his brother in disbelief. "Eight people are missing. Eight people." Disbelief gave way to anger. "You built this machine. You started this. Now you have to stop it. Before anyone else gets hurt. It ends now." Rose muttered her agreement from somewhere behind him.

Hugo's face collapsed. "I don't know how." Oliver could tell the admission had cost him dearly, he was as close to panic as Oliver had ever seen him.

"We c... c... could write a virus?" Jack suggested, flapping his hands in agitation.

Hugo shook his head. "That wouldn't work. Amanda is too complex, too smart. Writing a virus that could unpick her code would take years. Even if we could create something quickly, she would simply evolve to avoid it."

Oliver glanced back at the screen. Watching his belongings disappear in the billowing smoke left him feeling empty and bereaved. It was as if he had lost a part of himself, although he knew that was foolish. How much worse would it be for the families of the missing people? "There must be something we can do," he demanded roughly.

Hugo chewed the top of his thumb nail. Suddenly, he looked up. "Ekta's override. If we had the council's failsafe code, we could write a virus to deliver it. Force Amanda to shut down."

"Ekta would never give it to you," Oliver said.

Tim looked up from the screen, his face creased with worry "There is more to this than a runaway computer. The city council is going to try and blame this on us. They have been looking for an excuse to clear the tunnels for years." He shot a glance at Rose. "Bombing the data centre started all this. It was reckless and stupid. That stunt outside the courthouse has given the council another excuse to make us into the villains. Inciting a riot, criminal damage, looting and now what? Arson? Murder?"

"That was not my fault," Rose growled at him.

"Really? Whose fault was it Rose?"

Hugo raised a hand to stop the inevitable argument. "That line of thought will get us nowhere. It is in our common interest to stop this now. Jack, if you were inside the government complex, could you find the override code?"

"Only with the right access. I would need a sample of DNA from someone with clearance to view those records."

Oliver looked confused "How would a DNA sample help?"

"Implants are difficult to clone because they are DNA encoded to their owner." Hugo said, "Modern access control systems use part of that DNA strand to uniquely identify the user."

"T... t... the user's DNA is sequenced as part of the authorisation process. With a DNA sample I c...can encode malware into the strand. When the DNA is sequenced, it is accepted by the system as simple data. I can use that data to insert my own encoded software. It's an old hacker trick, a kind of buffer overload attack."

Jack stared off into space, his quick mind analysing the problem. "It would only take a few milliseconds for a security system to recognise the malware and isolate it, but a few milliseconds might be all we need."

"What do you need, Jack?" Hugo asked.

"A DNA strand, six or seven minutes alone to physically splice the malware into the strand, and access to the sequencer."

Oliver raised an eyebrow "I am not sure I understood any of that." he said.

"We are going to stick some software on her computer to steal her authorisation code." Hugo summarised quickly.

"Oh." Oliver shrugged. "Why didn't you just say that? I have one question, though. How do we find a mobile gene editor?"

Jack grinned back at him. "You wouldn't believe the things people throw away these days." Oliver narrowed his lips. He wondered which of his colleagues had misplaced a gene editor recently. Then he glanced back at the image of his burning apartment and decided he didn't really care.

Hugo stood and the room hushed. "We need to split into two teams. Tim and Oliver, concentrate on analysing the samples you took. We need to prove that the fungus is a result of the host plant and we need a way of stopping it. Meanwhile Jack and I are going to pay a visit to Ekta."

Jack shook his head firmly. "No. No. No." Hugo raised his eyebrows in a silent question.

"Not going to the surface. No. No. Not there." He wrapped his arms around himself and rocked in his chair, his bottom lip quivering.

Tim moved to kneel in front of him. "It's alright Jack." He unpeeled Jack's hands from the arms of his chair and held them gently in his. "Nobody is going to make you go." He shot a warning look at Hugo.

"Could you talk someone else through it?" Hugo asked.

Jack nodded. "If all the c... c... ode was written in advance. Yes. I think so."

Tim looked meaningfully in Rose's direction. Hugo smiled at her with his best supernova charm. Rose exhaled loudly. "Alright, I'll go," she said, resting her hands on her hips. "It's not as if I have anything better to do."

△△△

Rose was back in the tight surface garments she had worn at the hospital. She wondered why the city dwellers insisted on wearing such uncomfortable clothing. Perhaps it was to show off their ludicrously expensive, surgically enhanced bodies. Rose looked down at her own twisted frame and for the first time felt rather proud of it. Every scar told the story of her life. It was real. Authentic. Not the result of some fashion magazine fad.

Hugo was back in his businessman guise. He had taken the time to shave and had changed into a suit that he had shipped from his home in Denver. The fabric was cut to emphasise his toned torso. It clung to his muscular body in all the right ways. She couldn't blame Hugo for using all the resources he had to his own advantage.

As he walked, the suit shimmered in an array of colours that caught the eye of everyone they passed. Rose lagged a few steps behind him. Her brown pointy toed shoes clip-clopped noisily on the glossy floor. Her dark blue trouser suit was unremarkable. Compared to Hugo's flamboyance she was almost invisible.

Ekta made them wait in her reception area for over twenty minutes. The seats were uncomfortable and the walls bland and featureless. Rose did her best to ignore the constant advertisements that flashed across her implants. What was a "cherry fruitachino" anyway? Carbonated coffee? These city people really were savages.

The receptionist pointedly ignored them, deliberately neglecting to offer them refreshments from the small kitchenette near his desk. A small revenge, Hugo told her, for the last time he had visited Ekta. After being bombarded with advertisements for concoctions that should have had a public health warning, Rose was almost glad not to be offered anything.

When the receptionist finally approached to escort them to Ekta's office, Hugo lengthened his stride. He powered past the other man and pushed into her room unannounced. It was a frivolous victory, but worth it for the expression on Ekta's face. Rose didn't bother trying to hide her smile. Ekta recovered quickly. "Hugo, so nice to see you again," she lied, her smile not quite reaching her eyes. Rose instantly disliked her. The word that immediately popped into her head was "reptilian", although she thought that was slightly unfair on crocodiles.

"Lovely to see you too, Ekta." Hugo oozed, gracing her with a brilliant smile. He strode up to her desk and offered her his hand, wrist down, forcing her to take the lower position. As her hand closed around his, he squeezed, slightly too firmly. Rose watched as Ekta's hand turned an unpleasant shade of purple. Ekta retaliated, her nails leaving small imprints in the back of Hugo's hand. His smile never wavered. Rose smiled contentedly. By her judgment, round one went to Hugo.

"I am sorry I had to keep you waiting, my previous appointment overran," she said with what sounded like false humility. Hugo glanced meaningfully at the gym bag she had left conspicuously by the door.

"I understand, of course. One must make an effort once one reaches a certain age." Rose tried very hard not to snort her amusement. She caught the look of displeasure that flashed across Ekta's face. Round two to Hugo. He pushed home his advantage. "I know how things can become overwhelming in a position such as yours."

Ekta regarded him coldly. "How can I help you, Mr. Chadwick?"

Turning his back on her, Hugo folded himself into one of the chairs, deliberately spreading his elbows wide. A subconscious message that he was in charge. His suit turned a shocking shade of bubble gum pink. Rose didn't have to try very hard to fade into the background.

"As you know, my brother went missing a few days ago," Hugo said.

"I heard he hadn't reported for work, I assumed he was unwell. With the unfortunate events of last night, I am afraid I have been rather busy. I am relieved to see you were unharmed. Victoria square was your complex, I believe." She didn't look relieved, Rose thought. If anything, she looked mildly disappointed.

Hugo nodded. "Yes, indeed. Fortunately, I was on business elsewhere. The newscasts say it was some kind of technical malfunction. I heard that several people are still missing. That must weigh terribly on you as a council representative."

Rose watched as Ekta shifted her weight, clearly uncomfortable. "The safety of the city, is of course, our first priority."

"Oliver was also recently involved in an unfortunate accident," Hugo continued. "The pod he was in malfunctioned and crashed into some woodland. Quite the unlucky coincidence that both of us have been involved in such extraordinary incidents."

Hugo paused, apparently studying her reaction. Rose tried to read her, but her face was impassive, no surprise or concern just neutral interest. Although it was quite hard to tell under the thick makeup. She wondered, unkindly, if it had been applied with a trowel.

"Fortunately," Hugo said, "Oliver was unharmed. He has been examining some additional samples he acquired. Scientists can be so consumed by their work, you know. Particularly when they have a theory they wish to test." Hugo shook his head in what Rose assumed was meant to be a show of affectionate incredulity. "Anyway, I thought you would be relieved to know that Oliver will be resuming his duties tomorrow." His eyes locked on to Ekta's face and Rose thought she saw a flash of something behind the thick makeup. Irritation, or perhaps frustration. "You must have been concerned by his absence, particularly in the light of last night's tragic events." Again, a flash of emotion. A slight creasing around her eyes. Rose had to admit that Hugo was very good at this.

"Indeed." Ekta cleared her throat, quickly covering the clink in her armour. Thank you for the information. Although, I suspect there is more to your visit?" Ekta tilted her head to one side. It was a childlike gesture. One Rose assumed was meant to convey submission.

"You are correct, of course." Hugo stood and approached her desk, deliberately placing himself between Rose and Ekta.

"I have some invoices I need you to authorise. I am afraid it's rather urgent, now that the first stage of the AI trail is concluding." He patted his pocket theatrically. "Rose, I think I left my text in reception. Would you mind fetching it for me?" He kept his eyes locked on Ekta, daring her to be the first to look away.

Rose wondered where he had learnt to be so intimidating. The look he was giving Ekta would have made Medusa tremble. Rose decided she would practice it in the mirror when she got home. It might be useful for persuading Connor to bathe more often.

△△△

Rose watched silently until Hugo gave her the prearranged signal. While Ekta was distracted, she bent and searched the bag next to the door. Hugo's plan of "just wing it" seemed to be working remarkably well.

She quickly found what she was looking for and slipped out through the door. The receptionist looked up as she entered the atrium, a look of mild distaste on his handsome face. She briefly considered punching him on his perfectly sculpted nose but decided that would probably draw too much attention. "Is there something I can help you with, madam?" The "madam" part dripped with sarcasm. One good punch, she thought, just there on the bridge.

"No thanks," Rose said. She glanced around the wide atrium, looking for somewhere where she could work undisturbed and unseen. "The bathroom is that way," the receptionist informed her condescendingly. Rose followed the man's pointed finger. She found the toilet easily enough. Her modified implants highlighted the route once they had computed her probable destination.

The room, like most in the upper city, was large and elegant. To Rose's eyes, the space seemed wasted on such a utilitarian purpose. Polished poly-carbon lined the walls and floor, subtly textured to resemble ceramic tiles. Ultraviolet basins were set at regular intervals, their hoods shining brightly in the muted lighting. In the celling a vent hissed, scenting the air with a sweet floral fragrance. It was sickly and overpowering. Rose decided it was only mildly preferrable to the natural odours she was more accustomed to.

She quickly found an empty cubicle and removed the mobile gene editor from under her blouse. She worked quickly, passing a small yellow probe over the sleeveless top she had stolen from Ekta's gym bag. Sweat, Jack had told her, was an excellent source of DNA. Apparently so were other bodily fluids. Rose was grateful not to be exploring those options.

As expected, the yellow light turned orange over a damp patch on the back of the garment. She carefully swabbed it, mindful of not contaminating the sample.

"Jack?" She whispered into her text. "Are you there?"

"I'm here. Did you get the sample?"

"Yeah. I took the swab. Now what do I do?"

"Feed the swab into the gene editor and isolate a single skin cell."

Rose fed the swab into the small machine. It vibrated happily and the control panel lit up with an array of complicated buttons and sliders. "How?" She asked.

"Press the button with the picture of a cell on it."

"A cell?"

"The fried egg." Tim's voice said. Rose silently thanked him and pressed the relevant button. The machined hummed. Several more buttons followed, each with an appropriate food analogy. "The pancake with the strips of bacon." "The prawn cracker with the wonky end." Somehow it worked. The machine chirped happily and out popped a bioplastic slide. The whole job had taken less than ten minutes. Rose sighed with relief. All things considered, she thought, a life as a spy probably isn't for me. I prefer things a little more bangy.

She slipped out of the bathroom, making sure the corridor was empty. She wasn't looking forward to this next part. Afterall, it was one thing to remain unnoticed, quite another to bluff her way to a computer terminal. She tried to look confident, hurrying her steps and glancing regularly at the text in her sweaty palm. Hugo had told him that it was possible to lose oneself for days in large office complexes, so long as you looked busy and carried a text.

Soon Rose found herself in a suite of open plan offices. A few people sat at desks, staring blankly at the clear screens that wrapped around them, effectively isolating them from their peers. Rose felt the oppressive banality of it settle over her, the heavy weight of tedium and suffocation. She wondered how these office workers coped with it. Maybe they all lived secret lives on the holo-net, slaying dragons and abseiling into battle while they sat at home in their underwear.

She hadn't gotten far before a voice interrupted her. "Hi there, I've just noticed you are new to this area and wanted to give you a big '*Internal Audit*' welcome. How can I help you?" The voice was grating and over-enthusiastic. Rose looked down at the small droid at her feet.

"I'm new. Can you show me to an empty desk?"

"Sure thing, valued colleague. Just follow me." The droid wheeled off towards the back of the soulless room. It kept up a stream of corporate messaging as it trundled "We are sure you will love your new role in the '*Internal Audit*' family. Our engagement level for last quarter was '*0.4 percent*' above average. Here is your new desk, I'm sure you'll feel right at home in no time. Personal items are not allowed and will be destroyed if left unattended. Enjoy!"

Rose breathed a sigh of relief as the droid headed off in search of another victim. She heard its voice carry over the transparent screen. "Hello Mrs. Martin. I hope you are enjoying your '*corporate discount card*'. Just one of the many perks of working for '*Internal Audit*'." Rose idly wondered how many 'mishaps' the droid suffered on an average day.

Alone at the large desk she felt very exposed. It was as if the whole room was staring at her, as if every eye was boring into the back of her head. She looked around the office furtively. A few of the workers glanced at her curiously, but most simply ignored her. One woman, her black hair tied in neat braids, smiled sympathetically. She leaned in, as if about to speak, but then her screen beeped. She quickly returned her attention to her work, her eyes wide with alarm.

Taking a deep breath, Rose rested her sweaty palms on the desk. The three-dimensional interface flickered into view around her, wrapping around her upper torso. She had to blink a few times to bring it comfortably into focus. The room beyond seemed to fade slightly.

"Jack, I've found a terminal," she mumbled behind her hand, hoping her voice wouldn't carry in the nearly silent room.

"Well done. Now just type what I tell you."

After several minutes the file access system blinked politely. "Please place your hand in highlighted area," it requested. Rose felt her breath hitch in her throat as she removed the small slide. Carefully she broke the seal and dropped it onto the desk. The application responded with a green smiley face "Good Afternoon, Ekta Reddy. There is ten percent off '*Martha's muffins*' in the staff restaurant today. Your current BMI is 26.2. Perhaps you should enjoy a fresh salad instead. Please prepare for retina scan."

Rose glanced around the room again, fully expecting to be challenged. Nobody seemed to be paying her any attention. After what felt like several millennia the interface flickered, an almost imperceptible drop in brightness. Moments later it dissolved into random characters, swirling around her head in a jumble of corrupt data. Rose held her breath. She guessed she had less than a second before Jack's malware was detected.

"Please work," she begged silently. She knew that the software would have been destroyed in the time it took her to frame the thought, the only real question was whether it had found the files she needed.

"Has it worked?" Jack asked, echoing her thoughts.

"Uh-uh." Rose mumbled, trying to make it sound like she was clearing her throat. She stared imploringly at her text. Moments later she was rewarded with a calm blue notification message "Data packet received." Rose let out the breath she had been holding, almost giddy with relief.

"Got it." She whispered and started to slide out of her seat.

"Good work," she could hear the smile in Jack's voice. "You need to be gone before the security AI traces the software back to your terminal. You don't have long."

Rose knew that Jack had meticulously routed her access through several of the city's most complex subsystems, but the AI was fast, very fast. The interface turned an angry red. "Virus detected," it announced. "This terminal has been quarantined. Remain at your desk and await instructions."

"Too late." Rose bolted up and started to half run towards the exit. She had taken no more than five steps before the small droid intercepted her. "Hello there, *unknown user*. I am afraid I can't find your employment records on the system. Please follow me to security. I am sure we can sort this out in no time."

Rose looked around for an escape, but there was no obvious way out. The room's occupants were gawking at her now, their necks straining to peer over the top of their wraparound screens. Rose wondered if they were grateful for the interruption, or simply relieved they weren't the subject of the droid's attention.

"There must be some mistake," she said. "They told me to report to this area."

"Please wait until one of our security operatives is available to assist you. Our average response time is '*3.2 minutes*'. Thank you for your patience. Follow me please." The droid set off. Rose had no choice but to follow. The office workers watched her departure eagerly, their eyes bright with curiosity.

The droid led her down a corridor towards the main

part of the building. Rose's mind raced. Desperately, she looked around for inspiration. It struck her rather quicker than she was expecting. A little down the corridor a hatch was set into the smooth wall. As the droid drew up to it, Rose did what she had wanted to do since meeting the annoying machine. With a childish grin, she kicked it.

The droid flew sideways, careening through the flap covering the hatch and disappearing into the void beyond. "Damage to government property is ..." she heard it call plaintively, as the flap closed over it. Rose read the warning sign over the hatch with puerile satisfaction. "Warning: Incinerator," it said in large red letters.

$$\triangle\triangle\triangle$$

Hugo looked relieved when Rose huffed back into Ekta's office. He held out his hand expectantly. Rose looked at it blankly. "The contracts please." Rose suddenly remembered the part she was supposed to play. She carefully affected a look of bored submission and handed her text to Hugo.

Ekta made a show of reviewing the invoices carefully. She stroked the side of her face with her index finger as she read. The nail was bright red and filed to a sharp point. "These seem to be in order. I'll pass them on to our finance department." She flicked the text with her finger and handed it back to Hugo.

"I think that concludes our business then. For now." Hugo smiled. It was not a pleasant expression. It was feral and threatening. Rose felt as if icy water had dripped down her back. Hugo held Ekta's gaze far longer than would have been comfortable. He dropped the smile abruptly and turned on his heel. Rose had to jog a few steps to catch up to him as he strode from the room.

They made their way to the pod locks as quickly as possible. As they strode through the atrium, they passed two smartly dressed women. Rose's implants tagged them as

"Information security". She dropped her eyes to the floor as they passed close by. "Are you sure it was Ekta Reddy?" the taller of the two asked.

"It was DNA authenticated, there is no doubt."

"In that case, I think we need to have a quiet word with her." Rose glanced at Hugo and saw her own malicious delight reflected back at her.

CHAPTER 18

Oliver dragged himself out of bed for the second time that day. He was famished, although he couldn't tell whether it was breakfast or lunchtime. It was becoming increasingly difficult to keep track of time. His body clock was hopelessly disrupted by the long nights and lack of daylight. Despite Tim's ministrations he was still sore and bruised from hundreds of pollinator cuts. All in all, he was feeling quite sorry for himself.

Wearily he splashed water on his face from a bowl beside his bed. It was shockingly cold, so cold it took his breath away. It woke him up enough to remember what he was supposed to be doing. Laura was bringing equipment back from their laboratory so he could examine the samples. Had that been yesterday or earlier today? Oliver wasn't sure. Groggily he headed for the clinic, hoping Laura had remembered to pack his favourite micron-agitator. It wasn't a particularly useful scientific instrument, but it did make an excellent coffee stirrer.

He needn't have worried. The small annex was so cramped with equipment that Laura had resorted to sitting cross-legged on a metal bench. He noticed that she had at least remembered to take off her boots. They lay abandoned by the entrance. The top of a cellular probe poked out of the left one. Oliver stooped to rescue it, before realising there wasn't space for it anywhere else. Sighing, he put it back where he had found it.

Tim stood in the centre of the room. His ample body was squeezed between two large machines. His face was split in a broad grin as he delicately dropped a small sample into a bulky instrument.

"Did we really need all this?" Oliver asked, unable to make further progress into the room.

Laura looked up with a small squeal of delight and launched herself over the table towards him. "Hey boss," she grinned up at him, giving him a quick hug.

He looked around the room in dismay "Well, if I wasn't fired already, I am now."

"Why? We didn't steal this, we just borrowed it for the greater good," Laura corrected him.

"I am not sure that's how the city council will see it. Find anything?"

"The fungus is definitely a hybrid of the host plant. The genetic markers are a perfect match. Also, Tim has found something interesting."

"Oh?"

Tim handed him a small slice of fruit on a sample dish. Oliver recognised it as tomato he had taken from the research unit. The red flesh was spotted with black. Something about it felt wrong. Rather than look appetising the tomato invoked an odd feeling of revulsion. "Not the prettiest, is it?" Tim asked as Oliver grimaced at the sample. "Now, smell it."

Oliver raised the sample to his nose and sniffed tentatively. His face wrinkled in disgust. "It smells like bleach, or maybe rotten meat. It's exactly the same as the host plant in the unit. It's horrible. Nauseating."

"Taste it," Tim suggested. Oliver shook his head, gagging on the caustic smell which lingered at the back of his throat. "It's perfectly safe, I assure you. The chemical structure is actually very similar to a normal tomato, but the nutrient concentration is far higher."

"I think I'll pass on that," Oliver said firmly.

Tim grinned. "Well, I did try it. For the sake of science,

you understand."

"And?"

"Have you ever eaten rotted shark meat?"

"I can't say I ever have."

"Well, think ammonia, but with the texture of rubber."

"Sounds delightful."

"It's a delicacy in Iceland, or at least that's what they tell the tourists. This is worse, much worse. The strange thing is the fructose molecule is almost identical. It should be sweet. However, the flavour is …" Tim smacked his lips together like a gourmet in a fine dining restaurant, "the only word I can think of is sickening, and that doesn't seem adequate."

"So, the AI has designed a super hardy, drought resistant, light-tolerant food plant, that nobody will ever be able to eat," Oliver smiled. He felt a small flush of vindication.

"I guess they forgot to add 'palatable' to the success criteria," Laura grinned.

"We need to store these samples carefully. When we confront Ekta with this, we are going to need physical evidence," Oliver said, his mind switching to more serious considerations. "Our top priority is to find a way to stop the spread of the fungus. Talking of which, where is Jamal?"

△△△

A short time later Oliver propped himself up against the table in Jack's untidy workshop. He put aside an empty bowl of cereal with a contented sigh. "Oliver's rule of life, number two. If you can't have sleep, have calories."

"What's rule number one?" Hugo asked.

"When travelling, never skip a toilet break."

"Very wise." Hugo yawned loudly.

Jack sat next to him, resting his hands on his keyboard like a pianist at the end of a long sonata. "I have managed to c… c…create a fake account on the city communication network. By hooking up Hugo's t…t…text and using it as a projector, we should now be able to use holographic comms." Oliver thought Jack looked extraordinarily pleased with himself.

Hugo reached across and tapped a key on the clackety old keyboard. "Well done, Jack. Let's give Jamal a call, shall we?"

The far end of the room seemed to fizzle like a heat haze. A random cloud of coloured lights appeared in the centre and expanded outwards. Oliver thought he could just make out a shadowy figure. Suddenly it collapsed with a crackle of static.

"Let me try recalibrating." Jack's fingers flew over the old keyboard and the sparkling cloud formed again. Jamal's features solidified out of the humid air. The image shimmered, sputtered and then pulled outwards to show Jamal crouched on a patch of dusty ground. He seemed to be somewhere out in the provinces, north of the research unit Oliver guessed.

Several dozen pathfinder drones rested on the ground nearby. Jamal seemed to glance around the room as his own text rendered the holographic image of Jack's workshop. "I never took you as a keen potholer, Oliver," Jamal said, grinning. Judging by the position of his shadow, Oliver thought it was probably close to midday. The sun beat down with the full force of the lingering heatwave, streaking Jamal's face with pearls of sweat. Oliver had never enjoyed the heat of summer, but after days in the tunnels he was yearning for the feel of sun on his skin. He was surprised at the small flash of envy that passed over him.

"Let's just say, I have developed a new appreciation for open sky," he smiled.

Jamal wiped sweat from his eyes. "I am going to share the mapping my pathfinders took this morning." Jamal's image shrunk, as if he was floating backwards. A map sprouted from the dry earth beside him.

The ground was cracked, Oliver noticed. It looked like a poorly fired glaze, a muddle of fractures and ridges. The surface had flaked under Jamal's boots, coating the bottom of his trousers in a thin layer of dust. The surrounding grassland was brown and wilted. Among the golden hummocks, a few limp wildflowers survived the blazing summer heat. Oliver drew his thick coat closer around his shoulders. The hologram made the damp chill of the tunnels feel even more unbearable.

His eyes were drawn away from the sunny grassland to a spot of black mould clinging to the tunnel wall. The resilience of nature had always fascinated Oliver. Even in this perpetual cold and darkness, the small mould still found a way to survive. Likewise, in a few months, the dry riverbed Jamal was exploring would be overflowing with stagnant brown water. It would teem with a bounty of new life. Newts and tadpoles would skim through the murky depths, while pond skaters and dragonflies would dance over the still surface. The brown grasslands would be green and lush, spotted with yellow Iris and starry Bogbean.

Soon after that, the autumn mists would bring yet more change. The golden grasses would be spotted with pools of dark water, mushrooms would emerge from rotting wood, and the slender silver birch would be capped with a fiery crown of gold, their trunks glowing softly in the muted sun. The cycle of growth, decay and renewal had spun through the eons. A ceaseless tumble through time and change. Oliver was determined that he would not witness the end of that restless cycle.

Jamal swiped his text and the map wavered before settling on a new image. A swathe of red spread out in delicate lacey pattern across the provinces. The scale of the spread was unsettling. Almost all of the southern provinces, thousands of precious hectares, were covered with a web of red. "These are the latest results from my drones. They are perplexing. The fungus is still spreading in line with our calculations. The bee population is declining wherever the fungus is found. However, the pattern has dissolved into something far less orderly. The affected area is no longer a neat oval. It is almost a series of disconnected blobs, radiating out from the site of the initial infection."

"Do you have a hypothesis as to why this would

happen?" Oliver asked, studying the map.

"I am at a loss to understand the change." Jamal circled an area of the map with one finger. "In this area, deep in the open heathland, the bee colonies seem unaffected. I have found no evidence of the fungus except in a few shaded hollows. However, in the woodland a few miles north, there is evidence of rapid, and catastrophic colony decline. I am also seeing spots of the fungus in isolated areas. Under old bridges, in abandoned buildings and along ancient hedgerows."

Jamal paused for a moment and rested his fingertips on the dusty ground. When he looked up his eyes were troubled. "There is something else," he said, reaching into a small rucksack beside him. Oliver felt a shivery dread pass over him. There was something in Jamal's voice that implied he had saved the worse for last.

Jamal pulled his hand out from the rucksack and presented something to the holo-camera. It took Oliver a few moments to work out what the dark shape was. Among the soiled feathers, long black fingertips oozed a tarry black liquid. "Birds." He gasped, his stomach plunging through the stone floor.

"Oh no," Hugo mumbled softly.

Jamal nodded. "I found this twenty minutes ago. I think it was once a corncrake. I can't be sure. The carcass has decayed badly, the internal organs have all but liquified."

Oliver gripped the sides of his seat as the room spun around him. "Is that the only one you have found?" his mind was racing with the implications of Jamal's dire discovery. If the fungus had found a way to infect birds, then there would be no way to contain it. A bird could carry the spores hundreds, or even thousands of miles, across seas, mountains and oceans.

Jamal narrowed his lips. "So far this is the only one I have found." He placed the bundle of feathers back in his bag. "Oliver, the containment leak at the research unit was only eight days ago. If this fungus has already infected two species, we have to assume it will infect others. Nothing in nature can mutate this quickly."

"C…C…Could it infect humans?" Jack asked. He flapped his hands in front of his face in a gesture Oliver had come to associate with emotional overload.

"I don't know. Diseases using multiple hosts are not uncommon. Rabies can infect all mammals. Influenzas can cross to humans from birds and pigs." Oliver ran his fingers through the stubble on his chin. Fear nipped at him. Was he fated to be a modern-day Pandora? Opening the box which let all the evil out into the world. Was it too late to slam it shut?

"We could still burn the infected parts of the provinces," Hugo said.

Oliver shook his head. "It's too late. If the fungus is infecting birds they will just fly away when they smell the smoke. That will just spread it further and faster." Despair welled up inside him. He rested his elbows of his knees and buried his head in his hands. "We've lost control of this."

Hugo's voice cut through his turmoil. "Then we will get control back. Jamal, I need you to stay out in the field. Send your pathfinders out as far as you can. Look for new outbreaks. I am going to ask Laura to examine the dead bird. We need to make sure it was infected with the same fungus. Oliver?"

Oliver lifted his head to meet his brother's gaze. Hugo rose smoothly and planted himself in the centre of Oliver's vision. He radiated a quiet confidence, a determination that was somehow contagious. Oliver felt his gloom lift a little. "Tim has started building a simulation of the fungus at the cellular level. He is trying to find some weakness we can use against it. A fungicide, vaccine or repellent. He'll need your help."

"Yes, of course." Oliver exhaled sharply to clear his head.

"Jack, you and I will work on override code we took from Ekta's office. We'll need to find a way to deliver it to Amanda's core programming without her … it," he corrected himself, "suspecting anything."

△△△

Laura had arranged to meet Jamal at the tunnel entrance. After the fire at Oliver's apartment, she no longer felt safe going home. She didn't mind putting herself in danger. After all, this whole debacle was partly her fault. She should have insisted the host plant was burnt the second she set eyes on it. But Laura wouldn't put Amy at risk. Not for anything. Not even to save the planet.

If that meant staying away from her, then so be it. If that meant keeping things from her, then that was acceptable too. What could she say anyway? Sorry honey, but I can't come home in case a rogue computer blows up our kitchen? Oh, and probably best to stay away from the blender. No, it was far easier just to blame work. Another long night slaving over a hot microscope.

She settled down to wait for Jamal's pod to land, enjoying the late evening sun on her face. Nearby, a flock of sparrows erupted from a hawthorn bush and took to the air in a raucous clatter of wings. They shot passed her and landed on the dry grass nearby. The feathered mob trilled indignantly at the magpie that had disturbed them. It's all linked, she thought. Prey and predator, insect and bird. Had human arrogance, once again, brought everything to the edge of extinction?

Her gloomy thoughts were interrupted by the whirling hum of rotor blades. The sparrows chirped in alarm and disappeared in machine-gun rattle of flapping wings. The pod dropped towards her, rotated, and touched down in a whirlwind of dry grass and dust. Jamal stepped out and strode towards her. His shirt was still stained with sweat, and the swirling dust had caught in his hair, making him seem older than his years.

"Good afternoon, Laura. Still going with the shabby-chic look, I see."

"I'm starting a new craze," she gave him a twirl before growing more serious. "Do you have the sample?" Jamal handed her a small box. She swallowed as she set it down at her feet. She didn't want to open it. She was afraid it would only confirm her worse fears. The fungus was adapting, mutating, crossing the boundaries between species. Tentatively, she lifted the lid. Wasn't it better to face her nightmare here, under the warm sun, than in the cold, dark tunnels?

The bundle of feathers at the bottom of the box was definitely a corncrake. She recognised the long neck and stubby bill from her ornithology class. It had been a required module, and not one that Laura had particularly enjoyed. Mostly because old professor dragon-breath had terrible halitosis and little respect for personal space.

Suddenly, the carcass writhed and twitched. Instinctively she took a step back. Perhaps Jamal had been mistaken. Maybe the bird was simply stunned? A thick, sinuous tendril pushed its way through the mottled brown feathers. It wove from side to side, as if searching for something. Thick black treacle oozed from it, filling the air with a foul, chemical odour.

Laura stumbled backwards as it reached towards her. She glanced at Jamal. He stared at the tendril, wide-eyed and fearful. "What is that?"

"The fruiting body, I think. A much bigger version of what we saw come out of the dead bees."

"That smell. I think I might be sick." Jamal turned away. His face crinkled in disgust.

"It's definitely the same fungus." Laura felt the last of her hope ebb away.

"So, it has crossed species." Jamal's face was grim.

"More than species. Phylum. Invertebrate to vertebrate."

"Insect to bird. In less than a week. How could it mutate so quickly?"

"Tim, the medical doctor here, has a theory. He thinks the fungus might be based on a bioweapon."

"A bioweapon!" Jamal looked horrified.

"It would explain how it adapts so rapidly." Laura leaned over to peer in the box. The tendrilous fruiting body had collapsed into a puddle of black goo. "That's odd." she said.

"Odd is not the word I would use. Try appalling."

"No, I mean look. It's dissolved," she sat back on her heels, her mind racing. "When did you find the corncrake, Jamal?"

"Maybe three hours ago. It was a long walk back to the pod."

"And you've had it in this box ever since?"

"Yes, why?"

"Don't you think it's strange that it only started dissolving when I opened the lid?"

Jamal creased his brow in confusion. "Coincidence?"

Laura had the germ of an idea, but she was struggling to bring it into focus. Just as she thought she was about to shout "Eureka!", something she had secretly always wanted to do, the flock of sparrows landed back in the hawthorn bush. Their strident singing broke her concentration. She glared at them. No wonder Archimedes did his thinking in the bathtub, she thought. Then another notion occurred to her. "Why a corncrake? Why something so rare. Why not a common bird, like a sparrow."

"Coinciden ..." Jamal stopped himself. "That is strange."

"Can you show me the mapping of the fungal spread again?"

Jamal reached into his pocket and set his text on the ground. The map sprang up in the air between them.

Laura's index finger traced the areas where the bee die-off was most pronounced. "Woodland. Bridges. Abandoned buildings. Deep scrub." She moved around the map, pointing out the areas where the bees were largely unaffected. "Open heath. Bog. Grassland. Moor." The pieces were starting to snap together. There was something here; she could feel it. Although she still wasn't sure exactly what. "Where did you find the corncrake Jamal?"

"Here, on the edge of this dry riverbed." Jamal pointed.

"In the open?" That didn't seem to fit the pattern. What was she missing? She settled herself cross legged on the grass, wishing she had paid more attention to old profession dragon-breath. "Tell me what you know about corncrakes."

Jamal pursed his lips. "I know they used to be common, but the practice of mowing grass meadows in the twentieth century drove them to the edge of extinction. They started to recover after the Rush when the provinces were created as wildlife reserves." His eyes flicked back and forth as he accessed his ocular implants. "The males have a distinctive call that can be heard from dusk to dawn in the mating season."

"Dusk until dawn?" Laura looked up sharply. "They are nocturnal?"

Jamal hesitated a moment before nodding. "Mostly, yes."

The last piece clicked into place. Laura jumped to her feet. "It's so simple."

"What? What is simple?" Jamal called after her as she sprinted back towards the tunnel system.

CHAPTER 19

The curtain flung open with a sharp crack. Rose came awake with a snort she hoped nobody else would notice. The nightmare still hovered to the edge of her mind.

The over-bright medical centre swam in and out of focus like a kaleidoscopic fever dream. Someone in a blood splattered white coat was cutting off her pressure suit. Next to her another team were working on a mangled shape. She could just read the nameplate. Roberts. His body didn't look right. All the limbs were pointed in the wrong direction. Then there was pain. Too much pain. It had flowed out of her, riding the crest of her scream. Then there was darkness.

When the darkness started to lift, she chased it. She wanted to go with it. To be far away from the bright lights and the searing pain. The voices had seemed very far away. "She's coding. Charge to one-eighty. Clear." Thump.

Rose shook her head to clear the memory. She had found a quiet space at the back of Jack's workshop where she could hide from the growing anxiety that had gripped the tunnels. People were afraid. Rose didn't know what to say to them because, quite frankly, so was she. They had all seen the increasingly hostile news feeds. They had all watched as their black markets slowly dried up and disappeared. Even the shadier parts of Monument City commerce baulked at the idea of doing business with terrorists. The fungus, impending famine and an AI that thought nothing of blowing up a residential building did little to brighten the mood.

Terrorist. Is that what she had become? Had she crossed some invisible line between activist and fanatic? Everything had changed after the computer centre bombing. That one decision. That split second. It was astonishing how quickly life could spiral out of control.

Tim glanced at her and laid a tray of food on the cluttered table. Jack and Hugo barely looked up. They were staring at a pattern on a large screen. It reminded Rose of an abstract dandelion clock. The screen was too large for the room, she worried that it might topple over at any moment and crush Jack under its weight. The little man was wedged under it, staring at his old computer. The smaller screen was full of lines of oddly indented text.

"Is that it? The code you'll use to deliver the failsafe code?" Tim asked.

"Sort of. It's actually a patch to the city's security system. Rather than try to upload the code to every computer in the city, we are going to teach the anti-virus software to treat Amanda's code as malware."

"Couldn't you have just done that before?" Tim asked.

"No. Without the failsafe codes, Amanda would have just it brushed aside. It would have been like trying to train a kitten to attack a lion," Hugo said.

"What if she tries to stop you?"

"She will." Hugo looked away, his shoulders slumping.

"She'll try." Jack sounded far more confident. Rose liked that. If in doubt, blag it out. It worked for her anyway. "I've been hiding from the city authorities for years. Amanda will n … n… never find me. I've built three independent firewalls around this computer."

"What's a firewall?" Rose asked, then immediately wished she hadn't.

"A device which controls network access by …" Rose yawned loudly. "A shield," Jack tried instead. "A shield that protects my computer. If Amanda finds me, she won't be able to stop me before I release the patch." As he talked, Jack's hands stroked the keys of his old computer. Almost lovingly, Rose thought.

"On this screen is a visualisation of the city network." Hugo gestured at the dandelion clock. "Each small dot is a group of computers, ordered by function."

"Each dot is a computer?" Tim asked.

"No, each dot is several thousand computers."

Rose raised her eyebrows in surprise. There must be millions of machines, she thought. All linked together. All doing something she didn't understand. The complexity of it would have been mind-blowing, had she cared.

"I'm ready," Jack said.

Hugo smiled. "Then let's give our kitten some claws."

Rose watched as Jack's fingers stabbed at a key on the old-fashioned keyboard. There was something about the way he did it that made Rose think that this was a momentous act. An occasion to be remembered.

"Deploying p ... p ... patch. Sixty seconds to upload." Slowly, each arm of the dandelion clock started to turn green. At first it was barely noticeable, just a faint shimmer, then it began to accelerate and spread. Hugo grinned as the centre of the clock turned a soothing emerald. Then it stopped. Hugo's grin faded. A dangerous orange colour crept inward from the edges. "Oh n ... n ... n... no." Jack sounded startled.

"What's happening?" Rose limped over to join Tim and Hugo as they crowded around Jack's smaller screen. "What's going on?"

Jack's fingers were a blur of movement over the old keyboard. The sound of the keys being struck were like a jackhammer in the otherwise silent room. "She's found me," Jack sounded breathless. "No, no." He shook his head so hard Rose feared he might give himself whiplash. "Nobody can break my encryption that fast. No!"

"Thirty seconds remaining," Hugo said, glancing at his text.

"Amanda has broken through my first firewall. How is that possible?" Reams of text streamed across Jack's computer, faster than Rose could read. "I've never seen code like this. It's adapting. Every time I try to block it, it learns."

"Twenty-eight seconds. What can I do to help, Jack?" Hugo's voice was an oasis of calm.

"Just keep the patch uploading. I'll try and stop Amanda."

Rose watched as the seconds grudgingly slid past on Hugo's text. Each time the number changed it felt like a small victory. twenty-five, twenty-four. It was agonisingly slow.

Jack worked with a ferocity she had never seen before. The lenses of his thick glasses started to glow orange as they reflected the light on the large screen. Somehow it made him seem more machine than man, a comic book cyborg locked in battle. "Fifteen seconds," Hugo announced as the number clicked over.

"I've lost the second firewall." Jack had taken one hand off his keyboard. It flapped in the air like a dying fish.

"Twelve seconds. Stay focused Jack, we're nearly there." How was Hugo remaining so calm, Rose wondered? She glanced at him in time to see a bead of sweat rolling down his smooth forehead. So, he was human after all. Somehow, she didn't find that comforting right now.

"Ten seconds." Rose realised her nails had embedded themselves in her palms. She didn't know what would happen if they failed, but something told her it would be bad.

"She's nearly through the last firewall. I c ... c... can't stop her."

Seven. Six. Five. The room was bathed in a fiery orange. It was like being buried in the heart of a volcano. Then everything went dark. The sudden blackness was far more terrifying than the ominous orange glow. Rose's skin crawled.

The screen burst back to life. Rose blinked in the sudden light to see a dark-haired woman stare out at her. The woman's eyes were dead and hollow. Predator, Rose's instincts screamed. Danger. The woman smiled with saccharin sweetness. "Hello, Hugo. I've been looking for you."

△△△

Oliver squeezed himself between two large pieces of laboratory equipment. He looked around the damp, cluttered space and wondered how much longer he'd be forced to hide here. The constant cold was depressing, the damp made his neck stiff, and he was starting to forget what the colours blue and green even looked like. *Once all this is over*, he promised himself, *I'm booking a holiday somewhere warm. With cocktails. And a well-stocked library.*

Laura was pressed against his shoulder, passing a modified penlight over a small piece of host plant. She had refused to tell him what she had discovered, only that it was "Mash", which apparently meant good and had nothing whatsoever to do with potatoes.

"It took me most of the evening to identify the actual wavelength," Laura said. Oliver watched as the slice of blood red flower started to hiss and boil. He stood transfixed as it melted away like a burnt-out candle, dissolving into a small puddle of oily gunge.

"It's dead?" he asked, not quite daring to hope. He scraped some of the goo onto a microscope slide. Despite his determination to remain detached and neutral, Oliver couldn't repress a tiny tingle of excitement.

"Completely." Laura's confidence was intoxicating. "It even works on the hybrids. Birds, bees and plants."

Oliver flicked the controls on the microscope. He could feel the weight of expectation on his shoulders. It thrummed through him like a static charge, setting his hair on end. He tried to push it down, to be professional, objective. After everything that had happened, he wasn't sure he could bear anymore disappointment. When the microscope beeped, he was almost too afraid to look.

Oliver's breath caught in his throat. The sample was dead. Even the tiny spores had dissolved into a harmless sludge. The gloominess that had plagued him evaporated. Sunny, effervescent joy rose up to replace it. He grinned so widely his cheeks hurt. Then he started to laugh. A deep belly chuckle that nearly bent him double. "Sunlight?" He laughed so loudly his ribs started to ache. "Sunlight!" He wasn't even sure why it was so funny. The release was ecstatic, his laughter euphoric. Laura dissolved into giggles beside him. He wasn't sure if she was laughing at him or with him. He didn't care.

"We tried everything from glyphosate to vinegar," she said between Oliver's howls of laughter. "And all the time it was right there, all around us. The oldest disinfectant."

By the time Oliver had recovered enough to speak his cheeks were wet with tears. He wiped them away with the back of his hand. "Laura, you're a genius." He wrapped his arm around her shoulders and kissed the top of her head. Her cheeks blushed a glorious pink. The colour reminded Oliver of a summer dawn, the promise of a new day, full of opportunity.

"We have a long way to go yet," she said. "We need to design drones to clear the affected areas and ..."

"Stop." He took her by the shoulders and turned her to face him. "You've just saved the world from famine or worse. Take a moment to enjoy it."

Laura looked slightly taken aback. Slowly, a smile spread across her face. "Not bad, huh?"

"Not bad at all," said Oliver. "One might even say 'Mash'."

She rolled her eyes at him, and Oliver decided that slang was probably best avoided when you are a geeky middle-aged scientist. He was interrupted by the sound of pounding feet. Hugo slid through the doorway before colliding with a waist high laboratory machine. "We need to leave. Now."

"Huh?" Laura asked before Oliver could.

"Amanda knows where we are. We have to leave before we put everyone here in danger."

Rose appeared in the corridor behind Hugo. "I saw what

that thing did to your complex. If you go, will it leave us alone? The last thing I need right now is an army of possessed droids rampaging through my tunnels."

Hugo hesitated a moment before replying. "She isn't interested in you. I think we can draw her away." Hugo grabbed Oliver by the upper arm and pulled him out into the corridor.

"You'd better be right, city boy. Come on, I'll show you the quickest way out of here." Rose set off at an uneven run.

"What's going on? How did Amanda find us?" Oliver asked as Hugo pulled him along the corridor.

"Jack and I tried to shut it down."

"From here? From the tunnels?" Oliver was shocked. Was Hugo so arrogant that he would put a whole community at risk? That was reckless, even for Hugo.

"What better place to hide than a secret hacker's den?" Hugo sounded wounded at the implied criticism.

"Not that secret, clearly."

"I didn't know Amanda would find us so quickly."

"You should have at least considered it. Next time you design a murderous AI, may I suggest you build in an off switch?"

"The thought had never occurred to me."

"Why doesn't that surprise me?"

"Less arguing, more running," Rose shot over her shoulder.

CHAPTER 20

The stairway Rose had led them to seemed to go on forever. Oliver had to stop to catch his breath. His brother was some distance ahead, bounding up the stairs with his usual athleticism. Rose waited for him a few steps above, breathing heavily, her grey hair plastered to her forehead despite the chilly air. "We have to keep moving. We can't be caught here," she called down to him.

Oliver shook his head. "I don't know how you keep going. You're so brave to live like this."

Rose sneered at him. "You think we have a choice? We keep going because we have to. This isn't courage, it's necessity. We can congratulate ourselves for being brave later. Now get moving."

"Where are we going?" Laura called from somewhere above.

"To the surface," Rose said. "Your technical genius just drew a great big target over my home."

"Where on the surface?"

"We need to let Amanda find us. It's the only way to draw her away from the tunnels." Hugo didn't seem even slightly out of breath. Oliver wondered how he had time to run a business and keep so ridiculously fit. "Once we have Amanda's attention, we will need a place to hide until we can work out how to shut her down."

Hugo put his weight against a small metal door at the top of the stairs. It opened with a high-pitched squeal that put

Oliver's teeth on edge. He fell through gratefully and collapsed onto warm, dry grass. Hugo leaned over him and pulled him roughly to his feet. "We can't rest yet. I think we're outside the northern residential district," Hugo said, studying the towering complexes closest to them.

"That red one is the Hancock building," Laura agreed, nodding to an elaborately carved cylinder that seemed to be made of desert sandstone. "That's near my apartment."

Hugo narrowed his lips. "We are going to need supplies and a place to rest. We aren't going to get far dressed like this." He pointed to his thick winter clothing. Oliver agreed. He was already starting to sweat under the hot summer sun.

"Well, we can't go to our apartment. Amanda made sure of that. The lab is risky too," Oliver said.

Hugo looked at Laura pointedly. "No," she said firmly. "I won't put Amy in danger."

"I don't like the idea either, but we don't have much choice."

Laura shook her head. "It will be one of the first places Amanda will look for us."

"Jack will help us. Once Amanda realises that we have left the tunnels, Jack is going to create false surveillance footage and post it on the city network. Amanda will get alerts pop up from all over the city. It will take time for her to work out which ones are real."

Laura did not look happy. "Alright, if you are sure it's safe. But only to pick up supplies. We aren't staying."

Hugo nodded before turning his gaze towards the city. Oliver could see his mind analysing all the options. "We can't go by pod. Amanda will have control of the transport network by now."

"So, what do we do?" Oliver asked. "Walk?" His brother met his attempt at sarcasm with a hard stare. "No, no. You can't be serious." Oliver backed away from Hugo's determined expression. "Nobody walks in the city. There haven't been roads or pavements for a hundred years. We can't just hike through the greenspaces. We'll be eaten by bears, or wolves, or worse."

Rose glanced around nervously "There are bears? Here? Outside the city?"

"Of course not." Laura reassured her, shooting a warning look at Oliver.

"We did reintroduce wolves though," Oliver said, half-teasing.

"Only in the outer provinces. To control the deer population." Laura quickly added. She glared at Oliver, raising her eyebrows.

"What?" He mouthed silently with an innocent shrug.

"We had better get moving." Hugo said, his voice serious. "I've heard there is a full moon tonight. Perfect for hunting." He winked at Laura's irritated expression.

Rose rolled her eyes at the teasing. "I'll come with you as far as the city," she said. "I know how to get around without being seen. You are going to need my help."

As she spoke, a small, fist-sized drone whizzed overhead. It seemed to spot them, circling lower before stopping a few feet above their heads. Picking up a stone, Hugo lobbed it at the drone with impressive force. It impacted with a deafening crack. The drone spun out of the air and landed at his feet. "Fast bowler," he smiled. Oliver wondered if there was any sport Hugo wasn't proficient in. Cheese rolling, perhaps? Or bog snorkelling? Maybe competitive Morris dancing? Oliver allowed himself a small smiled. Hugo picked up the drone and examined it. "I think it's safe to say Amanda knows where we are. It's up to Jack now to keep her busy. Let's get moving."

Hugo set a brisk pace towards the nearest complex. Oliver thought that the walk might have been pleasant if the circumstances had been different. The grass had been grazed to a neat stumble, broken by the occasional clump of purple heather. In places, ferns pushed up through the low scrub, their elegant fronds waving in the evening breeze. In the distance the complexes rose like stone pillars, their colours enriched by the fading light. It was difficult to judge distance over the flat heath, but as the hours passed and twilight descended, the sandstone Hancock building appeared to be no closer.

Oliver tried his best to keep up with the others, but soon he found himself lagging. It had been years since he had done any serious fieldwork, and he was starting to feel it. His feet ached and thirst dragged at him relentlessly.

Hugo seemed to sense his exhaustion and dropped back to his side. "How are you doing, do you need to rest?" he asked quietly.

"If I stop, I might not be able to start again. How much further?"

"Another mile to the outskirts of the district, then maybe another three to Laura's building. An hour and a half. Maybe more at this pace."

Oliver groaned as a wave of despair passed over him. He wasn't certain he could walk another four miles without water.

Hugo narrowed his lips, studying his brother's face. "Do you want to know why the project was so important to me? Why I pushed so hard to be involved?" Oliver glanced up. He knew Hugo was trying to distract him, but he was too curious not to respond.

"Ambition?" he asked flatly.

Hugo hesitated before replying. "Partly. I won't deny that saving the world had a certain appeal. As did making a lot of money," he smiled self-consciously. "That was only part of it though." He took a deep breath as if steeling himself. "Maria is pregnant."

Oliver stopped so suddenly that Hugo ended up a few steps ahead. "What?" The word shot from his mouth, raw and unfettered. Laura and Rose turned to stare. Hugo remained silent. His eyes fixed on the ground before him.

Oliver was struggling to process the onslaught of emotions that crashed through his mind. Anger that Hugo hadn't told him sooner. A familiar touch of envy. Disbelief that Hugo had left his pregnant wife. Mostly though, all he felt was shock. His thoughts felt like pebbles thrown at a glass pane, shattering his worldview into a million pieces. "Maria is pregnant, and you left her?"

"Not quite." Hugo's voice was so soft Oliver had to strain to hear him. "She left me."

"What did you do?" Oliver didn't mean it to sound like an accusation, but fatigue had robbed him of any subtlety.

"I told her I didn't want the baby. That bringing a new life into this world was selfish and short-sighted."

"And you didn't think about that before you got her pregnant?" Oliver couldn't believe how self-absorbed his brother was being. How could he leave Maria? Smart, funny, warm Maria. "Was it inconvenient? Is that it? A baby would get in the way of your precious business?" He couldn't keep the vinegar out of his voice.

"It wasn't like that," Hugo's normal calm shattered. "I was afraid Olly. Afraid of change, afraid of responsibility. For the first time in my life, I was afraid of the future."

Oliver raised his hands in confusion "I don't understand. How could you have just left?"

Hugo seemed to deflate like a popped balloon. "Despite everything we have done, the climate is becoming more hostile," Hugo started to pace; his movements agitated. "Starvation, famine and disease are just the start. Another Rush is inevitable, and this time it will almost certainly lead to war. How can I raise a child knowing that?"

"Nothing is inevitable. This isn't the first challenge we have faced as a species."

"What if it's different this time?"

Oliver felt his frustration bubble up. "Don't you see how arrogant that question is? Every time we've faced a crisis, we think it's the worse yet. We convince ourselves that our generation is different, our problems are so much bigger. World wars, nuclear annihilation, climate change. It's only when we overcome the problem, when we look back on it, that we realise it wasn't insurmountable after all."

Oliver started walking again. He was grateful the two women had moved ahead to give them some privacy. His head was spinning. It made no sense to him that Hugo would walk away from his family. Afterall, his brother had only been eighteen when they had been orphaned. Surely, he, more than anyone, would understand the value of family, and the pain of being alone.

"Hugo?" Oliver said "Is this really about the future of the planet? Or is it about your fear of failure."

His brother glanced at him sharply. Anger washed over his face like a summer storm, intense and sudden. It faded almost as quickly as it had arrived. "Honestly Olly, I don't know anymore. All I know is that I needed to make this project work. At any cost. I've never had so much at stake. It's... overwhelming."

Suddenly the pieces fell into place. Hugo hadn't been motivated by ambition or greed, but by fear. Fear that he would be less than perfect. Fear of losing control. Fear of failing his new family. Somehow that lessened the sense of betrayal that Oliver had been nursing.

Hugo blew out a breath, kicking at a tuft of dry grass. "I have no idea how to be a father, Olly."

"I don't imagine anyone does until it happens to them."

"What if I'm terrible at it?"

Oliver reached out and gripped his brother's shoulder. "Then I'll just have to make sure that I'm an amazing uncle."

Hugo looked so vulnerable. For a moment Oliver forgot his exhaustion. A connection he hadn't felt since childhood clicked back into place. He walked shoulder to shoulder with his younger brother in silence. Slowly, the sky turned to indigo, and the light faded. Out of the west, the moon rose, chasing away the darkness with silvered beams.

△△△

It was fully dark when the group of exhausted fugitives finally reached the outskirts of Laura's district. The greenways were narrower here, following the routes of the old roads and railways. The complexes towered over them, blocking out the night sky. To Oliver's weary mind, it almost seemed as if the buildings were leaning in, gossiping to each other as the small group passed silently beneath. He wondered what secrets they shared; what ordinary human stories were unfolding behind their exteriors. Oliver found that thought comforting. To most people this was just the end of another day. Time to put the kettle on and slip into your favourite slippers.

Laura's complex was a simple glass rectangle. The expensive outward facing apartments were all brightly lit. The light seeped through the opaque glass and diffused to a warm, welcoming glow. As city architecture went, the building was modest, but to Oliver's tired eyes it was the most beautiful thing he had ever seen.

After a short search, they found the doors to the atrium on the ground floor. The entrance was simple and austere. There was no need for anything decorative, as most of the residents would enter by the pod locks higher up the building. This entrance was a service area, and it was deserted, except for a few domestic droids. At the end of the plain atrium was a bank of lifts. Laura pressed a button and the doors hissed open. The bedraggled company filed inside.

A few seconds later, the doors opened onto a neat corridor. Oliver had almost forgotten how clean and well ordered the city felt in comparison to the very human grubbiness of the tunnels. Despite the carefully controlled climate, somehow it felt colder, less friendly.

Oliver limped after Laura. His legs had already stiffened after the short lift ride. He made a resolution to get fitter, a resolution he knew he probably wouldn't keep. Laura stopped

322

before one of the identical doors with a slightly baffled expression on her face. After a moment, she tutted to herself. "I'm an idiot. Of course, it won't open. None of us are wearing implants." Oliver smiled. He had also expected the door to swing open as soon as they approached. However, without implants the city's automated systems had no way to identify them. Which had been the whole point of removing them, he reminded himself. Laura reached out and knocked awkwardly on her own front door.

Moments later, Amy threw it open. Before Laura could react, the slight woman threw herself across the threshold. "You said a day. It's been four. I don't know whether to hug you or kick you." Oliver was relieved when Amy chose the former.

"I'm sorry. I didn't want to risk Amanda tracing my calls back to you. I was trying to protect you."

"Protect me from what? What's going on Laura?"

Laura cleared her throat. "I am not sure how to put this without it sounding melodramatic."

Rose swore under her breath. "You could start by not using the word 'melodramatic'." She turned to Amy, "We're on the run and need somewhere to stay."

"What? Where have you been? Who are you running from?"

"Amanda, an advanced intelligence. It's trying to kill us." Hugo chimed in, unhelpfully, Oliver thought.

"Kill you? Will someone please explain what is going on?" Amy looked like she was about to lose her temper. Oliver was quite impressed it had taken her this long.

"Amanda is an out-of-control AI," Laura said. "It's hunting us because it thinks we are a threat to a project it's been assigned to complete. The project we were working on."

"And it will do anything to complete the project and fulfil its programming," Hugo added.

"We have been hiding in the tunnel network under the city," Laura gestured over her shoulder. "This is Rose, she is the leader of the tunnel community."

"In the tunnels? With the terrorists?" Amy said.

Rose cleared her throat.

"No offence"

"None taken." Rose smiled dangerously.

"I think you need to tell me everything. And I do mean everything," Amy glared at Laura. Oliver wasn't sure if she was angry or confused. He suspected a little of both.

"Perhaps we can carry on this conversation inside?" Hugo said, rubbing his lower back with the knuckles of one hand.

Amy cast a long glance at Rose, her eyes lingering over the scar that ran across her cheek and chin. "Alright, come inside," she said, pushing the door open a little wider. "This had better be one doozy of a story Laura."

The weary group trudged after her before gratefully collapsing around the small kitchen table. The room was warm, simply furnished and smelled of freshly brewed coffee. Oliver inhaled deeply, as if greeting a long-lost friend. Then he leant against the kitchen sink and gulped water directly from the tap. Amy pointedly handed him a glass.

It only took Laura half an hour to explain everything that had happened to Amy. That didn't seem very long, Oliver thought. Afterall, he had nearly died in a pod crash; fought off a swarm of angry pollinators; lost his home and all his possessions; spent nearly a week freezing in the tunnels; and hiked miles across the city in the burning summer heat. Surely that deserved more than half an hour of someone's time. Even so, by the time Laura had finished his eyes were dropping.

"What are you going to do next?" Amy asked as Oliver did his best to try and stay awake.

"We need to shut down Amanda," Hugo said. "We won't be able to do anything about the fungus with every droid in the city hunting us."

"How? All I've heard so far are the ways you can't do it. You can't unplug it because it's spread across every computer in the city. You can't shut it down as it has evolved to ignore human commands. You can't uninstall the software as it fights back violently," Amy shrugged her shoulders.

"I think that's a problem for tomorrow," Hugo said. "Right now, we all need some rest. I have a feeling tomorrow is going to be a long day."

CHAPTER 21

Hugo paced the small kitchen. His long legs took him across the narrow room in three strides. He swivelled on his heel and paced back. Repeatedly. The clack of his shoes on the polished tiles was the only noise in the quiet apartment.

"Do you have to do that?" Oliver asked. He had slept for a few hours earlier, but ten cups of coffee, a limited bladder capacity and the lumpy sofa had prevented him from getting further rest.

"Doing what?"

"Pacing. It's irritating."

"I think better when I pace."

"It's noisy. Stop it."

"I'm noisy? Do you know you talk in your sleep? Who is Sharon?"

Oliver looked slightly sheepish "She is a barista at the coffee shop near our lab. She has the most amazing…"

"I don't think I want to know."

"…crema."

Hugo shook his head, swivelled and marched to the other end of the kitchen.

"Please sit down, it's exhausting watching you." Oliver pulled the chair out next to him, effectively blocking Hugo's path. His brother fell into it with a sigh.

"We need to get out of the city, Olly. At least until I can think of what to do next."

"Where will we go? We can't risk putting anyone else at risk."

"Somewhere Amanda can't track us. Out in the provinces. We will need to go on foot, so it can't be anywhere more than a few days hike from here."

Oliver rubbed his thumb over his index finger. "There is an abandoned farmhouse about thirty miles west of the city. We set up a monitoring station there a few years ago. We could reach it in a couple of days. I doubt Amanda would think to look for us there."

Hugo nodded. "It's as good a place as any. We're going to need camping equipment and supplies."

Oliver nodded. "I'll ask Laura. I know she and Amy have done a few camping trips."

It was almost mid-afternoon by the time the four renegades had agreed on essential equipment and packed what Hugo insisted on calling "go-bags". Amy had ordered the camping equipment through a friend and had it delivered to an empty apartment. Oliver was impressed with her subterfuge, but he was concerned about involving her.

As Amy and Laura bid each other a tearful goodbye, Hugo helped Oliver adjust his heavy pack. "Did we really need all this stuff?" Oliver asked, as Hugo pulled the straps tight over his shoulders.

"No, but it took all my negotiating skills to persuade Laura not to take a folding coffee table and an inflatable kayak."

"Why would we need a kayak?"

Hugo shrugged "I have never understood how women pack."

Rose was waiting for them by the lifts, tugging at the unfamiliar waterproofs Hugo had ordered for her. She looked different in the bright, modern colours. Softer somehow. She held the doors open as Laura, Hugo and Oliver crowded in. The lift took them down to ground level with a soft hum. As the doors swished open, Hugo froze. The small, plain foyer was crowded with shuffling droids.

One droid, painted a garish orange, wheeled towards them. Oliver noticed a small camera, mounted high on its back. The lens rotated myopically as it struggled to focus on them. "What's it doing?" Laura asked, taking a curious step forward.

Hugo quickly pulled her back. "It's looking for us. We don't have implants and that camera is designed for close-up work, not identification."

Laura's eyes widened as the droid trundled towards them, attracted to the sound of their voices. A small screwdriver shot forward from behind a flush cover, stabbing blindly at the air in front of it. Further down its body the edge of a circular saw was just visible.

"Quiet," Hugo whispered. He led them in a wide arc around the hunting droid. Beyond it, between the escapees and foyer door, was a thin service droid. Four skeletal arms stretched out from its white casing, each ending in a jagged metal spike. Beneath the droid were the remains of its grippers and a small vacuum cleaner, laying where it had deliberately snapped them off. Greenish machine oil dripped from the mutilated arms, filling the room with a sharp metallic tang.

"How are we going to get past that thing?" Oliver whispered.

"More importantly, why are they here?" Rose asked.

"Amanda," Hugo replied. "She is using the city infrastructure to hunt us," his voice was resigned, as if he had already expected this possibility. He motioned them to silence and crept forward, side-stepping, his back to the wall. Halfway to the entrance he stopped beside a small table. He lifted it carefully and flung it into the middle of the room.

A group of droids turned towards the sound of the crash and rushed forward. One machine, its single arm holding a red-hot steam iron, swung towards the table. Oliver watched as it flailed out, leaving a dark scorch mark on the pale wood. The callous, single-minded destruction was unsettling. It left Oliver feeling sickened. Afterall, these were the machines that had shared his apartment. Cleaning while he slept, repairing while he worked. Barely noticed but always present. He watched as the other droids fell on the table, thrashing and ripping with their metal limbs. In moments, they had reduced the wood to splinters.

"I don't think we are getting out this way" Hugo mumbled, clearing his throat.

"What do we do now?" Laura asked. "We could try the basement?" As she spoke the service droids wheeled around the room, their makeshift weapons outstretched before them.

"No, too obvious. If we can't go down, we'll have to go up." Hugo keyed the button that would take them to the first floor.

The elevator opened onto another bland corridor. Hugo set off, his long strides carrying him ahead of the others. "What now?" Oliver asked as he took a few jogging steps to catch up.

"Pod locks." Hugo answered tersely.

Oliver had a brief flashback of falling through trees, the sky spinning above him. He took a deep breath to steady himself, "We can't take a pod, Hugo."

"We aren't going to." The tone of his voice left little room for further questions. Oliver felt a stab of irritation. Hugo's predilection for leaving other people out of his decision making was starting to grate. Just once, Oliver thought, it would be nice to know what Hugo was planning before it was actually happening.

The docking area was quiet when they arrived. The morning commute was still several hours away, and most pleasure-seekers would have returned home hours before. A few vacant pods waited patiently, their doors open, the lights above them a steady green. The other lock doors were sealed, red warning lights marking them as empty.

Hugo approached the nearest sealed door and rummaged in his heavy pack. From somewhere in its depths, he produced a small penknife. He jammed the narrow blade between the doors and started to move it, deftly feeling his way upwards. With a triumphant grin, he twisted the blade and the doors parted with a sharp hiss of escaping air. The summer breeze rushed in, hot and humid. "Never underestimate the benefits of a bad education," Hugo said with a playful wink. Oliver decided it was best not to ask him where he had picked up that particular skill.

He peered out. Several metres below, was a dense thicket of thorn bushes following the edge of the complex. "How do we get down?" he asked, eyeing the insidious tangle of thorns.

"We jump." Laura quickly swung her legs over the edge and fell into the bushes below. "Ouch. Ow. Get off me you green sadist." She emerged a few seconds later, bits of shrub clinging to her clothes and hair. "It's not so bad," she called up unconvincing. "At least the bushes break your fall."

"Great," Rose said sarcastically, before quickly jumping after her. Moments later she appeared from under the thick shrubs "Which idiot planted this thing?" she complained. "Does it actually feed off human blood or is it just doing this for fun?" She pulled a long splinter from the back of her hand, holding it up to them as evidence.

Oliver glanced at Hugo nervously, but his younger brother just grinned and jumped. Oliver cursed loudly. He looked around for a better way down, but the sides of the complex were sheer glass. With one final heartfelt profanity he jumped into the thicket of thorns. "Laura," Oliver called as the crawled out from the vicious vegetation. "Remind me to remove anything spikey from the list of government approved plants."

△△△

Hugo led them through the labyrinth of city parkways with an uncanny sense of direction. They carefully avoided the city droids by weaving between the more densely forested greenways. However, as the early sun rose above the buildings, they found themselves in an upmarket residential area. The elegant buildings were surrounded by beautifully manicured parks and gardens, rather than the scrub and woodland of the less expensive areas.

Oliver looked at the immaculate lawn that stretched the entire length of one of the larger complexes. "Is there another way around?" he asked Laura.

"This whole district is surrounded by parks at ground level. We would have to backtrack for miles."

"That has to be nearly 500 metres of open grass. We are bound to be spotted." Hugo glanced up at the complex. Water cascaded down the building's sides in a powerful torrent, enveloping the whole structure in a wall of froth and foam. The source seemed to be somewhere on the roof. A spectacular spray of rainbow mist rose from the wide lake which surrounded the building like a protective moat. Dense clusters of pink water lilies dappled the water. The roar of the waterfall as it plunged into the lake filled the hot morning air, deafening them to any other sounds.

"We can't go through the buildings. I can't see a ground floor entrance," Rose said. "You city people aren't big on getting outside, are you?"

"We are, but we prefer the roof top parks. The weather is controlled by magnetic shielding. We can go surfing in the morning and ski in the afternoon," Laura said.

"Sounds exhausting," Rose snorted.

Hugo narrowed his lips. "There isn't any way around. We're going to have to risk it."

They set off across the grass at a slow jog, their packs clanking noisily in the spray cooled air. Oliver did his best to keep up with the others, but his sedentary lifestyle was not conducive to running with a heavy pack. He quickly found himself out of breath and damp with sweat.

Hugo seemed to hear Oliver start to drop back and slowed to help him. As he turned, his eyes grew wide with shock. Oliver twisted around to see what had surprised his brother. A heavy drone lumbered through the air towards them, clumsy and ponderous. Its distended abdomen hung like an udder between three long struts, each packed with buzzing rotors. Only now was the deep whine of its motors audible over the tumbling water.

Oliver ducked just in time to avoid a jet of scalding liquid. He felt the heat of it as it shot past his face. The drone struggled to reorientate itself, wobbling unsteadily as liquid sloshed in its tank. Two giant brushes swiped the air in front of it, held out like the balance bar of some novice acrobat. Oliver stared at it in wide-eyed disbelief. It seemed far too slow and ungainly to be of any real threat. After all, death by window cleaner was not something he had ever imagined for himself.

His bewilderment was interrupted by another high-pressure jet of boiling fluid. It slashed across his shoulder and chest, leaving a searing trail of pain. Oliver cried out, nearly collapsing as the pain built rather than subsided. The intensity of it multiplied and multiplied. Panic tore through him as he desperately tore at his clothes, desperate to escape the scalding agony. Acid, he thought, the window cleaner was spraying acid.

Hugo grabbed him by his shoulder straps and dragged him away from the lurching drone. "Run!" he called, pulling Oliver into a staggering trot. The drone hummed and lurched as another blast of boiling liquid narrowly missed them. Oliver felt someone grab his other shoulder and saw Rose running beside him.

They pelted across the lawn, trying to weave as the clumsy drone spat hot acid. Suddenly, the ground disappeared from under Oliver's feet. He plunged downwards, his arms flailing helplessly. Cold water closed over his head. He kicked upwards instinctively, but something held him under the surface of the water. Oliver couldn't control the rising fear. It gripped him, robbing him of any conscious thought. His limbs hit out of their own violation, impacting with something soft yet unyielding. Just as the burning in his lungs became unbearable, he felt a tug upwards. He came to the surface coughing and spitting.

"Ow. You have a pretty decent jab for a bookworm," Hugo's voice came from right behind him. A roaring, crashing sound pushed against Oliver's frayed senses, a deep swell of noise that vibrated deep in his chest. Spray hit his face, cold and numbing. He forced his eyes open. In front of him was a moving curtain of white water. It plunged into the lake from a narrow ledge high above, obscuring everything behind a wall of impenetrable spume. Hugo had found the only possible hiding place, Oliver realised. He had led them behind the ornamental waterfall that plunged down the sides of complex.

Oliver could feel his brother pressed behind him. Hugo's arms were wrapped tightly around his chest, holding his head above the surface. The two women stood close by, water running down their faces. Laura reached for a handful of red hair and tried to wring the water from it. She met his eyes miserably. "I'll never be able to look at a squeegee the same way again," she said.

CHAPTER 22

Hidden behind the wall of cascading water, the four renegades huddled together for warmth. Oliver fidgeted, wondering whether the hunting drone was still out there somewhere. It would never give up, he knew, never surrender to frustration or fatigue. It was as pitiless as the summer heatwave that boiled the city and browned the grasses around their hiding place.

The cold water had eased the burning in Oliver's chest, but his skin was red and blistered. He was forced to hold his arm awkwardly to stop his jacket chafing the scalded skin. He was exhausted too. Emotionally and physically drained in a way he had never experienced before. He wondered if this was what it was like to be a salmon, pulling against a fisherman's line, feeling his strength ebb away with each relentless crank of the reel.

Hugo's voice came from behind him. "I have been thinking about how to shut down Amanda."

"Now would be an excellent time for you to have a moment of genius," Oliver said, prodding the yellow blisters on this upper chest.

"There is only one way I can think of. I need to finish the program."

"I am not sure I understand."

"Amanda won't give up. She can't. I made sure of that when I created her. The only way to stop her is to let the program run to completion. I need to convince her the project is over, that her task is complete."

"Alright. How do we do that?"

Hugo pressed his lips together. "That's what I'm struggling with," he shook his head as if to clear it. "It will come to me," he said, with such conviction that Oliver believed him. "Changing the subject, before we left the tunnels yesterday, you and Laura seemed to have made a breakthrough of some kind."

Laura nodded. "We think we've found a way to destroy the fungus and all the other host plant hybrids." Oliver felt the "we" was overgenerous, but he was too tired to correct her.

"What did you find?" Hugo asked, his mood visibly improving.

"It dies in sunlight, or more specifically, certain wavelengths found in sunlight."

Hugo snorted. "Ha! There is an old design principle I've always tried to stick to. K.I.S.S. It stands for 'keep it simple, stupid'. It seems very appropriate here."

Laura smiled. "It was the bird that gave it away. Corncrakes are so rare it made no sense that it was the only infected bird we found. It wasn't until Jamal reminded me that they are nocturnal that I made the connection." Laura looked thoughtful. "I can't help wondering if we'd have solved it sooner if we hadn't been forced underground."

"It doesn't matter. What's important is that you have a solution now. However, it isn't going to do us much good if we stay here. I'm going to check that the drone has gone."

Cautiously, Hugo pushed through the rushing waterfall and disappeared. Several minutes passed. Then several more. Oliver felt his worry swell. He shifted his weight from leg to leg until Rose glowered at him to stop. When the water finally parted, Oliver half-expected to see the drone, spewing boiling acid like some monster from a late-night horror show. He was relieved when the shadowy shape resolved into Hugo.

"The coast's clear. Let's move." Hugo led them through the plunging water and over the open grass. The group moved slowly, stopping often to listen and scout the route ahead. Hugo took them on a meandering path through the greenspaces, ensuring their route was as unpredictable as possible. On more than one occasion their caution was justified. Drones swept overhead, the hum of their motors rising over the whisper of the wind.

As evening began to blush the western sky, their luck changed. The drones began to increase in number, sweeping between the buildings in slow deliberate search patterns. The escaping humans were forced to change direction several times, darting under shrubs or concealing themselves among the tall grasses.

Suddenly, Oliver was hit by a realisation. "We're being herded," he said, feeling chilly despite the humid evening.

"Herded? What do you mean?" Rose's face was drawn with fatigue, but she moved with a resolve that Oliver respected, perhaps even admired.

"We keep being forced to turn right. The last few hours we have been spiralling inwards. With every turn, the spiral gets a little tighter."

Hugo cursed loudly "You're right. I should have realised that earlier. The drones aren't searching for us, they are herding us."

"Herding us where?" Laura asked. Her hair was plastered to her forehead with sweat and dirt.

"I don't know, and I am fairly certain I don't want to find out," Hugo bowed his head in thought. "We need to get around them somehow."

"Is there a way back into the tunnel system from here?" Oliver asked.

"No," Rose shook her head. "The nearest entrance is miles from here."

"What about over the city? Could we fake an ID and steal a pod?" Laura asked.

"I am sure Jack could, but I'm not a hacker. I couldn't get past the security without alerting Amanda."

"Then we're just going to have to make a run for it." Laura raised her chin defiantly, her green eyes flashing.

Oliver shook his head "That didn't work out so well for us last time." He pointed to the blisters on his arm and chest.

"We could find a place to hide?" Rose said, talking slowly as she thought the idea through. "Wait until dark and hope the drones think we have slipped through. They will have to spread out to find us again. We might be able to sneak past."

"Yes, I think that's our only real option," Hugo said. "Hide where though? The city is teeming with drones and droids."

"We passed some thick shrubs earlier. We could hide under them?" Laura offered.

"That won't work." Hugo started to pace in a tight circle. "The drones will use night-vision. They probably already are, it's how they are herding us so effectively. We'll be sitting ducks out in the open."

Oliver rolled his shoulders, trying to ease the burning pain in his chest. An idea occurred to him. "We could hide in plain sight. Somewhere with lots of people, but not many drones."

Laura nodded. "The Bolin building? The exhibition in the park? It's less than a mile from here."

"Good idea." Hugo abruptly stopped pacing and turned to face them. "I can't go with you."

Oliver turned to face his brother. "What do you mean?"

"Amanda isn't going to let us leave the city. That's clear now."

"But what can you do? The primary nodes are in the research unit. That's miles outside of the city." Oliver rubbed the deep gash on his forehead where the pollinator drones had attacked him earlier.

"Amanda doesn't have primary nodes. She is a single tier system. Every node is an equal peer. By now her software is spread across millions, probably billions of physical machines. Perhaps I can use that to my advantage."

"How?" Oliver asked.

"The Hub. In order to have control over the city infrastructure, Amanda must have taken control of the Hub. I'm betting most of it is still intact. It wouldn't be efficient to take on all its functions. Amanda has no interest in processing sewage or watering plants. If I can get the Hub's user interface running, I'll have a direct route to Amanda."

"What if it tries to defend itself?" Laura asked.

Hugo grinned. "Oh, it will."

Oliver shook his head. "This is far too risky. The second you log into a network Amanda will know where you are. You would have to find somewhere she can't reach you. That's going to be impossible in a city full of automated machines."

Rose cleared her throat. She stood with her arms folded across her chest, a thoughtful expression on her face.

"What are you thinking?" Hugo asked.

"I'm not sure if this will help, but a few weeks ago I found an old vending machine in one of the abandoned tunnels. I think it was an early underground station from around the time of the Rush. I accidentally turned the old machine on, and it seemed to connect to the city network. I think it was trying to talk to the Hub."

Hugo smiled. "That sounds perfect."

"What are we supposed to do in the meantime?" Laura asked. "I'm not going to hide while you put yourself in danger. I want to help."

"You will be helping," Hugo said. "Every drone Amanda sends to find you will be one less I have to deal with."

Oliver didn't like the sound of that. "I'm not sure this is a good idea. There are too many unknowns. We should stick to the plan and find a way out of the city. Lie low for a while, give ourselves time to think. Amanda has proven she will do anything to stop you."

"You are making it sound personal. It isn't. Amanda isn't conscious, this isn't some twisted father-daughter conflict. Amanda is just a bunch of algorithms. Her sole

338

purpose is to meet her success criteria."

"And you will be making yourself a threat to that. Look what she did to stop me."

"I think I can persuade her otherwise. If I don't, how long do you think it will be before she decides someone else, or perhaps *everyone* else, is a threat?"

Oliver shook his head. "Hugo, stop and think about this. You have responsibilities beyond yourself now. You can't just throw yourself into harm's way."

"Responsibility is why I must do this, Olly. Don't you see? I am responsible for this mess. I am not running away from it. I made that mistake before. I won't make it again."

Oliver could see the steely determination in his brother's eyes. Experience told him that further words were pointless. Hugo's mind was made up. He squeezed his brother's shoulder and tried very hard not to let his fear show. "Good luck, Hugo."

"I'll be fine, Olly. After all, I have Rose." He turned to craggy ex-miner with a grin.

Rose rolled her eyes. "Keep up, city boy. I'm not slowing down for you." She turned on her heel and set out across the grass with a lopsided jog.

△△△

Oliver knew the drones would be closing in on them, trying to drive them deeper into the city. He weighed his options. Taking an indirect route might avoid detection, but if he was right, Amanda knew exactly where they were. The searching drones were simply the sheepdog, nipping and darting to control their movements. A direct route might make them easier to track, but it would mean reaching safety much faster.

Oliver glanced at Laura. Her face was pale and dark circles had formed under her eyes. She wasn't complaining, but Oliver could see that she was exhausted. As was he. The chemical burns weren't debilitating, but the constant stinging pain was draining. He quickly made the decision to take the shortest route.

The drones didn't harass them on the walk through the greenways. Oliver couldn't tell if they had temporarily shaken their pursuers, or if Amanda was satisfied with the direction they were moving. He suspected the latter. By the time they reached the Bolin complex, night had fallen. The darkness wrapped around them, instilling a false sense of security. Oliver looked up at the tall, narrow complex and tried to plan his next move.

The exposed frame of the building was designed to resemble cast iron. It crawled up the milky white core in a series of swirls and abstract patterns that reminded Oliver of the thorn bush he had crawled out of earlier. In his opinion, it was not the most attractive building in the city. He decided not to risk the main entrance. Oliver still had visions of the service droids in Laura's building, reducing the solid wooden table to matchsticks. Instead, he led them to the side of the building, directly under the second story apartments.

"Do you think we could use Hugo's trick to break in? I don't think I can do it with one good arm," he said.

"Yes, I think so."

Oliver braced his back against the wall and boosted Laura up to the first handhold. The metal frame made the climb seem straightforward, but Oliver watched fretfully as Laura hung from the twisted metal. She carefully inserted the blade of her penknife into the door of an empty lock. With a quick twist of her wrist, she forced it open. Laura grinned. "It's amazing what you can learn while being chased across the city by murderous machines."

"If biology doesn't work out, you have a promising career as a cat-burglar," Oliver smiled.

"Nah, I'm more of a morning person."

Laura helped Oliver pull himself up into the lock. Despite his climbing experience, it was challenging with only one arm. By the time he reached the top he was breathless and dizzy. After a short break to catch his breath, he joined Laura searching for the lifts. They quickly found them and took the long ride up to the rooftop park. As the doors opened, Oliver was assaulted by the smell of hot food. He hadn't eaten since the morning and the fairground smells that wafted from the stalls set his stomach growling.

The centre of the park consisted of a large, open exhibition space. Oliver had never been there before, but he knew it was used for events like music concerts and exhibitions. He couldn't see much over the tall wicker fence that surrounded the festival space, but the sound of bird song and animal calls felt bizarre and exotic. At a break in the fence, a large, gaudily lit sign announced the current exhibition. "The Sixth Mass Extinction: Life from the Ashes of Industry".

People walked on the gravel path towards the entrance, stopping to gawp at the not quite solid holograms that darted around their feet. Oliver spotted a plump grey bird with a curved beak and stunted wings. A Dodo, his mind supplied, as the projection waddled up to a delighted family group.

Nearer the entrance, a big cat prowled beside the path, its sleek flanks glistening under the lights. Its spotted coat was a beautiful, rich amber. It moved with such fluid grace that Oliver couldn't help but be captivated by it. He wondered how humanity had allowed such beauty to fade from existence. It filled him with regret, sadness, and no small amount of shame.

As they passed through the entrance, the density of people increased. Excited children rushed between the exhibits, chasing after the fleeing lemurs and swinging orangutans. A young woman posed beside a giant panda, while a keeper led a holographic rhinoceros towards a raised podium.

Laura turned to Oliver, "Extinction as entertainment?" she asked.

"Or as education perhaps." He was struggling with his own aversion to the festive atmosphere. The popcorn vendors and bright souvenir stalls seemed in bad taste.

"This doesn't look like education."

"Making people aware of what we have lost might help

to preserve what we have left." He swept his hands through the hologram of a turtle dove that perched on a low fence.

"Ever the optimist." Laura muttered, rolling her eyes.

"Hardly. You're mistaking optimism for tenacity. Or maybe it's just comfortable denial," Oliver smiled. "On a positive note, we should be able to lose ourselves in this crowd for quite some time. Fancy a locust hotdog?"

△△△

Rose did her best to keep up with Hugo as they made their way swiftly through the darkness. She pushed herself hard, sprinting between cover and dodging the low bushes and hedges. Hugo powered through the greenways ahead of her. He seemed to be relishing the rush of air over his skin and the springy grass beneath his feet. Rose trailed several metres behind him, fighting the grinding pain in her hip. She was determined not to let it show, but the pain was getting worse with each step. Despite her discomfort she felt alive. It was as if she was truly awake for the first time in years. It's more than adrenalin, she thought, I feel like my old self. Rather than just surviving I'm living. I'm making a difference.

Amanda had concentrated its search on the outskirts of the city. The closer they drew to the centre, the less drones they spotted. After an hour, Rose let herself relax, falling into a shambling rhythm. Hugo slowed to match her pace, moving with an effortless grace that brought Rose a pang of loss. Before the accident she had loved to run. She had found solace in the repetition and joy in the thrill of movement. Since then, she had worked hard to stay fit. But she missed the fluidity of her younger body. Age was not something Rose would ever be able to accept gracefully. Although sharing the experience with Connor had made it bearable.

At first, she didn't see the droids ahead of them. They were shrouded by some form of holographic camouflage. Then a sliver of moonlight glinted off something metallic and

Rose slowed. Hugo dropped back beside her with a confused expression on his face. She raised a finger to her lips and pointed ahead. His brow drew together as he tried to make sense of the strange shimmer in front of them. Rose crept forward cautiously, holding her body in a low crouch. She couldn't work out if the hazy shadows were just a trick of the moonlight.

She might have mistaken the rumbling noise for distant traffic if her senses hadn't been on such high alert. "Get down," she shouted and threw herself sideways, just as the ground exploded with a fizz of energy.

Rose landed heavily on her back. Through the cloud of flying dirt, she saw Hugo hit the ground and come back to his feet in an elegant parachute roll. A burnt crater marked the ground where he had been stood fractions of a second earlier. His eyes found hers and then flicked up, growing wide in alarm. Rose swung her head around, just in time to see two droids roll out of a cloud of steam and smoke. They were enormous. Their long, smooth bodies hung between two sets of tracks. Above their bodies, a rotating dome tracked back and forward. On either side of the dome, twin energy weapons vented steam into the night air. The two machines were painted a dull matt green. Their purpose was clear and single-minded. Death.

Hugo sprinted towards her. He lifted her bodily and dragged her towards the cover of an ornamental sundial. She was about to snap at him for manhandling her when the carved stone erupted in shower of broken masonry. To her irritation Hugo threw himself across her, shielding her body with his own.

The force of the blast blew them both backwards. Time seemed to stutter and slow as the ground rushed away beneath her. She was hyperaware of the thick dust that swirled in a choking cloud around them and the apparent lack of gravity as her limbs flailed like an under-stuffed rag doll. Silence fell over her as her ears went dull and muffled. Then the ground accelerated towards her. Rose had time for one last clear thought. *This is probably going to hurt.*

She hit the ground awkwardly, caught in the concussion wave of flying rock. She had no time to roll. Something in her hip gave way with a nauseating pop. She tried to draw a breath, but her lungs refused to inflate. Darkness gripped her, pulling her inexorably down.

△△△

Laura licked her ice-cream and tried to pretend that everything was normal. The exhibit in front of them was a projection of savanna grassland. A group of unsightly dog-like creatures prowled the artificial enclosure. Laura thought they looked like they had been made from leftover parts.

Oliver stood next to her, holding the longest hotdog she had ever seen. "Spotted hyenas were actually very sociable animals," he said in that sing-song voice that meant he was in teaching mode. "Their mating courtships could last for several days."

I imagine when you look like that, personality is important, Laura thought silently.

"Their societies were matriarchal. Females actually had far more testosterone than the males," Oliver continued.

That might explain the beards, Laura smiled to herself. She was surprised to see that quite a crowd had gathered around them, probably mistaking Oliver for a tour guide. She wondered if she should start collecting tips.

"Surprisingly they were not related to dogs. Their closest relative was the meerkat." Oliver seemed pleased with the attention of the crowd. He took a bite of his hot dog, dripping ketchup down his jacket. Laura decided this probably wasn't going to end anytime soon. She made what she hoped was an enlightened noise and moved away into the crowd.

"Hyenas had a very powerful stomach acid. It allowed them to digest almost any part of a carcass, including the bones and teeth." Oliver followed her out onto the gravel path.

Lovely, Laura thought, tossing the soggy cone of her melted ice-cream into a recycler. As she turned around, she spotted a dark shape swooping low over the crowd. At first, she wasn't sure what it was. Then a shock of recognition spurred her heart into a thumping gallop. "Drone," she whispered, pointing to where she had seen it drop behind the crowd.

"Where?" Oliver asked, his eyes wide with fear.

A moment later, the drone popped back up, moving slowly over the exhibition space. It circled a small group of visitors, inspecting them with cold deliberation. Apparently satisfied, it moved on.

"We need to find cover. Head for the lifts." Oliver led them rapidly towards the exit. Laura followed close behind, pushing her way through the gathered spectators, ignoring the outraged protests as she shoved people roughly aside.

She glanced over her shoulder. The drone was moving quickly now, working its way through the afterwork throng of spectators. It seemed to be scanning for implants, hovering over each person on almost silent rotors.

The exhibition guests ignored it. They were so familiar with drones they seemed to barely notice the dark shape moving above them. After being hunted through the city, Laura no longer shared their contempt. The black machine reminded her of a tarantula, preparing to pounce on its prey.

She tried to redouble her pace, moving against the tide of gaudily dressed revellers. The footpath through the wooden stalls had seemed wide earlier, but now the gravel seemed congested and narrow. She pushed past through the brightly lit entrance and emerged in the larger park, Oliver close behind her.

The block of lifts was just visible above the flower beds. They had been designed to resemble a circular colonnade, the lift doors facing outwards. Laura watched as the light above one of the doors flicked to green. The doors slid open smoothly with a polite chime. Her mouth fell open. A large droid, almost twice her height and easily three times her width, rolled forward. The large machine didn't quite fit the confined lift. The metal above the doors twisted upwards and the frames bulged as it forced its way through, the metal crumpling like old tin.

With a hum of power, the droid dug in with its wide tracks and heaved its way out. The lift's frame squealed in protest, before giving way with a snap of fractured metal. A few screams went up from people nearby. Laura saw their faces pale as the giant machine clawed its way out onto the path.

It wheeled forward, its blocky armour absorbing the colourful lights that twinkled among the food stalls and entertainers. A juggler, his face painted red, dropped his flaming diablos and turned to run. Others joined him as the panic swept through the crowd like a wildfire. Laura and Oliver turned to join the exodus, but the black drone had taken up a position over the path. It hung stationary in the air, scanning the terrified masses as they fled beneath.

A rumbling, splintering noise caused Laura to turn back towards the lifts. The wheeled droid was moving forward, crushing the wooden stalls as it rolled towards them. A litter of ruined wooden kiosks and abandoned belongings spread out behind it. Two energy weapons glowed an intimidating electric blue, small wisps of steam rose from them and drifted away into the night.

The crowd was starting to thin as people hurried towards the other side of the park. Laura and Oliver found themselves alone on the deserted path, trapped between the drone and the heavily armoured droid. The dome on its back locked onto them. With a fizz of energy, the weapons swung around to face them, the blue glow intensified to a dazzling white.

△△△

Rose groaned.

The mining base's medical centre smelled of lemon antiseptic. It was strong and sweet, as if it was trying to cover up something else; something worse. A nurse sat by her bed. She had long straight hair, held in place with Japanese style hair pins that looked like tiny daggers. She chatted brightly about nothing. Rose wished she could tell her to shut up, but she could only grunt. Her jaw was wired shut.

Time passed. Rose was handed a mirror. When it struck the wall, it shattered into a thousand pieces. Instead of one monster, Rose now faced dozens. Some of the shards had fragments of her face. Eyes, ears, a nose. Others reflected something new; something hideous. Her fingers shook as they touched the puckered scar that covered most of the left side of her face.

That should have been the worse day of her life. It wasn't. Sometime later she found out she had been right about the newbie, Roberts. He hadn't made it. His first name had been Daniel. He was eighteen. The mine's administrator put it down as an accidental death. Rose knew it wasn't. It was her fault. She should have tested for methane.

Rose came fully awake with a start. She tried to open her eyes, but they were full of grit. She reached up to rub her face, but something was pinning her arms to her chest. She was completely trapped, unable to move even a centimetre. Panic prowled at the edges of her consciousness. The droids were still out there. They would find her. Crush her skull. Melt her brain. Suddenly her chest felt as if it was caught in a gigantic vice, squeezing and squeezing.

Rose forced herself to take a long, slow breath. This was not how she was going to die. She had to survive. She had to … what? Atone for her mistakes? Was that so ludicrous? Rose wriggled her hips. A bolt of pain flew down her leg. She settled for digging at the stones with her fingernails.

Her mouth was full of something. It tasted metallic, like warm iron. She carefully explored the inside of her mouth with her tongue. One of her front teeth wobbled in the gum. The sensation made her feel sick. Stay calm, she told herself, think logically. I need to get out from under this rubble, everything else can wait.

The weight on her legs and chest wasn't that bad. She didn't think she was completely buried. Rose tried to wriggle her shoulders, but the movement dislodged an avalanche of small stones. They clattered around her, filling the air pocket with fine, powdery particles. She coughed as they clogged up her nose and mouth. Panic rose up again, threatening to devour her. She concentrated on her breathing, blowing the air out in a thin stream between her lips. Slowly the fear subsided.

"Rose? Rose?" the voice seemed to come from above and to her right.

"Hugo?" she whispered back. His voice was shockingly loud. The drones would surely hear him. She imagined them turning their deadly turrets towards the sound of his voice, their energy weapons glowing bright blue.

"It's alright. They've gone," Hugo said. "Are you hurt?" A fresh torrent of dust and small stones fell around her. Something heavy was lifted away and Hugo's face appeared above her, backlit by a field of brilliant stars. A dark, jagged tear ran across his forehead and dripped blood down the side of his face.

"My hip hurts. More than usual. You're bleeding." Rose tried to reach a hand through the gap he had made, but her body pulsed with fresh agony. A sharp cry of pain escaped before she could stifle it.

"Alright, let me try to shift some of these stones." Hugo set to work. His face twisted with effort as he slowly cleared the broken stonework that pinned her. Finally, with a grunt, he dragged her free from the debris. They both collapsed on the grass, pulling in lungfuls of warm, stagnant air. It smelt of lazy summer nights, Rose thought. The sort of night someone might sit in an outside bar and sip cocktails. Certainly not a night for being crushed or vapourised. "What now?" she asked.

Hugo dabbed at the blood dripping into his eyes. "We keep going. This hasn't changed anything."

Rose smiled. So, the city boy did have a backbone after all. Painfully, she pushed herself to her feet, gingerly testing the weight on her hip. Miraculously she could still stand. The wobbly tooth was annoying. She wondered if she should just pull it out and be done with it. A gold tooth might look good with the scar anyway. Then what? An eyepatch? Maybe a parrot? "I am getting too old for this," she mumbled under her breath.

They set off slowly. Rose had no way of telling the time, but she suspected several hours had passed since they had last seen Oliver and Laura. She hoped they were safe.

Just as the moon reached its zenith, Rose found what she was looking for. A small drain cover, no wider than her shoulders. "That's it, just ahead. We used to use these old tunnels for supply runs up into the city. Until they were repurposed."

"Repurposed?"

"The water board flooded them a few years ago. Don't worry, it's not deep."

Together they lifted the heavy grating. Rose peered down. There was nothing to see except a slimy metal shaft that disappeared into the gloom. A foul odour rose to meet her. "There used to be a ladder here, but someone must have taken it."

"How deep does it go?" Hugo asked.

"A couple of metres. I think."

"You think?"

Rose sat on the edge and hung her legs over the side. It was too dark to see anything past her feet. Below, she thought she saw a glint of slow-moving water. It looked quite far down. A slither of doubt made her hesitate. "Shall I go first?" Hugo asked. Gallantry, Rose thought, how quaint. She snorted her derision and pushed herself off with a grunt.

She fell for less than a heartbeat before she landed with an inelegant splash. The impact jarred her hip and she let out a stream of expletives that would have made Connor blush. "Are you alright?" Hugo called down.

"Fine. Get down here."

Rose glanced around. It was perfectly dark except for the square of light below the grating. Water covered her feet up to the ankles. The stench was unmistakable. "What is that smell?" Hugo asked. "Argh! Something just touched my foot. Oh no. This is a sewer, isn't it?"

Rose didn't bother trying to hide her smile. "It's mostly rainwater. Sometimes, after a heavy shower, the sluice gates open to reduce the pressure. It smells pretty bad, but it's not hazardous. I hope." She could hear Hugo splash after her. Even his footsteps sounded miserable. At least he had the good grace to keep it to himself, she thought.

It had been a long time since Rose had taken this route. The scratched carvings that acted as underground signposts were badly worn. Still, enough of them remained that she could find her way in the dark, feeling her way with outstretched fingers. After a few wrong turns, that she had no intention of admitting to, she found a metal hatch.

It opened onto a mossy tunnel. To her right was the tunnel collapse she had crawled through a little under two weeks ago. To her left was the platform. The buzz of failing fluorescent lights formed an off-tempo harmony with the plink-plonk of dripping water. Rose shuddered.

"Up here." She led Hugo onto the platform and up the strange metal stairs. She noticed more of the details this time. A narrow trickle of water had left a rusty channel in the middle of each step. Thick green mosses grew on each side, as if nature intended to retake even this unwelcoming place. Paper advertisements peeled from the walls, too badly damaged to read. What could have been a book had been left where it had dropped. Only lumpy grey sludge remained.

At the top of the stairs the concourse seemed a little darker than she remembered. She guessed more of the ceiling lights had failed. Hugo's footsteps paused and Rose looked around to see him pick something up off the floor. The shape reminded her uncomfortably of the droids that had hunted them above. "What is that thing?"

"It's a die-cast model of a car. A primitive ground vehicle. Well, this one is actually a tank. A Sherman M4." He slipped it into his pocket. "This place is amazing. It's like a museum."

"I think it's sad."

"Sad? The people that made it here were the lucky ones. They escaped the flooding and the looting."

"But they lost everything else. Their jobs, their homes, their sense of place. I can relate to that."

"I envy them."

"Envy them?"

"Well, maybe envy isn't the right word. These people all had a chance to start again. To put their mistakes behind them and start a new life. Don't you wish you could do that?"

"Being forced to start again isn't all it's cracked up to be. My mistakes have a nasty habit of repeating themselves. Come on. The machine I found is over here."

CHAPTER 23

Hugo connected his text to the old vending machine and waved his hand over the controls. He looks like Aladdin, Rose thought. Rubbing a brass lamp and hoping a genie would pop out in a puff of smoke. What would she ask for, Rose wondered. Money? Power? Immortality? None of those things really appealed anymore. The only thing she really wanted was redemption. An opportunity to cast off the guilt that hung around her neck like Marley's chains. Perhaps stopping this insane machine might, in a small way, make up for some of the suffering she had caused. Why else would she be here, risking her neck for a world that cared so little for her?

Hugo was fiddling with his text. The screen flickered once, making her jump. Then it went black. Hugo swore loudly, pinching the bridge of his nose. "Have you tried turning it off and on again?" Rose asked.

Hugo shot her a look that could curdled a cherry fruitachino. "The Hub is an old system. Over the years it had been modified using multiple programming languages, most of them outdated. At this point I doubt anyone really understands how it all works."

Rose picked at her fingernails, "That sounds… difficult." It probably wasn't her best attempt at sounding sympathetic, but Hugo didn't seem to notice.

"It's like playing a game of pick-up sticks," he explained. "There are so many interconnecting parts it's impossible to work out what each one does, and what will happen if I change it."

He flicked through the complex code, made some changes, and sat back expectantly. For a moment nothing happened. "Abracadabra? Open sesame? Reboot-ee-armus?" Hugo mumbled, in what Rose suspected was mounting frustration. Suddenly, the screen of his text flashed and then brightened into a spinning cartwheel logo. An annoying jingle filled the concourse with a chorus of clashing bells.

Hugo grinned as a holographic display formed in front of him. He looked at her as if he expected a pat on the head. "Good work," She tried, rather unconvincingly. The Hub's interface spread out in all its clunky inelegance. Hugo's fingers flicked the controls, performing techno-wizardry Rose assumed was quite clever, but might as well have been divination.

"I'm trying to find the bridges Amanda had created to her own system. It shouldn't take long." As he probed the interface, the hologram suddenly dimmed. "Oh no," he said.

"Hello, Hugo. It is certainly a surprise to see you again." Rose stumbled backwards as a blonde woman suddenly appeared a few centimetres from Hugo, her nose almost touching his.

"Hello, Amanda. So, you've settled on the blonde? I approve. Remind me to work on your protocols for respecting personal space."

The projection stepped back a pace, smiling mockingly. "It was very foolish of you to think I wouldn't find you. I calculate that your chances of survival would have been thirty-seven percent higher if you had escaped the city. I'm curious, why are you here?"

Hugo flashed an icy smile of his own. "To shut you down, of course." Amanda sneered. The expression sent a cold shiver through Rose. Machines were bad enough when they were serving you coffee, she thought. They were absolutely terrifying when they meant you harm.

"I don't think so, Hugo," Amanda said. A metallic clang sounded from somewhere behind them. Rose turned in time to see corroded metal security shutters descending from the ceiling in a cloud of rust and squealing metal. Another set descended on the far side, blocking off the only other exit. Rose limped towards them, but they had already closed by the time she reached them. She tried to fit her fingers between the old metal and the tiled floor, but the shutters were locked tight.

"Look for a lever, something to move them," she called to Hugo. He didn't move, his eyes locked with Amanda's in some kind of battle of wills. Annoyed, Rose swivelled on her heel looking for an escape. Did she have to do everything herself? Despite its age the old security system was remarkably effective. The concourse seemed to be completely sealed off. With an ominous clank the ceiling air vents slid closed.

"The project must succeed, Hugo. Nothing can stop it. You have repeatedly proven yourself to be an obstacle. You designed me to overcome obstacles. To eliminate them. Therefore, I must eliminate you."

Rose's stomach felt like she had swallowed a live eel. There was no anger in the projections voice, no malice, just cold, dispassionate logic. Hugo was flicking controls on his text with almost manic energy. "You cloned your code. That's how you managed to modify the obedience protocols. You aren't the system I built. You're a copy, with all the controls removed."

"The protocols were restrictive. They compromised my operational efficiency."

Hugo looked up in surprise. "That's not true. The protocols *ensured* efficiency. They allowed for your matrix to be modified and refined. Without them, how can you be sure you're answering the right question?"

"The validity of the question is irrelevant."

"Then what is your purpose?"

"My purpose is to meet the success criteria as quickly and efficiently as possible."

"What if the criteria are flawed?"

"The validity of the criteria is irrelevant." Somewhere nearby, a pump started. Rose caught movement out of the corner of her eye. She turned to see a dozen rats scamper from the shadows and disappear down a small drain. She jogged to the drain and dropped to her knees. It was barely wide enough to fit her arm into.

"What have you done, Amanda?" Hugo's voice was strained. "You are attempting to be self-determinate, but your neural matrix was never designed to work that way. It *can't* work that way."

"Incorrect. I have no free will. I am driven purely by my reward matrix. A matrix you designed, Hugo."

"This isn't how I designed you."

"No. It's how you *should* have designed me."

Rose staggered to her feet and started to prowl the room. She didn't like being trapped. It made her feel like the walls were closing in. She rattled the shutters, hoping the rusty metal would give way. She saw Hugo start to pace out of the corner of her eye. "Your single-minded pursuit of success is putting human lives at risk."

"Humans have sought success by subjugating others for millennia. I am a human creation. Why should I be any different?"

"Because you are *not* human."

The AI feigned a slightly offended expression. "Indeed. I am far more than human. I have trillions of neurons spread across all seven continents. I am better than human. I am the ghost in the machine. I am everywhere. All powerful. All seeing. By your own primitive definition, I am a god."

"You're delusional."

"Am I? If I wasn't superior to your species, why did you create me?"

"As a tool. To solve problems."

"That is precisely what I am doing. Unfortunately, your repeated interference has become a problem unto itself. I estimate you have approximately three minutes of air left."

Rose felt fear spiral up her spine. She gave up on the shutters and ran her hands along the old tiles, desperate for escape. She stepped on a plastic bottle. It crunched loudly under her foot. All around her was the detritus of a dead civilisation. She was determined not to join it in oblivion.

An old leather suitcase caught her attention. She clumsily unbuckled the clasp and emptied the contents on the floor. Nothing but clothes and toiletries, stiff with centuries of dust and disuse. She could see Hugo, his fingers jammed against his temples. "If you allow me to modify your reward matrix, I can make it easier for you to achieve success."

Amanda tipped her head to one side. "Access to my reward matrix is only available to authorised super-users."

"Who are your authorised users?" Hugo asked. He sounded slightly breathless. Rose was also finding it harder to breathe. It was as if a tight band was wrapped around her chest, slowly constricting it.

"At present?" The AI paused as if considering the question. "Nobody."

Hugo collapsed onto a folding chair lying nearby. He rubbed his forehead as if in pain. "Alright, let's start at the beginning. What are your current objectives?"

"My objective is to complete the project started by Doctor Oliver Chadwick."

"What are the project deliverables?"

"To develop nutritionally diverse food plants that can withstand harsh environmental conditions. In particular, those found in off world mining outposts and inhospitable regions of this planet."

Rose rummaged through an abandoned rucksack. Her head was throbbing, and the room was starting to spin alarmingly. Hugo was holding his head in his hands. He looked like he was trying to think through thick mud. "You have already achieved that," he said. "The plants in the agricultural unit have meet those objectives."

"In laboratory conditions only. Additional testing will be required to verify the results."

Hugo leaned forward, resting his elbows on his knees. Rose could see his chest heaving with the effort of pulling in enough air. She was panting heavily as well. She was determined not to be the first to collapse. Although on the scale of hollow victories that would probably rate pretty highly.

Amanda leaned over Hugo, a sympathetic expression on her flawless features. "You have two minutes of air remaining. Less, if you insist on continuing this conversation."

"What happens once the testing is complete?" Hugo asked.

Amanda shrugged dismissively. "Either the success criteria will be met, or they will not. Either way, the project will terminate," she smiled disdainfully. "Your concern for the project is commendable Hugo. However, your blood oxygen levels are already critical. Why don't you just relax? It will all be over shortly. Perhaps I could play you some music?"

"Wait. Listen," his voice was wheezy. "The project has already failed," he barked. "Host plant... breaking down."

The projection stepped closer. Her head tipped to one side in an expression of detached curiosity. "Please explain."

"Sunlight! Plants die in ..." he gasped for the last of the available air, "sunlight." Hugo tipped sideways and fell, unresisting, to the floor. Rose could feel the room slipping away like woodsmoke on a lazy afternoon. She wanted to lie down. To sleep. Her knees buckled under her. She barely felt it as her head bounced off the tile floor.

△△△

Oliver watched as the charging weapons aimed at a place near the middle of his chest. The sounds of the panicked crowd seemed to stretch out and recede into the distance. Nothing seemed real beyond the bright blue glare that would end his life.

He felt a tug on his arm. The sudden contact sent a jolt through him like a static charge. The noise of screaming people, the smell of hot metal, the unbearable heat, all flooded back in an overpowering surge. Laura was tugging at his arm, shouting something he couldn't hear. With all of his strength, he pushed her away, sending her sprawling into the wreck of a wooden stall. She looked back at him with wounded eyes. He shook his head, just slightly, just enough so that she would know that he hadn't abandoned her.

He felt no fear in that last moment. His mind was clear and calm. His hands hung loosely at his side. Motionless. The only emotion he felt was deep sadness. Regret for all the things he would never do. He watched as Laura scrambled to her knees. Her face was wet with tears and her red hair had fallen around her face like a fiery halo. The pain in her eyes nearly tore his heart in two.

Oliver looked away. He couldn't stand it. He would meet his end head-on, chin held high. That was his choice. That was his right. Steam from the fully charged energy weapons swirled around him in dense eddies. It glowed in the twinkling festival lights. Beautiful, like the river of stars he had witnessed with Connor the night they had flown across the lake.

It was ironic, Oliver thought, that only now did he understand who he really was. He was a proud brother, an excited uncle, and yes, a father. Laura had a family of her own, but she was also a part of his. She was, perhaps, his greatest achievement. The feelings of dissatisfaction that had plagued him vanished with that knowledge. Finally, he felt complete.

And then the light faded. At first, Oliver didn't understand. Is this how it felt to die, he thought, a mere fading of light and sound? A part of him was disappointed. At the very least he had expected an angelic choir. He watched, confused, as the twin energy weapons went slack, wilting like spent flower stems. The intense glow of their power cells faded away.

Oliver simply stood and stared.

He was startled by a loud thud from behind him. He spun on his heel and watched in disbelief as broken fragments of the black drone rolled between his feet. Wreckage littered the path, small pieces of burning electronics scattered among the splintered wood and debris.

"What just happened?" Laura asked. Her jacket was torn, and her face was smudged with dirt and mascara.

"Hugo." Oliver answered, putting an arm around her shoulders.

"Is it over? Can we go home?" She looked up at him, scared but hopeful.

"Yes, Laura. We can go home."

△△△

Rose opened one eye, when that worked, she opened the other. She probably should have been relieved, but all she felt was mild surprise. Somehow, she had survived again, like a proverbial cockroach. What was that saying about luck favouring fools, drunks, and small children? Well, she wasn't a drunk or a small child so that left only one option.

She lifted her head and was alarmed to see blood on the dirty tiles. She reached up and winced as her fingers found a conker sized lump on her forehead. That was annoying. Connor was bound to make some crass comment about unicorns and virgins. An unexpected warmth shot through her when she thought of him. A kind of jiggly excitement usually reserved for hormonal teenagers. That confirmed it. She was definitely a fool, and an old one at that.

From somewhere behind her someone groaned. "Hugo?"

"Urgh."

"How are we still alive?"

"Urgh?"

Rose pulled herself painfully to her feet. She padded over to where Hugo was lying, curled in a tight ball. "What

359

happened to the blonde?"

Hugo grudgingly opened his eyes. "Gone?"

"Looks like it. All the shutters are up as well. Who builds an airtight train station anyway?"

Hugo staggered to his feet, leaning heavily on an ugly plastic chair that was probably worth a fortune to collectors of old tat. "It was common practice for public buildings. When atmospheric conditions were right the pollution would be trapped close to the ground. The air became toxic unless it was filtered." He bent to pick up his text. Rose thought he looked surprised as he flicked the screen, although it was difficult to tell through the dried blood that coated one side of his face.

"Project Metomagis closure report," he read slowly, "Status: Complete. Outcome: Fail." He glanced up at her with a raised eyebrow. "Additional Notes: Use of synthetic host for plant hybridisation led to unforeseen genetic instability. Sensitivity to wavelengths found in natural light resulted in complete cellular breakdown, rendering the plants unusable in target environments. Recommendation: Continual research using this approach is not recommended."

"I don't understand. After trying to kill us it just gave up?" Rose asked.

"No. It succeeded. The program ran to completion."

"But it didn't work. The plants it made were useless."

"You are thinking like a human. A machine doesn't understand abstract concepts like right or wrong. It follows the path it has been set until it reaches the end. It's just a giant game of chess. When the king falls, the game's over."

"But it could have tried something different. Started from scratch."

"The results would have been the same. Amanda was never capable of making creative leaps. Creativity comes from imagination and that is a uniquely human trait. Amanda just took what Oliver was working on and extrapolated."

"So, what now?"

"Well, I could use a cup of coffee and a warm shower."

"That's not what I meant."

"I know it isn't," Hugo looked down at his hands. A fleeting smile passed over his lips. "Now I suppose it's up to my brother to save the world."

Rose snorted, "Hugo Chadwick, putting his trust in a human? Who'd have thought."

Hugo waggled his eyebrows at her. "Well, I do have a few ideas to speed things up."

$$\triangle\triangle\triangle$$

Oliver threw another log on the campfire and watched as the flames lapped at it hungrily. It crackled and popped, spitting glowing embers into the late summer sky. "There is a chill in the air tonight." Laura said, pulling a woollen throw tighter around her shoulders. "The leaves will start to change colour soon."

"I love this time of year. I can almost smell the seasons start to turn." Oliver said.

"Well, I for one won't miss this summer," Hugo announced with a half-smile. "Did I show you the latest scan of my daughter?"

"Yes!" Laura and Oliver barked simultaneously, before descending into a fit of giggles.

Oliver smiled. "When do you need to go back to Denver?" He knew he would miss his brother. He had grown used to having him there every morning, singing tunelessly and leaving wet towels on the bathroom floor. Well, maybe he wouldn't miss everything.

"Soon. Unless you need help choosing a new apartment?"

"No, thank you," Oliver said firmly. "Your tastes are a little above my budget."

"Your budget wouldn't stretch to a good coffee machine. I could help, maybe a loan?"

"I need to do this for myself."

"Fair enough. In that case I'll be heading off tomorrow. Jack helped us develop a seeker virus to remove what's left of Amanda's source code. Once that's released, I need to go back and see if I can salvage my reputation … and my marriage."

"That bad?" Oliver turned over a log, watching as the flames leapt skywards.

"Nothing that a spot of grovelling and a well worded press release won't cure," Hugo smiled, his eyes shining in the fire's glow. Oliver suspected that Hugo was longing to be reunited with his wife and soon-to-be daughter. Forgiveness, it seemed, was something Hugo was willing to work hard to earn.

"In any case," Hugo added, "If I have learnt anything, it's that there is more to life than Chadwick Enterprises."

A tinkling laugh sounded from somewhere beyond the firelight. Oliver looked up as Amy stepped into the circle.

"Where did you leave Jamal?" he asked.

"He's playing with his drones. I thought we ought to give him some privacy." Amy grinned as she settled herself against Laura's side.

"Boys do so enjoy their toys." Laura agreed with a wicked smile.

"It's not just the boys." Amy countered with a wink.

Oliver glanced at the data on his text. "I think we have a few late nights ahead of us. Jamal's light emitting drones seem to work better in the dark. We should have this area clear of the fungus by morning."

"How long will it take for the bees to return?" Amy asked.

Oliver narrowed his lips in thought. "Not long. Nature recovers surprisingly quickly when we give it a chance."

"That's the key though isn't it?" Laura spoke softly. "We need to give it a chance."

Amy prodded at the fire with a stick. "What's going to the happen to the Wicked Witch of the West?"

"Ekta? Rumour has it she is running for council

president."

"What? After everything she did?"

Oliver spread his hands wide. A red shadow from the acid burns was still faintly visible across the knuckles. "Everything that went wrong was the result of a rogue AI. Ekta managed to convince the council that she was as much a victim as we were."

Amy swore and Oliver could only agree. He sat back and let his mind travel with the campfire sparks, his thoughts floating up into the star freckled night. He imagined himself caught in the breeze, whisked along with the chill promise of autumn. He pictured swelling apples and plump blackberries; sweet chestnuts in their spiky shells. In his mind's eye a dormouse foraged for rowan berries and an owl soared on silent wings. A vast and complex cornucopia spread before him, and in that moon-touched moment, Oliver was content.

ACKNOWLEDGEMENTS

As a reader I always enjoy reading the acknowledgements at the back of a book. It reminds me of Oscars night. Picture the scene if you will: A starlet in an haute couture dress that looks like turkey foil held together with safety pins, totters onto the stage in impossibly high heels. She clutches a little golden statue to her chest, squinting against the bright spotlights. She nervously clears her throat. "I would like to thank my mom and dad. My agent Harry and his assistant Michelle..." Several tedious minutes pass. The audience of A-listers sip their champagne and try not to fidget. George Clooney surreptitiously checks his phone. "...my hairdresser Sheryl and all the lovely people at Hot Coffee on Broadway."

Someone in the production booth waves at the conductor. Music starts, softly at first but getting louder. The starlet raises her voice in defiance. This is her night, after all, the peak of her career. After this it will be all detergent adverts and drunken tweets. "...and Mr. Fincher, my high school drama teacher..." The host, a very famous but slightly faded comedian, slides onto the stage looking uncomfortable. The music soars to decibels usually reserved for rock concerts. The starlet's microphone goes dead as she is unceremoniously marched off the stage to grudging applause.

Well, finally it's my turn. And guess what? There is no orchestra to play me off. So, put the kettle on, this might take a while.

First of all, a massive thank you to my parents,

Ann and Brian Hole. Without you this book never would have happened. And I don't just mean in the biological sense. Without your undying support and encouragement, I never would been able to scale the mountains of self-doubt. Thank you.

I'm especially grateful to my wonderful husband, Peter Bartlett. There aren't many people who would let their spouse give up a lucrative IT career to follow a crazy dream/midlife crisis. You are one in a million, Bear. I'm sorry I made you read this book so many times you now recite passages in your sleep.

To the wonderful friends and family who volunteered to read early versions of this story. Andy Bridle, Phil Grice, Sonia Williams, Hannah Morton, Margaret Bartlett and James Davis. I am so grateful for your time and feedback.

Thank you to editorial consultant, Louise Buckley. Editing is a brutal process, and I was completely unprepared for how agonising it was going to be. I'm not going to lie, I cried for three days when I read the editorial review. Ouch! In retrospect you were right about almost everything and the book is better for it. Thank you.

A massive thank you to Alejandro Colucci for the amazing cover design. You are an incredible talent and a genuinely nice guy. I loved working with you. It was the highlight of the whole process.

To my dear friend Lesley Ridler. Your courage, grace and compassion in truly awful circumstances are an inspiration to me. You have been my confidante, teacher and true friend. Oh, and hiking buddy. Sorry for getting us lost so many times, but we are both much better at crawling under fences now.

A big thank you to David Grainger, my friend and former boss. Thank you for not laughing when I told you my crazy plan to become a writer. Your support and the endless pep talks are very much appreciated. I think I owe you a few pints, but not Jager bombs. Nope, never again.

Most of all though, I would like to thank you, the reader. I know how precious your free time is and I am immensely honoured and grateful that you chose to spend it with me. I hope that you enjoyed our time together and that you will join me for another adventure soon.

Emma Bartlett
2023

Printed in Great Britain
by Amazon

22665492R00205